About

Born and raised just outside of Toronto, Ontario, **Amy Ruttan** fled the big city to settle down with the country boy of her dreams. After the birth of her second child, Amy was lucky enough to realise her life long dream of becoming a romance author. When she's not furiously typing away at her computer, she's a mum to three wonderful children who use her as a personal taxi and chef.

USA Today bestselling author **Catherine Mann** has over a hundred books in print in more than twenty countries with Mills & Boon True Love, Heroes, and other imprints. A six-time *RITA* finalist, she has won both a *RITA* and Romantic Times Reviewer's Choice Award. Mother of four, Catherine lives in South Carolina with her husband where they enjoy kayaking, camping with their dogs, and volunteering at a service dog training organisation. For more information, visit: catherinemann.com

Jennie Lucas' parents owned a bookstore and she grew up surrounded by books, dreaming about faraway lands. At twenty-two she met her future husband and after their marriage, she graduated from university with a degree in English. She started writing books a year later. Jennie won the Romance Writers of America's Golden Heart competition in 2005 and hasn't looked back since. Visit Jennie's website at: jennielucas.com

Princess Brides

December 2024
Enemies to Lovers

January 2025
A Second Chance

February 2025
A Marriage of Convenience

March 2025
Friends to Lovers

April 2025
A Cinderella Story

May 2025
A Royal Baby

Princess Brides: A Royal Baby

AMY RUTTAN

CATHERINE MANN

JENNIE LUCAS

MILLS & BOON

All rights reserved including the right of reproduction in whole or in part in any form. This edition is published by arrangement with Harlequin Enterprises ULC.

This is a work of fiction. Names, characters, places, locations and incidents are purely fictional and bear no relationship to any real life individuals, living or dead, or to any actual places, business establishments, locations, events or incidents. Any resemblance is entirely coincidental.

This book is sold subject to the condition that it shall not, by way of trade or otherwise, be lent, resold, hired out or otherwise circulated without the prior consent of the publisher in any form of binding or cover other than that in which it is published and without a similar condition including this condition being imposed on the subsequent purchaser.

® and ™ are trademarks owned and used by the trademark owner and/or its licensee. Trademarks marked with ® are registered with the United Kingdom Patent Office and/or the Office for Harmonisation in the Internal Market and in other countries.

First Published in Great Britain 2025
by Mills & Boon, an imprint of HarperCollins*Publishers* Ltd
1 London Bridge Street, London, SE1 9GF

www.harpercollins.co.uk

HarperCollins*Publishers*
Macken House, 39/40 Mayor Street Upper,
Dublin 1, D01 C9W8, Ireland

Princess Brides: A Royal Baby © 2025 Harlequin Enterprises ULC.

Baby Bombshell for the Doctor Prince © 2020 Amy Ruttan
His Pregnant Princess Bride © 2016 Catherine Mann
The Heir the Prince Secures © 2018 Jennie Lucas

ISBN: 978-0-263-41730-2

This book contains FSC™ certified paper and other controlled sources to ensure responsible forest management.

For more information visit: www.harpercollins.co.uk/green

Printed and Bound in the UK using 100% Renewable Electricity
at CPI Group (UK) Ltd, Croydon, CR0 4YY

BABY BOMBSHELL FOR THE DOCTOR PRINCE

AMY RUTTAN

For my readers.

I wouldn't be here, at this milestone,
without all of your support.

Much love.

CHAPTER ONE

Toronto, Ontario

Dang it!

She was late.

Imogen hated being late. Especially on the first day of the medical conference, in her first lab of the conference. This was a lab she'd specifically signed up for. This was her number one reason for coming to the conference and she was late.

Jet lag. It was jet lag and that was the story she was sticking to.

She'd been in Yellowknife a long time and hadn't traveled in a while. Jet lag usually didn't bother her.

Except today, of course. It had to be today.

She slipped into the room, hoping no one clocked her or noticed she was late for the simulation lab that was the talk of this conference. It was the whole reason why she had come. If it hadn't been for the lab and workshops, she would've stayed in Yellowknife, in her safe little bubble where she knew her routines, knew her patients, knew her work.

She tried to move quietly at the back of the lab, looking for any open seat.

"Dr. Hayes?"

She cringed as her name was called out.

"Yes. Sorry," she responded.

The instructor looked less than impressed. "Join group five over there. They've already started without you."

Imogen's cheeks heated with embarrassment as she slunk over to group five.

She sat down. The other two doctors briefly filled her in, but she knew they were annoyed she was late.

She was too. The last thing she wanted was to be the center of attention. She hated it, and arriving late had done exactly that.

Her ex, Allen, had craved the limelight and she didn't.

She loved helping her patients. She loved Yellowknife, but Allen had wanted more.

She was mortified to be the last one here.

"Another latecomer," the instructor piped up. "Honestly, people, let's not make this a precedent. Join group five, please."

Imogen looked up to see the other straggler, hoping to find a kindred spirit with whom she could commiserate. Her mouth dropped open when she saw who was walking toward her group.

He was six-three, at least, broad-shouldered, blue-eyed, and he had a neat beard. He reminded her of all those Viking heroes that she would see on the covers of her best friend's mother's romance novels. The ones she and her friend would sneak out and read at slumber parties.

It was like he had walked straight out of the pages of a book.

She was pretty tall herself, at five-eleven, so it was rare for her to find someone who towered over her and made her feel like she could actually wear a nice pair of heels with him and be swept off her feet.

Allen had never liked her to wear heels, as he was already an inch shorter than her.

What are you thinking about? Why are you thinking like this?

It had to be the jet lag. She wasn't thinking rationally. She shook those thoughts from her head.

He sat down next to her, smiling politely at her; she met his gaze, which was intense. It was as if he could read exactly what she was thinking and he in turn looked her up and down with a brief flick of his eyes.

She really hoped she wasn't blushing, because suddenly it was very hot in this room, especially after the chilly reception she had received from the others and the hotel air-conditioning, which was cranked up full blast.

"I'm Dr. Hayes," she whispered. "And I was late too."

He smiled. "Dr. Vanin."

He had an accent she couldn't quite place, but there was no time to talk, as they both had to catch up on what they'd missed.

And she got the feeling, by the way he sat so stiffly beside her, that he wasn't the chatty type. After the instructor gave them all directions, their group went to work in the simulation lab that had been set up. She was paired off with Dr. Vanin as they practiced using robotic technology to perform a surgery she would usually do with a laparoscope.

Their operation on the silicone abdomen was removing a gallbladder with a gallstone that was lodged in the common bile duct. One that could not be retrieved after an ERCP and that needed to be surgically removed.

Thankfully, this was her forte.

She was one of the top general surgeons in the Northwest Territories.

"Have you ever used this technology before?" Dr. Vanin asked.

"Robotic, no, but I'm pretty familiar with laparoscopic surgery, but when there's a situation like this with a stone lodged in a duct, I usually do a full laparotomy at that point.

It's why I'm here, to learn how to do this kind of surgery in the most minimally invasive way possible."

He nodded, seemingly impressed. "I do not do much general surgery, especially delicate work with laparoscopes. My specialty is trauma. I'm here to hone my skills."

"Well, I can help guide you." She stepped to the side. "Why don't you go first?"

He smiled warmly. "Thank you, Dr. Hayes."

"No problem." Imogen stood beside him. Her heart raced like she was a young girl standing beside her first crush. It was silly, but there was just something about him that made her feel out of control.

And she didn't like to lose control.

Control protected her. It had got her where she was today.

And she was kicking herself for offering to guide him with the instruments. The last thing she wanted to do was crow about her achievements. Allen used to get so defensive when she was lauded over him.

Allen's not here. He's gone.

"If I'm overstepping…" she started to say, and he looked up at her, confused.

"How? I appreciate the help from a more experienced general surgeon. Please, you are not overstepping."

She blushed. "Okay."

He nodded and turned his attention back to the instruments.

She watched him use the robotic controls easily. He was picking it up quickly.

"What stitch do you use on the common bile duct?" he asked.

"A running stitch using a monofilament absorbable suture. That allows me proper repair of the anastomosis of the bile duct. And it will hold well; the last thing a patient needs is a leak, which would lead to sepsis."

"Show me how you do it." He stood up and she took his spot. She showed him her running stitch, which she could do blindfolded.

"You do that so efficiently," he remarked.

"Thank you."

"No need to thank me. It is the truth," he stated.

She blushed. "Still, thanks."

Imogen couldn't remember anyone, other than her late father, complimenting her. But her father had *had* to compliment her—he was her father. He had been supportive and loving, but he'd also been biased.

Allen had never complimented her, but she'd never really worked much with him because the way they'd started out had been through professional rivalry, a torrid romance, then her broken heart when he'd left because he couldn't handle her popularity or life in the north.

She'd sworn she'd never again date another doctor.

Of course, with her workload in Yellowknife, she never had time to date, and the only people she interacted with besides patients were doctors, paramedics, nurses…medical people.

So she never bothered dating. Never thought about it.

And if she didn't think about it, she had control over her feelings. She didn't feel so alone or hurt.

Why are you thinking about it now, then?

She had to get a grip. She was not at this conference to date. She was here to work. Even if her friend and boss, Jeanette, had told her to loosen up and enjoy herself, Imogen had no time for that.

Once she finished her part of the lab, and the class was over, she was going to ask Dr. Vanin out for a cup of coffee. But when she looked up, he'd already left the room. She was disappointed, but it was probably for the best that she keep her distance.

***

All week she saw him. And as much as she tried to avoid him, they always seemed to sit next to each other and during labs they always partnered up. But when the class was done he'd disappear. Even though she made other acquaintances at the conference, when she'd spot Dr. Vanin, he was always on his own and he always seemed to disappear before she had the chance to really talk to him.

He wasn't really talkative, but he was smart and knowledgeable and, oh, so sexy.

So when she walked into the hotel bar for the mixer at the end of the conference, and saw him brooding at the bar rather than conversing with the rest of the physicians, she steeled her resolve to go and talk to him.

Even if this was so not her usual modus operandi, she didn't know anyone else. If she took control of the situation, then she could make a new friend. She could even call it networking, since he was a fellow professional and she absolutely, definitely was not going to date anyone medical ever again.

The way her own parents had ended up had made her a little gun-shy. Her father had been perpetually waiting for her mother to come back, but she never had.

She shook away the thought of the mother she'd never known.

This wasn't dating. This was a mixer and she didn't work with Dr. Vanin. All she was doing was going to talk to someone interesting.

And sexy.

Her stomach flip-flopped as she approached him.

"Dr. Vanin... Lev, isn't it?"

Dr. Vanin turned around on his bar stool and smiled. "Yes. And you're Dr. Hayes, if I remember, yes?"

"Yes, but you can call me Imogen." She extended her hand. "May I sit?"

He nodded and motioned to the empty bar stool next to him, and suddenly she felt very awkward and out of place.

Say something.

"We seemed to have been at every workshop together. Quite a coincidence, eh?" She cringed inwardly at using such an obvious Canadian colloquialism.

"That we do," he said. His eyes twinkled and she hoped he found her awkwardness cute rather than goofy.

"Where are you from?" she asked.

"I'm from Chenar."

"Where exactly is that again?" She knew it was in Europe but felt silly for not having a better grasp of geography.

He smiled and nodded. "Northeastern Europe. Our country was founded by Viking traders looking for access to the Silk Road by land instead of by sea. It's why we appear more Nordic than Russian. I get asked that all the time. Not many people know where it is. They just assume I'm Romanian or Russian."

"Now I remember. It's a small, unique country. I've been there, but a long time ago."

His smile brightened. "You've been there? How unusual."

"My father loved to travel. It was just the two of us and we went to a lot of places when I was young."

"Does your father still travel?"

"No. He passed a couple of years ago." Imogen tried to swallow the lump in her throat as she thought of her father, a scientist, who had been working up in Alert. He'd passed away from a major hemorrhagic stroke. Gone before he'd even hit the floor.

Imogen had been traveling to smaller communities up in Nunavut when it had happened. It was a sore spot for her that she hadn't been there when he'd passed. He'd been her only family. It had been just the two of them for so long.

Her throat tightened.

"I'm sorry to hear that," Lev said gently.

"Thank you." She cleared her throat, trying not to cry.

"And now that I have thoroughly depressed you," he teased, "what should we talk about next?"

Imogen smiled at him. "No. I'm fine. Really."

He cocked an eyebrow. "Are you sure? I mean, this social thing is kind of sad, and then I went and depressed you further..."

"You're not depressing me."

"Good." He took another sip of his drink. "I would hate to drag you down with me."

Imogen glanced over her shoulder. He wasn't wrong. It was summer and this was Toronto. She'd lived in the city when she was at university and then medical school. They were in a stodgy hotel with cheap drinks and bland food. Outside, Toronto was just coming to life.

"Do you want to get out of here?" she whispered conspiratorially.

He perked up. "Really?"

"I used to live in Toronto. I could take you on a quick tour if you'd like?"

Lev grinned and there was a twinkle in those deep blue eyes. "I would like that very much."

"Good." She set down her drink. "Let's go, before someone else decides to talk to us."

Lev finished the rest of his Scotch and followed her out of the bar.

It was kind of exciting to sneak out of the hotel, dumping their name badges on a table just outside the reception room.

In only a few minutes they were out of the hotel and on Front Street. The sun was only just beginning to set, though it wasn't late. Where she lived now, in Yellowknife, the summer sun wouldn't set for hours. It was one of her favorite things about living so far north, but there was still something magical about sunset in a bustling city like Toronto, with the city lights coming on and reflecting in the water of Lake Ontario. Toronto never seemed to sleep. It was exciting and thrilling. She'd forgotten that.

"There is one thing I want to do," Lev said as they walked along Front Street. "Something I've wanted to do since I came to Toronto."

"What's that?" she asked, curious.

"Go up that!" Lev pointed to the CN Tower.

"Sure. We can see if it's still open." Without thinking, Imogen took his hand. She froze for a moment when she realized what she'd done, but he didn't pull away or seem to mind as they headed in the direction of Union Station. They ran across the road, dodging and weaving through the parked cars and the small evening traffic jam in front of the train station.

There were people on their way to some concert at the Scotiabank Arena and there were others trying to make their way home, taxis dropping off and picking up in front of Union Station. She led him through the train station and to the walkway that connected the station to the major attractions that hugged the Toronto waterfront.

They were lucky and able to get two tickets, which Lev insisted that he pay for because she was his tour guide.

It was a quick elevator ride up, and Imogen had to plug her ears as they popped. Soon they were on the observation deck of what used to be the tallest freestanding structure in the world.

They stood side by side, looking out over the city, which was lighting up as the sun sank on the west side of the city. Lev didn't say much and Imogen stood beside him, her pulse racing with the anticipation of something new and exciting.

Something she hadn't felt in a long time.

"So big," Lev whispered. "This city is about the size of my country."

"It's a pretty big city. All the years I lived here, this is my first time on the observation deck."

He cocked an eyebrow. "Really? Why?"

She shrugged. "I was at medical school. I was focused. I didn't make time."

She hadn't made time for a lot of things and that saddened her.

They wandered along the perimeter of the observation deck until they were looking south at the lake. When she looked out over Lake Ontario, she closed her eyes and imagined she was back home in Yellowknife, on her houseboat and listening to the sounds of Great Slave Lake. She hated being so far from home. No matter where she and her father had traveled, they'd always come back to Yellowknife. She opened her eyes and looked out over the city and Lake Ontario.

Lake Ontario was smaller than Great Slave Lake, but you couldn't tell when on the shoreline, as both were vast and she didn't really care to think about it. Not now. Not when she was standing next to a man who made her body thrum with excitement, in a way Allen never had.

It's just lust.

Allen had been her boyfriend for three years, and lust didn't last forever.

She'd just met Lev. He was new.

She needed to get a grip on these crazy emotions. She had to get back in control. Only she liked this feeling of living a little. It was fun and new. It wasn't going to be anything serious.

This was what she should've done when she was younger, but she'd been too afraid. She was still afraid, but she was going to savor tonight. It was the first step she needed to take, to put the burning mess of what had happened between her and Allen behind her.

Her first step in moving on.

Even if Allen had moved on a couple of years ago.

"I have never seen a lake so large."

"This is the seventh largest in Canada." She winced. Her father had always called her an encyclopedia and Allen had hated her little trivia facts.

Lev's eyebrows rose. "Only seventh? Which is the largest?"

Imogen frowned. "Uh, I think Lake Superior. It's farther north, but still in Ontario."

Lev leaned forward. "I like Canada. I have only been here a short time and I wish I could stay. A man could get lost here."

He said the last bit almost wistfully, like he wanted to get lost, and she didn't really blame him for thinking that way. It was why she liked working in the north. Even though Yellowknife was a city, it was far from anything else.

Only a thirty-minute drive out of the city and it was wilderness, trees and rock that had been exposed by glaciers.

It was easy to get lost up there, but it was a place where she'd found herself after Allen had broken her heart and her father had died.

"What is on the islands?" Lev asked as they watched a ferry slowly make its way from Queens Quay to the islands.

"Some homes, parks, a nudist beach," she teased.

Lev chuckled. "Wouldn't it be cold?"

"Not in the summer. We don't all drive a snowmobile to work." She did, in the winter.

"I never thought that. Do people think that?" he asked.

"Some," she said dryly.

He shook his head. "Well, I just meant it's night and the water looks cold."

"Yes. It can be cold, but I doubt people are at the beach now."

A lazy grin spread on his face. "Why not? Darkness hides a lot."

Her heart skipped a beat and she felt the blush rise in her cheeks as she tried not to think of the two of them alone on the nudist beach with only the moon lighting up the sky.

"Where can we get a drink?" he asked, breaking the tension.

"I know a nice place down by the waterfront."

"Good. Lead the way." Lev took her hand and it sent a jolt of electricity through her. It just felt right to hold his hand. It made her forget all the rules she'd set up to protect her heart. It made her feel carefree. It made her feel hot and gooey, all the things she'd never really felt before. Or if she had, she'd forgotten and Lev had woken something up inside her.

And as they walked slowly along the waterfront toward the patio, it felt like they had been doing this walk for some time. They didn't talk much, but then, during the whole week at the conference they hadn't really spoken a lot. There had just been this instant camaraderie the moment they'd both walked into the robotic lab late. Like they knew each other, even though they'd never met before.

Kindred spirits. Although she didn't believe in that. Not really.

Still, she felt at ease with him.

Like this was right.

You're crazy. He lives halfway across the world from you.

She knew all her friends in Yellowknife had told her to let loose and live a little when she was down in Toronto, but this was ridiculous. She couldn't be interested in Dr. Vanin. Long-distance relationships never worked and she wasn't leaving Yellowknife. She couldn't.

She'd tried it when she'd been a traveling doctor and it had crashed and burned, hard. She wouldn't date someone from far away again.

Who said anything about dating?

All this was... Well, she didn't know what it was, but she was enjoying herself. She couldn't quite believe that she was here with Lev, walking along the waterfront, hand in hand, talking about the city, enjoying the summer evening.

She didn't want to go to the patio and be around other people, because she liked this so much. It was as if they were in a little bubble together and she didn't want anyone to burst it.

Of course, it would burst eventually when they both went home tomorrow, but for now, it was nice, just the two of them.

They stopped and Lev leaned over the railing, watching the water and the city lights reflecting in the lake.

"It's a beautiful night. It's nice out here. So calm. So quiet."

"It is a nice night, though I would hardly call Toronto calm or quiet."

"Well, it seems quiet here."

"I prefer the country," she said.

"Do you?" he asked, surprised.

"Why are you shocked by that?"

"I thought you were a city girl."

"What made you think that?" she asked.

"You could navigate that traffic outside the hotel. You seem not to be bothered by crowds of people."

"I went to school in Toronto for many years. I'm used to it, but I'm not a city girl. I much prefer a quieter setting. A smaller setting."

"Tell me about it."

"What would you like to know?" she asked.

"You're a surgeon where you're located?"

"Yes. I did some work with a flying doctor service, but now I'm based in a hospital."

"Flying doctor?" he asked. "I have heard of this, but I'm intrigued about how it works."

"There are so many small communities that have no other way to connect them. You're at the mercy of the weather, though, as a flying doctor. Food and medical supplies are all brought in that way for some communities."

"And if the plane can't fly?" he asked.

"People can die." She thought of her father again. Maybe if he'd been in a city...

She shook that thought away. His stroke had been so catastrophic that even if he'd been in a hospital, he would've died.

"You have to be tough to live there."

She nodded. "Being a flying doctor is not for everyone."

"It's for you, though," he said softly, and he touched her cheek as he said that, which caused a flush to bloom in her cheeks. "When you blush, you look so...beautiful."

Imogen's heart raced. Her body seemed to come alive at his touch. His compliments made her swoon. It had been a long time since someone had touched her so intimately, and the fact it was Lev made her heart beat just a bit faster.

It was like she'd been asleep for years, walking around in a haze.

Numb.

"Well, your job as a flying doctor is admirable," he stated, breaking the heady tension that had fallen between them.

Another compliment. It caught her off guard.

"You could be so much more if you'd leave Yellowknife," Allen huffed, annoyed with her.

"Why would I leave Yellowknife? My services are needed here."

Allen shook his head. "Being a flying doctor? You could earn so much more if you came south."

"Are you asking me to marry you and come south?" She was shocked and a little thrilled at the prospect of marrying Allen.

"No," Allen said bluntly. "I'm going south. You can come if you want, but you know I don't believe in marriage."

"I'm not going south."

Her heart broke, but she couldn't choose a man who couldn't commit.

"Then I guess this is it." Allen turned his back on her and left.

"How is it admirable?"

"I take it not many physicians want to do what you do," Lev said, interrupting her thoughts.

"No. You're right. They don't." It was an ongoing problem that the north had a hard time keeping people. "I don't anymore. I do like the hospital I work at."

"Still, you amaze me."

"I don't know why. I love my life. Perhaps I'm selfish," she said sheepishly.

"No. Not selfish. Not to live like that. I'm envious of you. In Chenar, I work in the capital city and deal with… the elite of my country. It's not what I like. Not at all." His tone was one of dissatisfaction. "I much preferred my military work, but that came to an end and I was discharged."

"You don't sound happy."

"No. I'm not. I enjoyed it, but…my time was up."

"You could always leave," she offered. "Go somewhere else."

"If I could, I would." He took her hand again. "I wish I could be free like you, Imogen. I envy you."

Was she free? She didn't feel free.

"Last time I checked, Chenar was a free country. Sure, there's a king...but I don't think he's cruel."

A strange smile passed over his face. "No. Not at all. But let's not talk about it anymore. You promised me a drink."

"I did. It's just over here."

It was a short walk to the patio that she had been thinking of, but when they got there, it was closed. Instead, a small boutique hotel had opened up in its place. And though it didn't have a public bar, it had a rooftop patio for guests.

"Well, that's a shame. We can find somewhere else," she suggested.

"Didn't you say this was a good place?" he asked.

"I did, but the bar is only for hotel guests."

He grinned, a devious look in his eyes. "Let's get a room together."

Her pulse quickened. "What?"

"Get a room so we can have a drink."

"You're crazy." It was a mad idea, but still kind of thrilling.

"What do you think? We get a room, have a drink and then leave."

Live a little.

"Okay," she said excitedly. "Let's do it."

This was perhaps the craziest thing she'd ever done, but this whole night was so out of the norm for her, it was exciting. Her heart was not in danger and then she'd return to Yellowknife and her normal routine.

Lev was going to take a room just so they could have a drink on the rooftop. All that was left was a penthouse suite, but he paid for it anyway.

Soon they were on the rooftop patio of a penthouse suite that overlooked the lake, drinking glasses of champagne, like it was the most natural thing in the world.

"I still can't believe we did this," she said.

"Have you never done this?"

"No." She laughed.

He grinned and clinked her champagne flute against his. "Well, there's a first time for everything."

"Oh?" she asked, intrigued. "You do this a lot, do you?"

He took a sip and shook his head. "No. This is my first time too."

Her blood heated when he said that and she tried to swallow the bubbly liquid, but it was hard to do that with her heart racing, her body trembling, while the rational part of her brain was still trying to process why she was here.

The limbic part of her brain told her she was in the right place and it keenly reminded her that Allen had left a long time ago and she was single and had been alone for quite some time.

One glass of champagne led to another and another. It was a beautiful summer evening and somewhere they could hear the muted strains of jazz music from some piano bar, somewhere down there.

"I would like to dance," Lev announced, setting down his flute and standing up. "Dance with me."

"Does everyone follow your orders?" she teased, although she wanted to dance with him too. She'd been swaying to the music because she couldn't help herself. The champagne was getting to her.

"Yes. Because where I work I am the Chief of Staff." He grinned. "Dance with me, Imogen, and then we'll get a cab back to the conference hotel."

She set down her flute and took his hand, letting Lev pull her into his strong arms. It felt so good to be held by him, one hand holding hers and the other on the small of her back as they slowly moved together to the echoing music that was intermixed with the sounds of the waves lapping against the shore. Her body thrummed with desire.

It was magical and she didn't want the night to end. She

didn't want the moment to end and she didn't want to go back to the conference hotel.

Warmth bloomed in her cheeks as she thought about kissing him.

She wanted to kiss him.

He smiled down at her. "You look so beautiful I almost don't want to leave."

"I don't want to leave either." She bit her lip and then leaned in, standing on her toes, because she'd worn flats and he was so much taller than her. She pressed her lips against his for a quick kiss.

She was doing what she had always been afraid of doing—getting involved with a doctor.

You don't work with him. He won't hurt you.

This was out of her comfort zone, but she was really enjoying what it felt like to live a little. There had been so many times that she'd been afraid to take a chance on something she'd wanted and had let the moment get away. This time, with Lev, she wasn't so afraid. She was only afraid she would regret *not* having this stolen moment with him.

The kiss was light at first and then deepened. His arms went around her back, pulling her close, and suddenly it was no longer a light, butterfly kiss but something deep with longing.

It had been so long since a man had made her feel this way. Since she had felt this need to relinquish her careful control and just feel.

The kiss ended.

"I'm sorry, Imogen. I didn't mean for that..." he whispered against her ear, his voice deep and husky.

"Don't apologize," she whispered, and kissed him again, running her hands through his overlong blond hair, wanting to have more of him.

Even if it was just for one night.

She didn't care. She wanted something to remember

him by. She pressed her body against him, not wanting an inch of space separating them as she melted in his arms, his hands hot through the thin fabric of her summer dress. She couldn't help but wonder what they would feel like on her skin.

All she knew was that she wanted more.

"Imogen, are you sure?" he asked.

"I am." She had never been so sure of anything. Even if nothing came of this, even if she never saw him again, she wanted this moment.

She'd been wandering in a fog for too long and Lev had awakened something deep inside her. He scooped her up in his arms and carried her off the patio into the room. She was glad it was just the two of them, far from the rest of the conference, far from what they both knew.

Just the two of them in this moment.

CHAPTER TWO

LEV WATCHED HER SLEEP. He couldn't help himself—she was so beautiful.

He'd thought so the moment he'd first laid eyes on her at the conference when he'd arrived late. She'd been the only friendly face in the crowd.

And a beautiful one at that.

Usually he avoided women.

He'd been so in love with Tatiana.

His father hadn't approved of her, but he hadn't cared. He'd believed they were meant for each other. He'd been about to propose to her when he'd caught her cheating.

She'd acted like it was no big deal. His father had cheated on his mother. It was all about position and wealth in Tatiana's eyes. There was no such thing as love.

To the world they had seemed perfect, but Lev remembered how sad his late mother had been in her marriage and he felt that same sadness and hurt too. He'd broken it off with Tatiana and joined the Chenarian armed forces as a trauma surgeon.

He'd been burned before. They never saw *him*, only his position.

His plan had been to keep far away from Imogen, but the fates seemed to have another plan, because every time he turned around, there she was.

And he was glad to see her, even though he knew he should keep away, but there was something genuine about her.

He knew he shouldn't have gone to that mixer, he knew he shouldn't have engaged with her, but he couldn't help it. She was beautiful, with long, soft, silky light brown hair, big expressive blue eyes, and her pink full lips were ones he could kiss for a long time. He liked it that she was tall and could almost look him in the eye. She held her head high with confidence, and she was funny, intelligent and dedicated to learning and furthering her career as a surgeon.

When they had been working in the simulation lab, he'd seen her ace the new surgical technique with skill, and the way she'd handled a laparoscope with such grace had been admirable. And she'd been willing to help him.

As a trauma surgeon, he had to get in fast and do repair work, but he wanted to learn all he could.

Imogen's had been the only friendly face in the crowd.

Everything about her was admirable.

His father and brother would not find that particular quality, intelligence, something to admire in a woman, but that was what he always looked for. He wanted an equal partner, and in his circle of Chenar society, that was almost impossible to find. Especially after Tatiana.

Imogen was a rarity in his world and he wished he could stay here forever with her. He hadn't planned on making love to her tonight, but he was glad it had happened. It had been a momentary lapse when he had forgotten who he was and who his family was. He had been caught up in the moment with her.

One stolen moment with her...

He reached out and touched her arm. She murmured in her sleep but didn't wake up. He smiled and couldn't help but think of how it felt to taste her lips against his, have those arms wrapped around him and be buried deep inside her.

Everything else in his life was a complete blur.

It was just her and him at that moment. It was an escape. One he desperately wanted.

Lev's phone buzzed and Imogen stirred in her sleep. He cursed inwardly, angry that it was intruding on their time together, and picked up his phone, to see a stream of texts that he'd ignored all night.

The last one made him angry as he realized that they had tracked his phone's GPS and were in the lobby. His bodyguards. Lexi and Gustav had been plastered to his side all weekend, not giving him a chance to breathe, and he felt bad for them. He knew they were bored out of their skulls, attending a medical conference, but his father had insisted when he'd given Lev permission to attend.

Lev wasn't to leave Chenar without Lexi and Gustav. His father had become so overprotective lately, not that his father really showed any affection. It was all about preserving his male heirs.

It was why his father had forced him to leave the military. His father had ordered it so. In his father's words, it was high time he used his foolish medical degree for the benefit of the cream of Chenar society.

He was actually surprised he'd been able to slip away from them at the mixer with Imogen. It had been an act of defiance, and a thrill of freedom to do that.

He didn't want Imogen to know who he really was. He didn't want the truth of his family to cloud her judgment of him, like it almost always did when women found out that Dr. Lev Vanin was just an alias. He was a doctor, but he tried to keep it quiet that he was the spare to the heir and really Prince Viktor Lanin of Chenar.

Women, once they found out who he was, changed. They wanted the fantasy. The prestige and power of being with a prince. Women like Imogen put their careers first, instead of duty to a country, and he couldn't begrudge them that. He envied Imogen's freedom and he would give almost anything to stay here in Canada and move to the north to get lost.

He loved the wilderness and loathed the pomp and ceremony surrounding his birth. Especially his ever-present bodyguards.

Lev quickly got dressed and texted Lexi that he was on his way down, that there was no need to come up. He'd get rid of them and then he would go back to Imogen and tell her he had to leave and why—because of who he was.

It would change everything. He was sure it would—it always did, even if part of him wanted to think that Imogen was different.

He slipped out of the room and headed downstairs. He knew that Lexi and Gustav, who had been with him since medical school, would be more than annoyed that he'd managed to give them the slip and go to an unsanctioned hotel with a woman.

And he was sure his father, once he found out, would be none too happy, but Lev didn't care. He didn't regret a single moment of his stolen freedom. It had been worth it.

The moment he got off the elevators he could sense there was something in the air. Lexi was acting strangely and his stomach knotted. Something was wrong. Gustav was on the phone, Lexi's gun was visible on his holster, and he was pacing. Outside, through the glass doors connecting the small lobby to the outside world, he could see black SUVs waiting and more guards.

Canadian bodyguards.

Something was wrong.

"Lexi," Lev said, coming forward, speaking Chenarian, which had developed over centuries from a blend of

Norse and Romanian, so that no one else would understand. "What's wrong?"

"There's been a coup," Lexi responded, his face somber. "Your father... I'm sorry, Viktor."

Lev couldn't breathe for a moment as Lexi's words sank in. That his father had been overthrown and was dead. It was something his father had talked about. It was one of the dangers of ruling a country with an unstable government, and though Lev had logically known something like this could happen, he'd never really thought it would.

He lived in an idyllic bubble where his father and his family were impervious to the machinations of those who sought power.

"What about Kristof?" Lev asked.

"Missing in action and presumed dead, but in reality he's safe. He just wants the world to think he's dead...and he wants you to go into hiding. Here," Gustav responded, ending his phone call. "It's a mess in Chenar. We've been speaking with the Canadian government and we need to protect you in case..."

"In case something happens to Kristof," Lev finished.

"The insurgents don't know where he is or where you are, because they don't know your alias. They don't know you're a surgeon," Lexi said. "The Canadian government has agreed to hide you. Embassy cars are outside and a plane is waiting. We have to go."

"I can't go into hiding. My father, my brother...our people."

"There is no choice, Your Highness," Gustav responded. "Our allies are sending in troops. This will be resolved, but until then we need to keep you hidden and safe."

"I cannot hide away. Not when there's trouble in Chenar. I need to go and—"

"Your Highness, there is no other option. This plan was

put in place by your father if something like this were ever to happen."

Lev was furious. It was just like his father to do something without telling him or Kristof what was going on. And even though he had no desire to be King or even a prince, for that matter, he hated knowing that his people were in danger.

That there was suffering, violence, and he was powerless to do anything.

He was safe and that was not right. He clenched his fists in frustration, but he knew he couldn't make a scene. It was late at night and he didn't want to draw attention to himself or his bodyguards, who were just as worried, upset and powerless to do anything to help their country.

They are helping their country by keeping you safe.

And then it really hit him that his father was gone and he didn't know where his brother was. At least Kristof was safe, or that was what he'd been told. He really didn't know.

He was being selfish by standing here and arguing with Gustav and Lexi about what needed to be done. Even though it drove him mad that he couldn't be on the front line, giving help to his people during this time of crisis, he had to do his duty and he had to go into hiding.

Imogen.

He looked back to the elevator with regret. He wanted to tell her everything now more than ever. He wanted to tell her why he was disappearing, but that wouldn't be safe.

It certainly wouldn't be safe for her.

Lev knew he had no choice but to leave. He was glad the room was paid for and that Imogen could just check out. He grabbed a piece of hotel stationery and quickly scrawled a note, apologizing to Imogen for his abrupt departure but not telling her why.

"Would you please give this to my guest when she leaves tomorrow morning?" he asked the concierge.

"Of course," the concierge responded, taking the envelope.

"Thank you," Lev said.

He wished he could go up to the room and tell Imogen in person why he was leaving. He wanted to tell her everything, but couldn't. She was the sacrifice he had to make for his country.

He couldn't let his people down. He couldn't let his brother down.

He couldn't let his father down.

"Your Highness," Gustav said gently. "We have to go."

"I know." Lev sighed. "Let's go."

Lexi and Gustav walked beside him. Their guns were visible at their sides, and Lev felt ill as he exited the hotel and saw the heavily armored dark SUVs waiting. The Canadian government had come to take him away to who knew where.

He just hoped that, wherever he went, he could still practice medicine while he waited for news from Kristof about when he could safely return to his country and mourn his father.

Properly.

CHAPTER THREE

Three months later, August
Yellowknife, Northwest Territories

"You can't live on a houseboat with a baby!" Dr. Jeanette Ducharme proclaimed, bursting into the doctors' lounge. Imogen knew instantly that the comment was directed at her for two reasons. She was the only one currently pregnant who worked at the hospital and the only one of the physicians who lived on a houseboat.

Imogen cocked an eyebrow in question at the Chief of Staff and her best friend in Yellowknife, who rarely got involved with people's lives, but seemed overly protective of her as of late.

Probably because she had been the one who had told Imogen to "live a little" at that conference in Toronto, which was how she had ended up pregnant in the first place.

Imogen liked to think that Jeanette felt bad, but only just a bit, and usually only when Imogen was having a really bad case of morning sickness.

Really, it was Imogen's fault she'd had a one-night stand in the first place, for throwing caution to the wind and momentarily forgetting she'd had her IUD taken out a month before because of the horrific migraines it had been causing. She'd forgotten in the moment that she'd had no other form of birth control, and she hadn't wanted Lev to stop.

Kids had never been in the plan, but now she was going to have a baby.

It was still kind of shocking, but she was excited and scared too.

Really scared.

She'd been raised by a single parent. She could do this.

Can you?

There was a fair bit of self-doubt buried deep down inside that told her she was crazy for even thinking of doing this alone. Her father had given her so much love and support, but there was always that piece missing, the weight of not knowing her mother.

Always wondering, always envious of those who had mothers.

She worried her baby would feel that way about not knowing its father.

It broke her heart and scared her.

Focus.

There was nothing to regret about her one night with Lev.

It had been unplanned, but she could do this.

She cleared her throat. "What're you talking about? Why did that thought just randomly pop into your head? Lots of people with kids live on the lake like me. It's called environmentally friendly living. I'm leaving less of a carbon footprint."

Jeanette rolled her eyes. "It has nothing to do with that. You're by yourself. What if you go into labor and there's a storm? Or your motorboat won't start or your anchor gives way and your barge just drifts away out into Great Slave Lake…"

"Jeanette, calm down. I'm only three months pregnant. The baby will come in the winter."

"Exactly. What if there's a blizzard or the ice hasn't formed…?"

"Right. Blizzards do happen in the winter," Imogen teased, trying to make light of a situation that she'd been thinking about too. "I don't live that far offshore and I have contingency plans. The ice should be formed by then and I have my snowmobile."

"Ice thickness has been tricky these last few winters. Winters are getting warmer… Ice road season is shrinking. Take it from me—I've lived here my whole life. It's not freezing as thick! Look how warm our summer was."

Imogen sighed and rubbed her temples. "Jeanette, what has gotten into you?"

"You know I like to think ahead." Jeanette sat down on the couch next to her. "I worry about you. Out there all alone and stuff."

Imogen chuckled. "I'm fine. Really."

What Imogen didn't tell her was that those thoughts had crossed her mind from time to time too. Ever since she'd found out she was pregnant and that she was alone. Truly alone. Her father was gone, she'd never known her mother, and she didn't have any extended family. She didn't have anyone to rely on.

It was just her. The way it had been for some time, and she was comfortable with that.

And Lev was gone.

The moment she'd found out she was pregnant she had called the Chenarian Embassy—or what passed for an embassy in the wake of the coup. She'd wanted to relay a message to him, but the consulate and Canada had repeatedly said they didn't know where he was, other than that he had returned to Chenar and was lost.

Lev was missing in action. No, not Lev. Prince Viktor Lanin. That had been a surprise she hadn't expected. A bigger shock to her than news of her pregnancy would be to him, she had thought.

It made her feel ill, thinking he was dead, but there was simply no information on him. Just reports. Prince Kristof and Prince Viktor were missing, and King Ivan was dead.

There was no sign of him and she'd tried all she could to find him.

Lev had vanished the morning all hell had broken loose in Chenar. There was no reliable communication with the war-torn country.

Her heart broke, thinking he might be dead, and she had no way of finding him or telling him about the baby. She also had a hard time believing he was gone—perhaps he had only got mixed up in the chaos and was unreachable? She knew she was foolish to cling to the hope that he was still alive, but somehow she couldn't let it go.

It upset her she couldn't tell him about the baby and that Lev might never know their child.

Would he even care? He was a prince and you were just a fling.

She didn't know. She liked to think Lev would care. After finding out Lev was really Prince Viktor, she'd looked him up online to try to force her brain to accept the truth. There were a few photos of him when he was young, but there weren't many of him as an adult—or even pictures of Dr. Lev Vanin, his alias.

Prince Viktor Lanin was different from the man with whom she'd had the one-night stand. His long blond hair was short and clean-cut. There was no beard, and he was clean-shaven and regal. It was the eyes that gave him away.

But now it was just her and her baby.

And she couldn't tell anyone who the father was.

And, anyway, there was no proof and she wanted to protect her child. She didn't want attention drawn to her or the baby, especially with such a politically unstable situation in Chenar.

She was terrified of being on her own, of carrying an heir to the throne of a country in chaos, and she was scared that she was living alone on the lake in the home her father had bought for himself to live in when he'd retired from his work in Alert.

All Jeanette's fears were her own. It was just that Imogen didn't want to say them out loud. If she said them out loud, it made them real. Not that they weren't real, but it was a way for Imogen to compartmentalize it all. Of course, Jeanette had done that for her instead, by stating the obvious.

"I didn't mean to freak you out," Jeanette said.

"I'm not freaked out." Although she was.

"You looked freaked."

Imogen sighed. "I'm okay. Truly. You don't need to worry."

"I just feel responsible."

"You didn't get me pregnant," Imogen said dryly. "I did that on my own...sort of."

She grew sad as she thought of Lev and the night she had thrown caution to the wind; when she thought of how he'd made her feel.

Lev was gone and her baby could never know his or her father. Imogen knew how that felt, how it felt not to know a parent.

Her mother had left shortly after she was born and her dad had never remarried.

She'd always had a feeling of being incomplete and she never wanted that for a child of her own, but here she was.

Alone. She touched her belly—not that she could feel anything, but it gave her comfort to ground herself. To think about all the possibilities. That was what she wanted to do right now—she wanted to think of the positives, because focusing on the negatives was just too scary.

Whatever happened, she was going to do right by her child. Her father had given her all he could, and although she had mourned and wondered about her mother, she had never been lacking in love.

And neither would her baby. Even if it completely freaked her out.

Jeanette chuckled, interrupting her chain of thought. "No, I don't suppose you conceived this baby on your own. I'm just worried about you. You're not only my colleague. You're my friend."

"Thanks, Jeanette. I appreciate it. I feel the same way about you, you know." She smiled.

Jeanette grinned. "I'm glad and I'm sorry for freaking you out slightly. That was not my intention."

"Well, to put your mind at ease, I've actually leased out the houseboat for the winter to a couple of scientists from Alert. They were colleagues of my father. They're coming down for an extended research trip and needed a place to stay, so they're taking over the houseboat for the winter season. I've found an awesome rental for the winter, which is not far from the hospital, so I'll be on the mainland for some time. I promise you the ice, or lack thereof, won't be a problem when the time comes."

"Oh, my God, that's so good to hear!" Jeanette gave her a side hug.

"So that's all you wanted to talk to me about on my break?" Imogen asked quizzically. "You just wanted to discuss my temporary living arrangements?"

"Yes. Well...no. I have a new assignment for you!"

Imogen groaned. Jeanette's code word for assignment meant a new doctor to the territory. When Jeanette used the word *case* it meant a new patient but *assignment* meant a difficult new doctor who even Jeanette was struggling with.

"Really?"

Jeanette stood. "I'll go and get him. He should be finished with Human Resources and you can show him the ropes."

"Why me?" Imogen sighed, getting up from the couch where she'd actually been enjoying a quiet morning until now.

"Because you're so lovable."

Imogen frowned. "I don't think that's it."

"Fine. Because you can handle these stubborn newbies."

"You're the Chief of Staff!" Imogen complained.

"Exactly! Which is why I'm so busy and need your help and your gentle but firm touch here."

Imogen rolled her eyes as Jeanette left the doctors' lounge, essentially giving Imogen no choice in the matter. As much as she didn't want to take over and show this new doctor the ropes, she knew that in a few months she'd be leaving Jeanette short one surgeon, in a place where there was already a shortage of doctors.

The least she could do was help this new doctor settle in.

She took a deep breath as Jeanette opened the door.

"Dr. Imogen Hayes, I'd like to introduce our newest member of the Yellowknife medical community, Dr. Lev Vanin!"

Lev took a step back, his eyes wide as he looked at her, and Imogen did the same, but she tried not to show her shock for too long. She didn't want Jeanette to suspect something, but Lev appeared just as shocked as she was. At least Jeanette couldn't see his expression.

And Jeanette wouldn't know he was a prince. He looked very different from the official photos online and he was using his alias.

Still, she couldn't believe he was here and he was alive! Her brain was trying to rationalize why a missing prince of a war-torn country was standing in front of her, in Yellowknife, of all places, while her heart was leaping and skipping. Of course she was glad he was still alive, but she was scared about what the future held for her unborn child.

She wasn't going to keep her child from its father, but really what did it all mean? All she could think was that her baby was in danger and there was no way to control the unknown. Her anxiety ticked up a notch.

Focus.

She had to keep calm so Jeanette wouldn't suspect anything.

"It's a pleasure to meet you, Dr. Vanin." Imogen stuck out her hand, hoping her voice didn't crack or sound too awkward.

"The pleasure is all mine," Lev said, taking her hand briefly.

"Dr. Hayes will show you around. She is Chief of General Surgery here in Yellowknife—at least until the winter, before she goes on maternity leave."

Imogen winced and could hear herself internally screaming. This was not how she wanted him to find out.

Lev's eyes widened again, his gaze falling to her belly, which really wasn't showing under her dark blue scrubs, as she was only three months along.

"I'm sure Dr. Hayes will fill me in on everything here," Lev said slowly. "Thank you, Dr. Ducharme, for such a warm welcome, and my apologies for the hiccup earlier."

Jeanette nodded. "Well, I'll leave you two to it."

"Thank you, Jeanette." Imogen was trying not to shake as Jeanette left the room. When they were finally alone, Lev crossed his arms.

"Pregnant?" he said, sounding astounded.

"Well, it's nice to see you too, Dr. Vanin. Or should I say Your Highness?"

Lev winced.

He suddenly remembered that he'd told her the truth in

the note he'd left for her at the hotel. He'd wanted her to know why he'd left. Why he'd had to leave. He'd thought he would never see her again.

He hadn't known where she worked and Canada was so large.

He was stunned to see her. Overjoyed to see her.

Since everything had fallen apart in Chenar, he'd been moved from one place to another. He had wanted to return to her that night, he hadn't wanted to leave her in the lurch like that, but he'd had no choice.

His brother, Kristof, who was also in hiding, had demanded Lev stay in Canada.

And, since their father was dead, Kristof was technically King and Lev had no choice but to obey. And he'd been shuttled from location to location ever since.

Lexi was in Yellowknife with him, but Gustav had had to return to serve in the military. Lexi wasn't alone in his duties. The Canadian government had provided protection.

Lev might be able to walk around freely, but he knew Lexi and the others were not far away.

Even though he was in Canada and hidden, he still wasn't free and he really didn't care about that. With his father gone and his brother also in hiding, Lev felt an even stronger sense of duty to his people. Once the situation in Chenar had de-escalated he would go back.

He'd go back to Chenar and properly mourn his father. They may have had their differences but Lev had made peace with their cold relationship.

He'd made peace with a lot of things since his homeland had been plunged into turmoil and he was stuck in Canada, powerless.

He couldn't let his grief take hold of him right now. The only way he'd make it through this whole ordeal was focusing on what he could do, and that was being a trauma surgeon…if he could just stay in one spot for more than a week at a time. He hoped the Canadian government and Lexi would agree that Yellowknife was a safe place for him and leave him here.

But then he saw Imogen and heard she was pregnant.

That took him a moment to wrap his mind around. Imogen was pregnant and not far along.

It might not be yours.

And that thought brought him back to reality.

Imogen was his secret joy, and he liked to remember their time together when the weight of everything that was happening to him dragged him down. She was the one good thing he could think of, even though he'd thought he would probably never see her again.

And now here she was, standing in front of him, and she was pregnant. Pregnant! And he could be the father. Most likely he was. Children had always been something he'd wanted, but it was hard to imagine that with his life the way it was right now. He was also terrified because he'd never had his father's love or affection. How could he be a good father?

So he never thought about kids. He'd entertained the notion when he'd been with Tatiana, but then she'd shown her true colors and all those hopes of having a real family had been dashed.

And now with Chenar in turmoil, he didn't want to put a child of his in danger.

"Am I the father?" he asked. In one way he was hoping that he was the father, because that meant there was no other man who had captured her heart, but he also worried about the burden of his family and the situation falling on his child. The thought of something happening to his child, to Imogen, because of who he was was too much to bear thinking about.

"Yes," she said quickly, apparently annoyed. "You are."

Not that he could blame her for being annoyed. First

he'd left her, leaving behind a hastily scribbled note with a bombshell of his own, and now he was questioning her integrity.

"I would ask why you didn't tell me, but I have been a bit out of touch with the world." Lev scrubbed a hand over his face.

"I know," she said gently. "The world says you're missing in action. I thought you were dead. You just vanished."

"It's better that way," Lev said quickly. At least Kristof seemed to think so. Lev wasn't so sure.

"Where have you been?" she asked.

"Everywhere, but no location was safe. Yellowknife is a small enough city that your government feels like I can be protected and work as a doctor, thus keeping up my secret identity."

"Okay," she said, but there was an odd edge to her voice. He didn't blame her. He was pretty sure he knew what she was thinking. She was as confused as he was. And he was terrified about her safety as well as his child's.

And he knew she was probably worried about their child. *Their* child.

He was still having a hard time wrapping his mind around that fact.

His stomach twisted in a knot. All he could think was that the danger that plagued his country now posed a threat to his child.

To Imogen.

It terrified him.

How was he going to protect his child? How was he going to protect Imogen?

Is it really your child, though?

And that niggling thought ate away at him. He remembered what had happened with his brother. His brother had fallen in love with a woman who was not of their father's choosing and that woman had become pregnant, supposedly with the next heir. Kristof had been over-the-moon happy. He'd been thrilled, and there had been a wedding planned.

And then it had come out that his brother's intended had been duping him. Just like Tatiana.

That the child was not really his.

His brother had been so broken and Lev never wanted to feel that kind of pain. He was wary about entering into relationships. He didn't want to feel that betrayal his brother felt.

He couldn't let himself get too excited. He had to protect himself, just as he wanted to make sure that Imogen wasn't in danger because of her association with him.

Why is she in Yellowknife?

She'd been safer when he hadn't known where she was. How had he not known she lived here?

Because she never said where she lived.

All she'd said was that she lived in the country and had been a flying doctor at one point.

Yellowknife was small, but it was a city. This was not country.

"You look like I feel," she said.

"How is that?"

"Stunned."

Yes. He was stunned, but he didn't want to talk about it.

"Why don't you show me to where I'm supposed to work?" Lev said, breaking the odd tension that had fallen between them. "I'm eager to get started. That's what I'm here for."

Imogen nodded. "Of course. I'll take you down to the emergency room. Follow me."

Lev followed her out of the doctors' lounge and through the halls. It wasn't a long walk from the emergency department. He would only be seeing those who required emergency surgeries. There were people in the emergency room who didn't have a regular family doctor, or those seeking help for mental health. Those patients fell under other doctors' jurisdiction. As much as he wanted to help more, he couldn't draw attention to himself. If someone figured out who he was, the truth could get back to Chenar and he'd be moved again...and now he knew where Imogen was, he didn't want to be moved.

"This is the emergency department. I'll take you over to the nursing station so you can be filled in on the protocols for triage. I know you're a trauma surgeon, but you'll be assessing more than traumatic injuries here. We're short-staffed and it's all hands on deck."

"That is not what I was told," he said.

"Well, that's how it is in the north. I made it clear that was how it was when we met," Imogen snapped.

"No. Not really," he said. "I had no idea you lived here."

If he'd known she was here, he would have told someone in the consulate so he wouldn't have been assigned here. He dismissed the wrench in his gut that said he would have done everything to ensure he was brought straight here.

"I told you."

"No. You said you lived in the country. This is not the country."

She rolled her eyes. "So I did, but I mentioned flying doctors to you."

"You did, but Canada is so large."

She sighed. "Well, you're here now."

"I am."

"And that means all hands on deck. As I said, we're short-staffed." Then she leaned over. "Sometimes we have to fly into remote communities. You will have to do that as well. Especially if there's an accident."

"I was not informed of this."

"Well, consider yourself informed." Imogen turned on her heel and headed toward the nurses' station. He followed after her, annoyed for a moment about the whole situation.

Yes, he was practicing medicine, but all he really wanted to do was go back to Chenar and assess the damage. Those were the people he should be helping. It was obvious his presence here in Yellowknife was not welcome. Lev could understand her coldness and knew it was for the best she keep her distance.

It would be the best for both of them.

It was safer for her and the baby. The baby...

And yet she was someone he could not get out of his mind. All those lonely nights, the nights he couldn't sleep and didn't know where he'd end up, he'd seen her face.

She'd been a comfort during all the chaos.

He didn't want to stay away from her, even though it was for the best.

She'd unknowingly been his rock since the collapse of his country. But now they were here in Yellowknife, things had to change. He didn't want to stay away from her—he was drawn to her. But he had to protect them.

Protect Imogen. Protect their child. And protect his heart.

CHAPTER FOUR

He was okay.

Of course she was relieved he was alive and not lost.

But she was also angry that the embassies had lied to her about not knowing where he was. She knew, logically, it had been to protect him. But that didn't change the emotions coursing through her body.

Imogen sat behind the nurses' station in the emergency room, watching Lev assess a patient. He was looking at the patient's imaging at one of the many computers in the central part of the trauma bubble, where all patients went when they had been triaged and there was a bed available.

When she'd received his note that first morning, she'd been floored. It had shocked her, and she'd thought of nothing else the whole way back to Yellowknife. Then the stick had turned blue and her world had come crashing down.

After she couldn't get hold of him, when she didn't know where he was—or whether he was even alive—she'd had to accept that she'd be raising this baby on her own. And she'd grieved the loss of him for her child. She'd grieved that her child would never know its father.

She knew what it was like, always wondering what they thought of you. Why they'd left. Worrying that you were the reason they'd left. That you hadn't been good enough for them. She'd never wanted it for a child of her own.

And suddenly there he was, standing right in front of her, in Yellowknife and under her supervision.

And she had to pinch herself to see if she was dreaming.

It felt like she was dreaming.

Lev glanced in her direction, as if sensing she was watching him, and she looked away quickly, but not gracefully. It was obvious she was watching him and she was mortified, but she couldn't help herself. Even though she was conflicted, she still found herself drawn to him.

Attracted to him.

Knowing exactly what it was like to be with him and craving that pleasure again.

Pull yourself together.

She sighed and tried to return to her work.

You don't get involved with or sleep with people you work with.

Only it was too late for that! She didn't regret their night together, but she was still reeling from the shock. Lev was here, alive and hiding in Yellowknife, working with her.

The missing Prince of Chenar was actually a trauma surgeon, and he was here, working in Yellowknife...and she was carrying his baby.

This seemed like something out of an offbeat comedy. *That ended with the hero and heroine falling in love and living happily ever after.*

She snorted at that thought and went back to her charting.

There was no way that could happen. She couldn't make the mistake of believing it could, of trusting someone in that way.

Allen had hurt her. She'd thought he was her home, her family, but he hadn't been. He'd left. Just like her mother had.

She didn't want their child to get hurt if it ended—or

rather, *when* it ended. Lev still deserved to be involved in their child's life and her baby deserved to have both of its parents. But she didn't want her child to feel the same rejection she did. The pain of being left behind.

Love was fleeting and never seemed to last. Not really. It was rare and Imogen had a hard time believing in happily-ever-after. There had been no happily-ever-after for her father. He'd been crushed when her mother had left him and he'd pined for her his entire life.

And then there was her one real, long-term relationship. That had ended badly and broken her heart.

Love was a fantasy not in the cards for her.

She wasn't going to get hurt. Lev could be involved with their baby, but not with her.

She had to protect her heart.

She couldn't—and wouldn't—deny her child access to its father.

She never wanted that for her child. But she couldn't pretend it wouldn't have been easier to tell her child that its father was dead, as cruel as that sounded, but it was the truth. Telling your child that it had been abandoned because its parent hadn't wanted it was a lot more painful.

"You can explain to her why you're not coming to see her. She's been looking forward to seeing you."

Her father looked at Imogen sadly as she stood by the door of their home in Toronto, waiting for her mother, who had promised to come and take her for the night.

Waiting for a woman who never came.

"Denise, this... Fine. Fine." Her dad hung up the phone and sighed.

"She's not coming, is she?" Imogen asked sadly, not unfamiliar with this disappointment.

"No, honey. She's not. How about we do something together?"

"No. It's okay, Dad. I'll just go read in my room for a bit."

Tears stung her eyes and Imogen swallowed the painful lump in her throat. She was angry at herself for letting that memory intrude. She didn't like to think of her mother. Didn't like to think about the pain and the disappointment she always felt when she was promised something and constantly disappointed.

Allen had promised her that they'd stay in the north. That he'd remain faithful to her.

That he loved her.

But all that had changed when he'd got a better job offer. He'd just left.

The only constant in life had been her father, but he was gone, and she was terrified that Lev would leave and not be there for their child.

Either way, she'd be the constant in their child's life.

She wasn't going to leave, but she wasn't going to force Lev into something he wasn't comfortable with. The moment the stick had turned blue, she had made her peace with the fact that she was probably going to do this on her own.

She glanced up again and Lev had moved on.

At least he was doing his work. Jeanette might've found him difficult, but really Lev wasn't being all that difficult, other than seeming not to understand the concept about the doctor shortage.

Not many physicians, nurses or even teachers came to the north. Yellowknife had it better than most communities, because it was a large city in the territory, but attracting qualified professionals to remote places was difficult.

The phone rang at the main station and Imogen answered

it, because it was a call from the dispatch phone and the nurse was working on triage.

"Emergency," she said over the line.

"We have an ambulance en route. Three injured. Boat capsized just off Jolliffe Island. One patient had to be intubated and vitals are weak," the ambulance dispatch answered.

"How far out?" Imogen asked, standing and motioning for the trauma team with hand signals they were used to.

"Five minutes."

"Okay. Thanks." Imogen hung up the phone.

Lev stepped out of the pod where he'd finished with a patient. "What's going on?"

"Incoming trauma," Imogen said. "You're the trauma surgeon on duty. I'll show you where to meet the ambulances."

Lev nodded and followed her as they quickly grabbed disposable gowns and gloves to cover their scrubs. He followed her outside, where they could hear the distant wail of the ambulance.

"What happened?" Lev asked.

"A boat capsized in the lake. One of the patients had to be intubated. You can take that patient and I'll assess the other two for injuries and then help you if you need it."

Lev nodded and she was glad he was here. His specialty was trauma, and though she'd worked on emergency situations, she much preferred the operating room over the accident scene. But this was the north, specialists were in short supply, and, as she'd tried to tell him, everyone mucked in when they were needed.

The ambulance pulled up and the doors opened.

Lev took over, as the first ambulance had the intubated patient. The ambulance driver rattled off instructions, while Lev did his own assessment, helping the ambulance crew push the intubated victim into the resuscitation room.

The second ambulance pulled up and the third followed. Imogen pointed one of her residents in the direction of the second ambulance when she realized the patient there had a superficial head wound that required stitching.

In the third ambulance, the patient had what looked to be a dislocated shoulder.

"What happened out there?" Imogen asked as she helped the ambulance crew to wheel her patient into another room.

"Wind whipped up pretty fast on the lee side of Jolliffe Island. It was something strange for sure and their boat wasn't that sound. Looked like it had seen better days."

Imogen nodded. "Gotcha. So it was probably taking on water."

The ambulance driver, Dave, nodded. "Yeah."

"I told my dad to get the boat fixed, but he said it would be fine," the young man said, grimacing as the ambulance crew helped him off the stretcher onto the hospital gurney.

"You're not from Yellowknife, are you?" Imogen asked, not that it mattered, but she wanted to distract her patient from the pain while they set him up with an IV, which would give him the pain meds he'd need to go through the X-ray and while they popped the joint back into the socket.

"How did you know?" the young man asked.

"I've never seen you come through here and I live out by Jolliffe Island. I notice new boats when they putter by."

The young man chuckled. "We're from Edmonton. Thought we'd come up a bit farther to do some fishing."

"What's your name?" Imogen asked, as the nurses working with her prepped his arm and she examined his dislocated shoulder.

"Tom."

"Are you allergic to anything, Tom?" she asked.

"No."

"Good. We're going to get an IV started and give you some pain meds, and then we're going to get some imaging on your shoulder here, which I think is dislocated. Is your father the patient in the first ambulance, the one who had to be intubated?"

Tom nodded, his face pale. "Yeah. My brother and I were able to get to shore and call for help. We thought Dad was behind us."

"I'll check on him. Is there anything I need to tell my team about your dad?"

"No. He's pretty healthy for sixty."

Imogen smiled. "Good. You just relax the best you can and we'll take care of you. Jessica, start an IV and give him some morphine for the pain. Let me know when his imaging comes back."

"Yes, Dr. Hayes," Jessica said.

Imogen left Tom to the capable team of nurses and checked on Tom's brother, who was getting sutures, and then she made her way to where Lev was working.

"How is he?" Imogen asked, joining in as the team worked on Tom's father.

"He has a head injury. Looks like he hit his head on a rock and he has water in his lungs. He had a brief moment of tachycardia, but we have his heart rate under control. There was no asystole," Lev said. "He's stable and his pupils are reactive. I just want to get some imaging done on his head. We have a central line started and I would like to keep him intubated until after the imaging."

"Okay. Well, let's get him down to CT." Imogen helped Lev wheel Tom's father out of the resuscitation room.

They got their patient down to CT and waited together while the imaging came up.

"How are the other patients?" Lev asked, as they waited.

"Well, one of the sons has a superficial laceration to his head that's being stitched up and my patient has a dislocated shoulder. I just want to make sure that I can safely pop the joint back into place and that he doesn't need surgery."

Lev opened his mouth to say something when they heard an alarm.

"He's going into cardiac arrest," the CT technician said over the speaker as they hit the code button.

"Page Cardio!" Lev shouted as he dashed out of the room to the patient.

Imogen paged Dr. Snell and then joined Lev as they got the patient out of the CT machine and began chest compressions, and the nurse handed Imogen a dose of epinephrine.

Dr. Snell was there within a few moments and took the lead as the three of them rushed the patient out of CT and up to the OR floor.

"I have it from here, Doctor," Dr. Snell said, as his team took over the patient outside the OR. Imogen could tell that Lev wanted to continue to help, but Dr. Snell was one of the best cardiac doctors north of sixty.

Lev stood back. "I should be helping."

"Dr. Snell has it. And wasn't it you that seemed confused you would be doing more in the emergency room than you have in the past?"

A half smile crept on his face. "Yes. This is true."

"Be thankful we have Dr. Snell. He's the best in these parts." Imogen got a page that her patient's imaging was back. "Looks like my patient's X-rays are in. Want to help put a shoulder back in place?"

"Don't you have an orthopedic surgeon?"

"We do, but he's not on duty today, and it's most likely a simple fix. I'm sure you can handle it."

Lev nodded. "I've done a few."

"Come on, then. I much prefer the scalpel to popping a joint back into place."

By the time they got back to the pod where Tom was waiting, he was pretty high on pain medication, which would make their job easier.

"The images you ordered, Dr. Hayes." Jessica brought

up the imaging on the computer and Imogen was relieved to see that it was a simple dislocation.

"Thank you, Jessica. If you could assist Dr. Vanin here, we'd be grateful."

Jessica nodded and smiled shyly at Lev, who didn't pay much attention to her. A small pang of jealousy hit her. It surprised her. She shouldn't care. Lev wasn't hers, but it bothered her that another woman was interested in him too.

Don't let it bother you.

She understood exactly what Jessica was feeling. Lev was sexy and charming. He was handsome and a doctor.

Three months ago, Imogen had been feeling it too when Lev had swept her off her feet. Or maybe she had swept him off his feet. Either way, sweeping had happened, and now she was pregnant. She thought about that night. It flashed in her mind. It made her blood fire.

Focus.

"Are you ready, Tom?" Imogen asked. "Dr. Vanin here is going to put your shoulder back into place."

Tom grinned up at her. "You're tall! She's tall!"

Imogen rolled her eyes while Lev chuckled. "Yes, Tom, she is."

Tom's eyes widened. "You're like a Viking! You know there are Viking graves up here, eh?"

"Is that so?" Lev said, trying to hide his amusement. "Now, brace yourself, Tom. This will hurt for a moment. One, two…"

Lev didn't finish his countdown as he popped the joint back into place. Tom let out a shriek and then passed out.

"Is he okay?" Lev asked.

"He's fine," Jessica said. "Vitals are good."

"Good. Thank you," Lev said, and then he looked at Imogen. "How much pain medication did you order for this man?"

"The standard amount for his size." Imogen left the trauma pod and Lev followed behind her.

"I have never been referred to as a Viking before, although our ancestors are Scandinavian and not Russian. My mother was from Sweden."

Imogen chuckled. "Well, the first time I saw you I have to admit I thought the same thing. I thought you were more Nordic. That was before I knew where you came from."

Lev's brow furrowed in puzzlement. "What about me says Viking to you?"

"You're taller than me."

"Other men are taller than you," he stated.

"Not many. I'm five foot eleven."

Lev shrugged. "What else?"

Imogen felt her cheeks warm. "I don't know."

"Come on. There must be something?"

Imogen felt embarrassed. She didn't want to be talking about this with him in the middle of the emergency room.

She didn't want to talk about how blue his eyes were, how broad his shoulders were.

How strong he was.

How he'd made her feel when he'd taken her in his arms.

She shook her head.

"We're at work."

"And a patient said I resemble a Viking, so I want to know if this is some kind of Canadian thing," he teased.

She rolled her eyes. "Fine. Your beard is trimmed, but it's very Viking-slash-lumberjack. And your long blond hair with the shaved sides. You're muscular, fit." What she didn't mention was the tattoo she knew he had on his upper thigh. That strong, muscular upper thigh with its Nordic design. Maybe it was more Baltic—what did she know?—but either way, it was dead sexy. It crept up his thigh and onto his abdomen.

Warmth spread through her body and her pulse thundered between her ears.

Don't think about that.

"It's more hipster, surely?" Lev grinned.

"What is?" Imogen asked, clearing her throat and forgetting the thread of what they had been talking about.

"My look. Less military and more hipster."

"I suppose. But if you start wearing flannel you could fit in with the best of the lumberjacks," she teased.

Lev laughed. "I do like that wilderness look. So different from my military uniform and...well, I do prefer this look. I can blend in like this."

"I like how you look too." She groaned inwardly as she realized what she'd just said out loud.

Lev grinned. "Do you indeed?"

"I think you know I do. I don't usually rent a hotel room with a man I hardly know."

He smiled, the corners of his eyes crinkling. "That was a magical night."

"It was." Her pulse began to race and she was very aware of how close he was standing to her.

"Do you think about that night often?" he whispered.

Her heart skipped a beat. Yes. She did think of that night, but she wasn't going to admit it. She had to remove herself from this situation.

"I'm not answering that," she said dryly.

"Why not?" he asked.

Because I refuse to get involved with someone I work with.

Because my heart can't take it.

Because you will leave.

Because Yellowknife is not your home.

Only she didn't say those things. They were hers to know. No one else.

"We're at work. At work, we talk about work things.

That's it. I don't like to discuss my personal life here and definitely not in the emergency room when there are patients waiting for us." She blurted it out, hoping he wouldn't press her further.

"Then perhaps we should have a meal or something together tonight so we can talk? I think we have a lot to talk about."

CHAPTER FIVE

THEY DID HAVE a lot to talk about. Lev wanted to ask her so many things, especially about her pregnancy. He was still having a hard time wrapping his mind around that.

He was struggling to believe her. He'd been hurt by Tatiana, had watched his brother be betrayed and watched his mother's heart break every time his father had cheated.

Imogen is different.

Was she?

He couldn't be sure. He wanted to believe she was, but he barely knew her...other than intimately. He tried not to think about her saying she liked the way he looked, and he tried not to think about the way her cheeks had flushed pink, and he definitely tried not to think about how her creamy skin would flush pink in the throes of passion.

How her full lips would swell with their passionate kisses.

Focus.

Imogen was obviously struggling with this whole situation too. He couldn't blame her. She'd all but admitted she'd thought he was dead. And she was smart enough to know that his true identity put the child in danger. He struggled too with all the implications.

It was overwhelming.

Yes, they had a lot to talk about. He'd have to talk to

Lexi about a safe place they could go for dinner. Lexi would need time to make sure the place was cleared of all security threats. He didn't want Imogen in any danger.

"I would like to talk more about it and would like to have dinner with you tonight, so why don't you come to my place?" she asked.

"Where is your place?" he asked. "I have to have my security team do a sweep."

"I live on the lake."

Now he was confused. "You live by the lake, you mean?"

"No, I live on one of those houseboats out in the bay. Near Jolliffe Island. I have a motorboat instead of a car. We can walk to the docks and I can ferry you out to my houseboat and take you back to shore afterward. That's if your security team would be okay with that. I mean, my place is pretty private."

"If it's private, I'm sure it will be fine." Imogen lived surprisingly unconventionally.

Lev couldn't be one hundred percent sure how Lexi would feel about Imogen's home, but he was intrigued by the prospect of Imogen living on a houseboat. In Chenar there were people who lived on barges. They weren't very big, but they were long and able to maneuver the slender canals and lakes in his country and the neighboring countries.

As a boy he'd been fascinated by the lifestyle that came with barge living. Until he'd grown to be over six feet tall and realized very quickly that the small, cramped confines were not for him. Imogen was tall too, so he couldn't see her living in a cramped space.

He was excited to see what the houseboats out on the bay looked like on the inside. When he'd first seen them a couple of days ago, he hadn't been able to believe what he was seeing—dozens of brightly colored homes floating out on a huge lake.

And the fact that Imogen lived on one of those boats just

solidified what he had suspected about her when he'd first met her: she was interesting as well as sexy.

Don't think like that.

She could never be his woman.

Not with the state of things back home. He didn't want to put her life in danger, but her life was already in danger because of the baby. He had to talk to Lexi and the Canadian officials about extending protection to Imogen.

At least until this whole situation with his government was settled.

Until Kristof said it was okay to come out of hiding.

And even though he and his brother had never had the best relationship, the thought that his brother was in danger ate away at him every single day.

Lev hadn't been in Chenar when everything had happened.

He hadn't been there when his father had been killed.

He hadn't been there.

"I can come back to Chenar," Lev said, annoyed that he was being denied by Kristof again. "You can't keep me here in Edmonton with nothing to do."

"No. You're to stay in Canada. It's for the best."

"How? I can't help here, Kristof."

"You need to stay," Kristof said coolly.

"No. I don't. I must get back to Chenar and do my duty!"

"Your duty is to your King and country."

"Father is dead!" Lev snapped.

"I am your King!" Kristof shouted. "You will do as I say and not be so selfish as to put your life and Lexi's at risk. You will stay there until I order otherwise!"

And maybe that was what Kristof had meant by saying that Lev was selfish.

Maybe he was. He just felt so helpless.

"So how about I meet you down by the docks off Franklin around seven?" Imogen said, interrupting his morose chain of thoughts.

"Okay. I don't know where that is," Lev said. "I haven't been here long enough."

"Any cabdriver knows the way and it's not a long walk from here. It's down near the Bush Pilot Monument."

"And I will be able to find your berth easily?"

Imogen chuckled. "Yes. You'll be able to spot me."

"Okay. I will see you at seven, then."

"Good. I'll see you then."

Lev watched her walk away and he scrubbed a hand over his face. He wasn't sure how he was going to explain this to Lexi, but he and Imogen needed to talk about what was going on.

He finished up his first shift and then made his way outside.

There was a heaviness in the air, a smoky quality that caused a haze to settle over the city, even though it was still light outside.

Lexi was waiting in front of the white pickup truck he'd acquired in Edmonton, Alberta. It had dark tinted windows and Lexi said it would help them blend in. At the time Lev hadn't been so sure, but as they'd made their way north, he'd seen that Lexi was right. Everyone seemed to drive a big white truck.

Lexi had taken his job seriously and had blended in. Gone was the clean-shaven military look he usually adopted.

He too had grown a beard and let his hair grow longer, but only on the top.

He no longer wore designer suits, but had settled into denim and plaid, just like Lev.

"How was your first day?" Lexi asked, opening the door for him.

"I thought we talked about this," Lev said gruffly.

"What?" Lexi asked.

"You can't act like my bodyguard any longer," Lev said, as he slipped into the passenger side and closed the door. Lexi came around and got into the driver side.

"Force of habit," Lexi responded gruffly. "I suppose you want your own vehicle."

"Yes. In fact, I do, and you're going to have to figure out something else to do while I'm working. I know it can't be easy on you, being here with me and just doing nothing."

Lexi grunted. "It does not matter. Your father tasked me to protect you and that's what I'm doing."

Lev rolled his eyes. "I appreciate that, but I'm well looked after."

"I can't go back to Chenar. I don't have family like Gustav, and I was discharged from the military because of my shoulder. What am I to do? This is all I know. All I know is protecting you."

Lev could feel his frustration. He felt it too.

"Lexi, I just feel bad you're stuck here with me."

Lexi grunted again, but he was smiling. "Your Highness, I've been watching over you since you graduated from medical school, and before that we were in school together. I know you're my Prince, my leader, but you're also one of my best friends."

"Thank you."

He sighed. "I suppose I could work down at the wharf. I spent the last couple of days watching them load floatplanes. I could do that work."

"You still have your pilot's license?" Lev asked.

"Yes," Lexi said cautiously. "Why are you asking?"

"You can be a bush pilot."

"I'm not leaving you in Yellowknife alone!" Lexi snapped. "The Canadians are doing a good job, but I promised your brother. I'm not becoming a bush pilot."

"So you just want to load planes at the docks?"

Lexi shrugged. "It's something to do. I can walk there and you can take the truck."

"Well, if it gives you something to do." Lev glanced out of the window. "What's with the smoke?"

"Wildfires, but they're not nearby. Apparently the jet stream causes the smoke to settle down here in Yellowknife. I don't mind it."

"It's a bit heavy out there, the air." Lev was trying to approach the subject about Imogen and the baby, but he didn't know where to start. "I'm going out tonight."

"Pardon?" Lexi said, stunned.

"Do you remember the woman I met in Toronto? The surgeon I—?"

"Yes."

"She's here."

Lexi's knuckles went white as he gripped the steering wheel tight. "So we have to leave?"

"No."

"Does she know who you are?"

Lev sighed. "Yes."

"Then we leave. I will call the consulate when we get back to the apartment."

"Lexi, she's pregnant."

"She's...what?" Lexi asked.

"Pregnant. With my child." If he said it clearly and simply, it would help him believe it too. Help him believe he'd been the only one since their night together.

Lexi didn't say anything for a few moments, but Lev could tell he was fuming.

"You've done a lot of irresponsible things..."

And he had.

He'd become a surgeon against his father's wishes, had been a military trauma surgeon and on the front lines, also against his father's wishes. He'd often left without the protection of his bodyguards; he'd rejected life at court.

"Did I know this was going to happen?" Lev snapped. "No! And I didn't know that my father was going to be assassinated and that our country would implode, trapping me here. I didn't know these things."

His guilt was heavy on his heart. It weighed on him like a rock.

"My apologies, Your Highness. I will speak to the Canadians about this delicate matter, but only after we confirm that the child is indeed yours."

"Well, that won't be for a few months," Lev grumbled. "Unless she's open to diagnostic testing beforehand, but I won't force that on her."

"I don't know if our Canadian friends will agree to protect her. If word gets out…"

"I don't even want to think about it. And how could they not protect her?" Lev snapped.

"What if she's lying? You said she knew who you were. May I ask, sir, with the utmost respect, what if it's not your child? Look what happened to Kristof. He was duped. And Tatiana…"

Just the mention of Tatiana brought the shame of being fooled right back up to the surface. He'd been foolish and, yes, selfish for not listening to his father about her, but that was in the past.

"You don't need to remind me of that," Lev snarled. "I'm fully aware of what happened."

"So, this going out tonight is with this other doctor?"

Lev nodded. "Yes. She has a houseboat out in the bay. She wants to take me to her place for dinner."

"You're not going out on a houseboat," Lexi stated.

"Lexi, you can hire a houseboat and do perimeter sweeps if that makes you feel better. She's not a threat and her houseboat is more than secure."

Lexi groaned. "I suppose so. I would like to meet her, though."

"Not yet. Let's not overload her. She was shocked to see me too. The world thinks that I'm missing, presumed dead, and she thought that I was dead too."

"All right, but I'm not happy about this, sir." Lexi pulled into the driveway of their small rental apartment, which was located at the top of a row house that sat down by the docks.

"I know you're not. I'm not either, but if the child is mine, I need to protect them both."

And he hated it that he had said *if*.

The child was his.

Imogen wasn't like Kristof's former fiancée. She wasn't like Tatiana. She was a different woman.

Is she? How do you know?

Lexi nodded. "I agree."

"Good." Lev climbed out of the passenger side and glanced out over Yellowknife Bay. He could see all the houseboats dotting the water from their vantage point on the top of a small hill, and he couldn't help but wonder which of those brightly colored homes was Imogen's. She was so close to him, yet still so far away.

After her shift, Imogen raced to the North Store Co-Op and grabbed something to make for dinner, since all she had in her fridge were a couple of yogurts and a really brown head of lettuce. She hadn't felt like cooking much recently and had yet to make it to the grocery store.

Usually when she got back to her houseboat after a long shift she made herself a bowl of soup and went to bed.

Tonight was different.

Tonight she wasn't so tired. Lev was here. So instead of feeding Lev a dinner of brown lettuce and yogurt, she opted to heat up a frozen lasagna and bought some garlic bread.

She'd been exhausted lately from the pregnancy and

trying to figure out how she was going to make everything work on her own, but she wanted to talk to Lev and to hear what he had to say and how they were going to deal with this.

The water of the bay was calm and it was an easy short ride from the docks to her teal blue houseboat that was moored off the edge of Jolliffe Island. Her plan was to get the lasagna started, do a quick clean and then watch for Lev to get to the docks.

She wasn't far from there, so she'd be able to see him when he got there and then she'd head over to pick him up.

Pick him up?

It made her stomach swirl at the thought he was coming here. There were so many emotions she was feeling.

What if he doesn't show?

That thought subdued her. How many times had her father waited for her mother to show, only to be disappointed?

Lev's not like that.

But she didn't know. She wanted to believe he wasn't, but she didn't know.

Feeling anxious, she started to tidy. It kept her mind off her swirling thoughts and nauseous belly.

She cleaned up and straightened a few things and had the lasagna on in her propane oven. She checked her water tank, which was still full, and then wandered out onto her deck to watch for Lev.

It was getting close to seven and she hoped he'd be punctual, because from what she recalled during that surgical conference in Toronto, he tended to be a bit late to sessions. Now she understood why.

He probably had a security team trailing after him and they likely wouldn't let him go anywhere without them.

Oh, no. What if his team is coming with him?

Imogen bit her lip, worrying that she didn't have enough food for his bodyguards and worrying about what her neighbors would think seeing guys in dark sunglasses and suits standing on her houseboat. If Lev wanted to keep his identity hidden, then that was not the best way to go about it.

This is a bad idea.

The only problem was she had no way to call him off.

There was no way to change plans until she met him at the docks. She was worrying about all of this when she saw him arrive and look around, and she was relieved to see he was alone.

Her stomach did a flip-flop. She'd never thought she'd see him again.

Now he was waiting for her. He'd come to the dock, like he'd promised, and it was a relief.

Be careful.

She had to control herself.

All they were going to do was talk about the baby and managing their co-parenting.

That was it.

Is it?

She got into her motorboat and pulled away from her houseboat, making the short five-minute ride to the docks and pulling up close to Lev.

"Hey!" she shouted over the engine as she moored her motorboat.

Lev grinned and waved at her as he made his way down the long dock to her berth. "I thought I was late and you had given up."

"No. Not late. I live just over there and I could see you approach." She pointed behind her. "The teal houseboat is mine."

"Ah! I was wondering which one was yours." Lev climbed down into the boat with relative ease and Imogen looked around.

"Is it just you?" she asked.

"Yes." Lev motioned up the hill where some row houses sat. "My place is just up there. Lexi, my…"

"Roommate?" Imogen offered, suddenly aware that he might not want to admit that Lexi was really his security guard.

"Yes. He's watching. He wanted to meet you, but I said that might be a bit overwhelming, given that you only found out I was alive this morning, and, you know, the baby…"

"Does Lexi know?" Imogen asked as she released the moorings on her boat and handed Lev the lines as she untied them.

"He does. I told him."

"I'm sure he's thrilled," Imogen said.

"He has…concerns."

She chuckled. "How very diplomatic of you."

There was a twinkle in Lev's eyes. "Well, I am a bit up on international relations."

"It's a short ride, so have a seat and I'll show you my place."

Lev settled into the seat next to her and she started the engine and navigated her boat away from the dock and headed out over the calm waters of Yellowknife Bay, before pulling up beside her houseboat. Lev helped moor the boat and then climbed out with ease onto her dock and then helped her up, lifting her slightly like she weighed hardly anything.

She stumbled slightly and fell into his arms.

"Whoops. I've got you," he said as he steadied her, his arms around her, holding her. She remembered the last time Lev had held her like that. She could feel herself blush, her blood heating as she looked up into his eyes.

She was so close to him again and she had forgotten how he made her feel. How good it felt with his arms around her. When it came to him, she was so weak.

She hated that.

Focus.

"Thank you!" she said breathlessly, pushing herself out of his arms. "Let me show you around."

"Sure."

Imogen opened the door and motioned for Lev to go in ahead of her.

"It's so spacious!" he said in shock.

"I'd hardly call it spacious."

"I do. Compared to the houseboats in Europe." Lev walked around her living space. Her place was open concept with the living room and dining room one big open space. There was a bathroom off to the side and another door connected to a small shed where she kept her snowmobile in the summer months and her motorboat in the winter months. Also housed there was her father's canoe, which she barely used anymore, but which she didn't have the heart to part with.

Her bedroom was up a set of stairs. It was a loft over the kitchen. And she had a lot of windows and a couple of good skylights to let in the sun when she could. In the winter it was a bit harder to get the sun in, but it was nice to lie on her bed at night and watch the aurora.

"Is this your childhood home?" Lev asked, staring up at the ceiling.

"No. My father had a house on the mainland, but this was always a dream of his and my mother…"

She trailed off, not wanting to think of her father's broken dreams. "When he died I couldn't bear to sell it. He built it, so I had to take it over."

"He built this?" Lev asked, impressed. "Amazing!"

"The houseboat doesn't leave a large carbon footprint. My water comes from the lake. There's a large freshwater tank and filter through here, as well as the septic system and the panels for my solar power and propane." She opened the door to the shed. Lev stepped through and examined everything, taking it all in.

"Your home is fueled by solar power too?"

"Only in the summer when I can take advantage of the midnight sun. In the winter, I rely on propane or hot water."

"It's incredible," Lev said with awe.

"Yeah. It was always my dad's passion to live off grid. I finished off the rest of this barge when he died."

"I'm sorry that your father never got to live here."

"Thanks, but I don't want to dwell on that." She didn't need extra emotional turmoil on her plate tonight. They were here to talk about the baby. "Do you want something to drink? I don't have any alcohol."

"Water is fine."

"Good." Imogen went to get a cup of water from the tap and watched as Lev wandered around, staring up at the ceiling. She handed him his glass of water. Lev took a seat on her couch and she sat down in the easy chair nearby. "So, I suppose you have questions."

Her stomach did another flip-flop as she braced herself for questions she wasn't sure she could answer because her brain decided to skip out on her.

Lev nodded. "When is the baby due?"

"February. Around Valentine's Day, funnily enough."

"I'm really concerned about how to protect you both, and my bodyguard Lexi is afraid that the baby is not mine. I'm sorry—he's not a very trusting individual. He's been trained to question everything."

But there was something in his tone that made her think that maybe he didn't quite believe the baby was his either. And although it hurt her, she couldn't blame him.

They were strangers.

Strangers who had shared one incredible night.

Don't think about it.

"I get it. I'm sure if you do the math, you can figure out the conception date, but I am willing to do paternity testing if that's what would make you and Lexi happy."

Lev set down his glass of water and scrubbed his hand over his face. "I don't want to put the baby at risk by doing invasive testing."

"I'm going to be having an amniocentesis. There are some genetic tests I want to have done, some genetic concerns on my side, and honestly, when I thought you were dead, I wanted to see if there was anything else I should be concerned about. I had no information about your side of the family."

Lev smiled gently. "There is nothing overly debilitating in my family, as far as I know. When is your amniocentesis scheduled?"

"In a couple of weeks. You're more than welcome to come—that way you can get the paternity confirmed and put your mind at ease."

Lev's brow furrowed. "I have no doubt that it's my child you carry."

"No doubt?" she asked, skeptical. She had a hard time believing that he would blindly trust her. She didn't think he was as foolish as she'd been.

"You wanted to be sure of the paternity."

"There are extenuating circumstances. I was skeptical, but... I believe you."

"I'll say," she said. "I just have a hard time trusting you."

"I believe you, Imogen." Lev stood and then knelt down in front of her. "I believe that it's my child you carry. I know I don't know you well, but my gut tells me it is the truth. Lexi may have his reservations, but I don't care. I want to protect you and our child. The only way I can bring about the same level of protection that I have is to make you my wife."

"What?" Imogen asked, stunned. "Say that again?"

"It's simple, Imogen. To protect you and our unborn child, you need to become my wife. I want you to marry me."

CHAPTER SIX

"What?"

Her world had stopped turning there for a moment, and she felt like she was going to be sick.

She was pretty sure that it wasn't morning sickness. She was a thousand percent sure that it was shock.

"What?" she said again, her heart racing. "I didn't hear you correctly."

"I'm asking you to marry me," Lev said, annoyed. "I thought I was clear."

Imogen got up and sidestepped around Lev, who was still on one knee in front of her chair. She needed to put some space between them.

This was just supposed to be a dinner to talk about the baby, to talk about what had happened since and what would happen next. To talk about what was going on in Chenar and how it would affect her and the baby.

She was not expecting a marriage proposal. Neither could she accept one. This was just too crazy. And all she could think about was when Allen had left her, when she'd thought he was proposing but wasn't, and how foolish it had made her feel to think that anyone could want to be with her.

Her mother certainly hadn't.

And then there was her parents' marriage. That had been a disaster.

"I think… I think you may have lost your mind," she stated, her voice shaking in partnership with her body.

Lev frowned. "How have I lost my mind?"

"You're proposing marriage to me. We barely know each other."

"We've had sex." He smiled knowingly.

She was very aware they'd had sex. She thought about it often, and if that wasn't enough, there was a baby growing inside her. But sex didn't mean they had to get married.

They were strangers.

"Sex doesn't mean you know someone. Like whether or not you like them as a person with a real personality or whether you can live with them or tolerate them. Sex is just…" She didn't even know how to finish that sentence. She ran her hand through her hair. Didn't know what to say.

"Something is burning."

"What?" Imogen asked, confused.

Lev stood and pointed, and she spun around and remembered she had a lasagna in the oven.

"Crap!" She ran over to the kitchen, grabbed her oven mitts and pulled open the door. Thankfully, some had just bubbled up over the side and had burned on the bottom of the oven, but the rest of the lasagna was perfectly salvageable for dinner.

It was at instances like this when she remembered she didn't like cooking. Not really. She didn't mind grilling, but anything else to do with the oven beyond boiling a pot of water on the range top she didn't seem to have the aptitude for.

"Is it okay?" Lev asked.

"Yeah. Some bubbled over. It's just a ready-made one I got. I've never actually bought a frozen lasagna before." She peeked under the tinfoil. "It looks okay."

Lev came over. "Test the middle."

She cocked an eyebrow. "The Prince of a kingdom is familiar with frozen lasagna?"

"What do you think I've been living on since I went into hiding? Lexi and I have learned to cook a variety of things. Frozen meals being the most common. Do you have a knife?" he asked.

Imogen reached into the drawer and pulled out a knife. He took it from her and cut into the middle, pulling it out and touching the side of the blade.

"It's hot. It's done. I'm sure it's excellent. Not as good as home made, but it will do at a pinch."

Imogen cocked an eyebrow. "And you've made one from scratch?"

"I have. I told you, Lexi and I have learned to manage things. I don't mind actually." He proceeded to cut the lasagna and then pulled out the garlic bread, which hadn't fared as well and looked a little blackened.

"You're full of surprises."

Including proposals and coming back from the dead.

"Well, seeing how you said we're strangers, I suppose that shouldn't be surprising..." His eyes twinkled and Imogen groaned.

"It's true, Lev. We're strangers and Lev isn't even your real name."

"No. That's true. But it is my middle name. Vanin is just a combination of my given name and my last name."

"See, this is why I can't marry you. I don't know you."

Lev sighed. "I know it's not ideal and it's not like I'm expecting anything from you."

Imogen's eyes widened and her pulse raced. "What would you be expecting?" Although all she could think of was sex.

Would that be so bad?

She shook that thought away. Last time she'd thought like that she ended up pregnant.

"To share my bed."

Her cheeks heated. "What?"

"Wifely duties."

She cleared her throat. She wouldn't mind a few "wifely duties" with Lev. When it came to Lev, it wouldn't be a duty and she would never think of it that way.

Nothing about that one stolen night they'd shared had resembled anything unpleasant. In fact, it had been the exact opposite.

Focus.

Imogen cleared her throat. "What are you talking about?"

"Imogen, it would be a marriage on paper only. That way you and our child would be protected."

"Because we're in danger," she stated.

Lev sighed. "I don't know. I really don't. Lexi seems to think so, as do the Canadians. There have been some unsettling experiences when I was placed in other locations and then was moved quickly, but mostly I was moved because they were worried I'd been recognized. I'm afraid that once they get wind of you, I will be moved again, and I don't want to leave you or the baby."

Imogen chewed her bottom lip. "I don't know, Lev. I mean, it's one thing to say it's a marriage of... I guess convenience, if that's even a thing, but wouldn't it raise suspicions if you were to marry me and not live with me?"

"I won't invade your life, Imogen."

"You already have, Lev," she said in bemusement, and touched her belly.

"Yes. I suppose I have." He smiled and her heart skipped a beat.

Imogen sighed. "I can't marry you."

"Think on it. Please."

* * *

Lev had never thought he would ever be asking anyone to marry him after what had happened with Tatiana, but he couldn't leave Imogen so exposed. He didn't want her or the baby at risk, and the only way he could offer her protection was to have her marry him. It was his duty to protect them.

At least on paper she would be protected.

Once this was all over and he knew that she and his child were safe, he would grant her a divorce. He didn't want to trap her into a life of protocol. He didn't want to take her away from this place she seemed to love so much.

And he understood why she felt that way about the north.

Despite being forced to come to this place for his protection, despite his every step and every move being watched, he still saw the appeal of life up here.

The drive up from Edmonton had been eye-opening. Endless farm fields, bright yellow with canola, to forests of birch, pine and cedar, crossing mighty rivers surrounded by rolling hills that reminded him of the badlands in America's Midwest.

The land had changed the farther north they'd traveled, and then the traffic had dropped away. Once in a while they'd drive through a small town or meet a transport truck going south, but then those signs of civilization would melt away into forest and rough rock that jutted through the loam, like the soil had been scraped away, the only sign of life the occasional bear or bison crossing the road.

Trees were slender, some burned away from a previous fire, but all reached up toward the large blue sky, reaching their leaves and needles to catch the last rays of summer sun as the days grew shorter.

And the quiet.

That was hard for Lev to get used to, but he liked it.

And then coming here to Imogen's simple houseboat. He could get used to living this way.

You can't.

It was all just a dream, because he couldn't have this life. He was a prince. He had responsibilities. He'd known that his whole life.

Lev set the knife down.

"Are you okay?" Imogen asked as she set the table.

He didn't even realize that she'd gone about setting the table. The last thing he could remember was asking her to think about his proposal and then his thoughts had run away with him.

"What?" he asked, shaking his head and picking up the lasagna tray with the oven mitts again.

"You drifted off there. You totally zoned out."

"I'm fine. I was just…thinking." Which wasn't a lie.

"I will consider your proposal, Lev, but I can't see how it would be a good idea." Imogen went to get a couple of glasses of water while Lev served the lasagna onto the plates. He got it. It really wasn't a good idea.

"You could always move in with me and Lexi." Then he frowned, because his place with Lexi was even smaller than her houseboat and Lexi wasn't thrilled that Lev had got someone pregnant.

"I don't think so." Imogen chuckled. "Those places on the hill are okay, but they're tiny."

"I could move in here. I mean, we work together and your couch looks comfortable enough."

Imogen's eyes widened and Lev pulled out her chair for her at the table. She sat down and was still sitting there looking stunned.

"You want to live with me?"

"If we were going to pretend to be married to keep you and the baby safe, you're right. We would have to live together to keep up pretenses, and it makes no sense for you to cram into my apartment with Lexi. So I'll move in here with you."

"Do you think my houseboat is safe?"

Lev shrugged. "It is exposed, but to move you would seem suspicious."

"And what about Lexi?" she asked.

"He'd stay where he is. He would be close enough to keep watch. He's already keeping watch."

"What do you mean?" she asked.

"The boat that keeps going by, which you probably haven't noticed, that's Lexi."

Imogen went to stand but Lev motioned for her to sit.

"Don't draw attention to him. He won't like that. This is the only way I could get him to agree to allow me to come out here."

Imogen sighed. "We're talking like we're going to go through with this charade and get married."

"It makes sense, Imogen, and it protects you and the baby. Please, let me do this for you. I feel so helpless right now and so worried about you both."

"I will think on it. That's all I can offer right now, Lev. I'm sorry."

He got up from his seat and knelt down beside her. "Don't be sorry. I'm sorry I got you into this predicament."

"I think I had a little bit to do with it too," she teased.

Lev smiled up at her.

Yes. She was definitely involved in their little mistake. He couldn't forget that and he didn't want to forget it.

The memory of that night together haunted him, and if he weren't now heir to the throne of Chenar and in hiding, he would go about this differently.

You don't really know her. She's right about that.

And that niggling thought brought him back to reality. Imogen was right. They really didn't know each other beyond that one night, and lust wasn't something you based a marriage on. His parents' marriage had been based on that and they had both been miserable.

They'd remained married, but neither of them had been faithful to the other, and his mother had died unhappy.

He didn't want that kind of marriage. He didn't want a marriage of duty. He wasn't sure he wanted a marriage at all. None of this had been in his plans.

"How about we eat before the food gets cold?" Imogen suggested. "Besides, my stomach is growling."

Lev nodded. "Sounds good."

He returned to his seat and they ate their lasagna and slightly charred garlic bread. The sunlight was slipping away and it was growing darker.

"What time is it?" he asked.

"About nine."

"I thought this was the land of the midnight sun?" he said, as he picked up his dish and took it to her sink.

"Only near the summer solstice. We're headed into autumn and it'll get dark earlier and earlier. The aurora should be coming back soon too."

"I hope to see it." He turned on the tap and let the sink fill.

"You don't have to do the dishes. I can do that. You're my guest."

"And the only reason I'm your guest is because you're carrying my baby and I'm apparently resurrected from the dead," he teased. "I have this. It's okay."

"Thanks." She packed up the leftovers in a plastic container. "Maybe Lexi would like some dinner."

Lev nodded. "He probably would. Knowing him, he hasn't eaten."

"Will he stay out there on that boat until you head back to the mainland?"

Lev nodded. "Probably. He's not only my bodyguard—he's my friend. We grew up together. Went to the same military school. My father wanted me to be a soldier like my brother, Kristof, but I preferred healing to anything else.

Lexi was in the military for a while, until an injury forced him out and my father appointed him as my personal bodyguard. I was a bit reckless in my youth."

"Oh?" Imogen asked, intrigued.

"I liked to party a bit too much, even though I was training to be a military doctor, and Lexi helped me see the error of my ways. He takes his job a little too seriously sometimes."

Imogen smiled. "It's nice to have someone looking out for you."

Lev shrugged. "I suppose, but why should he have to? He has no real life of his own. He used to be a pilot in the military and I know he would like to fly again. I suggested he take a job as a bush pilot if we're up here for the foreseeable future, but he won't do it. I'm his job, but I know he's bored."

"Well, he could get a job at the hospital."

Lev frowned. "What?"

"There are security jobs to fill in the hospital. He would still be close to you and doing something."

"Why are you insisting on torturing me?"

"I thought you said Lexi was bored. I was offering a solution." Imogen put away the dishes he had just washed.

She was right. It was a perfect solution, even if he hated the idea that Lexi would be so close. But maybe that way he could protect Imogen, the baby and himself all at the same time. Lexi would definitely like it.

Imogen was staring out of the window and she was worrying her bottom lip, thinking. She did that often. He'd noticed it when they'd been in Toronto and again at work today.

Those lips he remembered kissing. How he wished he could take her in his arms and kiss her again. She was so beautiful, and the memories that sustained him did not do her justice.

He couldn't think about her like that, though.

He had to keep his distance. This marriage was to protect her and his child from the situation at home. He refused to trap her into a life of protocol.

She belonged here in the north.

She deserved to be free. Even if it meant free of him.

"Lexi must really think there's a threat," she whispered.

"Yes. There is a threat. I've been moved all over. I've had places compromised. There are insurgents out there, trying to finish the job and eradicate all the heirs to the throne of Chenar." He reached down and, with a quick check to make sure it was okay, touched her belly. He knew he wouldn't be able to feel anything yet but he couldn't stop himself. "All heirs."

"Okay." She turned to face him. "Okay."

"Okay?" he asked, mystified.

"I'll marry you." She worried her lip again.

"You will?" he said, stunned but also relieved that she was agreeing to the marriage.

"But there will be some ground rules," she said.

"Ground rules?" he asked.

He couldn't help but wonder what kind of trouble he'd got himself into.

CHAPTER SEVEN

"What kind of ground rules?"

She could tell by his expression, his furrowed brow and pursed lips, that he was worried.

"Well, the marriage is on paper only. That much we've established."

Lev sighed. "Right. I understand."

"You're moving in here."

"Yes, but I don't think Lexi will approve," he groused.

"I understand that, but my place is bigger."

"Okay, what else?" Lev asked. He sounded exhausted and she felt bad.

"The baby... I have custody after this marriage ends." She was worried he wouldn't agree, because her child had royal blood, but she couldn't leave Canada for an unstable country. This was her home. This was where she wanted her child to grow up. Yellowknife was all she knew.

"I would never take the child from you, Imogen."

She was surprised. "You wouldn't?"

"Of course not. A child needs its mother more than its father." There was a hint of sadness in his voice.

"A child needs its father too," she said sadly, as she thought of her own father. And she couldn't really comprehend a child *needing* a mother because she had never had that experience, though she had surely wished for it.

"My late father was not...loving. He wasn't very warm and I rarely saw him. My mother, she loved me. She loved to be with me, but I lost her when I was seven and then spent many years being raised by governesses."

She felt bad for the little boy he had been.

"I didn't know my mother," she said. "But I wouldn't trade my time with my father for anything. Lev, I want you to be in our child's life."

She did. She just couldn't leave Yellowknife. This was her home. It would be their child's home.

She was scared. She couldn't see into the future, she couldn't control the future, and it felt overwhelming.

Lev took her hand. "I appreciate that, but when our marriage ends, our child will stay with you. It's better for our child that he or she grows up away from the life I knew. I'm not doing this to take the child from you. I'm doing this to protect you."

"I know," she whispered. And she believed him, but she was terrified of being hurt or her child being hurt.

"Come on," he said gently. "I think I've overwhelmed you enough for one night. Let's get me back before Lexi loses his mind."

Imogen chuckled. "Good idea."

They walked out and he helped her untie her motorboat. She made her way slowly to the mainland, the lights on shore and years of experience guiding her through the darkness.

"Lexi will be around here somewhere. I would like you to meet him and I'll explain to him what's going on." Lev got out of her boat and helped her tie up.

"Do you think that's wise?" she asked as she handed him the lines.

"Why wouldn't it be?" Lev asked.

"I don't think he'll exactly be thrilled."

"Thrilled about what?"

Imogen startled as Lexi, or the man she assumed to be Lexi, seemed to materialize out of the shadows.

"Lexi, I want you to meet Dr. Imogen Hayes." That was all Lev said but she knew he would tell Lexi about their agreement later. She knew they couldn't talk about it out in public, and anyway, Lexi looked like he was still processing this whole thing too.

Imogen got where he was coming from.

"It's nice to meet you." Imogen held out her hand, but Lexi just crossed his arms and nodded.

Lev said something under his breath in what sounded like Chenarian and Lexi took her hand grudgingly.

"I was thinking that Dr. Hayes could come up to the apartment and we can go over plans."

Lexi cocked an eyebrow. "If that is what you wish."

His bodyguard seemed a bit grumpy, but she couldn't blame him.

Lev reached out, took her hand and led Imogen away from the dock and up the hill toward where their apartment sat.

"Where is Lexi?" Imogen whispered to Lev.

"He's behind us somewhere. He'll show up."

"This is kind of freaking me out." She wasn't used to this kind of thing at all. What had she got herself into? She knew she should have kept away when she'd seen Lev at the conference. Why had she listened to Jeanette about living a little?

You don't regret it. You know you don't.

Even though this whole thing was more than she was expecting, more than she really wanted to deal with, in reality she was glad that she was pregnant and she was glad to have had that night with Lev.

Lev, as if sensing her apprehension, squeezed her hand in reassurance. They walked up the steps that led to the top of the row house and he unlocked the door.

The apartment was smaller than her houseboat and had what appeared to be two bedrooms, one bathroom and a kitchenette that connected to a small living-dining area. There was a set of windows that overlooked the bay, and from this high up on the hill she could see beyond her little houseboat to where the bay became Great Slave Lake.

There was just a hint of pink from the sun setting in the west, and with the remnants of the smoke in the air, there was a haze to the sky, and a few stars were starting to peek out.

The apartment was sparsely furnished, but that was to be expected given that Lev had nothing. Only what he'd brought with him to the medical conference and whatever he'd accumulated since.

She felt bad for him.

She couldn't imagine being cut off from the only home you knew and being forced to stay in a foreign country, not knowing what had happened to your loved ones. Although she did know what it was like to be alone.

"Have a seat." Lev motioned for her to take a seat on the couch. She sat down just as the door opened and Lexi came in.

"Everything is secure," he murmured.

"Good." Lev poured Lexi a cup of coffee, which Lexi took, but he didn't sit down. He remained standing. "Dr. Hayes has agreed to marry me."

A strange look passed over Lexi's face. It was as if he had expected it, but she got the distinct impression he was still mightily suspicious. As if he thought she was agreeing to all of this because Lev was a prince. Like this had happened before.

"I fought him," Imogen blurted out, annoyed with the face Lexi made. "I didn't want to marry him, but if my baby is in danger I don't see what choice I have."

Lexi didn't respond to her. "What is the plan now, Your Highness?"

"You need to obtain a license for me to marry Imogen and we will get married as soon as possible. Then I will live with her on her houseboat," Lev stated.

Lexi said something in Chenarian and Lev snapped back, causing Lexi to stand down.

"You don't want him to move out to the houseboat, do you?" Imogen asked. She didn't understand Chenarian, but she knew by his body language that Lexi was against all of this.

"No. He does not," Lev said. "But to protect you and the baby, it is the smartest decision. It is the only decision. You can see the houseboat from here, Lexi."

"I can't protect you out there, Your Highness. Neither can I properly protect your wife and heir."

"I'm not moving in here," Imogen stated. "No offense, but this apartment is very small, and so is my place. I'd offer you my couch, but that's where Lev will be sleeping. And, I might add, I wouldn't even be considering this if not for the dangerous political crisis that's happening right now in your country."

Lexi bowed at the waist. "My apologies, Dr. Hayes. I do understand your frustration. We shall try and make it work. May I be excused, Your Highness?"

Lev nodded. "You may."

Lexi gave another curt nod and retreated to his room.

"Not to be bothersome, but how am I going to get home?" Imogen asked.

"There's a Canadian agent waiting downstairs to escort you." Lev held up his phone. "I've explained the situation to those in charge of my protection, and the prime minister has been informed as well."

Imogen did a double take. "The prime minister knows?"

Lev nodded. "It's a matter of national security. This is how I can protect you and the baby."

"Okay." Imogen nodded. "Well, I guess this is going to come as a shock to those in the hospital. I mean, our marriage... I know they can't know the real reason we're getting married. I just don't like everyone knowing my business and now everyone will know you're the father."

"I understand. I value my privacy too, but this is the only way, Imogen."

Imogen nodded. "Let me know when we need to go to the courthouse. Or let me know if there's anything else I can do."

Lev closed the distance between them and placed his arms around her, and then took her hands, bringing them up to his lips for a kiss. His blue eyes were focused intently on her, making her heart skip a beat. The feel of his lips on her skin sent a tingle through her body.

She hated this effect he had on her. Both hated and loved it.

"Thank you for doing this, Imogen."

"Good night, Lev." She opened the door and headed down the steps where a plainclothes Canadian security agent was waiting to escort her down the road to her boat.

Usually, she wasn't all that bothered walking down Franklin at night, even though it was down by the docks, but tonight she felt like there were a million eyes on her. She felt unsafe for the first time in her ten years in Yellowknife, felt like she wasn't safe in her own city, and she didn't like that.

She didn't like having to rely on Lev for her safety.

For her baby's safety.

Her father had taught her to be resilient. To take care of herself.

Relying on someone usually just brought disappointment and heartache.

Like all the times her mother had promised to come and see her. Like Allen promising he'd never leave her, and that he'd stay in the north with her.

She felt powerless.

She felt helpless and it scared her that all these feelings involved Lev.

She was scared of it all.

"Wait, hold up... What?"

Imogen groaned inwardly. She looked up from her chart and saw that Jeanette was headed her way.

Here we go.

"Hi, Jeanette. What's up?" But Imogen knew exactly what was up. She knew exactly what Jeanette was going to say to her, because Imogen and Lev had gone to Human Resources to fill out the documentation that dealt with spouses working together at the hospital.

"You know what's up!" Jeanette said. "We need to talk."

Imogen sighed, set down the chart she was reviewing and followed Jeanette into an empty exam room. Jeanette flicked on the lights and closed the door.

"Imogen, I know I told you to show the new guy around, but...marrying him?"

"Jeanette, he's the father of my baby. Remember how you were bugging me since I got back from Toronto about the mystery guy I hooked up with, the guy who got me pregnant? It was Lev."

Jeanette's mouth opened in shock, and she sat down on the wheelie stool, sliding back to the wall. "I had no idea."

"Well, we didn't exchange emails or anything. I mean..." She had to straighten out her story. She couldn't tell Jeanette the truth. She couldn't tell Jeanette that Lev was from Chenar and she hadn't known where he was for a couple of months, and she couldn't let Jeanette think that her marriage to Lev was a marriage of convenience either. "It was supposed to be a one-night stand and I wasn't expecting anything to happen but something did. We connected and... I was embarrassed to tell you that your newest surgeon was actually the father of my baby."

Jeanette's eyes narrowed. "There's something else you're not telling me, but I'm too tired to figure it out."

"We're going to have a quick civil ceremony tomorrow afternoon and Lev is moving out to my houseboat. We're going to raise this baby together."

Liar.

She didn't know how long she had with Lev, but she wasn't completely lying.

She hadn't wanted Jeanette to know when she was getting married, because she didn't want her to make a big thing about it, but it was no use trying to hide it from Jeanette. She seemed to be able to figure stuff out and find out information so quickly. She was good at reading people and that was why she was Chief of Staff.

"What're we doing for the wedding?" Jeanette asked, going straight into planning mode.

"Nothing."

"Nothing? You can't have nothing. You need to do something."

"I just want something simple, Jeanette." Imogen shook her friend's shoulders playfully. "I don't need anything complicated or crazy."

"What're you going to wear?"

"I don't know. What I usually wear?"

Jeanette frowned. "You're not going to wear buffalo plaid and denim. I'll get you a dress."

"No. I don't need a dress."

Jeanette made a dismissive hand motion. "You're getting a simple, nice dress, and I'll pick it out for you and I'll be your witness."

"Okay." Imogen knew when she was defeated.

"What if we have dinner at the Grayling after?" Jeanette was smiling. "I can make a reservation."

"Sure. Lev's best friend is in Yellowknife too, and he'll be there, so if you and Dave come, make the reservation for five."

Jeanette nodded and then hugged her. "This is awesome. I feel like I'm responsible."

Imogen cocked an eyebrow. "How are you responsible?"

"I hired him and I sent you to that conference in Toronto where you hooked up!"

"Wasn't it a federal transfer?" Imogen asked.

"Yeah, but I had the spot." Jeanette winked. "Okay, I'll take care of the dress and the Grayling for dinner after. This is so exciting."

Imogen just shook her head as she left Jeanette to plan. She wasn't sure how she was going to break this to Lev and she was pretty positive that Lexi wasn't going to like the idea too much. Lexi hadn't said much to her at all, but Imogen knew that the government agents had made sure that their house, the dock and the hospital were now secured.

She was being watched now too, but none of it made her feel any more at ease. It didn't make her feel safe at all. She'd lost control and she hated that.

"Imogen!"

She turned to see Lev coming toward her.

"What's up?" she asked.

"I have an emergency appendectomy in the ER. It's about to rupture and I'm hoping you can help me in the operating room. I know from a certain simulation lab you're pretty handy with a laparoscope."

She was surprised Lev had asked for her assistance. Allen never had, but then, Allen hadn't liked to be upstaged. Especially not by her, which should've been a huge red flag, but she hadn't seen it at the time.

Now she knew better and she was happy Lev thought nothing of asking for her help.

"I'll meet you on the operating room floor in ten minutes."

Lev nodded and ran off back toward the emergency department. Imogen took a deep breath to calm her nerves. She couldn't think about government agents watching her or the fact that she was going to have to marry Lev just to protect her baby.

She had an emergency appendectomy to do.

She had her job to focus on and a life to save.

Lev was glad to see that Imogen was already in the scrub room by the time the emergency patient was being wheeled into the operating theater.

"So, tell me about the patient," Imogen said, scrubbing at the sink.

"The patient is thirty-two-year-old Fudo Fushita, a tourist from Japan. No territorial health card—this is a travel insurance job. He was complaining of worsening stomach pains the last day or so when his wife brought him in. Pain over the McBurney point and worsening pain on release rather than when I press down."

"Did you get an ultrasound?" she asked.

"I did and blood work. The appendix is about to rupture. I started the patient on a course of antibiotics, in case it did before we could get to it."

"Well, let's get in there before it does." Imogen headed into the operating room. The patient was already under general anesthesia in preparation for the procedure, so Imogen took her place on her side of the operating table, waiting while the scrub nurses finished draping and sterilizing the field. Lev stood on the opposite side of the table, ready to provide assistance to her in her role as general surgeon and the lead surgeon on his case.

Usually he had a hard time letting go and relinquishing control over one of his patients, but he didn't feel that unease with Imogen. He was just glad that he was able to assist, and as they started the surgery, he was pleased to realize how easy it was to work with her in the operating room.

They were in sync, like they had always seemed to be when running simulations at that conference. It was like she knew exactly what he was thinking. She made the same moves that he would and her skill was unsurpassed.

It made Lev admire her all the more.

She was such a strong woman. He couldn't believe she was here in Yellowknife and that she was so close to him now. When he'd kissed her hands last night it had made him want to kiss more than just her hands.

He wanted all of her, but he couldn't have her. He didn't deserve to have her since it was his background and circumstances that had put her life in danger.

He rolled his shoulders, trying to ease the tension in his back as he assisted Imogen on the surgery.

And as they removed the appendix and stabilized the patient, he was glad that she was here in Yellowknife, even more than he had been before.

They closed up and the patient was taken in a stable condition to the post-anesthesia recovery unit. They got out of their surgical gear and were at the sink, scrubbing out.

"I need to let the patient's wife know that he'll be okay, but she only speaks Japanese," Lev said. "Do you know where I can find an interpreter?"

"I know some Japanese. I can speak with the patient's wife."

Lev was surprised. "You know Japanese?"

"My father traveled a lot when I was young, remember. Also, I felt it was important to learn some basics, as Yellowknife gets a lot of tourists from Japan in the late summer, fall and into the winter. They come to see the northern lights. This isn't the first tourist I've worked on."

"I didn't know Yellowknife was such a tourist hot spot."

"It is when it involves the northern lights." Imogen smiled. "I also know French and Dene."

"Dene?" he asked.

"It's an indigenous language. My Dene is rusty, but Jeanette is Dene and her husband is Métis, and they've taught me a few things to get by."

"You'll have to teach me," Lev said. "I would like to know, because I don't know much about the indigenous people in Canada or even what Métis is."

And he did want to know. He was intrigued, and if he was going to be staying here for some time, he wanted to get to know the people. He wanted to be able to blend in. It would be safer for all of them if he could.

Imogen smiled. "There's time for that. Come on. Let's let Mrs. Fushita know that her husband is going to be okay."

"Right." She and Lev left the scrub room and made their way to the waiting room. Lev introduced Imogen to the patient's wife, and Imogen explained the procedure, how Mr. Fushita was faring and that someone would come soon to take her up to him, as well as making a translator available.

After Imogen had reassured the patient's wife, they left the waiting area.

"So, we're going to have a reception," Imogen blurted out as they walked down the hall.

"A what?" Lev asked.

"Jeanette found out that we're getting married. I had to tell her you're the father of my baby."

Lev stiffened. "What else did you tell her?"

"That we had a one-night stand in Toronto and that we're going to raise the baby together."

"And she didn't suspect?" Lev asked.

"No. She's just excited she was matchmaker. Or she thinks she was."

He frowned. He wanted to believe she was telling the truth, but something was bothering him about it. The way she was acting was a bit odd.

"You okay?" he asked.

"Yes. Why?"

"You seem out of sorts."

Imogen sighed. "Just nerves. Jeanette is making a big deal out of this wedding."

"Oh." Lev's stomach knotted. He was worried too. It was getting out of hand. "It'll be okay."

But he wasn't so sure. If something slipped, Lexi and the Canadians would make him leave.

And if he left, he wasn't sure that Imogen would follow.

And he couldn't blame her for that.

CHAPTER EIGHT

IMOGEN PACED NERVOUSLY on the deck of her houseboat. She'd lent her boat to Lexi when he'd dropped her off and now he was headed back to pick up Lev and his meager belongings so that Lev could move in with her, so they could start this pretense of being a happy couple, in love and getting married and about to have a baby.

Is it a pretense?

When he'd disappeared, she'd thought about him. She'd wished she'd got to know him more and been able to tell him about the baby.

Now they were getting married.

All so that Lev could protect their child, because of who he really was.

The whole thing seemed absurd. And she had to remind herself it wasn't real.

After Allen, she'd never wanted to get married. Marriage didn't last. So logically she knew this was fake, but it still seemed crazy and over the top.

You agreed to it.

She was doing the right thing for her child. She knew that. This was the right thing.

Is it?

"Why am I so nervous?" she said out loud, almost as if to ground herself.

It wasn't like she'd never lived with a man before, but she remembered how that had turned out before. She'd thought she and Allen had been in it for the long haul, because they'd been together a long time, but it hadn't worked.

It had hurt her.

She had felt rejected when Allen had left. Just like her mother had left.

She didn't want to have another broken heart. She couldn't.

This isn't real. You're not in love with Lev.

It made her question whether she had ever really been in love with Allen at all. She thought she had, but not the way her father had been in love with her mother and had ached over her mother's abandonment of them.

She'd got over Allen and learned from her mistakes. But her father had never moved on from his heartbreak.

"Why did you never move on, Dad?" Imogen asked.

"Why are you asking me this?" he asked, puzzled.

"I was always curious."

"I loved her."

"But she clearly didn't love you as much as you loved her."

"I know, Imogen, but try as I might, she still has my heart, broken as it is. I can't move on."

She wondered if she was incapable of such a love, and that made her even more wary about any kind of relationship. She had walls and her walls protected her. But they also protected Lev.

He just didn't know it yet.

And she didn't know why she was thinking like this. Right now.

Anxiety.

Which made sense. Her mind would not stop running.

The boat pulled away from the dock on the mainland and headed toward her. She took a deep breath. She had to keep reminding herself that this wasn't real.

Her marriage tomorrow would only be on paper. This was all for their child. This was to protect their baby. That was the important thing.

Their baby.

The only reality about this situation was that she was still attracted to Lev. She cared about him and she recalled how she'd felt when she hadn't known where he was, the shock she'd felt when he'd walked into the doctors' lounge. That was why she was doing this, and she had to keep reminding herself of it in order to make it through this whole charade.

But there was another part of her that desperately wanted this to work so her child could have two loving parents, but she banished that thought.

She didn't want to get her hopes up.

Yellowknife was her home, not Lev's, and one day he'd return to Chenar.

The boat pulled up to her dock. Lev was by himself.

"How did you enjoy your first solo ride?" she asked as she took a rope from him, tying it off.

"It was fine. Do people swim in this lake?" he asked, changing the subject abruptly. Which took her mind off her anxiety and jumbled thoughts.

"Some. It's quite cold. Why? Do you want to swim?"

"I might. I liked to swim back home, for exercise."

"It's cold, but I suppose if you wanted to you could. Will Lexi approve, though?"

Lev frowned. "You're right. Probably not."

They stood there awkwardly, a weird tension between them. It was like they were frozen in their respective awkwardness.

She worried her lip and he stood there, his back ramrod straight.

"Why is this so hard?" Imogen finally asked, breaking the silence.

"I don't know," Lev mused. "That's why I talked about swimming, to be honest. I didn't know what else to say."

Imogen smiled. "I thought as much."

"Perhaps because we're living a lie. A noble lie, but a lie nonetheless," he offered.

"Yes. Maybe," she said, but she wasn't completely convinced that was the only reason. "Well, we might as well get this thing started."

She opened the door to her home and Lev followed her inside.

"I'll have to show you how everything works," she stated. "How to pump water and turn on the propane."

"Yes. That would be helpful. I don't want to be a burden to you." He set his duffel bag down on the floor by the end of the couch.

"You're not a burden. I agreed to this as well. For the baby." She folded her hands in front of her and still remained frozen to the spot by the door. "Are you ready for tomorrow?"

"As much as I can be." He gave her a half smile. "I'm sorry to have dragged you into this situation, Imogen. I didn't want to entrap you in my complicated life."

"I wasn't exactly dragged, if you recall." And she blushed, thinking about it. No, she hadn't been dragged. She'd gone quite willingly with him.

And you'd do it again too. Admit it.

She shifted awkwardly because she was trying not to think about Lev and their night together.

Say something.

"Would you like a cup of tea or coffee?"

"I would love some, but please show me where and how to do it and let me make you a cup of tea."

"Okay."

It was a simple task to put on the kettle, but it kept her mind off worrying as she showed him how the kitchen was laid out and how to work the stove. When the tea was steeping she showed him how the solar panels worked and how to pump water from the lake. Then they took their cups of tea and headed out to the back of her houseboat, where she had a couple of Muskoka chairs sitting on the deck.

She liked sitting out there in the evening, watching the water and listening to the waves lap against Jolliffe Island. It always calmed her down.

They sat there in silence.

"This lake is larger than the one in Toronto?" he asked. "You told me there were larger ones."

Her heart fluttered. He remembered their discussion. He remembered their night in detail like she did.

"Yes. It is. It's a world record breaker, in fact, but there's one farther north of here that you can access by plane and it's even larger."

"What's it called?" he asked.

"Great Bear Lake."

He chuckled softly to himself. "It seems almost impossible to me that there is more to this country. I've been all over it and it still amazes me how large it is. How vast. I can't believe there is more."

"Well, it's a bit different up there. The tree line ends and it's mainly tundra. You can see musk ox and caribou migrating."

"That's what I love about Canada. The scenery is so different. It can change in a moment."

"Why don't you tell me about Chenar? I have been there, but it was so long ago," she said, though she knew she'd broached a touchy subject when she saw his lips purse.

"It is difficult for me to talk about it. It's small, and for the most part it resembles Romania with green forests and mountains. There are castles and old buildings, older than in your country, but you can see the Scandinavian influence in the style."

She smiled. "And that's what I love about Europe, about small countries like Chenar."

He nodded. "I just hope that I can return there one day."

"I hope so too." And she meant it.

Then that thought made her sad because she couldn't go with him if he left.

Yellowknife was where she belonged.

She was safer here.

She knew this place. This was where her father had been planning to retire. This was where her roots were firmly planted.

"I just never planned on returning there without my father as King." He set down his mug. "Kristof will be King. I am not prepared for that reality."

"Kristof is hiding too, right?"

"He is but my father is..." He trailed off and Imogen understood what he didn't say.

It was the grief talking now. If he didn't say it, then it wasn't true. When she'd first heard her father had died, she'd hoped they were wrong, that when she got up to Alert her father would still be alive. Deep down, though, she'd known that he was gone.

But not saying it out loud had given her control of the situation.

It was compartmentalization.

It was survival.

"I hope your country returns to its former glory too."

Lev smiled. "Thank you, but I would like to change the subject if it's all the same to you."

"Of course. What would you like to talk about?"

"Tomorrow. What is happening? Lexi is in a state and knows nothing. Jeanette has phoned me twice to ask me about a suit, which I do have, but what is going on?"

Imogen groaned and then laughed. "Jeanette has insisted on me wearing a dress and that we have dinner afterward—her, her husband, us and Lexi—at the Grayling Bistro."

Lev grinned. "Ah, so that is what Lexi was grousing about. I thought it was just about me moving in here with you."

"Oh, dear." Imogen sighed. "I do feel bad for Lexi. I'm sorry this whole thing is stressing him out."

"He's not the only one," Lev said dryly.

"This is all so complicated." She sighed again.

"A child does that. Especially an unplanned one."

Imogen was taken by surprise by that statement, but Lev had a point. This child had changed their lives already. Everything was so complicated now.

"Perhaps we should set some ground rules so we can live together comfortably." She didn't want to talk about rules, but they had to find a way to make this arrangement amicable.

It was a marriage of convenience, not a love match.

Give it a chance. It could be...

She dismissed that thought. It couldn't be.

"Like what?" he asked.

"Like what will be done when this marriage comes to an end?"

"What do you mean?" he asked.

"Well, if your country is settled you'll have to return back to Chenar. You said I could keep the baby."

"Yes, I've been thinking about it, and for the sake of the child you would come with me. I wouldn't divorce you."

Imogen blinked a couple of times. "What?"

"You both would come with me. I have no desire for this marriage to come to an end. Imogen, it will be a long time before things settle down at home, and even then there will always be danger for an heir to the royal family."

* * *

He knew she was shocked, but it was the truth. He'd been thinking about it a lot. He wanted to be in his child's life. Imogen would have to come to Chenar to make that happen.

He wished he could stay in Canada with them both, but that was not an option. His duty, as a prince, meant he had to reside in Chenar. Even if he'd rather stay here.

Sure, he groused about being trapped, but the more time he stayed in Canada with Imogen, the happier he was.

The freer he felt.

But he had been born into duty, and one day he'd have to go back to Chenar and the life he'd never wanted.

It wasn't ideal, but the baby would be his heir and this way he could protect them both. Forever.

"I'm not going to go with you," Imogen stated. "I'm doing this to protect the baby, but I'm staying here."

"And if the worst happens and something happened to my brother, I would become King and you will need even more protection."

"Lev, I'm not leaving Canada. I'm not leaving the north," she said firmly. "This is my life. I belong here, and if you can't handle that, if you try to force me to leave, then I won't marry you."

Lev said nothing as she got up and went back inside.

He sat there for a few minutes.

Imogen was stubborn, but so was he.

He knew he had scared her, because he was terrified too.

This might be a marriage of convenience, but he didn't intend for this marriage to end, not where his child was concerned.

He had not planned to marry Imogen, but now that it was to be done, he wasn't going to end it. He was going to change Imogen's mind about the whole thing. One step at a time.

He followed her inside, where he saw her cleaning up in

the kitchen, wiping the counter quite vigorously, like she was trying to wipe her way through it.

"Are you all right?" A foolish question. Clearly she wasn't.

"No. I'm a bit bowled over by what you said. I thought I made it clear when I agreed to this arrangement. It wasn't going to be forever. It wasn't going to be permanent." Her voice was shrill and anxious. He couldn't blame her, but he was only stating the truth.

He'd been thinking about this since last night.

As much as he wanted to let her go, he couldn't.

"Fine," he agreed, but only so she wouldn't change her mind. "You're right. We agreed to do this for as long as I am in the country."

She cocked a thinly arched brow and he knew she didn't believe his capitulation. She was perceptive, he was learning that, but to be a good surgeon you had to be.

"Are you sure?" she asked.

"Yes. You're right—it's what we agreed to. I can't force you or my child to come with me. So I will do everything in my power to protect you after our marriage ends, but for now, let me do this."

"Okay. Everything will go as planned tomorrow. Or as Jeanette planned tomorrow."

He laughed softly. "Yes. As Jeanette planned."

Lev nodded and headed back out on the dock, this time to the front of the houseboat. He could see that Lexi was out on their small balcony. Lev didn't wave to him because Lexi wouldn't like the attention, but Lev was annoyed that Lexi was stuck here too.

Lexi had the freedom to go back to Chenar, except for his vow to his father to protect Lev, and Lexi took vows seriously.

So do you.

Lev sighed.

He hoped Kristof got the situation in Chenar straightened out soon.

He wasn't completely sure that he wanted to go back, if it came down to it, but Lev had already let his father down so much and he wouldn't do the same to his brother.

Being unable to move, to be hidden and trapped here, was one thing, but to be free to make his own choice was another, and he envied Imogen and even Lexi their freedom.

Lexi straightened his tie. Lev could tell Lexi was anxious. As was he. He told himself that this was for the baby.

For Imogen.

"You're sure?" Lexi asked.

"Yes. It's the right thing to do. It's my duty to protect them."

It might be his duty, but he *wanted* to protect Imogen and the baby. The thought of something happening to them was too much to bear and it unnerved him how much Imogen affected him.

Lexi nodded, but he couldn't relax, which was making even Lev more nervous.

The doors opened and Imogen walked into the courtroom. She looked both a bit green and a bit pale at the same time. He hoped it was morning sickness and not that she was ill at the prospect of marrying him.

He wasn't exactly thrilled with it either, but he hoped he was hiding it better.

As she approached him, his anxiety melted away. She looked so beautiful.

He smiled at her. He was glad it was her. If he had to fake marry someone, he was glad it was Imogen.

She smiled back and he took her hand as they were married by the justice of the peace.

The only one in that room who was anywhere near happy was Jeanette, and by extension her husband, Dave.

The newlyweds had to put on a show.

They had to appear happy while they were out in the public eye. Everyone, including Jeanette, had to believe that this was real.

That they were in love.

You could be.

Only he didn't let himself think like that. There had been a brief time, before everything had happened at home, when he'd thought he could be, that he might want to fall in love with a girl like Imogen, but that wasn't a possibility.

He would stay married to her to protect her, but he wasn't sure he could open his heart to her without feeling a sense of guilt for burdening her with a life she didn't want. Every day he struggled with this sense of guilt.

And he hated himself for it.

After a very awkward dinner at the Grayling, it was time, as Jeanette put it, for the two newlyweds to go home.

Home.

This wasn't his home, but there had been times in the past when he hadn't felt that Chenar was his home either. Not since his mother had died. The longer he stayed in Canada, the more comfortable he was here.

"Are you okay?" Imogen asked, as he helped her tie up her motorboat at their houseboat's dock. *Their* houseboat.

"Yes. Why?"

"You seem a bit shell-shocked."

Lev chuckled as he finished securing the boat. "Maybe a bit. Marriage wasn't..."

"Me neither," Imogen said. "But it's for the baby."

"Yes." And that was what he had to keep reminding himself. It was for the baby.

She opened the door to their houseboat, and they went in. Lev sat down on the couch and watched Imogen putter around her place. He smiled. She was wearing the flowery dress Jeanette had picked out for her.

It was flowy, but still clung to all the right places, showing off her curves and a slight swell in her abdomen where his baby grew.

His baby.

She turned, a pink flush in her cheeks that made his blood heat as he thought of the flush in her cheeks when she'd been in his arms back in Toronto.

"What?" she asked.

"What do you mean, 'What?'"

"Why are you staring at me?"

"Just admiring you." Which was the truth. She was beautiful. He always thought that.

She blushed again.

"So, in the morning, is Lexi going to meet us to drive us? He doesn't have to. We can walk."

"Lexi will be there. I know you two were arguing about that, but unless you want to move into our place, we have to let Lexi do his job."

"I can deal with that." She stood up. "I'm exhausted. I think I'm going to bed."

Lev stood and took her hand. It was so small and delicate.

Don't get attached. This isn't permanent.

Nothing about his life was permanent.

"Good night, Imogen." He kissed her hand, hearing her gasp ever so slightly. She took her hand back. He'd stepped too far, but he couldn't help it when he was around her.

"Good night, Lev."

Lev made them tea. Decaf for Imogen and the real stuff for himself. The morning was a bit awkward. He knew he shouldn't have kissed her the night before, but he hadn't been able to help himself. All he could do was pretend it had never happened, even if he couldn't stop thinking about it.

"Morning," she said, but her voice sounded a bit tense.

"I made you tea." He held out a travel mug. "It's decaf."

"Thank you. I wish it wasn't decaf, though," she murmured.

"I know, but full caffeine is not good for the baby."

"I know." She sighed. "You ready for today?"

"Work?" he asked. "I always am."

"I mean work as a married couple. I'm sure there will be a lot of gossip."

"Why do you think that?" he asked.

She worried her lip. "I have made a point not to date anyone I work with."

"We're not dating. We're married," he teased.

"Be serious…"

"It'll be okay, Imogen."

"Sure." Though he could tell she wasn't. They left the houseboat and Lexi was waiting for them at the dock to drive them to the hospital.

She was tense and worried, and he didn't know how to ease her anxiety.

On arriving, they went their separate ways. He went to the emergency department and she went up to the postoperative care floor to check on her patient.

He was hoping that some distance between them would help him not worry so much about her and what her association with him had put her through.

He knew that was a pipe dream. She was his wife. He wouldn't stop thinking about her.

"Dr. Vanin, there's a patient in bed three who is in some distress," Jessica, the nurse, said, handing him the triage report.

"Thank you." He glanced at the chart and the labs that had been done. He went straight to the patient, who was not so much in distress as in pain. Lev suspected it was acute cholecystitis.

"Can you page Dr. Hayes?" he asked Jessica.

"Of course." Jessica left the pod.

"Mrs. Doxtater? I'm Dr. Vanin. Your blood levels are showing elevated pancreatic enzymes. You're having a gallbladder attack and I'm going to have a general surgeon talk to you."

"Thank you, Dr. Vanin," the patient said weakly.

"I'm going to give you something for the pain." He injected some pain medication into her IV line.

Imogen showed up a few minutes later.

"What's going on?" she whispered.

Lev handed her the chart. "I think this patient needs a cholecystectomy."

Imogen read through the chart. "I think you're right. Based on the levels of enzymes in her blood, her pancreas is taking over. I'll check her."

Imogen slipped behind the curtain and he listened to her talk to the patient. She was so gentle and sympathetic, instantly easing the patient's anxiety.

And she was good at cholecystectomies, or so she had said at the conference when they'd done their first simulation together. It was one of the first things he'd found attractive about her.

He was watching her now as she stepped out from behind the curtain, making notes in the chart, and the more he watched her, the more he started to feel for her, and that was a dangerous thing indeed.

You can't feel this way.

More to the point: he didn't deserve to feel this way about her.

Why not?

How could he love someone when he had never had a shred of love from anyone? How could he give love when he didn't know what it was? He didn't deserve it. Especially not when he was safe and the people of Chenar weren't.

Lev sighed and scrubbed a hand over his face.

He was exhausted from all this guilt, from all these feelings.

"You were right," Imogen said, coming up to him, leaning over the nurses' station where he had been sitting.

"She needs her gallbladder removed?"

Imogen nodded. "The ultrasound showed a gallstone the size of a golf ball, possibly bigger, and the gallbladder is elongated. I'm worried it could rupture. Do you want to assist me?"

"Of course. When do you want to do the surgery?" he asked.

"Tomorrow morning if I can. I've admitted her, and I think she's stable for now. I gave strict instructions for her diet and to start her on some antibiotics."

Lev nodded and stifled a yawn. "Good."

She frowned. "Are you okay? You seem a bit distracted today and tired."

"To be honest, it's your couch. It's not that comfortable."

"I'm sorry about that. Maybe you should take the bed tonight?"

"Absolutely not. I'm not pregnant."

"Maybe we can check the furniture store and see if they have a futon or a pullout? Of course, Lexi will hate that, running errands," she teased.

Lev chuckled. "Yes. He will."

"Why don't you let him work here at the hospital?" she asked. "He's coming here every day as it is. He would do well as a security guard and it would give him access to both of us while we're here."

"Security guards work irregular shifts. He won't like it much if he has to work and we're not here. He would be fired for leaving his post."

"True. I never thought of that," she said. "I feel bad that he's alone."

So did Lev.

Lexi really had no life and he knew how much his friend wished he could be in Chenar.

"It was a good thought, though."

"We should have him over to dinner tonight," Imogen said.

"I'm sure he would like to come for dinner." Although Lev wasn't completely positive that was true. They may have lived together, but Lexi tried to keep his distance when he could, because he didn't want people to think that they were connected. He didn't want people to recognize him or Lev.

Not that Lev was in the spotlight. The world knew who Kristof was. They didn't care much for the spare.

And he preferred it that way.

Still, Lexi tried to keep a low profile where possible, but Imogen hated to see him on his own. She might act like a tough surgeon and not be bullied by patients or coworkers, but there was a soft side to Imogen Hayes that he really admired.

"Oh, there's Lexi now," Imogen said.

Lev glanced over at the door to the emergency room and saw Lexi had walked in and was scanning the room.

"I'd better go and see what he wants." Lev got up and walked to the waiting room, catching Lexi's eye and motioning him forward. Lexi looked concerned and they found a private spot to speak.

"I have news," Lexi whispered.

"I'm listening."

"Your brother has sent word about the situation in Chenar. It won't be long until it is over and we can go home!"

CHAPTER NINE

IMOGEN WAS WATCHING Lev and Lexi. Something was up and she hoped it wasn't bad news.

Lexi left and Lev returned.

"Is everything okay?" she asked.

"I think so." But he hesitated like he wanted to tell her more and couldn't.

Then she thought it might be the location of where they were standing. They were in the hall of the hospital and anyone could walk by.

"Do you need some air?"

"That would be great," he said, sounding relieved.

They headed for the ambulance bay and stepped outside, where they were hit with cool crisp air, a sure sign that autumn was on its way. The cooler air was nice as they stood outside in the empty ambulance bay, taking in deep breaths.

"Seems early for this change in weather," he remarked, but she had a feeling that wasn't what he wanted to talk about.

"Autumn comes early here." She'd noticed the other day some of the trees were starting to change color. "So, what did Lexi want?"

He smiled. "You don't beat around the bush, do you?"

"I can't help it."

"Just word from my brother. He's fine… Well, he's more than fine. The situation in my country may be over soon."

"Well, that's wonderful!"

"Is it?" he asked, his voice tense.

"Isn't it?" she asked, confused.

"I would have to leave."

"Oh." Then it hit her. He would leave her. Just like she'd known he would all along.

You knew this could happen.

The only reason they'd got married was for the baby, and though she knew he wanted her to go with him to Chenar, she wouldn't leave Yellowknife.

This was her home.

"Imogen, right now I'm here," he said as if reading her thoughts and trying to reassure her.

"Right." His words did little to reassure her.

Nothing in life is permanent.

Except her home here. Yellowknife had never failed her.

"This is your home, Imogen," her father had said. *"Never forget that. Yellowknife has never failed us or let us down or left us. It's home."*

"So is Lexi leaving, then?" she asked, clearing her throat, trying to forget all the self-doubt she was feeling.

"Yes. For now. Some restrictions have been lifted. I can't leave the territory, but there's no immediate threat and Lexi needs to go to my brother."

"So you have some freedom?"

"A bit. Not much."

"Maybe we can go together on my rounds in Fort Smith?" she suggested, trying to change the subject from him leaving her and their unborn child.

Lev smiled. "I'd like that. Work will help keep my mind off everything. I'd like to keep busy until…" He trailed off, but Imogen knew what he'd been about to say.

Until he left.

Even though she had built up these walls to protect her heart, it was hard to breathe at that moment. When had she let him in? She'd known this would happen, she'd reminded herself of it at every turn, so why was it so hard to contemplate him leaving?

You could go with him...

She shook that thought away. Her pulse thundered in her ears. It was deafening and she felt like she was going to be sick.

You knew this wasn't forever.

Her emotions were in turmoil and she had to put some distance between herself and Lev.

"Imogen, you look pale. Are you feeling well?" he asked, putting his arm around her, like it was habit. But it wasn't.

She stepped away from him.

"I'm fine." Which was a lie. She was trying to process everything, all the emotions she seemed to have lost control over. "I've finished my shift early and I was going to walk back to the dock. I can get a water taxi to take me to the houseboat. I'll leave my boat for you."

Lev nodded. "Okay, but be careful and I'll be home as soon as I can."

Home. But this wasn't his home. He'd made that clear.

"Sure." Imogen walked away from him. She had to get her purse and change out of her scrubs. She needed space to calm down and process the fact that Lev would be leaving sooner than she'd thought.

She shouldn't have got her hopes up because she'd known this was coming.

And she'd been disappointed too many times.

Imogen tried to stay up and wait for Lev, but she had a headache when she got back to the houseboat.

She was so tired and she was worrying about what Lexi

had said to Lev. She didn't have the strength or stamina to deal with her emotions tonight.

She had to clear her head properly and make plans to move on. But when she got home, she went straight to bed. All this turmoil was making her feel nauseous and exhausted.

The moment she got home she fell asleep, and when she woke up the houseboat was quiet and still, and it was dark out. She wasn't sure how long she'd been out.

She got out of bed, but didn't turn on the lights, because she didn't want to blind herself and she was hoping to take herself back to bed until the last remnants of her headache were gone. She crept down the stairs and headed straight for the bathroom, only to walk straight into a wall of warm, wet flesh.

"What the heck!" she screamed as she jumped back, knocking over a vase that was on a small end table.

"Imogen, it's me!" Lev said in the darkness.

She rubbed her eyes. She could barely see him because all the lights were off downstairs and there was no moon tonight, a rainstorm having moved in from the northwest. She took a deep breath to calm her racing pulse after being scared senseless.

"Lev, what are you doing, lurking around in the dark?"

"I had a shower."

"Okay." Imogen moved past him to turn on a light. There was no sense hanging around in the dark now.

"No, don't..."

But it was too late and she'd already flicked on the light, gasping when she saw that Lev was standing in her kitchen stark naked. All she could do was stare and admire Lev in her kitchen, the intricate tattoo she thought about often, his well-defined muscles and a few other attributes that she admired on full display.

Don't think about it.

She tried to look away, but she couldn't. Her heart, which had been racing before because she'd been scared, was now beating faster for a completely different reason. Staring at him, standing there naked, she recalled every little detail about him and how he'd made her feel that night.

His strong hands on her skin, caressing her. The taste of his lips on hers and the hot, heady, endless pleasure they'd shared that night. Her blood began to heat, her pulse thundering, and she bit her bottom lip in a desperate attempt to keep the blush she felt from rising in her cheeks.

She turned away quickly. She had to regain control. She hated the way he had this effect on her body; that she was so attracted to him, that she still thought of him and the way he made her feel. Where Lev was concerned, she couldn't resist. He seemed to be the exception to all the rules she'd put in place, and it drove her crazy.

"Why are you standing in my kitchen completely naked?"

"I told you, I took a shower. I'm not dripping over your floor. I did dry off in the bathroom and hung up my towel. I thought you were asleep and that's why I didn't turn on the light, but your bathroom is small and I preferred to put on my boxer briefs out here."

She spun around and saw that he was standing there still, with his hands on his hips, not in the least embarrassed that he was naked. She wasn't exactly embarrassed either. It was just rather too tempting to see him this way and right now she was in no mood to tempt fate.

He had an amused smile on his face, which was a huge change from the frustrated and tense man she'd left behind at the hospital. This seemed more like the fun guy she'd met at the conference.

"You need to put some clothes on," Imogen said, her voice shaking.

"Fine." He walked over to the couch, pulled his boxers out of his suitcase and slipped them on. "Is this better?"

No.

Only she didn't say that aloud. She much preferred him naked, although the boxers made it easier for her to have a rational conversation with him, despite not really hiding anything.

She could still see his tattoo, peeking out from the top of his briefs and a bit from the bottom of the leg. It was hard not to stare at it. It was intricate, sexy and in an intimate spot she was all too familiar with.

"You like my tattoo?" he teased.

"What?"

"You're staring at it." He sat down on the couch, which he'd made up into his bed.

"It's quite large." Her face flushed again and then she groaned, laughing, while Lev chuckled.

"Thank you."

She rolled her eyes. "I was talking about the tattoo."

"I know, but this whole situation is actually quite funny. You brought me out of my funk."

"Good." She wandered over and curled up in her chair. Truth be told, she was feeling better too.

"How was the rest of your shift?" she asked.

"Quiet. Lexi left for the airport. He's off to see Kristof." He sighed. "The Canadians arranged it. I don't know where he's going."

"You sound a bit upset."

"I'm worried about Lexi leaving. He's the only connection I have to Chenar."

"Funnily enough, I'm going to miss him too. I miss seeing him standing out on his deck with binoculars or going by in a boat," she teased, trying to lighten the mood.

Lev chuckled. "Yes, well, as I said, he takes his job seriously. Although we never did get him to buy that futon."

"Well, we can go to the furniture store tomorrow, after I do that surgery and after my prenatal checkup."

"You're having a prenatal checkup tomorrow?" he asked. "Why didn't you tell me?"

"I booked it before I knew you were still alive and before we got married. It slipped my mind until now. It's routine. You're more than welcome to come. I hope you know that."

Lev nodded. "I would like to."

"I'll book my amniocentesis, so eventually you should get positive proof of your paternity."

"Thank you."

"You never told me why you need this. I mean, you married me. Do you really not believe that the baby is yours?" She wasn't sure she wanted to know the answer.

Maybe if she knew his real reason she could rationalize it and make sense out of this whole situation.

"It was because of two things." Lev sighed. "First was my brother. He fell in love with this woman and she became pregnant. He was thrilled, although our father was less than thrilled that she was pregnant and they were not married. Kristof was going to rectify that, though. He was head over heels for this woman. Actually, we all cared for her, and so in a way it hurt us all."

"What happened?"

"Kristof discovered she'd been having an affair. The baby he'd thought was his was not. He was so excited to be a father and to get married, but she was just after the title and the money. She didn't love Kristof. He never trusted anyone again and the pain he was put through was unbearable to watch."

"And the second one?" she asked.

"It was me."

"You?" she asked, confused.

"There was no baby, but I fell in love with a woman who also betrayed me. I was going to marry her. I was planning a life, a life she didn't want." Lev scrubbed a hand over his face. "Women don't see the man. They see only the title, the prestige."

"I'm sorry," she said gently.

"No woman, besides you, has ever got pregnant and claimed it was mine, but I have been burned before. I tend to keep out of the spotlight. I'm not as actively pursued as Kristof. And after Tatiana, a wife and child were never in my plans."

"I understand. That would test the faith of anyone."

"I'm sorry that I couldn't trust you right away."

"No apology necessary. This pregnancy wasn't in my plans either. I never thought I would have a family—I wasn't really sure that I wanted one."

"Why?" he asked.

"My mother abandoned me. She broke my father's heart and... I never really knew any extended family. It was just me and my dad for so long. I guess I was afraid."

"So you've never had a long-term relationship before?"

"I have." She didn't want to talk about Allen, but he had been so forthright about his brother and why he'd wanted to prove the paternity, she wanted to be truthful with him too. "I was in a long-term relationship with another doctor. I thought I knew what love was, and we were building a future together. He knew how important it was to me to be up here in the north. He knew that was my plan and told me he wanted the same, but he didn't and he left, but..."

"But what?" he asked.

Her cheeks heated in embarrassment. "I thought he wanted to marry me, but he didn't. He said that was never in his plan, but when he left here... Well, he's married now with a child. Of course, his wife could never upstage him like I apparently did."

"Upstage him?" he asked, confused.

"He liked the limelight and hated it when I got accolades. Between him and my mother, it's hard."

"So it's hard for you to trust too, then?" Lev asked.

"Yes. It is."

It was hard to trust anyone, because everyone eventually left.

No one stayed.

Not even her mother.

"Well, we certainly know how to have a good conversation, don't we?" Lev teased.

"Yes. We do." Imogen chuckled. "Well, I'm going to go back to bed. We have an early morning tomorrow and a surgery. I hope you're still able to come and assist?"

Lev nodded. "Of course. When is your prenatal?"

"One o'clock on the third floor. I hope you're able to come to that too."

"I will be there. For both. What time would you like the alarm set?"

"Five in the morning should do the trick."

"Very well. Good night, Imogen."

"Good night, Lev." She got up from her chair and quickly used the bathroom. After she was done she flicked off the light and made her way back up to her loft. She looked back once to see Lev spread out on the couch, looking uncomfortable and cramped as he moved around, trying to find a comfortable position.

He couldn't sleep like that. Not when they had to get up early in the morning to do a surgery.

"That's not working," she said, from her loft.

"I know, but I'll eventually find a comfortable spot," he answered back.

"I doubt that." And even though she knew it probably wasn't wise, she knew she had to offer. "Why don't you come and sleep beside me? I have a queen-size bed. You need a good night's sleep for surgery tomorrow."

"Do you think that's wise?"

No.

"It'll be fine. We're married. We're supposed to be sharing a bed anyway. At least for sleeping."

"Thank you. I wouldn't mind a good night's sleep." Lev got up, taking his pillow, and followed her up the stairs to the loft.

She climbed in on her side and Lev took the other side. Imogen tried to get comfortable, without disturbing Lev too much, and she hoped that she would be able to sleep tonight, but it was hard, knowing that he was so close.

Within arm's reach.

And it was dark and private here.

"Good night, Imogen," he whispered in the dark.

"Good night, Lev."

It wasn't long before she heard him breathing deeply, asleep, but she knew that it would be some time before she would find her own rest. She just hoped that she'd be able to get some more sleep before her long day tomorrow.

Imogen stifled a yawn from behind her surgical mask and blinked a few times. The one thing she hated about being pregnant was the fact she couldn't have her usual caffeine intake. She missed her black, fully caffeinated coffees in the morning.

Especially when she had spent all night tossing and turning, very aware that Lev was sharing her bed.

At least she had managed to go home early the night before and have that nap, but just thinking about the nap had brought back another keen memory of her walking into Lev when he had been naked and fresh out of the shower.

Just thinking about him standing there made her blush, and it didn't help matters that he was standing on the opposite side of the table, assisting her with the cholecystectomy.

Don't think about it.

She rolled her shoulders and turned her focus back to the monitor as she maneuvered the laparoscope to remove the inflamed gallbladder.

"Dr. Vanin, can you move the camera five degrees to the left?"

"Yes, Dr. Hayes."

Lev was operating the camera and light portion of the surgery while she was in there, working to seal off the bile duct and making sure she didn't nick the liver or the common bile duct while she removed the gallbladder. She wanted to make sure she took the whole thing out with the stone intact.

Usually, these were simple operations that she could do with her eyes closed, but truth be told, she was a bit worried about the size of the gallstone and whether she could remove the whole thing out of the belly-button incision. She didn't want to have to open the poor patient up.

With an adjusted movement, Imogen breathed a sigh of relief when she carefully separated the gallbladder and was able to bag it with the gallstone still in place. She was worried that the extremely inflamed gallbladder, which had some necrotic patches, might erupt.

She also didn't want a piece of the large gallstone to chip off and get lodged in the common bile duct, which could then cause pancreatitis.

And damage to the common bile duct could cause a whole mess of other issues for the patient. She'd have to open up the patient and the surgery would be longer. It reminded her of the simulation lab at the conference she'd done with Lev.

The robotic equipment made a bile duct injury very simple, but they didn't have that new equipment here. The only good thing was that Lev was familiar with the procedure and he was here, working with her.

She hoped it didn't come to that.

Thankfully, she was relieved when she was able to bag the nasty gallbladder and remove it with relative ease through the small incision she had made, with no damage to the bile duct.

"There!" she said with triumph as she removed the laparoscope with the bagged gallbladder hanging on the other end. "Got it!"

"Excellent work."

"Now, to make sure everything else is okay." She did a last check of the cavity, making sure she hadn't nicked a biliary artery or left something behind. Her sutures were all in the right place and the ducts had been clear. There was no sign of gallstones or pieces of gallstones anywhere.

Everything looked good. The patient's vitals were strong and she was happy to pull the laparoscope out and suture up the small incisions. Once she had done that, the patient was wheeled out of the operating room and she went to work recording the procedure on the patient's chart so she wouldn't forget later.

"I'm glad that was easy," Lev said, as he headed to the scrub room. "When you told me what was going on with her morning blood draw, I was worried that the gallbladder might have ruptured, which would have been worse."

"I was worried too," she said. "If it had ruptured I wouldn't be making it to my prenatal. I would be doing a much larger surgery and trying to clean up a mess."

"So what is being done at the prenatal today? You told me you had an appointment, but other than booking your amnio, you haven't told me what else is involved."

"It's just a routine checkup. I can't remember when they do the dating ultrasound, but I'm pretty positive that's not right now."

"That's too bad. I wouldn't have minded seeing it. I could use some cheering up."

"Yeah, I wouldn't have minded either, but what can you

do about doctors, eh?" She was teasing, hoping to get him to laugh again. Even though they had reached an understanding about the nakedness incident, there was still a sadness about him. Even if he didn't want to admit it, she knew that Lev was worried and that he was anxious to get home to Chenar.

And she wouldn't go with him.
She couldn't.
She wouldn't.
Yellowknife was her home.
Yellowknife had never let her down.

CHAPTER TEN

OF ALL THE places he'd imagined he'd be in his life, this was not one of them. He never thought that he'd be sitting in a prenatal exam room in Yellowknife with his wife, hoping that his baby was okay.

He'd already accepted that this baby was his.

Are you sure?

He hated that voice of doubt. He knew what had happened to Kristof and how Tatiana had shattered his trust, but Imogen was nothing like them.

Imogen was different and he had to keep telling himself that.

Stop. Focus on the baby.

He closed his eyes and took a deep breath to center himself. As much as he tried to clear his mind, all he could think about was last night. The way Imogen had looked at him, the flush in her cheeks, and then sharing a bed with her.

He'd been worried about that, but he'd been so tired he'd fallen asleep easily.

When he'd woken up she'd been snuggled up against him and he'd hated having to disturb her so they could go to work.

He hadn't wanted to leave. It had been so nice to have her in his arms.

It had felt right. It had felt like a home, although he wasn't sure what a real home felt like, but he liked to think it felt like this.

Warm. Safe.

He knew she wanted to stay, but if he wanted any relationship with his child—or with her—he had to convince her to leave with him when it was time to go. Even if he wanted to stay too, he couldn't. It was his duty to go back to Chenar.

Just because the unrest in his country was ending, Imogen was still carrying a royal baby. It was his duty to protect her. He was torn. He wished he could stay here in Yellowknife, but he couldn't be in two places at once. He had to make a choice.

He had to help Kristof rebuild Chenar. It was his duty. But he also had a duty to Imogen, to his child, as well as a duty to his country. His late father had always put the country before his children and had tried to teach his sons that too.

Lev was torn between guilt over duty and his longing to stay here and live a normal life.

Then he thought of her again, as she had been last night. It had not been his intention to have Imogen catch him unawares like that.

When he'd arrived home from his shift, he'd found the place dark, and for one split second he'd feared the worst, until he'd crept up into the loft and found out she'd been sleeping soundly.

If he hadn't been so uncomfortable and so tired that night, he wouldn't have slept in her bed, but it had been so nice to finally be able to stretch out completely and not be confined to such a narrow berth.

Why did it feel so right with her?

He'd never wanted this.

Yes, you did.

After Tatiana his life had been too complicated. Now it was even more so. And he couldn't do charting or see a patient to ease his anxiety.

He was in an exam room, waiting to hear what the doctor had to say about his wife and his baby.

"You're fidgeting," she said.

"Am I?"

Imogen reached out and took his hand. "What are you worrying about?"

"Nothing much. It's nothing really."

He wanted to tell her how he'd enjoyed waking up beside her and watching her sleep, but he couldn't say any of those things because he knew she didn't feel that way.

She'd made it clear that this marriage was on paper only and that she was staying in Yellowknife no matter what. How could he put his heart at risk?

Lev shook that thought away.

There was a knock on the door and the obstetrician, Dr. Merton, came into the room.

"Good afternoon, Dr. Hayes. How are we today?" Dr. Merton looked up from her chart. "Oh! Is this the baby's father?"

"Yes," Imogen said. "Dr. Merton, I would like to introduce you to my husband, Dr. Lev Vanin."

Lev stood up and shook the doctor's hand. "It's a pleasure to meet you."

The doctor stared at him for some time. "Do I know you, Dr. Vanin?"

He could feel the blood draining from his face and he worried that he would be recognized.

"Well, he's been working here for a couple of weeks now, Dr. Merton. I'm sure you've probably seen him in the halls. He's our new trauma surgeon," Imogen explained, seamlessly covering up the truth.

Dr. Merton nodded. "That must be it."

Lev breathed a sigh of relief and squeezed Imogen's hand in thanks. He'd never seen Dr. Merton before, even in passing, but it was enough to change the subject and throw Dr. Merton off the scent.

"Well, your blood work came back normal," Dr. Merton said, not missing a beat. "I would like to check the baby's heartbeat today through my stethoscope. You're far enough along now that we can probably pick it up."

"Probably?" Lev asked, worried. "You mean you weren't able to pick it up before?"

"No," Imogen said sadly. "No, but Dr. Merton doesn't think it's unusual early on. We've used Doppler before to hear it."

"Have you had the first ultrasound?" he asked.

"Yes," Dr. Merton said. "At twelve weeks and everything was fine."

Lev was disappointed. He'd missed it. A couple of weeks ago he'd been in limbo in another town. He'd missed out on so much already.

"I'm sorry," Imogen whispered.

"It's okay. I'm glad the baby is healthy. That's the main thing."

"Now, lie back on the table and lift your shirt. We'll find that heartbeat and take measurements," Dr. Merton said.

Lev stood, helped Imogen up onto the exam table and stood by her head.

"Sounds strong." Dr. Merton measured her. "And your measurements are right on track."

"I don't suppose you could use the Doppler again?" Imogen asked. "Lev was traveling before and missed out."

Dr. Merton smiled. "Of course."

Dr. Merton pulled out the Doppler and placed it on Imogen's abdomen. At first all Lev heard was static. Imogen squeezed his hand and he could tell she was a bit anxious as well. They were both a bundle of nerves.

Then they heard it, whooshing from the placenta and then a fast heartbeat. Dr. Merton smiled and Imogen let out a sigh of relief. He couldn't stop smiling. He looked over at Imogen and she was smiling too, her eyes twinkling. They both were sharing in this moment, the first time he was hearing the heartbeat.

It was amazing.

And surreal.

As a resident, he'd done a round on the obstetrics floor, like every good surgeon in their training, and he'd heard other babies' heartbeats. He was familiar with Doppler and ultrasound, but it was something quite different when it was your own child's heart.

The only thing he wished was that his life wasn't in such a topsy-turvy state.

He wished he could provide stability, wished his child wouldn't need bodyguards and security. Where there were always people watching you.

For that he was sad.

"That's a good strong heartbeat," Dr. Merton said as she finished up.

"Thank you, Doctor." Lev glanced down at Imogen. She was still smiling. "When will you perform the amniocentesis?"

Dr. Merton was recording measurements. "Between fifteen and twenty weeks. I like to wait until a happy medium between the two. Dr. Hayes, were you still thinking of having the procedure done?"

"Yes," she said, and she worried her bottom lip. He knew she was embarrassed. "I'm hoping you can also confirm paternity."

Dr. Merton looked confused. "We can in the amnio, but you two are married... Surely...?"

"There's a complicated situation, Dr. Merton," Lev interrupted. "Quite delicate and we'd both appreciate it if you could."

Imogen's cheeks bloomed pink and he knew she was embarrassed and worried that rumors could spread. He hoped that Dr. Merton wasn't the kind of physician to spread rumors. It was bad enough that people in the hospital were gossiping over their hasty marriage.

"The test can confirm paternity and it will be kept between us, I assure you," she said quickly. "I will remind you there are risks with the procedure."

"I'm aware," Imogen said.

"Risks?" Lev's heart sank. He'd forgotten that and now he wasn't so sure it should be done.

He didn't want anything to harm his child because this was *his* child. No matter what a test said.

"Perhaps we shouldn't," Lev said.

"I'm having it," Imogen said.

"It's a standard procedure," Dr. Merton tried to reassure them. "But, as with any procedure, there are risks."

"Thank you, Dr. Merton. I know that." Imogen sat up. "I would like to schedule one for week eighteen."

"I will have my secretary call you." Dr. Merton closed her chart. "And I will see you for your regular checkup in a month. My secretary will also call you with the date for your second ultrasound and with information about some more blood work and the glucose tolerance test."

"Fun!" Imogen replied sarcastically to the glucose test.

Dr. Merton smiled. "I know. Get used to it. Have a great day, Dr. Hayes, and it's a pleasure to meet you, Dr. Vanin."

Dr. Merton left the room and Imogen let out a sigh of relief. "That was a lot more awkward than I thought it was going to be."

"I'm sorry. I didn't mean to blurt it out…"

"No. It's okay. We had to ask or they wouldn't have tested for it and I understand your reasoning."

"Do you think Dr. Merton will keep our request secret? There has already been some gossiping and I don't want to embarrass you further."

"She'll keep it secret. She's a good physician." Imogen stood. "You seem distracted today. Any word from Lexi?"

"No." He let her think that he was worried about Lexi, but he wasn't. Not really. He was worried about her, the baby, about having to leave before he could convince her to come with him. So he let her think it was about Lexi and Kristof.

"I'm sure Lexi is fine." She touched his arm.

"I'm sure." They left the exam room and walked back together.

"Why don't we go out for dinner tonight?" she asked. "Just the two of us."

"I would like that, but you know that it won't be just the two of us," he teased.

He realized it was the first time he'd thought about the baby beyond being something he had to protect. Hearing that heartbeat had made it a reality for him.

"Well, I know that there will be agents watching and that they're never really far away, but they don't have to eat at the table with us, like Lexi does."

Lev chuckled. "True, but that's not what I meant."

Imogen looked confused. "What did you mean, then?"

He stopped and touched her belly. Although he couldn't feel anything, his heart warmed, thinking about the life growing inside her.

"There will be three of us."

She smiled, tears welling up in her eyes. "Right. The three of us."

"I would like a dinner with you two tonight."

She cleared her throat and blinked a few times. He moved his hand and they continued walking.

"Great. So we'll go back to the houseboat, change, and

I'll take you to one of my favorite places. Of course, I will have to rent a car."

"Lexi left me the truck. We can take the truck." He cocked an eyebrow as they stopped at the junction. One way led to the emergency department and one way back to the general surgery floor, where she was working today. "Where is this place? We usually just walk everywhere."

She smiled. "You'll see."

"Should I be nervous?"

"Nope. I'll see you at five downstairs by the main entrance?"

"Yes."

She nodded and he watched her walk away. He couldn't help but wonder what she had planned, and then he smiled when he realized that she'd succeeded in getting his mind off everything he was worrying about.

The night they had met, he'd been stewing over something as well. Something that wasn't important and he couldn't even remember what it was, but it would have been trivial compared to what was on his mind now, and she had walked up to him and just started talking.

And he'd forgotten everything.

He'd forgotten who he was when he was around her.

And that was a dangerous thing indeed.

"Where are we going?" Lev asked. She could tell he was curious and possibly slightly worried, but he was intrigued all the same.

She knew he was feeling a bit lost without Lexi, even if he had complained about Lexi's constant presence in his life, and he was in a bit of a rut. He'd been moved from place to place for the last four months. Everything about his life was dictated by government agents or by Lexi or by his job.

So Imogen had taken it upon herself to arrange a little

outing. She'd cleared it with the security detail and they wouldn't be far away, but she wanted to take him out of town. There was a small restaurant about twenty kilometers down the highway, just outside the city off Highway 3.

It looked like a little hole-in-the-wall place, but appearances were deceiving. Inside was a great little restaurant that she rarely got to visit unless she rented a car. And Imogen knew it would soon close for the winter.

This was their last chance and she thought it might be a nice change of pace for Lev. It would get his mind off whatever was worrying him and it would distract her too.

"To a restaurant I like."

"So you said, but where is it that we have to drive out of Yellowknife to get to it?"

"You'll see." She reached over the console and punched the coordinates into the GPS. "Just follow the directions and you'll be fine."

Lev cocked an eyebrow. "I don't know if I should trust you."

He was teasing and she laughed gently. "I think you can trust me."

"Can I?" he teased.

"Would you just drive?"

He was laughing as he pulled out of the parking lot onto the main road headed for downtown Yellowknife. "Fine, but I should also point out I don't like listening to the GPS too much."

"Well, you don't want to end up going in the opposite direction or we'll be driving until the road peters out and there's not much east of Yellowknife."

"So we're headed west onto the highway?" he asked.

"Yes. And make sure you watch for bison."

"I remember," he said dryly.

"Oh? You've had a run-in with one before?"

"Yes. We were delayed by a large group of them that

decided to walk down the middle of the highway. Lexi had already been warned that there wasn't much he could do and, really, those beasts are massive. I didn't want the truck wrecked."

"You should meet a moose."

"I have yet to see one. I would like to."

"Not if it's walking in front of your car you don't! Working as a trauma surgeon, you'll probably soon get a case or two of people involved in an accident with a moose. It can prove to be fatal."

Lev frowned. "That's good to know and I really hope I don't encounter one of those traumas."

"I hope not either, but I think it's inevitable."

They drove in silence past the large Yellowknife sign and out past the airport until they were on the Mackenzie Highway, also known as the Frontier Trail Route. Back when she had still been with Allen, they would take his car out as far as Fort Providence, having picnics in the different territorial parks that lined the highway.

One time, they had taken a few days and driven over the Deh Cho Bridge and headed down toward Fort Smith and Wood Buffalo. They hadn't stayed long, as Allen didn't particularly like hiking or the town, but Imogen loved it there. She wished she could go back.

She didn't mind long car trips.

Not in the summer, anyway.

"This really is out in the middle of nowhere," Lev remarked as they drove past the Yellowknife Golf Club and Fred Henne Territorial Park. "Now I'm worried what you have in store for me out here."

"Well, since we're both off tomorrow, I thought it would be the perfect time to take this short trip. Also, the place we're going to is seasonal and will be closing for the winter shortly."

"It's not even fall."

"We get snow in October," she reminded him. She had told him this before.

"That sounds awful, if I'm honest."

She chuckled. "It's not so bad, but, yeah, you don't want to be stuck on this highway in a snowstorm. It's not impassable, but it's slow. A simple eight-hour drive to Fort Smith can take somewhere around sixteen hours in a snowstorm."

"Sixteen hours?" Lev winced, and then frowned at a diamond warning sign on the side of the road.

"You need to slow down when you see those diamond signs," she warned, because he wasn't slowing down.

"Why?"

"It's where the permafrost has buckled the road. If you hit it the wrong way your car could get some air!"

Lev slowed. "What is get some air?"

"It can cause your car to roll, quite violently. It's the worst kind of bump you could imagine. It's fun for no one, and your wallet will hate you for the repairs needed on your vehicle's suspension."

"Okay." They took the dip slowly, but even then it was rough enough to cause her stomach to slosh and do a flip.

"So, this place is a seasonal restaurant?" Lev asked.

"Yes."

He made a face again. "Is it Ratchet Ronnie's?"

"It is! Have you been there before?" she asked, excited.

"That place looked like a dive when Lexi and I drove past. We opted to eat what we bought in Hay River at the North Store rather than test the water at that place."

"Appearances can be deceiving. It's a great place."

He shot her a look that said he wasn't too convinced.

"Trust me," she said.

"You've been asking me to trust you a lot tonight, which makes me even more worried."

"Look, I won't steer you wrong about the food. Trust me."

They drove for about an hour until there was a little

gravel road turnoff from the highway. Ratchet Ronnie's sat not far off that gravel road and there was a sign with neon blinking lights to show that it was open. There were several vehicles in the parking lot and Lev pulled the truck alongside them and stopped.

"See," she said triumphantly. "People love this place."

"It just looks like a clapboard shack. Like something out of an old horror movie."

"Just wait!" she teased. "I haven't steered you wrong yet."

"Well, you did once."

"What do you mean?" she asked.

"That little bar on the waterfront that you swore was wonderful, but it turned out to be a hotel. That was a pricey drink," he teased.

She'd forgotten about that momentarily. She had wanted to take him to that little bar after they'd gone up the CN Tower, only to find her favorite little haunt had turned into a boutique hotel. They had impulsively rented a penthouse suite because it had been the only room available and had drunk champagne on their own rooftop terrace before they'd made love.

It had been a wonderful night.

Of course, taking that suite had had bigger consequences than just a hotel bill. They were married. They were going to be parents.

Don't get used to this.

She had to keep reminding herself of that. Even though they were married, that didn't mean it was permanent. She could still end up raising this child alone.

Don't think about it now.

Right now, all she wanted to focus on was having a nice dinner at Ratchet Ronnie's. She didn't want to think about their marriage of convenience. She didn't want to think about security guards, lines of succession or danger.

"It was expensive," she admitted.

"But worth it." He took her hand and kissed it, making her melt and forget her worry.

"Come on. Let's eat!" She took Lev's hand and led him inside the restaurant.

The look of surprise on his face when they walked into a retro fifties-style diner, complete with red leather booths, jukeboxes and chrome, made her smile, and she gave him a small punch on the arm.

"See? What did I tell you? Appearances can be deceiving."

"This is amazing and it's in the middle of nowhere," he said, astounded.

"Yeah, it's a local secret only to be discovered by adventurous travelers."

They were led to a corner booth and they took a seat to look over the menu. It was classic diner food, featuring things like milkshakes and hamburgers, but also had a touch of territorial traditional foods like bannock, buffalo and arctic char.

"I have to say," Lev said after they'd ordered. "This is a nice distraction."

"I thought it might be."

"You're very pleased with yourself."

"I am rather," she teased. "We have a couple of days off and I thought it might be nice for you to see something outside the city."

He smiled and nodded.

"And we're going down to Fort Smith in a couple of days to help the doctors there."

"Where is Fort Smith?"

"South of here. It's my turn on rotation to do some surgeries at the hospital there. Just routine stuff. I get flown down, as it's an eight-hour drive. So I spend a day there and fly back in the evening. I asked Jeanette and cleared it all—you can come too if you'd like. I could use the help."

"I would like that. It would be a good change of pace."

"My thoughts exactly."

"So what is there to do in Fort Smith, besides work?"

"To do?"

"I would like to see something besides a clinic. I want to enjoy my time here."

Before he left.

He didn't have to say it, but Imogen knew that was what he was thinking.

"Well, you need more time there to see everything. It sits inside Wood Buffalo National Park, which is bigger than Switzerland."

Lev's eyes widened. "Impressive. It amazes me how vast your country is."

"We could go on a small hike in town to see the pelicans in Slave River before they migrate back down south."

"That sounds like a plan."

"Other than that, there's not much to do there." She remembered the way Allen would complain. He hated Fort Smith.

Looking back, she should have realized he hated the north.

"You okay?" he asked.

"Yes. Why?"

"You zoned out and you seemed sad."

"I was thinking of my ex. He hated Fort Smith. He preferred the city."

"Don't think about him," Lev said. "The city has merits, but I prefer this rugged place. Of course, I was used to mobile military hospitals."

"You're a prince," she whispered. "Surely you're used to much more glamorous cityscapes?"

"Used to and like are two very different things."

Her heart swelled. She was glad he liked it here. It gave her hope.

Of what?

Just because he liked it here it didn't mean he wanted to stay, or could stay.

Don't think about it.

She shook those thoughts from her mind. She just wanted to enjoy tonight.

The rest of their evening at the restaurant was exactly what they both needed: a distraction from everyday life. They didn't think about Chenar or work or anything. They enjoyed each other's company, just like they'd done when they'd first met. Imogen was sad to see the evening come to an end, but they had to drive back to Yellowknife and the restaurant would be closing soon.

They paid their bill and walked outside. There was a nip in the air and it was dark but clear.

"It's cooler than the other night," Lev remarked.

"I told you fall is coming, even though it's still August. September isn't far away. Just a couple more days."

Her phone buzzed and she glanced at it. She'd set up an alarm for an app that tracked a certain phenomenon, one she knew Lev wanted to see.

The alert was telling her the chances were high and it would happen soon.

"Is everything good?" he asked. "Is it the hospital?"

"No, but let's go down the road a bit. There's a park and I want to show you something away from this artificial light."

"What?"

"Just trust me."

They got into the truck and drove down the highway to one of the many territorial parks that lined the road.

Not a soul was there.

It was just the two of them.

They got out of the truck and walked toward a lake,

which was calm. The only sound was the gentle lapping of waves against the shoreline. Above them was a clear, dark sky.

"So what have we come here for?" he asked.

"Just wait," she whispered.

Then what she'd been waiting for, watching for, happened.

Across the sky a wave of undulating colors broke out against the inky blackness. The green light glowed, danced and arced above their heads in true aurora borealis fashion.

Her heart soared with excitement. She was used to seeing it, but she never got tired of seeing a full aurora moving and rippling across an inky dark sky.

It was magical.

Lev stood there and stared, his mouth open in awe.

"I've waited a long time to see this," he whispered.

"It's beautiful, isn't it?"

"It is." Lev continued to stare up at it, but then he turned and looked at her, touching her face. "It is beautiful, but not as beautiful as you."

Before she knew what was happening, he leaned down and kissed her, gently.

And even though she shouldn't, she melted in his arms as the kiss deepened. It was a brief kiss, but it made her pulse race in anticipation. She didn't know what to say. There was nothing to say as they stood there in the darkness next to the truck, watching the lights dance across the sky.

His arm slipped around her, pulling her close, and she leaned her head against his shoulder, enjoying this stolen moment with him.

Savoring it, while she had the chance.

CHAPTER ELEVEN

IMOGEN COULDN'T STOP to think about that kiss they had shared while watching the northern lights by the shore of Great Slave Lake. The kiss had been gentle, controlled, but nevertheless it had been like a kiss from a lover. It was nothing like their first kiss in Toronto, which had been fueled by passion and champagne.

This was deeper, emotionally.

It had been so simple, so innocent, but it had made her feel connected to him.

It had made her feel safe.

It had made her feel wanted.

Something she hadn't felt for a long time, and it scared her because she didn't want to rely on that feeling. The only person she could rely on was herself. It was what her father had taught her.

Her self-reliance and survival had got her through her father's death and Allen's departure.

She was a safe bet.

Lev was not.

They hadn't said much to each other on their drive back to Yellowknife. Imogen had gone to bed, but Lev had wandered out onto the back dock with a cup of tea to watch the northern lights dance over the water.

She wished she could have joined him, but she was exhausted and she had an inkling he wanted to be alone. And she too needed to be alone to process what had happened.

So she'd gone to bed and when she woke in the morning he wasn't next to her in bed or on the couch. She panicked. She checked out the back porch to see if he'd spent the night on one of the Muskoka chairs, but he wasn't there. She headed out onto the front deck and her boat was still there.

Where had he gone?

He couldn't have walked anywhere.

He left you.

Panic started to rise up in her. Last night had felt so right. She'd let her guard down and now he was gone. Or someone had taken him.

She took a deep breath. There was a rational explanation.

The sun was shining and that cool nip in the air from the night before was gone. It was warm, unusually warm for late August.

It was almost September and fall had been in the air last night.

And then she saw the towel on the deck and his head in the water.

Swimming.

She did a double take as he swam toward her.

"You're insane," she said, when he stopped and saw her.

He looked up from where he was treading water. "Why?"

"It's cold!"

"It's not too bad. I had energy to burn and I used to spend a lot of time swimming in Chenar, so I thought why not."

Imogen shook her head. "I still think you're crazy. Where did you swim to?"

"To the shore and back," he said nonchalantly, as if it were nothing.

She raised her eyebrows. "You're joking."

"No. It's not a bad swim." He swam over to the edge

of the dock and hoisted himself out of the water. Imogen squeaked when she realized that not only was he swimming but he'd been swimming au naturel.

"What is with you and being naked?" She handed him the towel.

He chuckled, a devilish glint to his eye. "It was refreshing."

"I should say so." She chuckled.

He grinned. "It was fine. No one saw me!"

"Oh, no?" Imogen waved to her neighbor, Mrs. Smythe, an elderly woman who was staring from her deck, where she had been enjoying a cup of coffee. She was now staring at Lev, mouth agape. "Good morning, Mrs. Smythe!"

Her neighbor waved, barely, still staring at Lev.

Lev's eyes were twinkling and he was trying not to laugh. "I didn't know she was there. I swear."

"Well, she might not have been there when you started out, but she certainly got an eyeful when you came out of the water."

"I'm glad you think it's an eyeful," he teased.

She shook her head at his bad joke, trying not to laugh. "Aren't you cold?"

"I am getting a bit chilly now."

"Let's go inside and I'll make you a cup of tea while you dry off and get dressed."

"That sounds good."

They headed inside, where Lev proceeded to dry off in the living room, buck naked, and Imogen tried to focus on making him tea and not stare at him.

Get a grip.

"I'm glad you're so comfortable here that you don't mind changing in front of open windows," she remarked dryly.

Or changing in front of me.

She kept that thought to herself.

Lev laughed. "No one is out there."

"You almost gave poor old Mrs. Smythe a heart attack!"

"I told you I didn't know she was there. I had a hard time sleeping and I decided to burn off some nervous energy. Besides, I'm a doctor. I could have resuscitated her."

"What are you anxious about?"

He sighed. "Lexi and Kristof. I'm glad things are settling down, but not knowing is driving me crazy."

"You mean if you stay or go?"

"Yes," he said quietly.

She swallowed a lump that formed in her throat. She didn't want to think about all of that. Not when last night had been so wonderful. And she felt foolish for panicking that he'd left her. She hated it that he was creeping in through her walls. Hated it that she cared whether he stayed or left.

You cared when he was missing.

"How late did you stay up, watching the northern lights?" she asked, changing the subject.

"Late. I think I tried to go to sleep about two in the morning."

"Did you get any sleep?" she asked, shutting off the kettle and pouring the water into the teapot.

"Not really, but I don't feel tired. I just feel like doing something." He pulled on his jeans and then picked up a plaid shirt and buttoned it up, his long hair tied back.

"We could go to the museum today."

"Museum?" he asked. "There's a museum here?"

"Yeah. You can learn all about the Mad Trapper."

He gave her a strange look. "There was a mad trapper?"

"Well, you'd have to go to the museum to find out."

He snorted. "You don't know about this mad trapper either. You just heard the name."

She narrowed her eyes. "Fine. I don't. I've never been to the museum, but I thought it might be nice. It would be something to do and maybe we can hike up to the bush pilot monument."

"I've been there," he said. "It's a beautiful lookout."

"I haven't been there either."

He looked at her, confused. "How long have you lived up here?"

"Shut up!" She laughed and handed him his tea as he came over to the island counter. "I was working. Before I started at the hospital I did a lot of flying to remote communities. When I was home, Allen and I would travel outside Yellowknife, but only when the weather was good."

His expression tensed when she mentioned Allen.

"He was a fool."

"I wanted to stay in the north and he didn't. So he left." It was more complicated than that, but she didn't want to talk about Allen. She didn't want to think about him. "I should've seen the signs before I got involved."

"It's not your fault," he said softly.

Only it was. She'd let Allen in and it had caused nothing but pain, just like Lev would cause her pain too.

"Let's not talk about him," she said.

"Well, I guess I can go to the museum and then we can go to the bush pilot monument. It's still early. When does the museum open?"

Imogen glanced at her clock. "Not for a while."

Lev finished his tea. "Then I'm going to go for a walk."

"What? Where?" she asked, confused.

"On the island behind you." He motioned out of the window.

"What?" she asked, setting down her mug.

"The island behind you. It's not a far jump. It seems to be mostly rock and I'm going to climb to the top of it and see what's on the other side."

"You're crazy."

"Come with me if you want. Have you ever done it?"

"No." She worried her bottom lip. "Fine."

She followed Lev out onto her back dock. There was a small gap between the houseboat and the island.

Lev easily leaped across and she hesitated.

"Come on." He held out his hand. "I've got you."

She reached out, took his hand and made the quick jump onto the rocky shore. His arms came around her, steadying her. It felt good to have his arms around her.

"Was that so hard?" he asked gently.

"No, but I still think you're a bit crazy."

He chuckled softly. "We can all use a bit of crazy once in a while. Come on. Let's see what's at the top."

He held her hand as they scaled the rocky island, using trees to balance, picking their way through the brush to the top.

"I can tell you what's at the top," she said, as her calves screamed in pain from trying to balance while walking up the slanting slope. "More rock and tree and lake."

"Still, it's something different." He got onto level ground and helped her up the last little bit. His hand was strong and steady. It was reassuring. Suddenly, it didn't seem like a silly thing to do.

It felt fun.

"Come on. Haven't you ever explored this place?"

"No. I work and that's about it."

"Where's the fun in that?"

"Your attitude has certainly changed."

"Yeah, well, I have to live while I can before I can't take any more risks like this."

She felt bad for him, but she was enjoying this moment with him as they made their way to the top of Jolliffe Island. When they got there they could see the other side of Yellowknife Bay and the road to Detah.

To the south of them Yellowknife Bay opened up like a great mouth to the rest of Great Slave Lake.

"This is also a pretty nice view," he said.

"It is. I don't know what took me so long to come up here." But she did. She'd got completely wrapped up in her work so she didn't have to think about anything else. So she didn't have to deal with the pain of her father's passing or the fact that Allen had left her. Or that her mother had left her.

Yellowknife was the first place her father had put down roots. He'd still flown to remote villages, but Yellowknife was the first place she had called home.

It was her home. Her work was her life, and that was the way she liked it.

Until recently.

Lev had changed everything.

He had made her see that there was more than work. When she was around him, she wanted to do more and see more.

"I can see why you love it here."

"Of course," she said. "It's my home. My father always came back. I was born here. It's where my mother was from..." She trailed off.

She knew why her father had stayed in Yellowknife. It was where he had met her mother.

Some part of him had always hoped she'd come back.

"Anyway, Yellowknife is my home," she said gently.

"It's a beautiful home," Lev said with a hint of sadness in his voice.

She was going to say something else when her belly fluttered. It was a quick flutter that shocked her and she gasped, touching her belly, startling Lev.

"What is it?" he asked. "Are you okay? Is the baby okay?"

She laughed and smiled, tears stinging her eyes. "Yeah, I'm fine. It was the quickening. The baby, I felt the baby for the first time."

The baby zoomed across her belly again and she laughed.

For all the people who had left her, this baby would be with her always.

This baby was her family.

"I wish I could feel it," he whispered.

"I wish you could too."

She smiled up at him and touched his face, and then this time she initiated it. This was what she wanted. She was in his arms again, kissing him, and she didn't want it to end. But it had to end. This wasn't permanent and she couldn't let him any farther into her heart.

She broke off the kiss, annoyed with herself for starting something she couldn't finish.

"Why don't we get back and head to the museum?"

A strange expression crossed his face. "Of course."

Imogen turned her back and made her way slowly down, back to her boat, her home.

She was angry at herself for kissing him.

And she was mad that she hadn't wanted the kiss to end.

She would've liked it to go on a lot longer.

Maybe even forever.

But that was not in the cards and she had to remind herself of that fact.

When they got back to the houseboat her phone was ringing. She rushed to grab it off the counter and saw that it was Jeanette.

"Jeanette, what's up?"

"We need Lev. There's been a major accident on the highway and we need a trauma doctor to go out to the scene. Seemed a truck collided with a herd of buffalo and flipped over, trapping a car."

"I'll go too," Imogen said.

"Great. Thank you. Get here fast," Jeanette said.

"On our way." Imogen hung up the phone and turned

to Lev. "It looks like our trip to the museum is canceled. There's been an accident on Highway 3 and they need us to go out to the scene of the accident with the paramedics."

"Moose?" Lev asked.

"No. A transport truck driver thought he could plow through a herd of buffalo and flipped himself over, but there were other cars involved too. Lots of injuries."

Lev nodded. "Let's go."

Imogen grabbed her purse and locked up. They got into her motorboat and made their way to shore. They went to the truck in the parking lot and Lev drove them to the hospital, where they changed into their scrubs. Lev packed emergency gear with Imogen before they got into an ambulance and headed off down the highway to the airport, where they'd be transported to the scene by helicopter, with the ambulances following as quickly as they could by road.

As they sat in the back, the rocking movement of the ambulance made Imogen start to feel a bit sick, and she popped an anti-nausea pill. She wasn't the best on helicopters either and there was something of a breeze picking up.

Lev helped her out of the ambulance and into the helicopter, buckling her in. The helicopter took off and Imogen tried to focus on the sky rather than the ground as they headed south, cutting over the choppy water of Great Slave Lake toward Behchokǫ̀ Rae-Edzo.

It didn't take long before she could see smoke rising in the sky and the flashing lights from the RCMP and other emergency personnel from the surrounding villages who had come out to assist in the accident.

The surviving buffalo had been corralled and moved off so the emergency crew could go in and help those who were injured.

The helicopter landed with a small bump, and once it was safe to get out, she followed Lev through all the chaos, the noise and the smoke of the accident scene.

"Are you two the surgeons from Yellowknife?" an RCMP constable asked.

"Yes," Imogen said.

"Great. We have the driver pinned and then there's another man we managed to extract who's in bad shape. We managed to get his wife out, but he's trapped."

"I'll help with the pinned man. I've done complicated extractions before," Lev said. "You check on the man they've already pulled out of the wreckage."

Imogen nodded.

She followed another paramedic to where the man was. A fire team from Behchokǫ̀ was putting out a smoldering car, and nearby, on a tarp, covered in a blanket, was a man. Her heart sank to the soles of her feet when she saw how badly injured he was, barely conscious, under the blanket.

She knelt down beside him and took his hand, assessing his vitals. He was in bad shape; his vitals were not good. She needed Lev's help, but he was working on someone else who was pinned under the transport truck.

She motioned for a paramedic and an RCMP officer to help her move the injured man away from the rubble. She could tell from the bruising on his abdomen as she assessed him that he had a ruptured spleen and would need surgery.

"Is he okay?" a woman asked, coming forward. She was heavily pregnant and had her arm bandaged. "I'm his wife. Marge."

"What's his name, Marge?" Imogen asked.

"Henry," Marge said nervously. "His name is Henry."

"We need to get Henry to Yellowknife." Imogen needed to order a CT scan and get Henry into the operating room, but she didn't want to put any more stress onto Marge. "Get him to the hospital," she said to the paramedic, "and I will be there as soon as the other patients have been helped."

The paramedic nodded and loaded Henry into another

helicopter that had landed to transport the seriously injured to the hospital.

Lev came from behind the other side of the wreck, looking grim.

Her heart sank.

"The driver?" she asked.

"There was nothing to be done. He was gone."

"I need to get back to the hospital to work on my patient—"

There was a sharp cry and she spun round to see Marge, Henry's wife, clutch her belly.

Imogen and Lev raced to her side.

"Marge, are you okay?" Imogen asked.

"I was in labor when we left our home in Behchokǫ̀."

Imogen's eyes widened. "You're in labor?"

"With the accident..." The woman cried out again. "...it stopped."

"It's started again." Lev turned to the RCMP officer who was with him. "I need some blankets. I think we're about to deliver a baby here!"

"Have you done an emergency delivery?" Imogen asked.

"Yes. It wasn't always soldiers I attended to."

While paramedics were dealing with the other minor injuries from the multicar crash, Imogen and Lev were able to get Marge into the back of an ambulance.

Lev checked her while Imogen assisted.

"The ambulance won't make it to the hospital in time. The baby's head is crowning," he said. Imogen looked and saw there was no way they'd make it to Yellowknife.

"Marge, you need to push when I say," Imogen coached.

"What about Henry?" Marge cried.

"He's on his way to Yellowknife to get help. Dr. Vanin and I will take care of you now."

Marge nodded.

"Come on, Marge. Push!" Imogen urged, as she braced

Marge's shoulders while Lev helped guide the little life into the world.

The birth happened so fast it startled Imogen.

Lev cut the cord and took the baby to the other side of the ambulance, where there was another gurney and oxygen.

Her heart sank.

"My baby?" Marge asked.

"Your baby has been born. Dr. Vanin is assessing—"

"It's a boy," Lev said.

"Your son is being assessed." Imogen helped Marge deliver the placenta and cleaned her up, but she was bleeding heavily and they needed to get her help too. Imogen watched Lev cradle the little, silent new life.

The baby was so small and fragile in Lev's big strong hands. He was so gentle, the way he cradled the infant, studiously keeping the baby warm and holding the large oxygen mask over the baby's face.

"Come on," he whispered. Then he said something in Chenarian.

It sounded like a prayer and Imogen's heart sank, but then a thin little wail sounded in the back of the ambulance and Imogen smiled, relieved, a tear slipping from her eye.

Lev beamed. "He'll be fine. Your son is fine, Marge."

Marge cried and Imogen helped Lev bring the baby and oxygen over to Marge.

"He needs some oxygen support," Lev said, carefully placing the wrapped bundle back in her arms. "We need to get you two to the hospital."

"There's a helicopter ready now, Dr. Vanin," the paramedic said.

Lev nodded and turned to her. "You go with Marge. Keep the oxygen over the baby's face. Keep him warm."

"Why don't you go?" Imogen asked. "You delivered him."

"You need to get back to operate on her husband. Go."

Imogen nodded. The paramedics wrapped and stabilized Marge, who was bleeding more heavily than Imogen would've liked, while she held on to the precious bundle. They were loaded into the helicopter.

"I'll be back soon," Lev said, and then he kissed her forehead before the door to the helicopter shut.

Imogen sat back as the helicopter rose and Lev grew smaller and smaller.

She didn't want to leave him behind.

She didn't want him to go, and it had nothing to do with leaving him behind at the crash site and everything to do with the fact that she wanted him to stay in Yellowknife, for her, as well as for their child. But she knew he wouldn't.

He couldn't.

CHAPTER TWELVE

Lev finally arrived back at the hospital. The baby was in the pediatric critical care unit, but he was assured the boy was doing well. Then he went to check on Marge, who was stable and resting. It was then he learned that Imogen was still in the operating room with Henry, Marge's husband.

He went to the viewing gallery, where some residents were observing the surgery.

He kept to the back to watch Imogen work. He'd done emergency splenectomies in the field, but he was glad for the patient that a hospital had been a short trip by helicopter away and that Imogen was the surgeon working on him.

A smile crept over his face as he watched her. She'd remained so calm under pressure in the field and she'd been a true help when delivering that baby, especially when he hadn't been sure the baby would live.

He'd attended a birth like that in a war zone. Only they hadn't had oxygen and a hospital had been hours away. Both mother and baby had died. It had torn him apart back then. This time the story had ended better, but it made him worried about what would happen to Imogen if he wasn't there when her time came.

She had to return with him to Chenar. He couldn't leave her behind. He had to be there for their child's birth.

He wasn't going to miss that.

And what if she won't come?

He didn't know what he would do if she didn't come with him. He wanted to do everything in his power to make sure she came, but he also knew how strongly she felt about staying in Yellowknife, working in this community. No matter what he did, someone would get hurt.

Maybe this trip to Fort Smith would decide it. It would be just the two of them together and he could woo her and convince her to go back with him.

You could always stay.

It would be a dream to be free to make that choice, but he had a duty.

Imogen had to go with him.

The surgery finished and he left the gallery to meet her on the OR level, outside the scrub room.

She looked exhausted, but she smiled when she saw him. "You're back!"

"I am. I checked on the baby and Marge. Both are well. How is Henry?"

Imogen sighed. "He lost a lot of blood. The spleen was a mess. I couldn't resect it, it had to come out, but I'm hopeful he'll pull through. He's on his way to the intensive care unit now. He's stable, but, still, you never know."

"You look tired."

"I am," she said wearily. "I am really tired, as a matter of fact. This is not much of a day off."

"No. Not really."

"I still have to pack for Fort Smith."

"I'm looking forward to that. I hope I can be of some help."

"Of course you can. I really appreciate you coming."

They walked side by side down to the cafeteria. He wanted a coffee and she wanted a tea.

Imogen had been in the operating room for hours and

Lev had stayed behind to make sure all those who were injured were taken care of.

They got their drinks and sat down at a table.

"So, did you find out how the accident happened? I mean, I know there were buffalo involved."

Lev took a sip of some old, bitter black coffee. "The transport truck collided with a herd. One of the bison was thrown up and over the truck as it hit one of those dips you warned me about. As the truck was thrown, the bison bounced onto Henry and Marge's truck. Then it was a chain reaction of a couple of vehicles behind them."

Imogen winced. "It's unfortunate that the driver of the transport truck was killed."

"Yes, but lucky that no one else died. You seemed surprised when Marge mentioned they'd left Behchokǫ. Is that far?"

"Yes, about two hours, but there are currently no nurse practitioners, no doctors or midwives in their village. They had no choice but to come to Yellowknife. No one wants to stay in the north."

"Except you?" He felt bad all over again about trying to snatch her away. If he could stay, he would, in a heartbeat, but his life was not his own. It belonged to Chenar. And now he'd forced that same duty onto Imogen and their unborn child.

"Why don't we go back to our place and get ready for our flight tomorrow?" she suggested.

"Good idea."

They finished their drinks and made their way to the doctors' lounge to change out of their scrubs and collect their belongings before they headed back to their home.

Or rather, her home.

Not their home.

It could never be that. Even if he wanted it to be.

***

The first stop the next morning before their trip south was to the hospital, where Imogen picked up the supplies she was taking down to Fort Smith.

Lev helped her pack up.

"This is a lot of mini first-aid kits," he remarked. "What are these for?"

"I like to take them down to Fort Smith and hand them out at the community center. They're for emergency situations, or for people's cars. There's a lot of national park and no decent cell service in a vast area. I want them to be prepared. Plus, there are always the natural disasters, rock slides, forest fires...tornadoes."

"Tornadoes in Fort Smith?" he asked, confused.

"They had one recently. It's rare, but it happens." Imogen zipped up her duffel bag. "It's part of the outreach program I do. I'll hit some other communities too. Fort Smith has a great hospital... They just have a shortage of surgeons. I promised to cover today and I thought it was a good time to distribute the kits."

"It's a good cause." Lev did up his duffel bag. "You ready to go?"

"Yes. I think so. I don't think I'm forgetting anything."

"Did you check on Henry?" Lev asked.

"Yes. I did. He's still in the intensive care unit and the surgeon on call will keep me informed. I've left instructions."

"Good." Lev smiled and slung the duffel bag over his shoulder. "Should we make our way to the airport?"

"Yes. There's a cab waiting and a chartered plane. It should be a short trip. We'll be back late tomorrow night. We'll stay overnight in Fort Smith and I'll do the couple of surgeries I have booked tomorrow morning. Today we'll see patients."

"Okay" was all Lev said.

He was acting odd. He seemed to be on edge.

He's probably worried about not hearing anything from Lexi or his brother.

Still, something was eating away at him. She wasn't convinced it was that.

You don't have time to think about it now.

There was a lot of work to do and she had to get her head in the game. The cab took them to the airport and the private jet was waiting for them. Once the plane was taking off, Lev seemed to visibly relax.

"Are you okay?" she asked.

"Why wouldn't I be okay?"

"You just seemed tense."

"I am a bit nervous about this trip. Nervous about my newfound freedom, I suppose."

"You are?" She had a hard time believing that. It didn't seem like him, or the man she thought she knew.

The man she was falling for.

Don't think about him like that.

But it was hard not to. Before the accident, she'd enjoyed that moment on Jolliffe Island, when he'd put his arms around her and they'd kissed. And the prenatal appointment, and the kiss under the northern lights. It had all seemed so perfect. Then the baby had moved for the first time and everything had just seemed so right.

If anyone had been looking at them, they would have sworn they were a real couple, totally in love.

And that sobered her. It reminded her that their marriage wasn't real. They weren't really in love, no matter how she felt when she was around him.

She couldn't fall in love with him. Except she already was.

When that helicopter had taken off and she'd left him behind, she'd cried. It was silly, but she had. She didn't want him to leave because she couldn't go.

Why can't you?

She shook that thought away. She hated it that he was getting past her walls. She was terrified of the hurt it would bring. And she was scared of delivering her child alone. Seeing Lev hold Marge's baby so tenderly had made her wish for a future she simply couldn't have.

It made her sad.

And her sadness scared her. She was losing control. Unless she could convince him to stay. Although he was the heir to the throne now, he wouldn't be King. His brother would have children, and they would have children, and Lev could be free. Why couldn't he stay in Canada?

The flight was a quick up-and-down flight.

In Fort Smith they were picked up by another taxi and taken to a small hospital that was in the center of town.

Lev frowned when he saw it. "I thought you said this was a hospital."

"It is...sort of. They have the facility. It's just they don't have the surgeons. They have a nurse practitioner and a doctor, so my postoperative patients will be in good hands."

Lev didn't seem convinced, but didn't say too much else. She was worried he'd realize he hated the north, just like Allen, and leave.

Like her mother.

They were taken to a modular home that was owned by the hospital to put up surgeons and specialists who flew in, and they dropped their bags.

It was a cramped space and the couch was in no way big enough for either her or Lev to sleep on. There was one bedroom and one double bed.

"It looks like we're sharing tonight," he stated, and cleared his throat uncomfortably. "Are you okay with that?"

"Of course. I guess they didn't think too much about it when I told them my husband was coming."

"I remember the first time we shared a bed," he teased, taking a step closer to her, smiling deviously.

"I haven't forgotten," she said, her voice cracking, her body coming to life just at the thought of him. Of that kiss they'd shared on Jolliffe, of the night they'd shared together in Toronto.

The night they'd conceived their baby and the evening out under the aurora.

And now, here in Fort Smith, they were alone. They were away from everyone who knew them. It was just the two of them in a very confined space.

"Well," Imogen said, clearing her throat. "We'd better get these supplies over to the hospital. It's a short walk and my first appointment is in about an hour. I'm hoping you can check on the preoperative patients for me?"

Lev cleared his throat and took a step back. "Of course. Let's do that."

"Good."

Imogen took a couple of calming breaths as she collected up the medical equipment she'd brought. She needed to calm down and not think about Lev in that way, although it was getting increasingly harder to do that.

Lev was distracted.

Before, he had been worrying that he'd be caught, that Imogen would find out he was disobeying orders by accompanying her to Fort Smith to protect her, but now he was distracted by her.

When he saw that they would have no choice but to share a bed in that small little cottage, he couldn't help but think back on the kisses they'd shared, and then his mind had gone to that night in the penthouse suite in Toronto.

To the way she'd felt in his arms.

The way she'd felt when he'd been buried deep inside

her. How sweet her kisses were. How he wanted no one else and had never wanted anyone like he wanted her.

And all he wanted to do was whisk her away and show her how much he desired her. How he'd never stopped thinking about her. But he didn't want to scare her off and he knew that she didn't want to leave Yellowknife.

He couldn't do that to her. He couldn't drag her away from her home.

Who said you had to?

He wouldn't force her, but he'd put up a fight to make her want to come. It was all he could think about. This was tearing him in two.

And he was terrified she didn't feel the same things he was feeling. That she'd hurt him and he would have to leave her behind. He wasn't Canadian and Kristof would force him to return to Chenar. Force him to give up medicine and push him into a life of politics and court.

It would be better for his child to be raised here because Chenar would take years to rebuild. Canada was stable.

Lev knew he should keep his distance, that their marriage was just so he could protect them, but, try as he might, he just couldn't stay away from her. He loved being with her and he was glad he was here now, helping her in this small community to provide much-needed surgical care.

He was helping to save lives and that was what he'd always wanted. Politics had never been his thing. It had been his brother's thing, but then, Kristof had been trained for that life.

Medicine was his passion.

All he knew was medicine.

All he wanted to know was medicine.

And Imogen.

He cleared his throat and went back to his filing, but he couldn't help but watch and admire her from afar as she moved from exam room to exam room.

As if she knew he was looking at her, she glanced over and smiled. Her smile was infectious and he smiled back.

What is this spell she's put on me?

He didn't know, but he was losing the battle. He was falling in love with her.

"You ready to go back and get some dinner?" she asked.

"Are you done?"

"I am." She folded her hands on the counter of the nurses' station. "I think everything should go smoothly tomorrow."

"With you at the helm, I'm sure it will." And he meant it.

"Thanks. Are you hungry?"

"I am."

"Good. We can get changed and then head out for something to eat."

"How about I go and get some groceries and cook you something?"

She cocked an eyebrow. "I'm intrigued. You did tell me you and Lexi cooked, but I haven't tasted one of your creations yet."

"*Yet* being the operative word," he said. "Tonight you will."

"Okay. Well, there is a fully equipped kitchen and the grocery store isn't far from our lodging. But remember I am pregnant, so no raw fish or things like shark or swordfish."

He gave her a weird look. "Where am I going to get shark in Fort Smith?"

"Good point."

"I will be mindful, Imogen. I promise." He placed a hand on his chest and bowed at the waist ever so slightly.

She laughed. "Okay, well, let's get going."

Once they had changed, he left her sitting out on the small deck under the awning with a warm cup of tea as he strolled down the street to the co-op store.

The leaves had turned here already. There were bright

yellows, reds and oranges mixed in with the green from the cedar and pine.

It was a sleepy community, but there were a few people who stopped and stared at him for a few moments because he was new to town—at least he hoped that was why they were studying him.

Not that it much mattered now. The news was reporting that Kristof had returned to Chenar. The coup had been put down, but Lev had heard no details. Which didn't surprise him. He was an afterthought to his brother.

Still, it would've been nice to have been told.

Of course, peace meant his time here was almost over, and the thought of leaving Imogen made him feel ill.

Don't think about it.

The problem was he couldn't stop thinking about it. It was at the forefront of his mind. Always.

He gathered up ingredients to make a beef Stroganoff with egg noodles. Something his governess used to make. It was comfort food for him and he could use some of that starchy comfort just about now.

He bought a few other things for the night, some snacks, just in case Imogen got hungry, and then carried the bags back to where they were staying.

Imogen was sitting outside still, sipping her tea and reading over files in preparation for tomorrow's surgery. She looked up when he came up the gravel drive.

"How did it go?" she asked.

"The cost of food up here is ridiculous," he groused. "But I had fairly good luck. I'll see what I can make of it."

"I really can't wait to find out what you're making."

"Well, you'll just have to wait." He tried to open the door, but couldn't. "Could you help?"

"Sorry!" She got up and held open the door for him. He slipped inside and set the groceries down, and she followed him in after she'd retrieved her tea and files.

"You'll ruin the surprise if you watch me," he stated.

She shrugged. "Oh, well, I want to know."

"You're so impatient," he teased.

"I know." She rummaged through the bags. "Oh, sour cream. Interesting."

"That was expensive," he muttered.

"Yeah, it can be pricey. Seriously, what are you making?"

"You're kind of a pain."

She frowned. "You're mean."

He chuckled. "Fine. I'm making beef Stroganoff. It's cool out there, the leaves are changing, and it's a comfort food. My nanny used to make this a lot for us, especially when we had a bad day at school or something."

"I guess your mother really didn't have to cook. You guys had servants."

He nodded. "Well, my mother was raised to be Queen and she died when I was young. My nanny was very caring and doting. When I make her recipe it reminds me of her."

"I'm sorry. I forgot. You did tell me you lost your mother young."

"It's okay."

She sighed. "Well, at least you had a nanny who loved you. I had no one, save my father. I never knew my mother."

"You don't talk much about her," he said, as he started to prepare the food. "What happened to her? I'm sorry if it's insensitive, but did she pass on when you were young?"

"No. She left us."

"She left?"

Imogen nodded. "She didn't want to be a mother or a wife. She didn't want to move around so much with my father and his research. She wanted a completely different life, so she left and my father raised me."

"I'm sorry. I thought she was from Yellowknife?"

"She was."

"Did she have parents who lived in Yellowknife?"

"They died before I was born. Truth be told, Dad said she hated Yellowknife. Dad and I traveled, but we always came back to Yellowknife. I think he lived in hope she'd come back."

And then he finally understood why she didn't want to leave, but he kept that thought to himself.

"Well, I'm sorry all the same."

"Thanks, but I can't mourn a person I never knew."

"True, but you can mourn that you never knew her."

She smiled at him, her expression soft. "I suppose so. Either way, I want you to know that I'm here for this baby and I don't plan on leaving him or her. I may not know what it's like to have a mother who stayed, but I had a loving father who taught me so much about being a good parent."

"Then you're one up on me. My father wasn't very loving," he said, as he dumped the chopped meat into the skillet and then washed his hands. "I didn't know my father at all."

Yet he still mourned him. It hurt that his father was gone and he wouldn't get the opportunity to know him. Their chance was gone. There was no turning back, and though he grieved the loss of what could have been, he didn't have time to process it. Over the years Lev had tried to reach out to his father and had been met every time with a cold reception.

Maybe Imogen was right. You couldn't mourn someone you never knew.

"We should think of something happier, like this delicious meal that I'm preparing for you." He grinned and she laughed at him.

"Deal. I look forward to trying it."

"That's a lot of pressure to put on me," he teased.

"I'm sorry, but it does smell good and you seem to know the recipe by heart, so that's encouraging!"

He grinned. "Well, I hope I please you."

"You do." And then he saw a blush creep up her cheeks, as if she was embarrassed he'd caught her admitting something that she might not want him to know, and it thrilled him.

Lev tried to stifle a yawn as he scrubbed out after a simple cholecystectomy, one of the two general surgeries Imogen had performed today. He hadn't got much sleep last night and it was all his fault. He'd opted to sleep on a very hard floor rather than risk temptation and sleep next to Imogen.

Dinner had gone well and thankfully Imogen didn't think his cooking skills were a waste. She had cleaned up—since he had cooked, she'd said—and then they'd both gone outside to enjoy an autumn evening before their early morning start.

The problem was that in that small double, Imogen had kept rolling over to curl up against him. He would try to move and invariably brush something or touch something he shouldn't.

It had been hard to sleep with her curled up beside him. So instead of trying to make the most of a tight situation, he'd slept on the floor, and now he had a crick in his neck and was exhausted. If he was going to be exhausted, he should have just opted to stay in the bed with her. At least then he wouldn't have had a crick in his neck all day.

"You okay?" Imogen asked, as she came into the scrub room.

"Tired."

"I woke up in the middle of the night and saw you on the floor."

"You were taking up most of the bed," he groused.

"I'm sorry."

He shrugged. "It's okay."

"Well, at least we'll be back in Yellowknife tonight and you can get a good night's sleep."

They finished cleaning up and headed out, but when they got their gear to head to the landing strip, they were told by the director of the hospital that all flights were grounded. There was a massive thunderstorm in Yellowknife and there wouldn't be any flights tonight. That meant they were stuck and both of them were too tired for a hike to the rapids.

So they went back to the modular home. Lev hoped he wouldn't have to spend another restless night on the floor.

The weather in Yellowknife might have been grim, but in Fort Smith it was beautiful. They sat outside, watching the sun go down and waiting for the stars to come out.

"It gets so dark here," he said. "And it's so quiet. Quieter than the city."

"That's because Fort Smith is in Wood Buffalo National Park and it's a dark night preserve."

"It's nice just sitting out here with you." He looked over at her. "I hope we see the northern lights again."

"Me too. It's a bit early for that."

"Well, it's worth the wait."

"It's a spectacular show."

"My favorite part about that night was being with you." He saw her blush.

"Lev, that... I liked being with you too."

"Do you?" he asked.

"I do. I often think of that night in Toronto." She tucked a loose strand of hair behind her ear. "You made me feel alive that night, Lev. I've never forgotten it."

Her words stirred his blood. Ignited him. It thrilled him to know that she thought of him the same way he thought of her. That she desired him the same way he desired her. The way he wanted her and no one else.

He got up from where he was sitting and knelt in front of her. "I've been thinking about something."

"What's that?" she asked, her voice quiet.

"I've been thinking about that kiss the other day. I've

been thinking about how this fake marriage of ours is actually very real to me. You make me feel alive, Imogen, and I haven't felt alive in quite some time."

His words stirred something deep inside her. "I feel the same way about you too, Lev." She ran her hand down his face. "I've never wanted someone more than I wanted you. More than I want you." And then she kissed him and she forgot all the reasons why she shouldn't, because she too had been thinking constantly about their kisses, about Toronto, about him.

She couldn't get it out of her mind.

Lev touched her cheek, brushing his knuckles down her skin, making her tremble with desire. She remembered the way he made her feel before and she wanted to feel that again, even if only for a moment.

If he were to go, she wanted one more night with him. One more chance to savor a moment with him and never forget.

"When you touch me, Lev… I forget everything. All I want is you," she whispered.

"I care about you, Imogen. I've never stopped thinking about you."

"I never stopped thinking about you either." A tear slid down her cheek. She was falling in love with him, only she wouldn't say it out loud. She couldn't. She was scared of what it all meant. Of how much it would hurt.

"I know we can't make any kind of commitment, but I want you, Lev. I know it's a bad idea, but I want you."

Imogen wanted just one more night with him. Just one night so she could get on with her life and know there would be nothing to hold her back. And she wanted more memories of this fantasy, memories of her Prince to sustain her. "Please."

Lev didn't say anything. He just pulled her into his arms and kissed her with such intensity she melted. His touch felt so good. Being in Lev's arms was so wonderful it was just what she needed. Lev made her feel safe and secure. He made her body tremble with desire and her blood sing.

When she was with Lev she forgot everything else. All she thought of was hot, sweet passion that made her blood fire and her toes curl.

She pressed her body against him.

"Imogen, how I've missed you. I've thought of you constantly since that night I had to leave you."

"I've missed you too."

Lev scooped her up in his arms and carried her to the bed they had shared the night before, when it had been awkward and he'd ended up on the floor. They'd both been so restrained since their wedding, but now there was no holding back.

Her body was humming with anticipation. They sank onto the mattress together, kissing. Lev's hands were in her hair, down her back, skimming up her thighs and between her legs, making her mew with pleasure.

There was no more talk. The only sounds were their hearts thundering in their ears, their breath catching, as they slowly undressed each other.

She ran her fingers over the tattoo on his thigh. It was a tree branch, the ink black and the design intricate. She traced the design with her fingertips, causing him to moan.

"You drive me wild," he murmured against her neck.

She smiled, but didn't say anything. Her body was shaking with need and she brought him close. He kissed her all over. Down her neck, over her breasts, making her body arch.

She wrapped her legs around him, urging him to take her, to possess her, to be with her.

Lev slowly entered her. She bit her lip as pleasure coursed through her. Never had anyone made her feel this way. She only wanted Lev.

Even though it scared her, she didn't want anyone else. Ever.

Just him.

She didn't want this night to end. She just wanted this moment to go on and on, the two of them moving together in bliss. It wasn't long before both of them came together in shared pleasure.

When it was over, he held her close, tight against his chest, as if he was afraid to let her go, and in return she clung to him.

He couldn't stay and she couldn't go, so they just lay there and held each other in the darkness.

CHAPTER THIRTEEN

IMOGEN WOKE UP to an empty bed. Lev was nowhere to be found.

She frowned. Her stomach churned. They had spent a blissful night together, and when she'd first woken up everything had seemed so rosy, so perfect.

So wonderful.

She got dressed and headed out into the kitchen, sighing in relief when she saw Lev was outside. She walked outside to join him.

"Good morning," she said, trying to stifle a yawn and hoping she didn't sound stressed, like she had been a moment before.

He smiled at her. "Good morning. Our taxi will be here soon."

"What time is it?" she asked, confused.

"Nine. Our flight leaves in an hour."

"Why didn't you wake me sooner?"

"I wanted to let you sleep." He wrapped his arms around her and kissed her. She laid her head against his chest, listening to his heart beating. It was comforting.

"I'd better get ready," she mumbled.

"Yes."

Imogen kissed him again and headed back inside. Her

heart was still hammering. She'd thought he'd left. Her paranoia was killing her.

He was still here.

But for how long?

It frightened her.

And she hated that.

It didn't take her long to pack, so she was ready when the cab came, and they boarded their flight back to Yellowknife. She planned to go straight to the hospital and check on Henry. She hadn't expected to be away this long and she hoped he was okay and out of the intensive care unit.

"What are you thinking about?" Lev asked.

"Lots of things." She didn't want to tell him she'd been afraid he'd left, afraid he didn't like Fort Smith, afraid he hated the north. He'd seemed so unimpressed, like Allen.

History seemed to be trying to repeat itself.

"What did you think of Fort Smith?"

He looked confused. "It was fine. Small, expensive groceries, but fine."

"No, seriously. You seemed underwhelmed when we landed."

"Not underwhelmed," he said. "More like sad that such a large town is so cut off and so lacking in care."

"Oh." She was surprised.

"It made me think of Marge and Henry having to drive more than two hours for medical care."

"Yeah. It's a serious issue. No one wants to stay."

A strange look passed over his face and instantly she regretted saying it.

It was a short flight, and as they were landing, Imogen saw government vehicles waiting on the tarmac.

"What's going on?" she asked. Then her heart sank. They were here for Lev.

The plane landed, and as soon as the door opened, Lexi walked into the cabin.

"Lexi," Lev shouted happily.

"Your Highness, it's over. We can go home!"

Lev grinned and started speaking Chenarian. Then he clapped Lexi on the back as Lexi left the plane.

"Isn't that wonderful?" Lev asked.

"It is. It really is." Her heart was breaking.

"It means we can go back to Chenar."

"Who's *we*?"

"You and me and Lexi, I suppose. Kristof has ordered me to return."

Imogen sighed. "I'm not going!"

"What?" Lev asked.

"I'm not going. I told you. Yellowknife is my home."

They didn't say much else. The car ride back to the hospital was tense. They were escorted into a private meeting room to discuss plans and details for Lev's return to Chenar. The staff now knew who Lev really was. There was no more need for secrets. He was safe.

Finally it was just the two of them again in a room and the tension between them was palpable.

"What happens now?" she asked, her voice trembling.

"You know what happens. We leave," he replied sternly.

"No, *we* don't."

His gaze locked on hers, his eyes sparkling. "I have no choice. It's my duty and I have to obey my King."

"But I do. I have a choice. You know that. You said this was to protect the baby and me, and now the threat is over."

"You married me!"

"For protection. This is my home."

"If our marriage was so fake, why did you spend the night with me? To manipulate me like other women have tried to?" It was like a slap to the face.

"I beg your pardon?"

"You heard me," he said. "You're selfish and you're afraid."

"How am I selfish? How am I afraid?" she demanded.

"Your past relationships failed because you refused to bend. You refused to leave Yellowknife! You refused because you're afraid to lose anything, to take a risk because of what happened to your father. You stay here thinking your mother will come back, but she won't, yet you refuse to go because here you have control. You're afraid, Imogen, and you're selfish."

His words stung and she didn't want to admit that there was an ounce of truth to them. She was too hurt for that.

"You're the selfish one. You lied to me. You promised me you wouldn't force me to go. Did you sleep with me in the hope I would blindly follow you? I'm not one of your subjects! You used me. Trying to seduce me to convince me to go when you knew it was the last thing I wanted. And for what? You don't love me. How can you? If you loved me, you'd know I can't go. You're not King. Why do you have to go?"

"I didn't ask to be born into this life. I didn't want this, but it's my duty. You know that."

"But it's not *my* duty."

"I'm not free. I have to obey Kristof." Lev's eyes narrowed. "You are my wife and you are part of the royal family now, and I order you to come with me."

"You *order* me? Don't be ridiculous. I'm only your wife on paper. That's it," she snapped.

"You carry my child!"

"You don't believe that."

"What are you talking about?" he asked coldly.

"You don't trust me. Not really. You think we're all like Tatiana, but we aren't. I didn't sleep with anyone else, but still you demanded a paternity test, so why do you care about me or the baby?"

"I care."

Imogen's eyes filled with tears. "If you cared for us, you wouldn't be giving me this ultimatum."

"It's no ultimatum, Imogen. It's the truth."

A tear slipped out of the corner of her eye and she hated herself for falling in love with him. She hated it that she was afraid to leave with him. So many people had left her, had hurt her.

Even her father had left her.

She was angry at herself, but how could she be with someone who didn't trust her, someone who didn't listen to her, who ordered her to follow him? Someone who called her selfish. Someone who didn't love her.

"Goodbye, Lev."

She turned to leave, and though she could hear him calling her name, she wouldn't look back. She couldn't. She was too hurt.

She felt betrayed. He'd lied to her and she didn't know how to come back from that, or if she even could.

Why not?

She shook that thought away and closed the door, knowing that she would never see her baby's father again.

And she hated herself for being too scared to follow him.

Lev stood outside Henry's hospital room door. Henry was awake and Marge was showing him their baby. Lev smiled at them. Then felt a pang of longing. He didn't want to leave, but he had no choice.

He'd let his father down enough. He had to be what Kristof needed.

He had hurt Imogen and he was hurt himself that she didn't love him enough to go with him.

You knew she wouldn't.

He sighed and walked away. He'd been too hard on her. If he wasn't duty-bound, he'd stay here with her. He could be so happy here. Being with her here felt like home. It felt right, but there was nothing he could do. Lexi found him wandering the hall.

"We're trying to get Kristof on the phone again," Lexi said. "He's heard about your wife."

"She's not coming to Chenar."

Lexi sighed. "So I heard."

"I have no choice but to leave."

"You do have a choice," Lexi stated.

"No, I don't. You know Kristof. I'm honor-bound to him. I was a disappointment to my father and selfish practicing medicine. Now Kristof is alone and has to rebuild by himself. I have to go."

"No, you don't. Talk to Kristof."

"He won't understand. He's just like my father."

"In some ways, but not all ways." Lexi rolled his eyes. "You're a fool, Your Highness, if you let her go. Don't be so afraid. Don't use your duty as an excuse not to make difficult choices. There's nothing standing between you and the life you want."

"I thought you didn't like Imogen."

"I never said that. I was worried about you both. She was just one more person to worry about, including the baby."

"What if she actually doesn't want me?" Lev asked. "Most women just want my title. If I stay here, I give that up."

"She doesn't want that and you know it." Lexi sighed. "You can be so distrusting, but it's time to let go of the past."

Lev scrubbed a hand over his face. "I've ruined everything. I don't want to leave Yellowknife. I like it here, but I am a prince…"

"You have a choice. You can stay, but are you willing to make a life here? Is Imogen willing to make a life with you?"

"I doubt it. I hurt her."

"You can make it up to her."

"How?" Lev asked.

"You can grovel." Lexi smiled. "Talk to Kristof. He will understand. The situation in Chenar has stabilized and everyone is focused on rebuilding. I will go back to help."

"And if I have to return, she won't follow. She had relationships that ended because she wouldn't leave Yellowknife. She lives on that houseboat that belonged to her late father and she won't leave."

"Perhaps she's still grieving. Perhaps she's afraid. Just like you."

The words sank in. He was afraid. Afraid he wasn't good enough. Afraid he wouldn't be a good father. He used Tatiana as an excuse to keep women away, to keep Imogen away. He was not his father and neither was Kristof. He had a chance for happiness here, if he'd only take it. Lev knew what he had to do. He had to find Imogen and tell her. He had to make it right. He loved her and he'd hurt her deeply. Of course she was grieving. Everyone she'd loved had left. And he'd broken her trust trying to convince her—and then order her—to come with him, two things he'd promised he wouldn't do when she'd agreed to marry him.

"I have to find Imogen."

Lexi nodded. "Good. Go and make it right."

He was going to make sure she didn't feel afraid. He wanted her to know that he was just as afraid as she was. He was uncertain of the future and what it held. He didn't know what was going to happen with his country.

The only thing he knew for certain was that he loved her and he couldn't let her go. He couldn't leave her behind and he wasn't going to force her to come with him either. As much as he loved being a surgeon, as much as he loved saving lives, he would give it all up to be with her.

Lev ran down the hall, searching for her, but she was

nowhere to be found, and then he caught a glimpse of her with her coat on and she was leaving.

"Imogen!" he called out.

She turned around and frowned when she saw him, then turned back to continue walking away.

He ran after her and grabbed her by the arm.

"Let me go," she whispered under her breath.

"No. I won't let you go."

She stepped back, stunned. "What are you talking about?"

"I won't let you go. I'm not leaving."

Her expression fell. "You have to leave. You said so yourself. You're duty-bound."

"No. I'm not. And I'm not leaving you or Yellowknife. If this is where you need to stay, if this is where you need to raise our child, then I'm staying."

"Lev, a prince can't stay in Canada."

"This one can. Kristof will understand. I'm staying here with you. This is my home now."

"Everyone at the hospital knows who you are."

"Then I won't work here." He shrugged. "All that matters is that we're together."

"You love being a surgeon… You can't give that up!"

"I can, to be with you. To stay with you. I love you, Imogen. I lost you once before and I won't lose you again. I can't live without you."

Imogen couldn't quite hear the words that were coming out of his mouth. She couldn't quite believe it.

It was what she had been wanting to hear for so long, she just didn't believe that it could be happening.

"I love you too, but…"

"I know you're still struggling with your father's death and your mother's abandonment. I know that's why you don't want to leave, but you've lived in other places before."

Her lip trembled. "This is where I was born and this is where my father was going to stay in case she came back. That's why I was staying here."

Lev pulled her in close and he held her. She wrapped her arms around him.

"Then this is where I'll stay. I need to stay with you. I can't lose you or the baby."

Imogen wiped away a tear. "What about the paternity test?"

"I know it's mine, Imogen. You've never lied to me. Never. The best I can do is ask for your forgiveness and hope that you will forgive me. I love you. I'm sorry I tried to force you to make a decision I promised you would never have to make."

"Oh, Lev." She kissed him and then leaned her forehead against his. "I love you too and I'm sorry. I will go anywhere with you. You're right. I was holding on to something that is never going to happen. I thought that by planting myself here, my mother would come and find me, but she won't. I don't even know if she's dead or alive, and I have been mourning what I don't know and what I'm never going to know my whole life. I do know one thing. If I let you leave without me, I'm throwing away something I've always wanted—a family. I'm throwing away a chance for our child."

"I love you, Imogen."

They kissed again and then they walked hand in hand back to where they knew the government officials were waiting to take him away.

He was going to tell them that he was staying. He'd talk to his brother and explain. This was his family. He would always be there for Chenar and, if it came to it, he now knew that Imogen would be there with him.

They were each other's family.

That was all that mattered.

When they walked into the boardroom she could sense a change in the air. There was a buzz and Lev felt it too.

"Your Highness," Lexi said as he bowed.

"I've come to tell you that I'm not leaving my wife. And I'm not leaving Yellowknife. I'm staying here."

Lexi smiled. "That is fine. King Kristof wants you to stay and be an ambassador for Chenar in Canada."

"An ambassador?" Imogen asked.

Lexi nodded. "You'll have to spend some time in Ottawa, though, at least half the year."

"Can you live with that, Imogen? Can you do that for me?" Lev asked.

"Of course," Imogen said.

Lev's eyes filled with tears and he held her close.

"It seems, Your Highness, that you don't require so much protection anymore. The civil unrest is over and your brother is King. You will be safe here in Canada."

Imogen hugged Lev and he pulled her in close.

"What does this mean now?" she asked. "Do we need to go to Ottawa now?"

"No. Prince Viktor still has to remain here and we're trying to patch through another call so he can talk to his brother. From there, we'll work with the consulate and the government to figure out the next steps. For now, you're both staying in Yellowknife."

Lev smiled. "Thank you, Lexi. I appreciate all your help. I will miss you."

"You might as well both go home and we can patch a call through onto your cell phone," Lexi said.

Lexi turned back to the others in the room as they went to work, making arrangements and figuring out the next steps.

"What would you like to do now?" Imogen asked.

"I would like to go home."

"Home to Chenar or the houseboat?" she teased.

"The houseboat. Wherever you are is my home, Imogen. One day, when my brother needs me, I will go back, but for now, there's a lot to figure out and I have to take care of you and our child." He reached down and touched her belly. Although he couldn't feel it yet, there was a nudge, and she placed her hand over his.

"Let's go home."

EPILOGUE

A year later

THE PLANE TOUCHED down and Lev's heart was soaring as he glanced out of the window and saw the familiar sights of Chenar.

A place that, at one time, he'd never thought he would see again.

His home.

Or at least the country of his birth. His home was now in Canada with Imogen and their daughter, Aurora, but he was still glad to be back for his brother's coronation, his wife and daughter by his side.

As the plane taxied toward the private hangar, he could see the royal motorcade waiting. He spotted Lexi right away, standing at the end of the red carpet.

Imogen was holding Aurora, who, at seven months old, wouldn't remember any of this, but at least she had the freedom now to come to Chenar with him. To understand her roots.

"Lexi is out there," Lev said happily.

Imogen smiled. "I'm glad he's here. I know your brother is working hard to rebuild, but I'm still worried."

"No more worries. Lexi will take good care of us, just

like he took care of us in Yellowknife. At least this time we won't be out on the water. We'll be in the palace."

"Aw, I kind of miss him driving by in his motorboat or hanging out in his apartment with his binoculars, watching."

Lev chuckled. "Don't tell him that or he'll come back to Yellowknife."

"Maybe he should. Maybe he wants to."

"I'll leave that up to Lexi. This time he can live on the houseboat instead of us renting it out to tourists."

"What? You don't want him living in our house near Jackfish Lake? There's lots of room to build him his own place."

"No! Don't get any ideas, Imogen. I lived with that man for too long and had him control my life. He's not moving into the guesthouse."

She laughed, but he could tell she was nervous about meeting Kristof and being formally introduced to the country as Prince Viktor's wife. She had a hard time thinking of him as anything other than Lev.

Lev didn't want her to think of him as anyone else. With her, he could be himself, whatever name she called him by.

In Yellowknife, he was still a trauma surgeon and she was still a general surgeon, or she would be when she returned from maternity leave.

He liked his life in his new home, but he was also glad to return to Chenar and hold his head up high. And most of all he was glad that his brother was restoring their country. The only downside to the formality of the coronation was that he had to shave his beard off, which he'd grown fond of, as well as cut his long hair, which his wife liked.

When they got back to Canada he could grow it all back.

The doors opened and Lev stood.

"Are you ready for this?" he asked.

"Yes. I think so."

"You'll do fine." He took her hand and kissed it. "You're with me and I'm so proud of you. Both of you."

He kissed his sleeping daughter on the forehead.

"I'm glad you're both here. I couldn't do this without you."

"You could have," she said.

"Perhaps, but the point is I don't want to. I was a fool when I almost walked away from you. I don't know what I was thinking."

"You were afraid, much like I was. I never thought I would ever get married, not after what happened to my parents. I didn't think that love and marriage could last. I didn't think it was possible, not for me."

"Me either, but I'm so glad we were wrong."

"Me too."

"And I'm glad that I'm able to bring you both to Chenar so you can see where I grew up and see my home. I wouldn't want to do this without you both."

Imogen kissed him on the lips. "And you don't have to."

Lev nodded. The door to the private plane opened and Lexi appeared. He had cut his hair and shaved his beard too. There were times neither of them had thought this day would come, when Chenar would be a safe place for everyone again.

Lev hugged Lexi in the privacy of the plane. He'd missed his friend, even though he tried to deny it. He'd missed having Lexi in Yellowknife.

"It's so good to see you, my friend," Lev said. "I've missed you nagging at me in Yellowknife."

"I've missed you—and Yellowknife too, if I'm honest." Lexi gazed at Imogen. "Your Highness, it's so good to see you and the little Princess are healthy."

Imogen stepped forward and kissed Lexi on the cheek. "It's so good to see you too, Lexi. I've missed you."

Lexi laughed. "Now, that is a bare-faced lie."

"How is Kristof doing?" Lev asked.

"He's ready to become crowned and he's thrilled the three of you are here. How long do you plan on staying in Chenar?" Lexi asked.

"A month at least, but then we have to get back before the fall...before the winter storms."

Lexi looked wistful. "I don't suppose you want a bodyguard? I mean, someone has to protect the little Princess."

"We would love to have you back in Yellowknife, Lexi," said Imogen. "In fact, we have a bunkhouse on our property..."

Lev glared at her, but only in jest.

Lexi bowed. "Thank you. You are too gracious. Now, if you'll head out, the car is waiting and I will follow."

Lev took a deep breath and took a step outside. His country's anthem was playing once again and there was a small group of people cheering. He waved, waiting for Imogen to come down the stairs. She was wearing heels and a dress, which he knew made her uncomfortable, just like his military uniform made him uncomfortable, but it was only for a short while.

Soon they could go home, to the north, where it was just the three of them.

A prince, his wife and their daughter.

A life where he was free and could be himself.

His home.

* * * * *

HIS PREGNANT
PRINCESS BRIDE

CATHERINE MANN

To my dear friend and former neighbour from Louisiana – Karen. Thank you for all the Mardi Gras cakes and celebrations!

Prologue

"I have to confess, I don't care for the football at all."

Princess Erika's declaration caught Gervais Reynaud off guard, considering they'd spent the past four hours in the private viewing box overlooking Wembley Stadium, where his team would be playing a preseason exhibition game two months from now.

As the owner of the New Orleans Hurricanes NFL team, Gervais had more important things to do than indulge this high-maintenance Nordic princess he'd been seated beside during today's event, a high-stakes soccer match that was called "football" on this side of the globe. A game she didn't even respect regardless of which country played. Had it been sexist of him to think she might actually enjoy the game, since she was a royal, serving in her country's army? He'd expected a military member to be athletic. Not unreasonable, right? She was definitely toned under that gray, regimented uniform decorated with gold braid and commendations.

But she was also undoubtedly bored by the game.

And while Gervais didn't enjoy soccer as much as American football, he respected the hell out of it. The athletes were some of the best in the world. His main task for today had been to scout the stadium, to see what it would be like for the New Orleans Hurricanes when they played here in August. He'd staked his business reputation on the team he owned, a move his financial advisers had all adamantly opposed. There were risks, of course. But Gervais had never backed away from a challenge. It went against his nature. And now his career was tied to the success of the Hurricanes. The media spotlight had always been intense for him because of his family name. But after he'd purchased the franchise, the media became relentless.

Previewing the Wembley Stadium facilities at least offered him a welcome weekend of breathing room from scrutiny, since the UK fan base for American football was nominal. Here, he could simply enjoy a game without a camera panning to his face or reporters circling him afterward.

He only wished he could be watching the Hurricanes play today. He'd put one of his brothers in charge of the team as head coach. Another brother ran the team on the field in the quarterback position. Sportswriters back in the United States implied he'd made a colossal mistake.

Playing favorites? Clearly, they didn't know the Reynauds.

He wouldn't have chosen from his family unless they were the best for the job. Not when purchasing this team provided his chance to forge his own path as more than just part of the Reynaud extended-family empire of shipping moguls and football stars.

But to do that successfully, he had to play the political game with every bit as much strategy as the game on the field. As a team owner, he was the face of the Hurricanes. Which meant putting up with a temperamental princess who hadn't grasped that the "football team" he owned wasn't the one on the field. Not that she seemed to care much one way or the other.

Sprawled on the white leather sofa, Gervais tossed a pigskin from hand to hand, the ball a token gift from the public relations coordinator who'd welcomed him today and shown him to the private viewing box. The box was emptying now that the clock ran out after the London club beat another English team in the FA Cup Final. "You don't like the ball?"

She waved an elegant hand, smoothing over her pale blond hair sleeked back in a flawless twist. "No, not that. Perhaps my English is not as good as I would wish," she said with only the slightest hint of an accent. She'd been educated well, speaking with an intonation that was unquestionably sexy, even as she failed to notice the kind of football he held was different than the one they'd used on the field. "I do not care for the game. The football game."

"Interesting choice, then, for your country to send you as the royal representative to a finals match." Damn, she was too beautiful for her own good, wearing that neat-fitting uniform and filling it out in all the right places. Just looking at her brought to mind her heritage—her warrior princess ancestors out in battle side by side with badass Vikings—although this Nordic princess had clearly been suffering in regal silence for the past four hours. The way she'd dismissed her travel assistant had Gervais thinking he wouldn't even bother playing the diplomat with this ice princess.

"So, Princess Erika, were you sent here as punishment for some bad-girl imperial infraction?"

And if so, why wasn't she leaving now that the game had ended? What held her here, sipping champagne and talking to him after the box cleared? More important, what kept *him* here when he had a flight planned for tonight?

"First of all, I am not a reigning royal." Her icy blue eyes were as cool as her icy homeland as she set down her crystal champagne flute. "Our monarchy has been defunct for over forty-five years. And even if it was not, I am the youngest of five girls. And as for my second point, comments like yours only confirm my issue with attending a function like this where you assume I must be some kind of troublemaker if I don't enjoy this game. I must be flawed. No offense meant, but you and I simply have different interests."

"Then why are you here?" He wanted to know more than he should.

The PR coordinator for the stadium had introduced them only briefly and he found himself hungry to know more about this intriguing but reticent woman.

"My mother was not happy with my choice to join

the military, even though if I were a male that would not be in question. She is concerned I am not socializing enough and that I will end up unmarried, since clearly my worth is contingent upon having babies." Rolling her eyes, she crossed her long, slim legs at the ankles, her arms elegantly draped on the white leather chair. "Ridiculous, is it not, considering I am able to support myself? Besides, most of my older sisters are married and breeding like raccoons."

"Like rabbits."

She arched a thin blond eyebrow. "Excuse me?"

"The phrase is *breeding like rabbits.*" Gervais couldn't quite smother a grin as the conversation took an interesting turn.

"Oh, well, that is strange." She frowned, tapping her upper lip with a short, neat fingernail. "Rabbits are cute and fuzzy. Raccoons are less appealing. I believe raccoons fit better," she said as if merely stating it could change a colloquialism on her say-so.

"You don't like kids?" he found himself asking, even though he could have stood and offered to walk her out and be done with any expectation of social nicety.

When was the last time he exchanged more than a few words with a woman outside of business? He could spend another minute talking to her.

"I do not believe I must have a dozen heirs to make a defunct monarchy stable."

Hmm, valid point and an unexpected answer. "So I take that to mean you're no threat to hitting on the players?"

Down on the field, the winning team was being mobbed.

"You assume correctly," she blurted so quickly and emphatically, she startled a laugh from him.

It was refreshing to find a woman who wasn't a sports groupie for a change.

He found himself staying behind to talk to her even though he had a flight to catch. "What do you do in the military?"

"I am a nurse by degree but the military uses my skills as a linguist. In essence, I'm a diplomatic translator."

"Say again?"

"Is that so shocking? Do I not appear intelligent?"

She appeared hot as hell, like a blue flame, the most searing of all.

"You're lovely and articulate. You speak English fluently as a second language. You're clearly intelligent."

"And you are a flatterer," she said dismissively. "I work as a translator, but now that I'm nearing the end of my time in military service, I'll be taking the RN degree a step further, becoming a nurse-practitioner, with a specialty in homeopathic treatments, using natural herbs and even scents, studying how they relate to moods and physiological effects. Stress relievers. Energy infusers. Or immune boosters. Or allergy relievers. Any number of combinations to combine an alluring perfume with a healthier lifestyle."

"Where do you study that?"

"I've been accepted into a program in London. I had hoped to pursue nursing in the military to increase my experience, but my government had other plans for me to be a translator."

A nurse, soon to become a nurse-practitioner? Now, *that* surprised him. "Very impressive."

"Thank you." She nodded regally, a lock of hair sliding free from her twist and caressing her cheek. She tucked it behind her ear. "Now, explain to me what I need to know to speak intelligently about what I saw down on the field with all those musclemen when I return home."

Standing, he extended an arm to her. "By all means, Princess, I know a little something about European football even though the team I own is an American football team."

She rose with the elegance of a woman who'd been trained in every manner to grace high-end ballrooms not ball games. And yet she chose to further her education and serve her country in uniform.

Princess-Captain Erika Mitras wasn't at all what he expected when he'd spotted a foreign dignitary on the guest list. He'd envisioned either a stiff-necked VIP or a football groupie bent on a photo op and a chance to meet the players. He didn't come across many people who dared tell him they didn't like football—European or American. In fact, he didn't have many people in his life who disliked sports. The shipping business might be the source of Reynaud wealth, but football had long been their passion.

How contrary that her disinterest in sports made her all the more appealing. Yes, she aroused him in a way he couldn't recall having felt about any woman before.

And quite possibly some of that allure had to do with the fact that for once in his life he wasn't under the scrutiny of the American media. Perhaps if he was careful, he could do something impulsive without worrying about the consequences rippling through his family's world.

He stepped closer, folding her hand into the crook of his arm, and caught a whiff of a cinnamon scent. "And while I do that, what do you say we enjoy London? Dinner, theater, your choice. Just the two of us."

Flights could be rescheduled.

She paused to peer up at him, her cool blue eyes roaming his face for a moment before the barest hint of a smile played over her lips. "Only if, after a brief outline of the differences in these football sports, we can agree to no football talk at all?"

"None," he vowed without hesitation.

"Then it sounds lovely."

Who knew cinnamon would be such a total turn-on?

One

2 ½ Months Later
New Orleans, Louisiana

Princess Erika Birgitta Inger Freya Mitras of Holsgrof knew how to make a royally memorable appearance.

Her mother had taught her well. And Erika needed all the confidence she could garner striding onto the practice field full of larger-than-life men in training. Most important, she needed all her confidence to face one particular man. The leader of this testosterone domain, the owner of the state-of-the-art training facility where he now presided. Players dotted the field in black-and-gold uniforms, their padded shoulders crashing against each other. Shouts, grunts and curses volleyed. Men who appeared to be trainers or coaches jogged alongside them, barking instructions or blowing whistles.

She'd finished her military stint a month ago, her hopes of serving her country in combat having been sidelined by her parents' interference. They'd shuffled her into some safe figurehead job that made her realize the family's Viking-warrior heritage would not be carried on through her. She'd been so disillusioned, adrift and on edge the day she attended the soccer game, she had been reckless.

Too reckless. And that weekend of indulgence brought her here. Now. To New Orleans. To Gervais.

Her Jimmy Choo heels sank into the most plush grass ever as she stepped onto the practice field of the New Orleans Hurricanes. She'd assumed this particularly American game was played on Astroturf. And assumptions were what she had to avoid when it came to her current adventure in the United States.

She had not intended to see Gervais Reynaud again after he left the United Kingdom. Their weekend of dates—and amazing, mind-blowing sex—had been an escape from rules and protocol and everything else that had kept her life rigidly in check for so long. She'd had relationships in the past, carefully chosen and approved. This was her first encounter of her own choosing.

And it had turned out to be far more memorable than she could have ever imagined.

She felt the weight of his eyes from across the open stretch of greenery. Or perhaps he had noticed her only because of the sudden silence. Players now stood still, their shouts dimming to a dull echo.

The rest of the place faded for her while she focused on Gervais Reynaud standing at the foot of the bleachers, as tall as any of the players. He was muscular, more so than the average man but more understated than the men in uniform nearby. She knew he had played in his youth and through college but had chosen a business route in the family's shipping enterprise until he had bought the New Orleans Hurricanes football team. The *American* football team. She understood the difference now. She also knew Gervais's purchase of the team had attracted a great deal of press coverage in business and sports media alike.

He had not told her much about his life, but before she made her trip here she had made a point of learning more about him and his family.

It certainly was amazing what a few internet searches could reveal.

Tracing their ancestry deep into Acadian history, the Reynaud family first built their fortune in shipping, a business that his grandfather patriarch Leon Reynaud had expanded into a thriving cruise ship company. Leon also turned a love of sports into another successful venture when he'd purchased shares in a Texas football team, learning the business from the inside out. His elder son, Christophe, inherited the shares but promptly sold them to buy a baseball team, creating a deep family rift.

Leon passed his intense love of football to his younger son, Theo, whose promising career as a quarterback in Atlanta was cut short due to injury and excess after his marriage to a celebrated supermodel fell apart. Theo had three sons from his marriage, Gervais, Henri and Jean-Pierre, and one from an earlier affair, Dempsey. All of the sons inherited a passion for the game, playing in college and groomed for the NFL.

While the elder two sons broke ties with their father to bring corporate savvy to the front office of the relatively new team, the younger two sons both continued their careers on the field. The Reynaud brothers were especially well-known in Louisiana, where their football exploits were discussed—as much a topic of conversation as the women in their lives. She'd overheard references to each in the lobby of the five-star hotel where she'd spent the night in New Orleans.

Would she be the topic of such conversation once her "encounter" with Gervais became public knowledge? There would be no way to hide it from his football world much longer.

Football. A game she still cared very little about, a fact he had teased her about during their weekend together, a weekend where they had spent more time undressed than clothed. Her gaze was drawn back to that well-honed body of his that had made such passionate love to her.

His dark eyes heated her with memories as he strode toward her. His long legs ate the ground in giant slices, his khakis and sports jacket declaring him in the middle of a workday. He stopped in front of her, his broad shoulders blocking the sun and casting his handsome face in shadows. But she didn't have to see to know his jaw would be peppered with the stubble that seemed to grow in seconds after he shaved. Her fingers—her body—remembered the texture of that rasp well.

Her breath caught somewhere in her chest.

He folded his arms over his chest, just under the Hurricanes logo stitched on the front of his jacket. "Welcome to the States, Erika. No one mentioned your intention to visit. I thought you didn't like sports."

"And yet, here I am." And in need of privacy out of the bright Louisiana sun and the even brighter curious eyes of his team and staff. She needed space and courage to tell him why she'd made this unexpected journey across the Atlantic to this muggy bayou state. "This is not an official royal visit."

"And you're not in uniform." His eyes glided over her wraparound dress.

"I'm out of the service now to begin furthering my studies." About to return to school to be a nurse-practitioner, the career field she'd hoped to pursue in the military, but they would not allow her such an in-the-field position, instead preferring to dress her up and trot her around as a figurehead translator. "I am here for a conference on homeopathic herbs and scents." A part of her passion in the nursing field, and a totally made-up excuse for being here today.

"The homeopathic scents for healing, right? Are you here to share specially scented deodorant with my players? Because they could certainly use it." His mouth tipped with a smile.

"Are you interested in such a line?" Still jet-lagged from the transatlantic flight, she was ill prepared to exchange pleasantries, much less ones filled with taunts at her career choice.

"Is that why you are here? For business before you start your new degree?"

She could not just banter with him. She simply could not. "Please, can we go somewhere private to talk?"

He searched her eyes for a long moment before gesturing over his shoulder. "I'm in the middle of a meeting with sponsors. How about supper?"

"I am not here for seduction," she stated bluntly.

"Okay." His eyebrows shot upward. "I thought I asked you to join me for gumbo not sex. But now that we're talking about sex—"

"We are not." She cut him short. "Finish your meeting if you must, but I need to speak with you as soon as possible. Privately. Unless you want your personal business and mine overheard by all of your team straining to listen."

She definitely was not ready for them to hear she was pregnant with the heir to the Reynaud family dynasty.

She was back. Princess Erika, the sexy seductress who'd filled his dreams since they'd parted ways nearly three months ago. And even though he should be paying attention to the deal with his sponsors, he could not tear his eyes away from her. From the swish of her curves and hips. And the long platinum-blond hair that made her look completely otherworldly.

He needed to focus, but damn. She was mesmerizing.

And apparently, every team member on the field was

also aware of that fact. From their top wide receiver Wildcard to running back Freight Train.

Gervais turned his attention back to finishing up his conversation with the director of player personnel—Beau Durant—responsible for draft picks, trades, acquiring the right players and negotiating contracts. An old college friend, Beau shared his friend's interest in running a football team. He took a businesslike, numbers approach to the job and wed that with his personal interest in football. Like Gervais, he had a position in his family's multinational corporation, but football was his obsession.

"Gervais, I'd love to stay and chat, but we have another meeting to get to. We'll be in touch," his former college roommate promised.

"Perfect, Beau. Thank you," he said, offering him a sincere handshake. Beau's eyes were on the princess even if he didn't ask the obvious question. Beau was an all-business kind of guy who never pried. He'd always said he didn't want others sticking their noses in his private life, either.

The eyes of the whole damn team remained on the princess, in fact. Which made Gervais steam with protectiveness.

He barked over to his half brother, the head coach, "Dempsey, don't your boys have something better to do than stand around drooling over a woman like pimply teenage boys?"

Dempsey smirked. "All right, men. Back to practice. You can stare at pretty girls on someone else's time. Now, move!" Henri Reynaud, the Hurricanes' quarterback and Gervais's brother, shot him a look of half amusement. But he slung his helmet back on and began to make his way into formation. The Bayou Bomber, a nickname Henri had earned during his college days at LSU, would not be so easily dissuaded from his obvious curiosity.

Dempsey scratched some numbers out on his paper. Absently, he asked, "What's with the royal visit?"

"We have some...unresolved issues from our time in England."

"Your time together?" Dempsey's wicked grin spread, and he clucked his tongue.

He might as well come clean in an understated way. The truth would be apparent soon enough. "We had a quiet...relationship."

"Very damn quiet if I didn't hear about it." Crossing his arms, he did his best to look hurt.

"You were busy with the team. As it should be."

"So you have some transcontinental dating relationship with Europe's most eligible princess?"

"Reading the tabloids again, Dempsey?"

"Gotta keep up with my players' antics somehow." He shrugged it off.

"Well, don't let her hear you discussing her eligibility. She's military. She might well be able to kick your ass."

"Military, huh? That's surprising."

"She said male royals serve. Why not females? She just finished up her time." Which had seemed to bother her. He understood well about trying to find where you fit in a high-profile family.

"Carole Montemarte, the Hurricanes' press relations coordinator, will have a blast spinning that for the media. Royalty for a girlfriend? Nice, dude. And she chased you clear across the ocean. You are quite the man."

Except that didn't make sense. She'd ignored his calls after he left the country. Granted, what they'd shared blew his mind, and he didn't have the time or energy for a transcontinental relationship. So his calls had been more...obligatory. Had she known that? Was that the reason she'd ignored him?

So why show up here now?

He sure as hell intended to find out.

Two

Limos were something of the norm for Erika. Part of the privilege of growing up royal. This should feel normal, watching the sunset while being chauffeured in the limo Gervais had sent to retrieve her from her hotel. Half of her childhood had been spent in the backseat of a limo as she and her family went from one event to another.

But today was anything but normal. As she pulled at the satin fabric of her dress, her mind began to race. She had never pictured herself with a brood of children like her sisters. Not that she didn't want them, but this was all happening so fast. And with a man she wasn't entirely sure of. Just the thought of Gervais sent her mind reeling. The thought of telling him about their shared interest made her stomach knot. She began to wonder about what she would tell him. How she would tell him. News she could barely wrap her brain around. But there were secrets impossible to keep in her world, so if she wanted to inform Gervais on her terms, she would have to do so soon.

Tonight.

And just like that, Erika realized the vehicle had stopped. Reality was starting to set in, and no amount of finery and luxury was going to change that. She had chosen the arctic-blue dress because it reminded her of her heritage. Of her family's Viking past. Of the strength of her small country. She needed these reminders if she was going to face him.

Try as she might, Erika couldn't get the way he looked at her out of her mind. His eyes drinking her in. The memory sent a pleasurable shiver along her skin.

The chauffeur opened the door with a click, and she stepped out of the limo. Tall and proud. A light breeze danced against her skin, threatening her sideswept updo. Fingers instinctively flew to the white-crusted sapphire pin that, at the nape of her neck, not only held her hair together but also had been in her family for centuries.

Smoothing her blond hair that cascaded over one of her shoulders, she took in the Reynaud family compound in the meeting of sunset with the moon, the stars just beginning to sparkle in the Louisiana sky. Though she had to admit, the flood of lights leading up to the door diminished the starlight.

She lifted her gaze to the massive structure ahead of her. Greek Revival with white arches and columns—no other word than *massive*, and a girl who grew up in a palace wasn't impressed easily.

As she walked up the stairs to the home, the sureness from touching her family heirloom began to wane. But before she could lose her nerve and turn back, the limo pulled away and the grand door opened in front of her. This was officially happening.

Though the lights outside had been clinical and bright, the foyer was illuminated by bulbs of yellow. The warmth of these lights reflected on what appeared to be hand-painted murals depicting a fox hunt. American royalty.

A servant gestured for her to walk through the room on the left. Gathering the skirt of her dress, Erika crossed the threshold, leaving behind the foyer and its elaborate staircase and murals.

This room was made for entertainment. She had been in plenty of grand dining halls, and this one felt familiar and impersonal, with wisps of silk that told their secrets to the glass and windows.

Erika had always hated dinners in rooms like this.

Quickly scanning the room, she noted the elaborately carved wooden chair and the huge arrangements of flowers and the tall marble vases. But Gervais wasn't here, either.

She pressed on through the next threshold and found herself in a simpler room. It was clear that this was a family room. The opulent colors of the grand dining room softened, giving way to a creamy palette. The kind of colors that made Erika want to curl up on the plush leather sofa with a good book and some strong tea with milk.

The family room sported an entertainment bar with

Palladian windows overlooking the pool and grounds. But if she turned ever so slightly she could also see an alcove that appeared to lead to a more private section.

The master bedroom and bath? She could envision that space having doors out to the pool, a hot tub, perhaps. She bit her lip and spun away.

It was not as if she was here to gawk at furniture. She had to tell a man she barely knew that they were having a baby. And that the press would have a field day if she and Gervais didn't get a handle on this now.

And there. She saw him. Chiseled. Dark hair, ruffled ever so slightly. His lips parted into a smile as he met her gaze.

Nerves and something else jolted her to life. Pushed her forward. Toward him and that wolfish smile.

She looked around and saw housekeeping staff, but no one else. Erika waved an elegant hand to the expansive room they stood in and the ones she'd already passed through. "Where's the rest of your family?"

"Dempsey owns the other home on the compound grounds, next door. My younger brothers Jean-Pierre and Henri share the rights to the house to the northwest on the lake. Gramps has quarters here with me, since this house has been in our family the longest. It's familiar. He has servants on call round the clock. He's getting older and more forgetful. But we're hoping to hold back time as long as we can for him."

"I am so sorry."

"They make great meds these days. He's still got lots of life and light left in him." A practiced smile pressed against his lips. It was apparent he was hopeful. And used to defending his grandfather's position.

"And where does the rest of your family live?"

"Are you worried they'll walk in on us?" He angled a brow upward, and she felt the heat of his eyes graze across her body. A flush crept along her face, heating her from the inside out. Threatening to set her nerves bounding out of control. She needed to stay calm.

"Perhaps."

"My father's in Texas and doesn't return often. Jean-Pierre is in New York with his team for the season and Henri lives in the Garden District most of the time, so their house here is vacant for a while."

Stepping out onto the patio, he nodded for her to follow. She hastened behind him. Intrigued. He had that way about him. A quality of danger that masked itself as safe. That quality that made him undeniably sexy.

And that, she reminded herself, was how she'd ended up in this situation.

Gervais surveyed the patio. She followed his gaze, noting the presence of a hot tub and an elaborate fountain that pumped water into the pool. The fountain, like the house, was descended from a Greek aesthetic. Apollo and Daphne were intertwined, water flowing from the statues into the pool.

Over the poolside sound system, the din of steel drums competed with the gentle echo of rolling waves on the lakeshore.

"You arranged dinner outside." Erika breathed in the air on this rare night of low humidity. She looked around at the elaborate patio table that was dressed for dinner with lights, fresh flowers, silver and china. Ceiling fans circled a delicious breeze from the slight overhang of the porch.

"I promised you gumbo—" he gestured broadly, before holding the seat out for her "—and I delivered."

She settled into the chair, intensely aware of his hands close to her shoulders. The heat of his chest close to her back. Blinking away the awareness, she focused on the table settings, surprised to realize he planned to serve her himself from the silver chafing dishes. "Your home is lovely."

"The old plantation homes have a lot of character." He slid into the seat across from hers. "I know our history here doesn't compete with the hundreds of years, castles and Viking lore of your country, but the place has stories in the walls all the same."

"The architecture and details are stunning. I can see why you were drawn to live here." When Americans talked about their colonial towns, they always spoke of the old-world charm they'd possessed. But that was selling it short. Cities like New Orleans were the distillation of cultures haphazardly pressed against each other. And that distillation yielded beauty that was so different from the actual Old World.

"If you would prefer a restaurant…" He paused, tongs grasping freshly baked bread.

"This is better. More private." She held up a hand. "Don't take that the wrong way."

"Understood. You made your point earlier."

Seafood gumbo, red beans and rice, thick black

coffee and powdery doughnuts—beignets. It was a spread that sent her taste buds jumping.

"Did you have a nice ride from the Four Winds Resort?"

"I did. The trees heavy with Spanish moss are beautiful. And the water laps at the roads as if the sea could wash over the land at any moment." The languid landscape was so different than her country's rugged and fierce Viking past. She'd liked learning about New Orleans so far.

"You could stay here, you know."

"I did not come here for that." She laced her words with ice even as her body burned with awareness of the man seated across from her.

"Then why are you here after walking out on me without a word or backward glance?"

So that hadn't escaped his notice. She began to prepare the speeches that had replayed in her mind since she had boarded the plane to make the transatlantic journey.

"I'm sorry about that. I thought I was making things easier for both of us. It was a fling with no future, given we live across an ocean from each other. I saved us both a messy goodbye."

At that time she had been thinking about the life she needed to get on track. But all her carefully laid plans were shifting beneath her feet, now that she was pregnant.

"And when I called you? Left messages asking to speak to you?"

"I thought you were being polite. Gentlemanly. And

do not get me wrong, I believe it honorable of you. But that is not enough to build a relationship."

"How much would it have hurt to return one call? If we're talking about polite, I expected as much from you." He cocked an eyebrow.

"You are angry. I apologize if I made the wrong decision."

"Well, you're here now. For your conference, right?"

"Actually, that wasn't the truth." She fidgeted with her leather band bracelet, inspirational inscriptions scrolled on metal insets providing support. Advice. And if ever she was in need of help, the moment was now. "I only said that in case others overheard. I'm here to see you. I want to apologize for walking out on you and have a conversation we should have had then."

"What conversation would that be?"

Oh, what a loaded question, she thought. "How we would handle it if there were unexpected consequences from our weekend together."

He stared at her, hard. "Unexpected consequences? How about you spell it out rather than have me play Fifty Questions."

She dabbed the corners of her mouth as if she could buy herself a few more seconds before her life changed forever. Folding the napkin carefully and placing it beside her plate, she met his dark brown eyes, her own gaze steady. Her hands shaky. "I am pregnant. The baby is yours."

Of all the things that Erika could have said, being pregnant was not what Gervais had been preparing himself for. He ought to say something. Something fast, witty and comforting. But instead, he just looked at her.

Really looked at her as he swallowed. Hard.

She was every bit as breathtaking as that first night they'd met. But there was something different in the way she carried her body that should have tipped him off.

Her face was difficult to read. She'd iced him out of gaining any insights in her eyes. Gervais examined the hair that trailed down her shoulder, exposing her collarbone and slender neck. This was the hairstyle of a royal, so different than the girl who had let her hair run wild over their weekend together.

And what a weekend it'd been. Months had passed since then and he still thought about her. About the way she'd tasted on his tongue.

He had to say something worthy of that. Of her. He collected his thoughts, determined to say the perfect thing.

Despite all of that, only one word fell out of his mouth.

"Pregnant." So much for a grand speech.

Her face flashed with a hint of disappointment. Of course, she had every right to expect more from him. But more silence escaped his lips, and the air was filled not with sounds of him speaking, but with the buzz of waves and boats.

The trace of frustration and disappointment had left her face. She looked every bit a Viking queen. Impassive. Strong. Icy. And still so damn sexy in her soft feminine clothes and that bold leather bracelet.

"Yes, and I am absolutely certain the child is yours."

"I didn't question you."

"I wanted to be clear. Although in these days of DNA tests, it is not a subject that one can lie about." She frowned. "Do you need time to think, for us to talk more later? You look pale."

Did he? Hell, he did feel as if he'd been broadsided by a three-hundred-pound linebacker, but back in his ballplaying days he'd been much faster at recovery. And the stakes here were far higher. He needed to tread carefully. "A child is always cause for celebration." He took her hand in his, as close as he could let himself get until he had answers, no matter how tempted he was for more. "I'm just surprised. We were careful."

"Not careful enough, apparently. You, um, did stretch the condom, and perhaps there was a leak."

He choked on a cough. "Um, uh…I don't know what to say to that."

"It was not a compliment, you Cro-Magnon." She shook her hand free from his. "Simply an observation."

"Fair enough. Okay, so you're pregnant with my baby. When do you want to head to the courthouse to get married?"

"Are you joking? I did not come to the United States expecting a proposal of marriage."

"Well, that is what I am offering. Would you prefer I do this in a more ceremonial way? Fine." He slid from his chair and dropped to one knee on the flagstone patio. "Marry me and let's bring up this child together."

Her eyes went wide with shock and she shot to her

feet. Looking around her as if to make sure no one overheard. "Get up. You look silly."

"Silly?"

For the first time since he'd met her, she appeared truly flustered. She edged farther away, sweeping back her loose hair with nervous hands. "Perhaps I chose the wrong word. You look...not like you. And this is not what I want."

"What do you want?"

"I am simply here to notify you about your child and discuss if you wish to be a part of the baby's life before I move forward with my life."

"Damn straight I want to bring up my child."

"Shared custody."

He reached to capture her restless hands and hold them firmly in his. "You are not hearing me. I want to raise my child."

"*Our* child."

"Of course." He caressed the insides of her wrists with his thumbs. "Let's declare peace so we can make our way through this conversation amicably."

Her shoulders relaxed and he guided her to a bench closer to the half wall at the end of the patio. They sat side by side, shoulder to shoulder.

She nodded. "I want peace, very much. That's why I came to you now, early on, rather than just calling or waiting longer."

"And I am glad you did." He slid his hand up her arm to her shoulder, cupping the warmth of her, aching for more. "My brother Dempsey grew up thinking our father didn't want him and it scarred him. I refuse to let that happen to my child. My baby will know he or she is wanted."

"Of course our child will be brought up knowing both parents love and want him or her."

"Yes, and you still haven't answered my question."

"What question?"

"The *silly* question that comes with a guy getting down on one knee. Will you marry me?"

Three

"Marry you? I do not even know you." Erika's voice hitched. Marriage? She had wanted him to be supportive, sure. But…marriage? The words tumbled over and over in her head in a disjointed echo.

"We knew each other well enough to have sex. Call me old-fashioned, but I'm trying to do the right thing here and offer to marry you. We can have a civil ceremony and divorce in a year. As far as our child knows, we gave it an honest try but things didn't work." His voice was level. Calm. Practical.

Her fears multiplied. This seemed too calculated. And she would not land in a family environment that was all for show again. Being raised royal had taught her she was not meant for a superficial existence. She had already chosen a meaningful career. A future where she could make a difference.

Swallowing back the anxiety swelling in her chest, she reminded herself to be reasonable.

"You figured all that out this fast? Or have you had practice with this sort of business before?" The notion cut her with surprising sharpness. She did not want to think about Gervais involved with other women after the way they'd been together.

"I am not joking." His hand inched toward hers.

She scrutinized his face, studied the way his jaw jutted. The play of muted lights on his dark hair, the way it was thickest on top of his head. Even now, he was damn attractive. But that fact wasn't enough to chase reason from her mind.

"Apparently not."

"I'll take that as a no to my proposal." Retreating his hand, he leaned forward, elbows on his knees.

"You most certainly can. It is far too soon to speak of marriage. And have you forgotten? I have plans to pursue my education in the UK."

Tilting his head, he lowered his voice. It became soft. Gentle. "You won't even consider my offer? Not even for the baby's sake? Let me take care of you while you're pregnant and recovering, postpartum and such. You can get to know my family during the football season. Afterward, we can spend more time with yours."

Even if the monarchy was defunct, she was a royal and sure of herself. She shot to her feet. "Do I get any say in this at all? You are a pushy man. I do not remember that about you."

He stood and stepped closer, very close, suggestively. His hips and thighs warm against hers. "What do you remember about our time together?"

"If you are trying to seduce me into doing whatever you want—" Erika needed to focus. Which was tougher than ever with him pressed up against her and that smolder in his eye setting her on fire.

"If? I must not be working hard enough." He slid his hands up her arms.

Her eyes fluttered shut, and for a moment she felt as if she could give in. But thoughts of her future child coursed through her mind. A ragged breath escaped her lips, and she reopened her eyes.

She clasped his wrists. "Stop. I am not playing games. I came here to inform you. Not demand anything of you. And certainly not to reenact our past together."

His hands dropped and he scowled. "Let me get this straight. If I hadn't wanted anything to do with the baby, you would have simply walked away?"

"You never would have heard from me again." The words escaped her as an icy dagger. She would have no use for such a man. And she had to admit that even if his proposal felt pushy, at least Gervais was not the sort of person to walk away from his child.

"Well, not a chance in hell is that happening this time. You may have brushed me off once before, but not again."

Had he genuinely wished to see her again after their weekend together? She had been afraid to find out at the time, afraid of answering his call only to discover that his contact was a perfunctory duty and social nicety. After what they had shared, she was not sure she could bear hearing that cool retreat in his voice. Now, of course, she would never know what his intentions had truly been toward her.

She took a deep breath. Regrouped.

"And you cannot command me to your will," she warned him, her shoulders stiff with tension. "I will not be forced into marriage because you think that is the best plan. I have plans, as well."

How many people had underestimated her resolve over the years because she had that label of "princess" attached to her? Her commanding officers. Teachers. Her own parents.

She would simply have to show Gervais her mettle.

"I understand that," he murmured, his voice melting into the sounds of waves and steel drums. "Now we need to make plans together."

Some of the tension in her eased. "Nice to know you can be reasonable and not just impulsive."

With a shrug, he began again. "In the interest of being reasonable, let's spend the next four weeks—"

"Two weeks," she corrected him. She had already disrupted her life and traveled halfway across the globe for him.

He nodded slowly. "Two weeks getting to know each other better as we make plans for our child. You could stay here in my home, where there are plenty of suites for privacy. I won't make a move that isn't mutual. We'll use this time to find common ground."

"And if we are not successful in your time frame?"

This felt like a business deal. But the time frame might be enough to bring him to reason.

"Then I guess I'll have to follow you home. Now, how about I call over to the hotel for them to send your things here? You look ready to fall asleep on your feet."

"You're honestly suggesting I give up my plans completely and stay here?" She gestured back toward the house. Two weeks. Together. Under the same roof.

That part sounded decidedly *less* like a business deal. The very idea wisped heatedly over her skin.

"Not in my bed—unless you ask, of course." He smiled devilishly. "But if we're going to make the most of these two weeks, it's best we stay here. There are fantastic graduate school programs in the area, too, if you opt for that later down the road. And I can also provide you with greater protection here."

"Protection?" What in the world did she need his protection for? And from what? And what was this later-down-the-road notion for her plans?

"We're a professional NFL family. That brings with it a level of fame and notoriety unrivaled in any other business domain. The fans are passionate. And while most of them are supportive, there is a segment that takes the game very personally. Some of the more unstable types occasionally seek revenge for what they perceive as bad decisions." His jaw flexed. "Since your child is my child, that puts our baby at risk as a Reynaud. If you won't stay here for yourself, then stay for our child. We are safe here."

He had found the one reason she couldn't debate. But she needed to be careful. To give herself time to think through the consequences of what she was agreeing to, and she couldn't do that now when she was so tired.

"I am weary. It has been a long, emotional day. I would appreciate being shown to these guest suites that you speak of and I will consider it."

"Of course." He picked up his phone and tapped the screen twice before setting it down. "You'll find all the toiletries you need at your disposal. I'll have someone show you to a room and make sure you have everything you need."

Before he finished speaking, a maid had arrived at the door, perhaps summoned by his phone.

Apparently, Gervais was serious about giving her some space if she elected to stay in the house with him. And while she appreciated that, she was also surprised at his easy efficiency. Hadn't her pregnancy announcement rattled this coolly controlled man even a little?

"Thank you." She looked at him, her breath catching at the raw masculinity of the man. She backed up a step, needing boundaries. And sleep.

"And I'll have a long Hurricanes jersey sent up for you to sleep in." His eyes remained on hers, but his voice stirred something inside her.

The last time they had slept under the same roof, there hadn't been much sleeping accomplished at all. And somehow, as she took her leave of him, she knew that he was remembering that fact as vividly as she did.

The door closed behind her, and she loosed a breath that she didn't realize she'd been holding.

This was...different from what she had grown up

with. The billowy sheer curtains thinly veiled a view of Lake Pontchartrain. Heels clacked against the opulent white marble as she made her way to an oversize plush bed. Instinctively, she ran her hand over the white comforter as she took in the room.

A grand, hand-carved mahogany-wood nightstand held a score of toiletries.

It was luxurious. She unscrewed the lid on one of the lotion bottles, and the light scent of jasmine wafted up to her. She set it down, picked up the shampoo, popped the lid and breathed in mint and a tropical, fruity flavor.

This house was old, not as old as her castle, of course, but it still had history. And such a different feel than her wintry homeland. This was grander, built more for leisure than practicality.

Plopping onto the bed, Erika was somewhat surprised to note the bed was every bit as comfortable as it looked. The bed seemed to wrap her in a hug.

And she needed a hug. Everything in her life was undergoing a drastic change. Untethered. That was where she was. Her career in the military was over. It left her feeling strange, adrift. The past few years, her path had been set. And now? A river of conflicting wants and obligations flooded her mind.

Yes, she wanted to pursue her dream. She wanted to be a nurse-practitioner and pursue her studies in the UK, wanted that so badly. But that dream wasn't as simple as it had been a couple months ago.

Even now, thousands of miles away, she felt the tendrils of familial pressure. When they learned she was going to have a child, they would be pressuring her.

Probably into marriage. And Gervais seemed to have the same ideas. How was she supposed to balance all of it?

In her soul, she knew she'd be able to take care of her child. Give her baby everything and have her dreams, too. But the weight of everyone's expectations left her feeling anxious. First things first, she needed to figure out what she wanted. How she would handle all of this. And then she could deal with the demands of her family and Gervais.

Lifting herself off the bed, she made her way to the coffee table where a stack of old sports programs casually dressed the table.

Dragging her fingers over the covers, she tried to get a feel for Gervais. For his family. The Greek Revival hinted at wealth but shed little on his personality. Though, from her brief time in the halls, she noticed how sparsely decorated the place was. On the wall, directly across from where she stood, were some photos in sleek black frames. They were matted and simple. The generic sorts of photographs that belonged more in a cold, impersonal office than a residence.

She walked over to investigate them further. The two images that hung on the wall were formal portraits, similar to the kinds she and her family had done. But whereas her family bustled with Viking grace and was filled with women, these pictures were filled with the Reynaud men.

The sons stood closer to the grandfather. Strange. A man who looked as if he could be Gervais's father was on the edge of the photograph, an impatient smile curling over his face.

Gingerly, she reached out to the frame, fingers finding cool glass. Gervais. Handsome as the devil. A smile was on her lips before she could stop it. She dropped her hand.

No, Erika. She had to remain focused. And figure out how to do what was best for her—their—child that didn't involve jumping into bed with him. Again.

Pulling at the hem of the jersey that cut her midthigh, a jersey she'd found on her bed and couldn't resist wearing, she resolved to keep her hands off him. And his out from under her jersey. Even if that did sound…delicious.

Father.
The word blasted in his mind like an air horn.

Gervais tried to bring his mind back to the present. To the meeting with Dempsey, who had stopped by after Erika retreated to a vacant suite for the night. Just because Erika was pregnant didn't mean his career was nonexistent. He needed to talk with his brother about the Hurricanes' development. About corporate sponsorships and expanding their team's prestige and net worth.

But that was a lot easier said than done with the latest developments in his personal life.

He swirled his local craft beer in his glass, watching the mini tornado foam in the center as he made himself comfortable in the den long after dinner had ended. Back when this house had still belonged to his parents, most of the rooms had been fussy and full of interior decorator additions—elaborate crystal light fixtures that hung so low he and his brothers broke a part of it every time they threw a ball in the house. Or three-dimensional art that spanned whole walls and would scrape the skin off an arm if they tackled each other into it.

The den had always been male terrain and it remained a place where Gervais felt most comfortable. The place where he most often met with his brothers. Dempsey had headed for this room as soon as he'd arrived tonight.

Now, sipping his beer, Gervais tried like hell to get his head focused back on work. The team.

Dempsey took an exaggerated sip from his glass and set it on the table in front of them. Cocking his head to the side, he settled deeper in the red leather club chair and asked, "What's the deal with the princess's arrival? She damn near caused Freight Train to trip over his feet like a first-day rookie."

"She came by to see me." Gervais tried to make it sound casual. Breezy.

"Because New Orleans happens to be right around the corner from Europe?"

"Your humor slays me." He tipped back his beer. Dempsey was a lot of things, but indirect? Never.

"Well, she obviously came to see you. And from what I'm starting to hear now from the gossip already churning, the two of you spent a great deal of time together in the UK. Are you two back together again? Dating?" A small smile, but his eyes were trained on Gervais. A Reynaud trait—dogged persistence.

"Not exactly dating."

"Then why is she here?" He leaned forward, picking up his glass. "And don't tell me it's none of my business, because she's distracting you."

He wanted to argue the point. But who the hell would he be kidding?

Instead, he dropped his voice. "This goes no further than the two of us for now."

"I'm offended you have to ask that."

"Right. Well, she's pregnant. It's mine."

"You're certain?" Dempsey set his glass on the marble side table, face darkening like a storm rolling out.

Gervais stared him down. Not in the mood for that runaround.

"All right. Your child. What next?"

"My child, my responsibility." He would be there for his child. That was nonnegotiable.

"Interesting choice of words. *Responsibility.*" Something shifted in Dempsey's expression. But Gervais didn't have to wonder why. Dempsey was Gervais's illegitimate half brother. Dempsey hadn't even been in the picture until he turned thirteen years old, when Yvette, Dempsey's mom, had angled to extort money from their father, Theo, at which point Theo brought Dempsey to the family home.

To say the blending had been rough was generous. It was something that felt like the domestic equivalent of World War Three. Gervais's mother left. Then it was just a houseful of men—his brothers, Theo and Gramps. And it was really Gramps who had taken care of the boys. Theo was too busy shucking responsibilities.

"I'm sure as hell not walking away." He'd seen too

well the marks it left on Dempsey not knowing his father in the early years, the sting of growing up thinking his father didn't care. Hell, their father hadn't even known Dempsey existed.

Not that it excused their father, since he'd misled Dempsey's mother.

"I'm just saying that I understand what it feels like to be an inconvenient mistake. A responsibility." His jaw flexed, gaze fixed over Gervais's head.

"Dad loves you. We all do. You're part of our family."

"I know. But that wasn't always the case."

"We didn't know you then."

"He did. Or at least he knew that he'd been with women without considering the consequences." Dempsey's eyes darkened a shade, protectiveness for his mother obvious, even though the woman had been a negligible caregiver at best. "Anyhow, it took us all a long time to come back from that tough start. So make sure you get your head on straight before this baby's born. Better yet, get things right before you alienate the child's mother. Because if you intend to be in the kid's life, you're not going to want to spend years backtracking from screwing up with words like *responsibility* at the start."

The outburst was swift and damning. Dempsey shot up and out of his seat. He began to storm away, heading for the door.

Gervais followed.

"Dempsey—wait, I…" But the words fell silent as he nearly plowed into his brother's back.

Dempsey had halted in his tracks, his gaze on the

staircase in the corridor. Or, more accurate, his gaze on the woman now standing on the staircase.

Erika. In nothing but his jersey that barely reached midthigh. And she looked every bit as tantalizing as she had in her dress.

Gervais's eyes traced up, taking in her toned calves, the slope of her waist. The way her breasts pushed on the fabric. That wild hair of hers… She was well covered, but he couldn't help feeling the possessive need to wrap a blanket around her to shield her from his brother's gaze.

"I heard noise and realized there was someone wandering around." She drifted down a step, gesturing toward a shadowed corner of the hallway outside the den, where Gervais's grandfather stood. "I believe this is your grandfather?"

Gramps must have been wandering around again. Leon Reynaud was getting more restless with the years, and forgetful, too. But it was Erika who concerned him most right now. Her face was emotionless, yet there was a trace of unease in her voice. Had she overheard something in their conversation in the den?

Gramps Leon shook a gnarled finger at them. "Somebody's having a baby?" He shook his head. "Your father never could keep his pants zipped."

A wave of guilt crashed against him. For years he had tried to avoid any comparisons between himself and his father. Purposely setting himself on a very different path.

His father had been largely absent throughout his childhood and teen years. Theo Reynaud was a woman chaser. Neglectful of his duties to his children, his wife and the family's business.

Gervais would make damn sure he'd do better for his child. Even if Erika wasn't on board. Yet. He'd be an active presence in his future child's life. Everything his father failed to be.

Dempsey moved toward their grandfather, face slightly flushed. He stood and clapped Leon on the shoulder. "Dad's not expecting another child, *Grandpère*."

"Oh." Leon scratched his sparse hair that was standing up on end. "I get confused sometimes. I must have misunderstood."

Dempsey looked back at Gervais, expression mirroring the same relief Gervais felt. Crisis avoided.

His brother steered Gramps toward the door. "I'll walk with you to your room, Gramps." He gave Erika a nod as they passed her, though his focus remained on Leon. "I programmed some new music into your sound system. Some of those old Cajun tunes you like."

"Thank you, boy, thank you very much." They disappeared down the hall. Leaving Gervais alone with Erika.

Her arms crossed as she met his gaze. Unflinching bright blue eyes.

"You look much better in that jersey than anyone on the team ever did." God, she was crazy sexy.

"Whose jersey is this?" She traced the number with one finger, tempting him to do the same. "Whose number?"

He swallowed hard, a lump in his throat. "It's a retired number, one that had been reserved for me if I joined the team. I didn't." He shook off past regrets abruptly. He'd never played for the team, so he'd bought it, instead. "So shall I escort you back to you room?"

He couldn't keep the suggestive tone from his voice. Didn't want to.

She tipped her haughty-princess chin. "I think not. I can find my own way back."

That might be true enough. But they weren't done by a long shot. He wouldn't rest until the day came when he peeled that jersey from her beautiful body.

Four

She was really doing it. Spending two weeks with Gervais in his mansion on the shores of Lake Pontchartrain. She'd slept in his house and now that her luggage had been sent over from the hotel, she had more than a jersey to wear. She tugged at the hem, the fabric surprisingly soft to the touch, the number cool against the tips of her breasts.

This was actually happening. Last night had been more than just an overnight fluke. True to his word, Gervais hadn't been pushy about joining her here. But she felt his presence all the same.

And she was here to stay. A flutter of nerves traced down her spine as she fully opened the pocket doors to get a better look at the guest suite. She crossed the threshold from the bedroom to the sitting room, clothes in hand.

But she paused, toes sinking into the rich texture of the red Oriental rug. The way the light poured through the window in the sitting room drew her eye. Stepping toward the window, she took a moment to drink in the twinkled blue of Lake Pontchartrain.

The morning sun warmed her cheeks, sparking prisms across the room as it hit the Tiffany lamps. Glancing at her reflection in the gilded-gold mirror that was leaning on the mantel of the fireplace, she tucked a strand of hair behind her ear.

Mind wandering back, as it had a habit of doing lately, to Gervais. To the way his eyes lingered on her. And how that still ignited something in her...

But it was so much more complicated than that. She pushed the thought away, moving past the cream-colored chaise longue and opening the cherrywood armoire. As if settling her belongings in drawers gave her some semblance of normalcy. A girl could try, after all.

Her hand went to her stomach, to the barely perceptible curve of her stomach. A slight thickening to her waist. Her body was beginning to change. Her breasts were swollen and sensitive.

And her emotions were in a turmoil.

That unsettled her most of all. She was used to being seen as a focused academic, a military professional. Now she was adrift. Between jobs. Pregnant by a man she barely knew and with precious little time to settle her life before her family and the world knew of her pregnancy. She had a spot reserved for her in a graduate nursing program this fall, and she wanted to take coursework right up until her due date. But then what?

A knock on the door pulled her back to the present. She opened the paneled door and found a lovely, slender woman, wearing a pencil-thin skirt and silky blouse, tons of caramel-colored hair neatly pinned up. A large, pink-lipstick smile revealed brilliant white teeth.

She extended her hand. "Hello, I'm Adelaide Thibodeaux. Personal assistant to Dempsey Reynaud—the Hurricanes' coach. Gervais asked me to check in on you. I just wanted to make sure, do you have everything you need?"

Erika nodded. "Thank you. That is very kind of you to look in on me."

"I've been a friend of Dempsey's since childhood. I am happy to help the family." She wore sky-high pumps that would have turned Erika into a giantess—exactly the kind that she enjoyed wearing when she wasn't pregnant and less sure-footed.

"Did you have my things sent over?"

Adelaide's brow furrowed, concern touching the corners of her mouth. "Yes, did we miss anything?"

"Everything is perfect, thank you," she said, gesturing to the room behind her. "The home is lovely and comfortable, and I appreciate having my personal belongings sent over."

"We want you to enjoy your stay here in the States. It will be a wonderful publicity boon for the team to have royalty attending our games."

Erika winced. The last thing she wanted was more

attention from the media. Especially before she knew how she was going to handle the next few months.

Adelaide twisted her hands together, silver bracelets glinting in the sunlight. "Did I say something wrong?"

"Of course not. It is just that I am not a fan of football, or competitive sports of any kind." It was a half-truth. Certainly, no matter how she tried, she just didn't understand the attraction of football. But she couldn't tell Adelaide the real reason she didn't want to be a publicity ploy.

"And yet clearly you're quite fit. You must work out."

"I was in the military until recently, and I do enjoy running and yoga, but I have to confess, team sports have never held any appeal for me."

"No?" Adelaide frowned. "Then I am not sure I understand why you are here— Pardon me. I shouldn't have asked. It's not my business."

Erika searched for a simple answer. "Gervais and I enjoyed meeting each other in England." Understatement. "And since there is a conference in the area I plan to attend, I decided to visit." Okay, the conference was a lie, but one she could live with for now.

"Of course." Understanding lit her gaze, as if she was not surprised that Gervais would inspire a flight halfway across the world. "If you need anything, please don't hesitate to ask."

"Thank you. I appreciate your checking on me. But I am independent." She had always been independent, unafraid of challenges.

"I wasn't sure of the protocol for visiting royalty," Adelaide said, her voice curling into a question of sorts.

As if a princess couldn't fend for herself. "You are a princess."

"In name only, and even so, I am the fifth daughter."

"You're humble."

"I have been called many things, but not that. I am simply...practical."

Pink lips slipped back up into a smile. "Well, welcome to New Orleans. I look forward to getting to know you better."

"As do I." She had a feeling she was going to get to know everyone exceptionally well. Erika's thoughts drifted back to Gervais. She certainly wanted to get to know him better.

Adelaide started to leave, then turned back. "It might help you on game days if you think of football as a jousting field for men. You were in the military and come from a country famous for female warriors. Sure, I'm mixing time frames here with Vikings and medieval jousters, but still, if you see the game in the light of a joust or warrior competition, perhaps you may find yourself enjoying the event."

The door closed quietly behind her.

A joust? She'd never considered football and jousting. Maybe...maybe she'd give that a shot.

Her gaze floated back to the window, back to Lake Pontchartrain. It stretched before her like an exotic promise. Reminded her she was in a place that she didn't know. And it might be in her best interest to find any way into this world.

To make the most of these days here, to learn more

about the father of her child, she would need to experience his world.

And that meant grabbing a front-row seat.

Yet even as she plucked out a change of clothes, she couldn't help wondering... Had Adelaide Thibodeaux welcomed many other women into this home on Gervais's behalf?

Today was quite the production. Gervais watched the bustle of people filling the owners' suite at Zephyr Stadium for a preseason game day. Tickets for special viewing in the owners' box were sold at a premium price to raise money for a local charter school, so there were more guests than usual in the large luxury suite that normally accommodated family and friends.

His sister-in-law Fiona Harper-Reynaud was a renowned local philanthropist, and her quarterback husband was the golden boy of New Orleans, which added allure to her fund-raising invitation. Henri—beloved by fans as the Bayou Bomber—was the face of their franchise and worth every cent of his expensive contract. He was a playmaker with the drive and poise necessary to make it in the league's most closely dissected position.

The fact that female fans loved him was a bonus, even though it must be tough for Fiona sometimes. But she seemed to take it in stride, leveraging his popularity for worthy causes. Today her philanthropic guests sat casually on the dark leather chairs that lined the glass of the owners' suite. Half-eaten dishes with bottles of craft beer peppered the table in front of them as the clock ticked down the end of the second quarter that saw the Hurricanes up by three points.

Yet Gervais's eyes sought only one person. Erika.

He'd been busy greeting guests and overseeing some last-minute game-day business earlier, so he hadn't gotten to spend any time with her yet. She was tucked away, in a leather sofa by the bar, sipping a glass of sparkling water with lemon, wearing a silky, fitted turquoise dress that brushed her knees and caressed her curves with understated sex appeal. He knew full well where those enhanced curves came from.

From carrying his baby inside her.

She scrunched her toes in her heeled sandals, reaching down to press her thumb along the arch of her foot. The viewing box was cool—downright chilly. But was the New Orleans heat bothering her? The climate was a far cry from where she lived. He wanted to help her feel more comfortable, to love his home city as much as he did so they wouldn't be forced into some globe-hopping parenting situation. He wished they could have had a private breakfast to talk, but he'd been called away to the game. Thank goodness Adelaide had offered to check on her personally. Dempsey's assistant and longtime friend remained the one good thing that had come from Dempsey's early years spent living a hardscrabble life before their father had found him.

Adelaide had texted Gervais this morning, assuring him that Erika had everything she needed.

Now he watched Erika eyeing the food the servers carried. Caviar nachos and truffles pizza. Delicious delicacies, but she declined the offerings whenever the waitstaff stopped in front of her. Though she certainly looked hungry.

"Is the food not to your liking?" He stepped toward her, smoothing his tie and wondering if he should look into the foods native to her homeland. "We ordered a special menu for the event today, but we can have anything brought in."

Nearby, a group of women cheered as Henri connected with one of the rookie receivers running a slant route down on the field. No doubt, it would be one of Henri's last big plays of the game, since they needed to test the depth of the quarterback position with some of the backup talent.

Erika stood, moving closer to him, the scent of magnolia pulling his focus away from the game and slipping under his guard, making him recall their weekend together. Making him remember the view of her long legs bared just last night in a jersey that had covered her only to midthigh. He'd barely slept after that mouthwatering visual.

"Gervais, this is all incredible and definitely far more elaborate than I would have expected at a football game. Thank you."

Her response had been polite, but he could see something tugging at her. So he pressed, gently, "But..."

She took a few steps toward the glass, gesturing to the seats below, where fans were starting to crowd the aisles as halftime neared. "Honestly? My mouth is watering for one of those smothered hot dogs I see the vendors selling. With mustard and onions."

"You want a chili dog?" He couldn't hide a grin.

Right from the start she'd charmed him with the unexpected. She was a princess in the military. A sexy rebel. And despite all the imported fare weighing down the servers' trays, she wanted a chili dog.

"If it is not too much trouble, of course." She frowned. "I did not think to bring my wallet."

"It's no trouble." He wouldn't mind stepping out of the temperature-controlled suite into the excited crowd. How long had it been since he'd ventured out from behind the tinted-glass windows during a game? It had been too long.

He leaned to whisper in her ear, hand bracing her on the small of her back. "Pregnancy craving?"

She blinked quickly, her breath quickening under his touch. "I believe so. Mornings are difficult with nausea, but then I am starving for the rest of the day. Today has been difficult, with all the travel yesterday and jet lag."

"Then I will personally secure an order for you." He smiled. "I have to say I wouldn't mind having one for myself." He touched her shoulder lightly, aching to keep his hands on her. "I'll be right back."

Erika moved closer to the glass and took a seat, looking down into the field, her eyes alert.

There was no fanfare in yoga or running, so Erika looked on at the halftime show with a sense of wonder. LSU's band performed in tandem with a pop star local to the area, sending the fans into wild cheers as a laser light show sliced the air around her. The scents of fog and smoke wafted through the luxury suite's vents, teasing her oversensitive nose.

This box was quite different from the Wembley luxury suite where she'd met Gervais. The Reynaud private domain was decorated with family memorabilia, team awards and lots of video monitors for comfortable viewing in the back of the box right near the bar.

But she enjoyed her front-row seat, watching intently. So this really did have a form of old-world pageantry mixed with a dash of medieval jousting. Her military training made her able to pick out various formations on the field below, the two teams forming and re-forming their lines to try to outwit one another. Viewing the game this way had been a revelation—and definitely not as boring as she'd once thought. And she couldn't wait to taste one of the chili dogs once Gervais returned.

Fiona Harper-Reynaud, the quarterback's wife and Gervais's sister-in-law, if Erika remembered correctly, tilted her head to the side. "Princess Erika, you look pensive."

"I have been thinking about the game, trying to understand more about what I've seen so far, since I am actually quite a neophyte about the rules. My sisters and I were not exposed much to team sports."

A few of the other women laughed softly into their cocktail napkins, eyeing Erika.

Fiona smiled, crossing her elegant legs at the ankles. "What an interesting choice, then, to spend time with Gervais when you're not a football enthusiast."

"I am learning to look at the game in a new light." She would read more about it now that she knew her child would be a part of this world.

She couldn't allow her son or daughter to be unprepared for their future, and that meant football. She could not sit in this box overflowing with Reynauds and fail to realize how deeply entrenched they were in this sport.

"How so?" Fiona traced a finger on her wineglass, her diamond wedding ring glinting in the light from a chrome pendant lamp.

Erika pointed down to the field, where the head coach and his team were now returning to the sidelines. "Adelaide Thibodeaux suggested I think of this as a ritual as old as time, like an ancient battle or a medieval jousting field. The imagery is working for me."

"Hmm." Fiona lifted one finely arched eyebrow. "That's quite a sexy image. And fitting. Armor versus shoulder pads. It works. I'll spin that for a future fund-raiser."

"That sounds intriguing." And it did. If it helped Erika to appreciate the game more, it could certainly appeal to someone else.

"Perhaps I should rethink the menu, too, as I may have overdone things with this event." She picked up a nacho and investigated it.

"The food is amazing. Quite a lovely, fun spread," Erika offered, smiling at her.

"But you want a chili dog—or so I overheard you say."

"I hope you did not take offense, as I certainly did not mean any." Erika fought the urge to panic. She bit down her nerves—and a wave of nausea. This was easily explainable. "I am in America. I simply want to experience American foods served at a regular football game."

A server walked by with another fragrant tray of caviar nachos—too fragrant. She pressed her hand to her stomach as another wave of indigestion struck, cramping her stomach.

Fiona's eyebrows rose but she stayed silent for a moment. "If you need anything, anything at all, please don't hesitate to ask."

Did Fiona know somehow, even though she didn't have children? There seemed to be an understanding—and a sadness in her eyes.

For a brief, fleeting moment, she wondered if Fiona had ever found herself in Erika's situation. Not the pregnant-with-a-handsome-stranger situation, but the other one. The one where she was an outsider who shouldered too much responsibility sometimes.

The weight of that thought bore down on her, making her stomach even more queasy. She fought back the urge, praying she could get to her feet and to the ladies' room before she embarrassed herself.

Erika bit her lip, shooting to her feet, only to find the ground swaying underneath her. Not a good sign at all, but if she could just grab the back of her seat for a moment to steady herself… There. The world righted in front of her and she eyed the door, determined. "I will be right back. I need to excuse myself."

And the second she took that first step, the ground rocked all the harder under her, and she slumped into unconsciousness.

Five

Gervais pushed through the crowds, eyes set on the chili dog vendor. As he weaved in and out, he saw recognition zip through their eyes.

The media had done a nice job planting his image in the minds of the fans even though he would have preferred a quieter role, leaving the fame to the players. But the family name also sold tickets and brought fans to their television screens, so he played along because he, too, loved the game and would do whatever was needed for the Hurricanes.

Many of the fans smiled at him, nudged a companion and pointed at Gervais. He felt a little as if he was in a dog-and-pony show. And while part of him wouldn't mind pausing to speak to a few fans and act as an ambassador for the team, he really just wanted to get Erika that chili dog. Pronto.

So he flashed a smile as he continued, stopping in front of the food vendor, the smell of nacho cheese and cayenne peppers sizzling under his nose. Of all the things Erika could have asked for, he was strangely intrigued by this request. It was the most un-princess-like food in the whole sports arena. He loved that.

Gervais's phone vibrated. He juggled the two chili dogs to one hand as he fished out his cell while taking the stadium steps two at a time. He glanced at the screen and saw his sister-in-law's name. Frowning, he thumbed the on button.

"Yes, Fiona?"

"Gervais—" Fiona's normally calm voice trembled "—Erika passed out. We can't get her to wake up. I don't know—"

"I'm on my way." Panic lanced his gut.

His hand clenched around the hot dogs until a little chili oozed down his fingers as he raced up the steps faster, sprinted around a corner, then through a private entrance to the hall leading to the owners' viewing box.

A circle of people stood around a black leather sofa, blocking his view. A cold knot settled in his stomach. He set the food on the buffet table and shouldered through the crowd.

"Erika? Erika," he barked, forgetting all about formalities. He dropped to his knees beside the sofa where she lay unconscious. Too pale. Too still.

He took her hand in his, glancing back over his

shoulder. "Has anyone called a doctor? Get the team doctor. Now."

Fiona nodded. "I called him right after I called you."

He brushed his hand over Erika's forehead, her steady pulse throbbing along her neck a reassuring sign. But still, she wasn't coming around. There were so many complications that could come with pregnancy. His family had learned that tragic reality too well from his sister-in-law's multiple miscarriages.

Which made him wince all the more when he needed to lean in and privately tell Fiona, "Call the doctor back and tell him to hurry—because Erika's pregnant."

Erika pushed through layers of fog to find a group of faces staring down at her. Some closer than others.

A man with a stethoscope pressing against her neckline while he took her pulse must be a doctor.

And of course she should have known that Gervais would be near. He sat on the arm of the sofa at her feet, watching her intently, his body a barrier between her and the others in the room staring at her with undisguised interest.

Curiosity.

Whispering.

Oh, God. Somehow, they knew about the baby and she hadn't even told her parents yet.

"Gervais, do you think we could have some privacy?"

He looked around, started, as if he hadn't even realized the others were still there. "Oh, right, I'll—"

Fiona stepped up. "I've got this. You focus on Erika."

She extended her arms, gesturing toward the door. "Let's move to the other side of the box and give the princess some air..."

Her voice faded as she ushered the other guests farther away, leaving behind a bubble of privacy.

She elbowed up, then pressed a hand to her woozy head. "Doctor, what's going on?"

The physician wearing a polo shirt with the team's logo on the pocket said, "Gervais here tells me you're pregnant. Would you like him to give us some privacy while we talk?"

She didn't even hesitate with her answer. "He can stay. He has a right to know what is going on with the baby."

The doctor nodded, his eyes steady and guarded. "How far along are you?"

"Two and a half months."

"And you've been to a doctor?"

"I have, back in my homeland."

"Well, your pulse appears normal, as do your other vital signs, but you stayed unconscious for a solid fifteen minutes. I would suggest you see a local physician."

Gervais shot to his feet. "I'll take her straightaway."

Erika sat up, the world steadier now. "But you will miss the rest of the game."

"Your health is more important. We'll take the private elevator down and slip out the back." He shifted his attention to the physician. "Doc, can you send up a wheelchair?"

She swung her feet to the ground. "I can walk. I am not an invalid. I simply passed out. It happens to pregnant women."

"Pregnant women who don't eat," Gervais groused, sliding an arm around her waist for support. "You should take care of yourself."

Even as she heard the grouchiness in his voice, she saw the concern in his eyes, the fear. She wanted to soothe the furrowed lines on his forehead but knew he wouldn't welcome the gesture, especially not right now.

So she opted to lighten the mood instead. Heaven knew she could use some levity after the stress she had been under. And how strange to realize that in spite of being terrified, she felt safer now with Gervais present.

She looked up at him and forced a shaky smile. "Don't forget my chili dog."

Gervais paced the emergency room. The hum of the lights above provided a rhythm to his pacing. He tried to focus on what he could control.

Which was absolutely nothing at this point. Instead of being in the know, he was completely in the dark. He couldn't start planning, something he liked to do.

Sitting still had never been his strong suit. Gervais wanted to be in the midst of the action, not hanging on the sidelines. That was how he'd been as a football player, how he dealt with his family. Always engaged. Always on.

But now? No one would tell him anything. He wasn't a family member. Not technically, even though that was his unborn child.

God, he hated feeling helpless. Most of all he hated feeling cut off from his family. His child.

What the hell was taking the doctor so long?

Sure, the place was packed with weekend traffic. To his left was a boy with what appeared to be a broken arm and a cracked tooth. His sister, a petite blonde thing, wrinkled her nose in disgust as he shoved his arm in her face.

The man on his right elevated a very swollen ankle. He was in the ER alone, sitting in silence, hands rough with calluses.

Gervais could hear snippets of the conversation going on in the far corner of the room. A young mom cooed over her baby, holding tight to her husband's hand. They were probably first-time parents. Nervous as hell. But they were tackling the problem together. As he wanted to with Erika, but the lack of information was killing him.

The whole ride over, Erika had been woozy and nauseated. He tried to tell himself that fainting wasn't a big deal. But he wasn't having much luck calming down his worries.

The possibilities of what could be wrong played over and over again in his head. He hated this feeling. Helplessness. It did not sit well with him.

A creak from the door called his attention back to the present moment. Snapping his focus back to the ER. And to the two men heading for him. His brothers Henri and Dempsey. Henri's sweat-stained face was grave as he caught Gervais's eye. Hell, he knew time had passed. But that much? And he hadn't even watched the rest of the game on the waiting room television.

He charged over to his brothers.

Henri hauled him in hard and fast for a hug, slapping him on the back. Smelled of Gatorade. Heavily.

The leftover jug must have been poured over his head, signifying victory. "What's the news?"

"I'm still waiting to hear from the docs." He guided both of his brothers over to the privacy of a corner by a fat fake topiary tree. "We won?"

Dempsey didn't haul him in for a brotherly hug, but he thumped him on the back. They were brothers. Not as close as Henri and Gervais, but the bond was there. Solid. "Yes, by three points. Even though we sidelined most of our starters to test depth at various positions. Henri's backup did a credible job marching the offense downfield for one more TD in the closing minutes. But that's not what matters right now. We're here for you. Is everything okay?"

Gervais shrugged. "We don't know yet. Nobody's talking to me. I'm not tied to her in any legal way."

Dempsey's voice lowered till it was something barely audible. He looked squarely into his brother's eyes. "Do you plan to be there for your child?"

"Yes." Gervais didn't hesitate. "Absolutely."

Henri shifted his weight from foot to foot. The three Reynaud men stared at each other, no one daring to utter so much as a syllable for a few moments.

Dempsey nodded. "Good. You know what? I'm going to get coffee for us. Who knows how long we will be here. ER visits are never short."

"Great. Thanks," Henri said as Dempsey walked back toward the doors. "Is she considering giving the baby up for adoption?"

"I didn't bring that up." Truth be told, he hadn't even

thought of that as a real option. It was his child. He wanted to provide for his child.

"Did she?" Henri crossed his arms, voice lowered so only they could hear each other.

"No. I'm not even sure how the royalty part plays into this." God, what if his power, prestige, money, wasn't worth jack and she took his child away altogether? "She discussed shared parenting."

Henri shrugged. An attempt at nonchalance that fell flat. "I just want you to know that if things change, Fiona and I are willing to raise the baby as our own."

Gervais looked over at his brother quickly, thinking of all the miscarriages his brother and sister-in-law had been through, the strain that had put on their marriage. This baby news had to be hitting his normally happy-go-lucky brother hard. "Thank you, my brother. That means a lot to me. But this is my child. Not some mistake. Not just a responsibility. My child."

Henri nodded and hooked an arm around his brother's shoulders. "I look forward to meeting my niece or nephew. Congratulations."

"Thank you." Gervais noticed how Henri's face became blank. Distant. "Are you and Fiona okay?"

"Sure, we're fine," Henri replied a bit too quickly.

"We need your total commitment to the season. If you're having any problems, you can come to me." And he meant it. He wanted to be there for his brother. For his whole family. They meant everything to him.

Henri shook his head, looking his brother in the eyes. Offering a smile that refused to light his cheeks or touch his eyes. "No problem."

Gervais shook his head, raising an eyebrow at him. "You never were a good liar."

Wasn't that the truth? When they were kids, Henri always cracked under pressure. His eyes would widen when he fibbed.

"No problems that will distract me from the game. Now stop being the owner of the team and let's be brothers."

Gervais was about to protest, but suddenly the ER waiting room was alive with movement. Dempsey strode back over to them, cups of coffee on a tray. A damn fine balancing act going on.

And following closely on his heels was a doctor. The same old, frazzle-haired doctor that had been treating Erika. His gut knotted.

The doctor cleared his throat. "Mr. Reynaud—Gervais Reynaud," he clarified. The whole town knew the Reynauds, so no doubt the doctor recognized them. "Ms. Mitras is asking for you."

All he could do was nod. Deep in his chest, his heart thudded. Afraid. He was afraid of what was wrong with Erika and his child.

The doctor opened a thick pinewood door to a small exam room and gestured for Gervais to enter.

In the center of the room, Erika was hooked up to a smattering of machines. Lights flashed from various pieces of equipment. Her blond hair was tied back into a topknot, exposing the angles of her face. Somehow making her seem impossibly beautiful despite the presence of the machines.

Within moments he was at her side. He wanted to

show her he was here. He was committed to their child and would not abandon her. Stroking her hand, he knelt beside her. "You're okay? The baby's okay?"

Her face was pale, but she smiled, her eyes serene. "We are fine. Absolutely fine."

"This child is important to me. You are important to me." She was damn important. He had to make her see that.

"Because I am the baby's mother." The words spilled from her mouth matter-of-factly. As if there was no other reason he'd be here right now.

"We had a connection before that."

A dramatic sigh loosed from her pink lips. "We had an affair."

"I called you afterward." She'd been imprinted on his brain. A woman he could not—would not—forget.

"You are a gentleman. I appreciate that. In fact, that was part of what drew me to do something so uncharacteristic. But it was only a weekend."

"A weekend with lasting consequences." A weekend that had turned him inside out. Given time, he could make her see that, too.

"More than we realized," she said with a shaky laugh.

"What do you mean?" Head cocking to the side, he tried to discern the cause of the uneasy laughter.

She gestured to the ultrasound machine next to her. "I am pregnant with twins."

Gervais tore his gaze from Erika, focusing on the screen. Sure enough, there were two little beans on the ultrasound. He and Erika were going to have twins.

Six

Exhausted, Erika relaxed back into the passenger seat of Gervais's luxury SUV. The leather seat had the smell of a woodsy cologne, a smell she distinctively recognized as Gervais. It was oddly comforting, a steadying moment in a day that had been anything but stable.

As the car pulled away from the hospital, she glanced out the window, craning to see the collection of Reynaud brothers who stood at the entrance. Her sisters would swoon over the attractive picture they presented, those powerful, broad-shouldered men. They had all come rushing to the hospital, filled with concerns. And likely, with questions.

But they had been polite in the lobby after her release. They didn't press for information—the conversation had been brief. They'd wanted to know if she was okay. And neither Gervais nor Erika had offered any information about twins. That was something that they still had to discuss together. Something she still hadn't processed.

But how should she broach this new development in an already emotionally charged day? How in the world could she bring up everything in her whirring mind? Her eyes remained fixed out of the car, even though the scene of the hospital had faded from vision, framed by wrought-iron fences and thick greenery. Now the vibrant pinks and yellows of the old French houses populated her view.

Glancing at an elaborate wood-carved balcony, she let out an emotional sigh. What had happened today had left her shaken. She'd never passed out like that before, never felt so disoriented in her life. She'd been blessed with good health, and she had pushed her physical endurance to the limit during her military training. Yet this pregnancy was only just beginning and it had already landed her flat on her back. But, thanks to Gervais's quick action, she and her children—*children*, plural, oh, God—were safe.

It was all that mattered. That her children were okay. The twins were fine. *Twins*. She turned the word over. Was it possible to love them both so much already, even though she'd just learned about them? And yet, she did. In spite of her nerves, in spite of not having a plan figured out. Sure, she was scared about the future, about having to deal with her family...but she was overwhelmed with a deep love for her children already.

She peered over at the man in the driver's seat beside her. Perhaps he felt her eyes on him, because soon Gervais's throat moved in a long swallow. "Twins?" he mused aloud. "Twins."

The simple utterance seemed to linger on his tongue and echo through the quiet interior of the luxury vehicle. Not that she could blame him for being overwhelmed by the news. There was a lot to take in. Still, even under Gervais's audible processing of the fact that he was about to be a father not to one but two children, she could hear a glow of pride in his tone. A protectiveness that caught her attention.

Of course, the raw, masculine appeal of his muscular body taking up too much space beside her might have something to do with how thoroughly he held her notice. How easy it would be to simply lean closer. Lean on him. She could almost imagine the feel of his suit jacket beneath her cheek if she laid her head on his shoulder and curled up against his chest.

She forced herself to focus on the conversation they needed to have instead. On their children.

"Yes, there are two in there. I even heard the heartbeats." Her heart fluttered with joy as she remembered the delicate beating of her—*their*—children. The sound had made her spring to life in a way she didn't know was possible. She felt bad he'd missed that. They were his children, too, and he'd deserved to have that same feeling of awe. Looking at him sidelong, she said cautiously, "Next time you can come with me if you wish."

"I wish." There was no mistaking the sound of his commitment.

"Then you should be there." She couldn't hold back

the smile swelling inside her as she drank in his eyes alight with honest excitement. "It is too early to distinguish the sex, you know."

He shrugged, clearly unconcerned. "That doesn't matter."

"It did in my family." It came out in a whisper, something almost like a secret. And each word hurt.

He glanced over at her briefly before turning his eyes back to the road as they drove west toward his home. "Be clearer for me."

She smoothed the skirt of her dress, wrinkled beyond recognition after being crumpled into a hospital bag during her exam. If only she could smooth over her past as easily. This was knowledge she carried every day. Knowledge that ate at her and had her entire lifetime. "A line of girls was always cause for concern in my home. The monarchy is technically inactive, but even so there is no provision for a female ruler. There are no male heirs. I am afraid…"

"Oh, no. No way in hell is anyone taking my children away." His brow furrowed, anger simmering in his eyes, the joyous warmth gone.

"Our children. These are our children." She felt all the same protective instincts he did, and she felt them with a mother's fierce love.

"And we can't afford to forget for even a moment how important it is that we work together for the children. If there's a chance we can have more than a bicoastal parenting relationship, don't you think it's worth figuring that out as soon as possible?" The look he gave her was pointed. Sharp.

But Erika wasn't about to back down. She hadn't decided how to handle whatever was between them. And that meant she had to think a bit more. She wouldn't be rash and impulsive. One of them had to think through their actions.

"I will let you know when I schedule my doctor visit. I will want to visit the doctor again before returning home."

He scowled. "Can we not talk about you leaving? We're still settling details."

"You know I do not live here." New Orleans was lovely, with its vibrant history, loud colors and live music that seemed to drift up from every street corner. But it was not home. Not that she really knew where home was these days...

"One day at a time. And today we are dealing with a big change, the reality of two children. I know that happens. I just never expected..." His voice trailed, his words ebbing with emotion.

"I have twin sisters." She had always envied them their closeness, like having a built-in best friend from birth. "Twins—how do you say?—walk in my family."

"Run in your family. Okay."

She blinked at him, filing away the turn of English phrasing that brought a funny image to her mind of twins sprinting through her family tree. This was all happening so fast, she'd never stopped to consider the possibility of twins. There was so much to figure out still. "My oldest sister also has twin girls. I should have considered this possibility but I have been so overwhelmed since I realized I was expecting."

"Thank you for coming to tell me so soon." He covered her hand on the center console. "I appreciate that you didn't delay."

"You are the father. You deserve to know that." Erika lifted her chin up, tilting her head to the side to get a better look at him. He was a good man. She knew that much.

"We're going to make this work." He lifted her hand and kissed the back, then the inside of her wrist over her rapidly beating pulse.

The press of his mouth to her skin was warm and arousing, stirring memories of their weekend together. The air crackled between them now as it had then. Her emotions were already in turmoil after the scare at the game. She ached to move closer, to feel his arms around her. To have those lips on her body again. Everywhere. Arousing her to such heights her head spun at the thought. How quickly she could simply lose herself in what he could make her feel.

But doing so would take away any chance of objectivity. And now she had twice the reason to tread carefully into the future.

The silver stain of moonlight washed over the lake. The water was restless. Frothy. Uneasy. A lot like the restlessness inside Gervais. But he had to pull it together in order to make this phone call.

He thumbed through his phone, finding his father in his contact list. How long had it been since they'd spoken? Months, no doubt. The bright screen blared at him.

He knew he had to call him about Erika's pregnancy.

Theo was in Paris for the week with his latest girlfriend. Which was, in some ways, fortunate. This way, Gervais had gotten to talk to Erika privately before his father had a chance at royally screwing the dynamic up.

But it also meant he had to make this call. Which was something he never looked forward to doing. Years of neglect and dysfunction had their way of clinging to their current relationship. Another lesson of how not to treat children brought to you by Theo Reynaud. Dear old dad loved football and his family, but not as much as romancing women.

Before he could think better of it, Gervais pressed Send on the screen. Feeling the pinch of nerves, he poured himself a glass of bourbon from the pool-deck bar, staring at where a few kids messed around with a stand-up paddleboard. Beyond them, the lights of gambling boats winked in the distance and even farther behind those he could see the bridge that spanned the lake.

Gervais wasn't sure why he felt the need to talk to his dad other than doing him the courtesy of making sure he didn't hear via the grapevine. Discretion wasn't Theo's strong suit. But if Gervais spun the news just right, maybe he could keep a lid on it a bit longer. Erika would appreciate that.

And tonight making Erika relaxed and happy felt like the first priority on a quickly shifting list in his life. But knowing that she carried his children had brought things into sharp focus for him today.

"Hello, son." His father's graveled voice shot through the receiver, yanking him from his thoughts.

Might as well cut to the chase.

"Dad, you're going to be a grandfather."

"About damn time. Damn shame Henri is still carrying a grudge and didn't tell me himself. The divorce was a long time ago."

In the background of the call, the sound of violin music and muted chatter combined with the clink of glasses. The sounds of a bar scene.

Gervais ignored the mention of his parents' dysfunctional marriage. "Henri and Fiona aren't expecting. I'm the one about to make you a gramps."

News about the twins could wait. One step at a time. He was still reeling from that news himself.

"With who? You didn't knock up some groupie looking for a big payoff from the family?" His voice crackled through the phone from across the Atlantic.

"Dad, that's your gig. Not mine." And just like that, he was on the defensive. Gervais was not his father. He would never be like his father. And the fact that his father thought he had that in his nature sent him reeling.

"No need to be disrespectful." Bells chimed in the background of the call, an unmistakable sound of a slot machine in payoff mode.

So much for keeping the subject of his parents' divorce off the table. "You destroyed your marriage with your affairs. You ignored your own sons for years. I lost respect for you a long time ago."

"Then why are you here now telling me about this baby?"

Gervais closed his eyes, blotting out the lights from the distant boats on the lake, listening to the sound of the water. With his spare hand, he pressed on his eyes, inhaling deeply. Exhaling hard, he opened his eyes, resolve renewed.

"Because this news is going to go viral soon and I want to make sure you understand I will not tolerate any inappropriate or hurtful comments to the mother of my child." That was something he absolutely would not allow. From anyone. Least of all his father. He would protect Erika from that.

"Understood. And who might this woman be?" An air of interest infused his words.

"Erika Mitras." He sat down, inspecting his ice cubes as he waited for his father to make some sort of off-color remark.

"Mitras? From that royal family full of girls? Well, hell, son. It's tough to find someone not out for our money, but kudos to you. You found a woman who doesn't need a damn thing from you."

The words cut him, even though, for once, his father hadn't meant any harm by them. Erika had said as much about not needing Gervais's help. But he wanted to be there for his children. For her. Seeing those two tiny lives on that monitor today had blown him away.

And knowing that Erika was already taxed from travel and devoting her beautiful body to nurture those children made him want to slay dragons for her. Or, at the very least, put a roof over her head and see to her every need.

"Thanks. That wasn't forefront in my mind at the time."

"When you were in England, I assume?"

"Not your business."

"You always were a mouthy bastard." Smug words from the other end of the receiver.

"Just like my old man." He downed half of his glass of bourbon. "Be nice."

"The team's winning. That always puts me in a good mood."

"Nice to know you care." Not that his father owned a cent of this team. The Hurricanes belonged to Gervais and Gervais alone.

"Congratulations, Papa. Name the little one after me and I'll give—"

"Dad, stop. No need to try so hard to be an ass."

"I'm not trying. Good night, son. Congrats."

The line went dead. So much for father-son bonding time.

Gervais tossed his cell phone on a lounge chair and tipped back the rest of the ten-year-old bourbon, savoring the honey-and-spice finish in an effort to dispel the sour feel left by the phone call. He didn't know what he'd expected from his old man. That he would magically change into...what? A real father? Some kind of reassurance that maybe, just maybe, he himself could be a good father to not just one but two babies?

Foolishness, that. Theo remained as selfish as they came.

Regardless, though, he knew one thing for certain. He was not going to ditch his responsibility the way his father had.

Tucked in the big guest bed in Gervais's house, Erika snuggled deeper beneath the lightweight comforter, hugging the pillow closer as sleep tugged her further under. She was exhausted after the hospital visit and the strain of pregnancy that seemed to drain all her physical resources. She would feel better after she rested, and she couldn't deny taking extra pleasure at sleeping under the same roof as Gervais.

During her waking hours, she did all in her power to keep the strong attraction at bay so she could make smart decisions about her future. Her children's future. But just now, with sleep pulling her under, and her body so perfectly comfortable, she couldn't resist the lure of thinking about Gervais. His touch. His taste…

Her memories and dreams mingling, filling her mind and drugging her senses with seductive images…

The press of Gervais's lips on hers sparked awareness deep in Erika's stomach. He pulled back from the passionate kiss, and she surprised herself when she was disappointed. She wanted his lips on hers. And not just there. Everywhere.

But he led her toward the couch in his den.

His den?

A part of her brain realized this was not a memory. She was in Gervais's house. In Louisiana. She could smell the scent of the lake mingling with the woodsy spice of his aftershave as he drew her down to the leather couch, tossing aside a football before he landed on the cushion while she melted into his lap. And it felt right. Natural. As if she belonged here with him.

Her heart slugged hard in her chest, the strength and warmth of his so incredible she could stay for hours. Longer. She wanted this. Wanted him. She'd never felt so alive as during those days when she'd been in his bed, and she couldn't wait to feel that spark inside her again. The hitch in her breath. The pleasure of sharp orgasms undulating through her body, again and again.

Now he tilted her chin up, searched her eyes for something. A mingle of nerves, anticipation and desire thumped in her chest as he kissed her forehead. Her lips. Her neck. She trembled as he touched her, her whole body poised for the fulfillment he could provide.

Her eyes closed, and the muted noise of a football game on a television behind them began to fade away until only the sound of their mingled breaths remained.

"Erika," he whispered in her ear before kissing her neck again. The heat of his breath on her skin made her toes curl.

"Mmm?" A half question stuck on her lips.

"Stay here with me." His request was spoken in clips between kisses, then a nip on her earlobe.

His hands tugged at the heavy jeweled collar around her neck. He removed it from her, the metal crown charms clanking against the coffee table. How good it felt to set that weight aside.

"Let me take care of you. Of them." Wandering hands found her shoulders, slipped underneath the thin straps of her dress. She burst to life, pressing into him with a new urgency. A want and need so unfamiliar to her.

As he kissed her, he rocked her back and forth. The scent of earthy cologne seemed to grow stronger. Demanded more of her attention...

"Erika?" a deep voice called, a man's voice.

Gervais.

Opening her eyes, she had a moment of panic. This was not the hotel room.

As the suite came into focus, she realized where—and when—she was. This was Gervais's house, his guest bedroom. She wasn't in London, but rather in Louisiana. Still, the memory pounded at her mind and through her veins.

She wanted to go back there now. To her dreamworld in all its brilliant simplicity.

But Gervais himself stood in the doorway of the guest suite.

His square jaw flexed, the muscles in his body tensed, backlit from a glowing sconce in the hall.

"Erika?" He crossed the threshold, deeper into the room, his gaze intense as he studied her. "I heard you cry out. I was worried. Are you okay? The babies?"

The mattress dipped as he sat beside her, stirring heated memories of her dream.

"I am fine. I was, um, just restless." The sensuality of her dream still filled her, making her all the more aware of his hip grazing hers through the lightweight blanket. The electricity between them was not waning. If anything, she felt the space between them grow even more charged. More aware.

"Restless," he repeated, eyes roving her so thoroughly she wondered what she looked like. Her hair teased along her bare shoulder, her silk nightdress suddenly feeling very insubstantial, even though the blanket covered her breasts.

Images from her dream flitted back into her mind,

and she bit her lip as her gaze moved down his face, to his hands reaching up to her exposed shoulders. Looking back at him through her eyelashes, she could tell he sensed the charged atmosphere, too. But his hands didn't move. Not as she'd expected—and wanted—them to. There was something else besides hunger in the way he held her gaze. Something that looked a bit like worry.

"Gervais, I truly am all right. But are *you* all right?"

He ran his hand through the hair on top of his head, eyes turning glossy and unfocused. "I called my dad tonight to tell him about the pregnancy. Not the twin part. Just...that he's going to be a grandfather. I didn't want him to hear it in the news."

She thought of how the day had gone so crazy so fast simply because she passed out. "I wish we could have told your family together."

"You didn't include me when you told your family."

She looked away, guilt stinging her. And didn't that cool the heat that had been singeing her all over?

"You've told your family, haven't you?" he asked, his eyes missing nothing.

"I will. Soon. I know I have to before it hits the news." She wanted to change the subject off her family. Fast. "What did your family have to say? Your brothers were quiet at the emergency room."

"My brothers are all about family. No one judges. We love babies."

Erika raised her eyebrows, unsure how to take the casual tone of what felt like a very serious conversation. She noticed he didn't include his father in that last part.

"That is all?" she asked, knowing she had no right

to quiz him when she hadn't shared much about her own family.

"That's it. Now we need to tell your parents before they find out."

"I realize that."

"I want to be with you, even if it's on the phone in a Skype session." His jaw flexed in a way she was beginning to recognize—a surefire sign of determination. He slid his arms around her and said, "I want to reassure them I plan to marry their daughter."

Seven

"You have forgotten we have *no* plans to get married. I have plans—other plans. Our plans are in flux."

Erika pulled out of Gervais's arms so fast he damn near fell off the bed. He wasn't sure why he'd raised the issue again, other than not wanting to be like his father, and certainly the timing of his proposal hadn't been the smoothest. But the least she could do was consider it, since they hadn't taken time to seriously discuss it that first night.

Time to change that now. He shifted on the bed so they were face-to-face. And promptly remembered how little she must be wearing under that blanket. A bare shoulder peeked above the fabric, calling his hands to rake the barrier down and away.

To slide between those covers with her.

"Why not even consider?" he ground out between clenched teeth, determined to stay on track with this talk. "We have babies on the way. Even if we have a civil ceremony and stay together for the children's first year." From the scowl on her beautiful face he could see he was only making this worse. "Erika?"

"I came here to tell you about being pregnant, see if you want to be an active father, and then make plans from there. I didn't come for a yearlong repeat of our impulsive weekend together."

He swallowed. Had his carnal thoughts been that obvious? No sense denying that he wanted her.

"And what would be so wrong with that?"

"I have a life in another country."

"You're out of the military now. So work here. You have more job flexibility than I do."

Red flushed into her cheeks, making her look more like a shield maiden and less like a delicate princess in need of saving. "You are serious?"

The more he thought about it, the more it felt right. A marriage of convenience for a couple of years. He stroked her hair back and tucked it behind her ear, the silky strands gliding along his fingers. "We have amazing chemistry. We have children on the way. You're already staying in my home—"

"For two weeks," she said, finality edging her voice.

"Why not longer? Things have changed now with the twins. Two babies at once would be a lot for anyone to care for."

He needed to be involved. A part of his children's lives.

"I have plans for this fall. A commitment to my career. You are thinking too far into the future." She shook her head, a toss of silvery-blond hair in the moonlight. "Please slow down."

She angled an elbow against a bolster pillow, reclining even as she remained seated. And damn, but he wanted to be the one she leaned against, the one who supported her incredible body through the upcoming months while she carried this burden for them.

"We don't have that option for long. And you yourself said you were concerned about the babies being boys and being caught up in the family monarchy as next in line. If they're born here and we're married here in the States..." He wasn't exactly sure what that would mean for the monarchy, but it certainly would slow things down. Give them time to become a family. And to figure out how everything would work together.

She clapped a hand over his mouth. "Stop. Please. I cannot make this kind of decision now."

The magnolia scent of her lotion caught him off guard. He breathed in the scent, enjoying the cool press of her skin on his lips. Would have said as much if he hadn't noticed the glimmer of tears in her eyes.

A raggedy breath before speaking. "Can we please think about our future rationally? When I am rested and more prepared?" Though she did her best to look past him, every inch a regal monarch in that moment, he could see the strain in her cheeks.

She'd had a helluva long day. Fainted. Found out she was pregnant with twins. And she still had not gotten her damn chili dog.

There was a lot going on.

He could cut her some slack, give her space to collect herself. It was no use pushing so hard while she was emotional. And she had every right to be. Hell, he'd been upset tonight, too, uncharacteristically irritated with his father.

So he would revise his approach until cooler heads prevailed. This tactic to get her to stay was not the right one. She'd dismissed it out of hand.

Who could blame her, though? He'd given her no real reason to stay. And, as much as he hated to admit it, Erika Mitras was a woman who did not need him for anything. She could afford the best care and doctors for her pregnancy the same as he could. She would have highly qualified help with day-to-day care in her homeland.

But what she hadn't realized yet was that they were so damn good together. There was something between them, a small spark that could be more. And they had the children to consider.

Rather than insist she stay, he'd convince her. Which meant she was in for some grade A romancing. That was something he could give her that she couldn't just find in a store.

He would win her the old-fashioned way. Because like hell if he was losing his children. Missing out on the lives of his offspring simply wasn't an option. He'd make sure of that.

The next evening Erika still could not make sense of what had happened the night before. But no matter which way she spun Gervais's actions in her bed last night, nothing made sense. She'd been so sure that he wanted her. That he felt that same sharp tug of attraction between them, but his decision to simply walk away and let her go to bed alone had left her surprised. Confused. Aching. Wanting.

He hadn't mentioned the baby issue at all the whole day, then he surprised her with this dinner date, a night out in the city they called the Big Easy.

Draping an arm along the white-painted wrought-iron railing of the patio, her hand kept time to the peppy jazz music playing. She hadn't realized her head nodded along to the trumpet until Gervais flashed her a smile.

Heat flushed her cheeks as she turned her attention away from the very attractive man in front of her. She pushed around the last bite of her shrimp and andouille sausage, a spicy blend of flavors she'd quizzed their waiter about at length. Every course of her meal had been delicious.

Attention snapping to the present, she caught a whiff of something that smelled a lot like baked chocolate and some kind of fruit. Maybe cherries, but she couldn't be sure. All she knew was that her senses were heightened lately.

As were her emotions.

What was Gervais up to with this perfect evening? Was he trying to charm her into changing her mind without discussing the logistical fact that he still moved too fast?

Setting her fork down, she inclined her head to the meal. "Dinner was lovely. Thank you."

His dark eyes slid over her. One forearm lay on the crisp white linen tablecloth, his tanned hand close to where hers rested. He made her breath catch, and she felt sure she was not the only woman in the vicinity who was affected. She liked that he didn't notice. That his gaze was only for her.

"I'm glad you enjoyed yourself. But the evening doesn't have to end now." His hand slid closer to hers on the table.

Her tummy flipped. Did he mean—

Standing, he folded her palm in his. "Let's dance."

She was relieved, right?

Oh, heavens, she was a mess.

She took his hand, the warmth of his touch steadying her as he guided her over to the small teak dance floor. Briefly they were waylaid by an older couple who congratulated Gervais on the Hurricanes' win the day before. But while he was gracious and polite, he didn't linger, keeping his attention on her.

On their date and this fairy-tale evening that Gervais had created for her.

Beneath the tiny, gem-colored pendants, he pulled her into him as the slow, sultry jazz saxophone bayed. With ease, his right hand found the small of her back, and his left hand closed around her hand. As they began to sway, he tucked her against him, chest to chest underneath the din of the music and the lights.

The scents and sounds were just a colorful blur, though, her senses attuned to Gervais. The warm heat of his body through his soft silk suit. His fingers flexing lightly on her back, his thumb grazing bare skin where a cutout in her dress left her exposed.

She swallowed. Each fast breath of air she dragged in pressed her breasts to the hard wall of his chest, reminding her how well her body knew his. What would it be like to be with him now, with her senses so heightened? It had been incredible two and a half months ago.

She couldn't hold back a soft purr. She covered by saying, "The music is beautiful."

"It's the heartbeat of our city. The rhythm the whole place moves to."

He whirled her past the bass player, where the deep vibrations hummed right through her feet.

"There's so much more about my hometown to show you beyond our sports. So much history and culture here. And of course, some amazing food."

Which she could still smell drifting on the breeze. The scent of spices thickened the air, making the heat of the evening seem more exotic than any of the places she'd ever been to during her stint in the military.

"I cannot deny this Big Easy fascinates me." She could lose herself in these brick-and-wrought-iron-laced streets, the scent of flowers heavy in the air. "But I want to be clear, as much as I enjoyed the food tonight, or how much I might like the sound of jazz, that is not going to make me automatically change my mind about your proposal. We have nothing in common."

His voice tickled in her ear, a murmur accompanying the jazz quartet. "Sure we do. We both come from big families with lots of siblings."

A shiver trembled along her skin, and she reminded

herself it was just the pregnancy making her so susceptible to him. It had to be. No man could mesmerize a woman so thoroughly otherwise. Her hormones simply conspired against her.

"I guess your family does qualify as American royalty." She held up her end of the conversation, hoping he could not see the effect he had on her. "So that is one thing we have in common. Just minus the crowns."

"True. No tiaras here." His head dipped closer to speak in her ear again. "Although thinking of you in a tiara and nothing more—that's an image to die for."

She knew he joked. That did not stop her from imagining being naked with him.

"An image that will have to remain in your mind only, since I do not pose for pictures. After what happened to my sister because of the sex tape with the prime minister," she said, shuddering, "not a chance."

Gervais almost missed a step, though he recovered quickly enough.

"Your sister was in a sex tape?"

"You must be the only person in the world who did not see it." That snippet of footage had almost ruined her family. The publicity was all the more difficult to deflect, since their monarchy was both defunct and not particularly wealthy. They'd had precious few resources to fight with.

"Never mind." Gervais shook his head, dismissing that conversation. "That's beside the point. First, I wasn't speaking literally. And second, I would never, never let you be at risk that way."

Her neck craned to look at him, eyes scanning his

face. There was no amusement in her eyes. "Perhaps more to the point, I will not put myself at risk."

"You're an independent princess. I like that."

"Technically, I am a princess in name only. The monarchy doesn't have ruling power any longer."

"Fair enough."

Gervais spun her away from him. There was a moment before she returned to the heat of his body that left her with anticipation. She wanted him to keep touching her, to keep pressing his body against hers.

After they resumed their rhythmic swaying, he said softly into her ear, "You are pretty well-adjusted for someone who grew up in a medieval castle surrounded by servants and nannies."

"What makes you think we had servants and nannies?"

A smile played with his sexy mouth. "That princess title."

She rolled her eyes. "The castle was pretty crumbly and we had some maintenance help, since we opened part of the palace to the public, and tutors volunteered just to have it on their résumé that they'd taught royalty. But definitely no nannies."

"Your parents were the involved types." Somehow they had gotten closer, lips barely a breadth away from each other. The thought of how close he was made it hard for Erika to concentrate. So she pulled back a bit, adjusting her head to look out over the crowd, toward the band.

"Not really. After class we had freedom to roam. We were quite a wild pack of kids. Can you imagine having your own real-life castle as a playground? We had everything but the unicorn."

"You make it sound fun."

"Some days it was fun. Some it was lonely when I saw the kids on tour with their parents." She hesitated. The last thing she wanted from Gervais was sympathy. She'd accepted what her family was and was not a long time ago. So she continued, "And some days were downright dangerous."

"What do you mean?"

"My sisters and I wanted a trampoline for Christmas." Which sounded perfectly normal. Except for the Mitras clan, there was no such thing as normal.

"Okay. And?"

"You do not get those on royal grounds. It does not fit the historical image, and without the tours we didn't have money. So, we made our own."

"Oh, God." A look of horror and intrigue passed over his face.

"We pulled a couple of mattresses down the stairs, stacked them under a window… And we jumped."

Gervais's eyes widened. "From how high?"

She shrugged. "Third story. And the ceilings were high."

"You're making me ill."

"It was only scary the first time when one of my sisters pushed me." And, later, when another sister broke an arm and the game ended for good.

"Pushed you?" Disbelief filled his voice. Surely his brothers had done equally dangerous things as forms of entertainment when they had been younger.

She'd seen the Reynaud males up close, and there was an air of confidence and arrogance about all of them that didn't exactly coincide with a sheltered upbringing.

"I was the test dummy," she informed him. "As the youngest and the lightest, it was my job to make sure the mattress had been placed correctly and had enough bounce."

"And did it?"

"We had to add some duvets and pillows."

"So it hurt."

"Probably no more than playing football without shoulder pads."

Tucking a loose strand of her hair behind her ear, he whispered, "You're such a badass. I expected a story like that from a family of boys, but not girls."

Not all girls were the descendants of female warriors. And that was usually the justification for their shenanigans as children. "We considered it our gym class. It was more interesting than lacrosse."

"Lacrosse, huh? I didn't expect that." He brushed his lips across her temple, his breath warm, his brief kiss warmer.

Her body even warmer still with want.

Just when she thought she would grip his lapels and melt right into him, he stepped back.

"I should get you home, Princess. It's late."

And just like that, the fairy-tale book was closing. She felt close to him all evening, physical distance aside. And every time it seemed as if there was something more between them, he pulled back.

While part of her was relieved that he'd stopped pushing for more, a larger part of her wanted him. She had to weigh her options. Had to be strong for her unborn children and make the wisest decision possible. It wasn't just her life in the balance.

After a sleepless night dreaming of Gervais's touch, Erika hadn't awoken in the best of moods. And now she had to make the phone call she had been dreading. The one that had sent her on edge all morning long until she found her courage and started dialing.

Erika sat on the chaise longue in the guest room as she hugged the device to her ear and listened to the call ring through on the other side of the world. She needed to speak with her parents and tell them that she was pregnant. With twins. There was no sense in avoiding the inevitable any longer.

Her mother answered the phone. "Hello, my love. What brings about this lovely surprise of a call?"

"Um, does there have to be a special reason for me to call you?"

"There does not have to be, but I hear a tone in your voice that tells me there is a reason. Something important perhaps?"

Her mother's surprise intuition tugged at her already tumultuous emotions.

"I am pregnant. With twins." The words tumbled out of her mouth before she had even had a chance to respond to the pleasantries with her mom.

So much for the long speech Erika had outlined and perfected. Glancing down at the piece of paper in front of her, she noted that her talking points were basically for show. There was no going back now.

Silence fell from the other end of the receiver for what seemed like an eternity.

"Mother?" she asked, uncertainty creeping into her voice.

"Twins, Erika? Are you certain?"

She nodded, as if her mother could see. "Yes, Mother. I'm certain. I went to the doctor two days ago and heard the two distinct heartbeats with my own ears. The tradition of twins lives on in the Mitras family."

"Who is the father?" Her mother's interest pressed into the phone.

"Gervais Reynaud, the American football team owner—" she began, but her mother interrupted.

"A son of the Reynaud shipping empire? And Zephyr Cruise Ships? What an excellent match, Erika. American royalty. The press will love this."

"Right, but, Mother, I wanted to—"

"Oh, darling, have you considered what this could mean for the family? If you have boys, well...the royal line lives on. This is wonderful, my love. Hold on, let me get your father."

Rustling papers and some yelling came through over the phone. Erika's stomach knotted.

"Your father is on speakerphone. Tell him your news, my love." Her mother cooed into the phone, focused on all the wrong things.

"I'm going to have twins, Father. And I'm just—"

"Twins? Do you know what this means? You could have a boy. Maybe two."

Erika nodded dully into the phone, the voices of her parents feeling distant. As if they belonged in someone else's life. The way they had when she was a child. The image of the royal family always seemed more important than the actual well-being of the family itself.

They weren't interested in hearing what she had to say but were already strategizing how to best monetize this opportunity. The press was about to have an all-access pass to her life before she even knew how she was going to proceed.

"Mother, Father," she said, interrupting their chatter, "I've had quite the morning already." They didn't need to know how much it taxed a woman to daydream about Gervais just when he'd decided to pull back. "Do you mind if I call you later, after I've rested?"

Tears burned her eyes for a variety of reasons that shouldn't make her cry. Pregnancy hormones were pure evil.

"Of course not, my love."

"Not at all, my dear," her father said. "You need your rest if you are going to raise the future of the royal line. Sleep well."

And just like that, they were gone, leaving her cell phone quiet as the screen went dark. They had disconnected from the call as abruptly as they often did from her life, leaving her all alone to contend with the biggest challenge she'd ever faced.

"Well, we're surprised to see you so early, that's all," Dempsey said from a weight bench, his leg propped up on a stool. He pressed around his knee, fidgeting with the brace. An old injury that had cost him his college football career. It was flaring up again. Most days, it didn't bother him. But then there were days like today.

Gervais understood Dempsey's position. He'd been sidelined from the field, as well. One too many concussions. But quite frankly, he enjoyed the business side of owning the Hurricanes.

There were new challenges, new ways of looking at the game and new styles of offense to develop as players came up stronger and faster than ever before. And he was still involved in football, which had been his ultimate goal anyway. This had just been another way to get at the same prize.

As an owner, he would not only strategize how to field the best possible team, he would also make the Hurricanes the most profitable team in the league. Corporate sponsorships were on track to meet that goal in three years, but Gervais had plans that could shorten that window to two. Maybe even eighteen months. The franchise thrived and the city along with it.

"I'm not sure what you two find so fascinating about my night out with Erika." Gervais curled the dumbbells, sweat starting to form on his brow as they worked out in a private facility within the team's training building.

The team lifted in a massive room downstairs, but Gervais had added a more streamlined space upstairs near the front offices.

"We just want to know what's going on in your life. With the baby. And you," Henri, their father's favorite, added. Theo had high hopes that Henri would one day wear a Super Bowl ring for the Hurricanes and continue in the old man's footsteps as a hometown hero.

The whole family was here, with the exception of their father and their brother Jean-Pierre, who played for a rival team in New York and didn't get to Louisiana much during the season.

And while Henri technically worked out with the team, he never minded putting in some extra hours in the upstairs training center to try to show up his older brothers in the weight room.

"That offer still stands, by the way, if you want it to," Henri said, his voice low enough so only Gervais could hear. Gervais knew that things had been hard for Henri and his wife since they hadn't been able to conceive. It affected everything in their marriage. But Gervais wasn't about to give them his unborn children. He wanted to raise them, to be an active part of their lives. To be the opposite of their father.

"Hey now, secrets don't make friends," Dempsey snapped, his face hard. Henri rolled his eyes but nodded anyway.

"So, Pops—" Dempsey shot him an amused grin "—have you decided what you are going to do?"

"Yeah, how are you going to handle fatherhood in the public eye with a princess?" Henri teased, huffing out pull-ups on a raised bar.

"I told you both, I'm taking care of my children." And Erika, he added silently. His main goal as they got ready for the game in St. Louis was to show her that they could be together. That they were great together. An unconventional family that could beat the odds. He was prepared to romance her like no other. And he might have shared that with Henri and Dempsey, if not for the man that rounded the corner, stopping in the entrance to the weight room.

From the door frame, a familiar booming drawl. Theo. "I'm here to meet the mother of my first grandchild."

Eight

As the limo driver faded from view, Erika sped into the Hurricanes' office building. She moved as fast as her legs would carry her, feeling less like royalty and more like a woman on a mission.

Twenty minutes ago, Gervais had called her. Urgency flooded his voice. He needed her in the office stat.

Pushing the heavy glass door open, she took a deep breath, feeling ever so slightly winded. The humidity was something she had yet to fully adjust to, and even small stints outside left her vaguely breathless. The rush of the cool air-conditioning filled her lungs as she crossed the threshold, a welcome chill after the New Orleans steam bath. Striding beneath the black-and-gold team banners hanging overhead, she struggled to figure out what was wrong that he needed her here.

Taking the stairs two at a time, she made it to the second floor and hung a right. Headed straight for the glass wall and door with an etched Hurricanes logo.

The secretary smiled warmly at her from her desk. Adjusting her glasses, she stood. "Princess Erika, Mr. Reynaud is expecting you—"

Extending a manicured hand, she gestured to another door and Erika didn't wait for her to finish. Hurrying forward, she reached the polished double doors made of a dark wood. And heavy. She gave one side a shove, practically falling into the huge office of the team owner.

Currently an empty room.

Erika looked around, heart pounding with nerves. And, if she was being honest, disappointment.

Spinning on her heel, she practically ran into the secretary. Grace was not on her side today.

"My apologies, ma'am," the secretary started in a quiet voice. "Mr. Reynaud will be back in a few minutes, but please make yourself comfortable. Can I get you anything while you wait? We have water, soda, tea. And of course enough Gatorade to fill a stadium."

"Thank you." As the words left her lips, she settled down. Slightly. "I'm just fine, though."

"Of course." The secretary smiled, exiting the room and closing the door with a soft click.

So she was here. In his office without him. While not ideal, it did give her a chance to feel out what sort of man he was. At least in the business sense.

A bank of windows overlooked the practice field below, the lush green grass perfectly manicured with the white gridiron standing out in stark contrast. Silver bleachers glimmered all around the open-air facility with a retractable dome. Funny they didn't have the stadium roof on today when it was so beastly hot outside, but perhaps the practice had been earlier in the day as there were no players in sight now.

Turning from the wall of windows, she paced around the office. She noted the orderly files, the perfectly straightened paper stacks on the massive mahogany desk. The rows of sticky notes by the phone. The walls were covered with team photos and awards, framed press clippings and a couple of leather footballs behind glass cases. The place was squared away. Tight.

Not too different from the way she kept her own living quarters, either. Impersonal. Spit-shined for show. They might not have done a lot of talking in London, but clearly they had gravitated toward each other for reasons beyond the obvious. After last night she felt as if they had more in common than they realized.

A tightness worked in her chest. So desperately did she want to trust him now that they found themselves preparing to be parents together. But trust came at a high cost. It wasn't a commodity she candidly bestowed. It was earned—her most guarded asset. Years of being royalty had taught her to be suspicious.

Shoving her past aside, she approached a picture on the farthest corner of his desk. It was different than the rest. It seemed to have nothing to do with the Hurricanes. Or football, for that matter.

The photograph was faded, old—probably real film instead of digital. But she would have recognized him anyway. Gervais. His brothers. A woman. His mother, she assumed. But no Dempsey. Which struck her as odd.

She would have continued to stare at the picture as if it could give her the answers she was after if she didn't hear a man clearing his throat behind her.

She glanced over her shoulder, through the blond strands of her hair. Gervais stood in the doorway. And he looked damn sexy.

He was disheveled. Not nearly as put together as his office. His hair was still wet from a shower, and his shirt was only half buttoned. For the quickest moment she had the urge to finish undoing it. To kiss him—and more.

The urge honestly surprised her. She had promised herself yesterday that after a good night's sleep, she would be levelheaded today. She needed logic to prevail while she figured out if he could be trusted. Only then could she decide what to do next.

Leaning against the desk, and looking at his lips with feigned disinterest, she asked as casually as possible, "What is the emergency? Is something wrong?"

He shook his head, closing the door behind him. "Not really. I just wanted to speak with you privately about—" he hesitated "—a…uh…new development."

Her smile faded. He was leaving. People always did. Her parents, who never remained in town with their kids for long. The vast majority of her friends who hung around only because she was royalty. The dozens of tutors who only helped for long enough to get a good reference before moving on to an easier job than five hell-raising sisters.

Schooling her features to remain impassive, she sat

down in a leather wingback chair. She needed the isolation that chair represented. She didn't need him tempting her by sitting next to her on the sofa or walking up to her to brush against her. Touch her. Weaken her resolve.

"Tell me." She met his gaze. Steeled herself.

"Remember that I told you I called my father a couple of days ago to tell him about the baby?" His dark eyes found hers for a moment before he stalked toward the wall of windows and looked down at the field. "Apparently, he decided to make a surprise visit."

"Your father is here? In the building or in New Orleans?"

The tight feeling in her chest returned, seizing hold of her. Erika was as unsure of how to deal with his family as she was her own. Selfishly, she had hoped they would have alone time together—without family making plays and demands—to figure out how to handle their situation. And to figure out if there was something there between them, after all.

"He was in the building but he's taking his girlfriend out to lunch before coming to the house later. I wanted to warn you in person and couldn't leave work."

More confirmation she didn't want to hear. But she felt compelled to hear it anyway. "Why do I need warning?"

"He's not a good person in spite of being charming as hell when he wants to be. I just want to make sure you're prepared. Feel free to steer clear of him."

"I can take care of myself. If he becomes too much to handle, I will flip him with Krav Maga I learned in the military." The warrior blood boiled beneath her skin. She would not be taken for a fool.

"You're pregnant."

"I am not incapacitated. But if you are concerned, I will simply pretend I do not understand his English." Uncrossing her arms, she gave him a wickedly innocent grin. Eyes wide for full effect. "It worked on almost half the tutors who showed up at the Mitras household prepared to teach the rebellious princesses."

"Good plan. Wish I'd thought of that as a kid."

A laugh escaped him and he turned toward her, a good-natured smile pushing at his cheeks. Funny how that smile slid right past her resolve to let logic prevail. To be levelheaded. That shared laugh stirred a whole wealth of feelings that had been building inside her ever since she'd stepped onto the practice field to face Gervais Reynaud.

Thinking back to the photograph on the desk, she had to admit, she was curious about him. His past. What it was like growing up in New Orleans. She had so many things to learn about him that it could take a lifetime. And wasn't it perfectly *reasonable* of her to learn more about him when her children would share his genes?

Emboldened by the rationalization, she thought she might as well begin her quest to know him better right now. "But you did not need to arm yourself with elaborate schemes to outwit the grown-ups around you as a child. You and your brothers are so close—or the three of you I've met."

The faintest pull of unease touched his lips. "We weren't always. Dempsey didn't come to live with us until he was thirteen. Our dad... Maybe you already know this."

"No, I do not."

"That's right." He shifted away from the windows to move closer to her, taking a seat on the edge of the desk. "You're not a big follower of football and the players."

"I am learning to be. You make me curious about anything that relates to you." Leaning forward, she touched his arm gently.

"I'm glad." A small victory. She could see him struggling with his family history, despite the fact that it was, apparently, public knowledge.

"Why did Dempsey come to live with you later?"

"We have different mothers."

"Your parents got divorced? But—" That certainly did not seem strange.

He met her gaze, his expression tight. "The ages don't match up. I'm the oldest, then Dempsey, followed by Henri and Jean-Pierre. Dad slept around on Mom, a lot."

"Gervais, I am so very sorry." She touched his arm lightly, which was as much sympathy as she dared offer without risking him pulling away or shutting down.

"My father used to go to clubs with his friends. Remember, this was before the internet made it possible to stalk your date before you'd ever met." He took another breath, clearly uncomfortable.

Erika's eyes widened, realizing that he was opening up to her.

"All families have...dead bones in the closet," she said quietly.

A smile pushed against his lips. "You mean skeletons?"

"Is that not the same thing?" She ran her hand over his.

"More or less, I suppose. Anyway, he hooked up with Dempsey's mom, Yvette, at a jazz club. She got pregnant. Worked a lot of jobs to raise Dempsey, but never found my father, since he hadn't even been honest about who he was, apparently. Until his image was blasted all over the sports page and she recognized his face. Yvette thought it was her ticket out of the slums. She arranged a meeting with my father. But he insisted Dempsey become part of the family. And Dempsey's mother agreed. For a price."

How horrible for Dempsey. And, from Gervais's perspective, how horrible it must have been for him to assimilate a new brother almost his own age when they were both young teens. She avoided focusing on him, however, guessing he would only shift gears if she did.

"That had to be strange for your mother," she observed lightly.

He bit back a bark of a laugh. "Strange? She wasn't much of a motherly type. After one more kid got added to the mix, she left."

"That is so much change for children." Her heart swelled with sympathy for him. She had no idea that there was so much struggle in the Reynaud family.

"We didn't handle it well. I was jealous. Henri was my shadow, so he followed my lead. We blamed Dempsey for breaking up our parents, which was ridiculous from an adult perspective. But kids can be cruel."

"What happened?"

He looked at her sidelong. "We were living in Texas then. Staying at our grandfather's ranch while our father chased our mother around, trying to work things out. Anyway, I dared Dempsey to ride a horse. The biggest, meanest horse on the ranch."

"Oh, my."

"You don't sound horrified."

She shrugged her shoulders. "Remember? My sisters threw me out a third-story window. I know how siblings treat each other even when they have grown up together."

"True enough." He nodded. "Of course, he had no idea how to ride—not even a nice horse. So he was... completely unprepared for a high-strung Thoroughbred used to getting her own way."

"That's scary. What happened?"

"She threw him clear off, but he landed awkwardly and broke his leg. We both almost got trampled while Henri and Jean-Pierre ran to get help."

"You did not mean to break his leg." Ah, sibling cruelty was something that existed in all countries.

"Things were difficult between us for a long while, even once we all made up. I don't want my children to live in a fractured family. Not if I can help it. I want them to have a firm sense of belonging, a sense of being a Reynaud."

"And a Mitras," she reminded him.

"Yes. Both." He reached out to take her hands in his and squeezed. "I want your strength in our children. They will need it."

His words warmed her even more than his touch, and that was saying a lot when a thrill danced over her skin.

Too breathless to answer, she bit her lip, unwilling to allow a dreamy sigh to escape.

"Erika, please stay here with me for a while. We need more time to get to know each other." He drew her to her feet, his eyes pleading with hers at a time when her resolve was at an all-time low.

Her heart beat wildly, her lips parted. Anticipating the press of his mouth to hers.

He rubbed her arms, sliding them up until his hands tangled in her hair. They kissed deeply, with open mouths and passion. Tendrils of desire pulsed through her as he explored her mouth with his tongue, tasting her as she tasted him right back. She had not been passive in their lovemaking before, and she could already feel the urge to seize control driving her to the brink now.

It could have gone on like that for hours, for days even, if not for the sound of the door opening. She pushed back. Looked down. Away. At anything else but him.

While Gervais spoke in a low voice to his secretary, Erika used the time to collect herself. Straighten her dress. Find her purse. She had to figure this out soon. It was apparent there was chemistry simmering hot just beneath the surface. But now there was also a tenderness of feeling. An emotional connection. How would she ever forget that look in Gervais's eyes when he told her about the guilt of seeing Dempsey hurt? Of course she understood why he wanted to keep his own family intact. His children connected.

That was admirable, and a deeper draw for her than the sensual spell he cast around her without even trying. It had been difficult enough resisting just one.

How would she ever keep her wits about her with both those persuasive tools at his disposal?

On the private plane to St. Louis later that week, Erika replayed the kiss in Gervais's office over and over again. Of course, she had already relived that moment in her mind more than once, awake and asleep. Every look between them was filled with so much steam she could barely think, much less trust herself to make logical decisions around him.

At least they were on different planes today, so she could avoid temptation for a few hours. All the wives and girlfriends traveled first-class, while the team went on a chartered craft. Gervais had a meeting in Chicago first, something to do with corporate sponsorship for the Hurricanes. But he would arrive in St. Louis at the same time she did.

With any luck, she could use this flight to get her bearings straight.

But even as she tried to focus on being objective, her mind wandered back to the kiss in the office. A kiss that hadn't been repeated despite the fact that they'd spent time together over the past few days. It felt as though he was always on the clock, managing something for the team or overseeing business for one of the other Reynaud family concerns. So he was a bit of a workaholic; not a flaw in her opinion. In fact, she respected how seriously he took his work. He expected nothing to be handed to him in life.

And when they were together, he was fully present. Attentive. Thoughtful. He'd even helped deflect an awkward run-in with his father and his father's girlfriend because she hadn't felt ready to face Theo after what she'd learned about him. And knowing how little his own son trusted him.

Erika's instincts had seldom failed her. In London, there had been something between them. Something she hadn't imagined. And the more she thought about the past few days, the more excited she was to be with him again. To have another kiss. To throw away caution as quickly as clothes peeled away in the heat of passion.

To make love again and discover if the fire burned as hot between them as she remembered.

Erika clutched a long silver necklace in her hand, running the charm back and forth. Just as she did as a child.

Fiona, Henri's wife, gently touched her arm. "You know, we have a book club to help pass the time when we're on the road with the guys."

"A book club?" She glanced at the row across from her, to where Gervais's father's girlfriend stared intently at a fashion magazine.

Fiona scrunched her nose. "I should have asked. Do you like to read?"

"Which language?"

Fiona laughed lightly. "No need to get all princess-sy on me."

"I apologize. That was meant to be a joke. Sometimes nuances, even though I speak all those languages, get lost. Tell me more about the book club."

"We choose books to read during all those flights

and then we have one helluva party while we discuss them."

"Party?"

Fiona nodded. "Spa or five-star restaurant or even the best room service we can buy."

"Did Gervais ask you to sit here and use the time to convince me it is fun to be on the road?" Try as she might, Erika couldn't keep the dry sarcasm out of her voice.

"I am simply helping you make an informed decision. It's not just about partying. We have homeschooling groups for families with children, as well." Shadows passed briefly through her eyes before Fiona cleared her throat. "It's amazing what you can teach a child when your field trips involve traveling around the country. Even overseas sometimes for the preseason. Our kids have bonds, too. There are ways to make this kind of family work. Family is important."

Damn. That struck a chord with her. Maybe Fiona had a point. She had just dismissed the women of the group without bothering to really get to know them. And that certainly was not fair.

Maybe she could strengthen her ties to Gervais's world this way. She already knew she wanted to explore their relationship more thoroughly—to take that first step of trust with him and see where indulging their sensual chemistry would lead. But in the meantime, why not work on forging bonds within his world? If things between them didn't work and they ended up co-parenting on opposite sides of the world, she would need allies in the Reynaud clan and in the Hurricanes organization. Growing closer to Fiona would be a good thing for her children.

All perfectly logical.

Except that a growing part of Erika acknowledged she wasn't just thinking about a rational plan B anymore. With each day that passed, with every moment that she craved Gervais, Erika wanted plan A to work. And that meant this trip was going to bring her much closer to the powerful father of her children.

There was nothing Gervais hated more than a loss. It rubbed him the wrong way, sending him into a dark place, even though he knew that a preseason loss didn't matter. The preseason was about training. Testing formations. Trying out new personnel. The final tally on the score sheet didn't count toward anything meaningful.

Opening the door to his suite, he was taken aback by what he saw on the bed. Erika in a Hurricanes jersey. On her, it doubled as a dress, hitting her midthigh. Exposing her toned legs.

His mind eased off the loss, focused on what was in front of him. "I wanted to catch you before you went to bed."

She closed the book she'd been reading and uncurled her legs, stretching them out on the bed. "I am sorry about the game."

"I won't lie. I'm disappointed we lost this one. But I'm realistic enough to know we can't win every time, especially in the preseason when we don't play all of our starters or utilize our best offensive strategies. The whole point of the preseason is like a testing ground.

We can create realistic scenarios and see what happens when we experiment." He told himself as much, but it didn't soothe him when he saw a rookie make poor decisions on the field or watched a risky play go up in flames.

"You have a cool head. That is admirable."

Her head tilted sympathetically.

Gervais was floored. Unsure of what to make about Erika's behavior. For the first time since her arrival in the United States, it felt as if she was opening up to him. But could that be?

She'd been so adamant on keeping distance between them, urging logic over passion. She was probably just being polite to him. After all, they would have to be civil to each other for the sake of the children. She had said as much more than once.

Still, damn it, he knew what he saw in her eyes, and she wanted him every bit as much as he wanted her. Back in his arms.

In his bed.

"Thank you. I'm sorry I've been so busy the past few days." He had taken a red-eye to Chicago to be there this morning for a meeting to secure a new corporate sponsor for the team. He was exhausted, but the extra hours had paid off, and he was one step closer to making the Hurricanes the wealthiest team in the league.

"You have been very thoughtful." She leaned forward, her posture open, words unclipped.

Her gaze was soft on him. And appreciative, he noticed. So maybe he hadn't been so off base. "I was concerned you would feel neglected having to fly in a separate plane."

"I understand you have other commitments. And I had a lovely conversation with Fiona—in case you were wondering, since you made sure we had seats beside each other." Erika raised her eyebrows as if daring him to deny it.

"Are you angry?" He couldn't help that he wanted to give her reasons to stay in New Orleans. But he knew she did not appreciate being manipulated.

He'd never met a more independent woman.

"Actually, no. She was helpful in explaining the logistics of how wives blend in to the lifestyle of this team you own."

He hadn't expected that.

"She answered all of your questions?"

"Most..." Shifting on the bed, she crawled toward him. "I had cats when I grew up."

All of his exhaustion disappeared.

His eyes couldn't help but watch her lithe form, the way her breasts pushed against the jersey he'd given her. An unforgettable vision.

And the sensory overload left him dumbly saying, "Okay."

"We had dogs, too, but the cats were mine."

Trying his damnedest to pull his eyes up from the length of her exposed legs, he stumbled over the next sentence, too. Focusing on words was hard. And he had thought that tonight's loss had left him speechless. That was nothing compared to the sight in front of him. "Um, what were their names?"

Erika's lips plumped into a smile as she knelt on the bed in front of him. "You do not need to work this hard or pretend to woo me."

"I'm not pretending. I am interested in everything about you." And he was. Mind, spirit...and body. He tried to keep his mind focused on the conversation. On whatever she wanted to talk about.

"Then you will want to know the real reason why I mentioned the cats. I loved my cats. And yet my children—our children—will not be able to have pets when they are traveling all over the country to follow this team that is part of their legacy." She gave him a playful shove, her smile still coy.

"Actually, I have a baseball buddy whose wife travels with her dog." He deserved a medal for making this much conversation when she looked like that. "I think the guy renegotiated his contract to make sure she got to have her dog with her."

"Oh," Erika whispered breathily. Moved closer to him, hands resting on his arms. Sending his body reeling from her touch.

"Yes, oh. So what other questions went unanswered today? Bring it. Because I'm ready."

"I do have one more question I did not dare to ask your sister-in-law." Her hands slid up to his neck. Pulled him close. Whispered with warm breath into his ear. "Will it mess up your season mojo if we have sex?"

Nine

Erika's heart hammered, threatening to fall right out of her chest as she stared at Gervais. All the time on the plane and waiting for him tonight had led her here. To this moment. And while the direction of her life may have been still uncertain, she knew this was right.

This was exactly where she needed to be. There was a closeness between them, one she had been actively fighting against.

Gervais's eyebrows shot upward. "What brought on this change?"

"I desire you. You want me, too, if I am not mistaken." Direct. Cool. She could do this.

"You are not mistaken. I have always wanted you. From the moment I first saw you. Even more now."

"Then we should stop denying ourselves the one

thing that is uncomplicated between us." And it was the truth. Everything was happening so fast, but it was undeniable that there was an attraction between them. In her gut, she knew that he would be there to support their babies. But it was more than that.

It was a deeper connection between them. When she had boarded the plane for New Orleans, she hadn't expected much from him. People had a nasty habit of leaving her, using her for the minimal privileges her royal status awarded her. She'd never expected to be welcomed and treated so well. In the past, her friends were dazzled by the idea of her world, rarely seeing beyond the outer trappings to the person beneath.

She also hadn't thought his family would be so accepting. It had scared her a bit, how many people were in the Reynaud clan. The number of people suddenly fussing over her and trying to get to know her had been overwhelming.

But they had also been kind. And maybe, just maybe, she'd be able to see past her preconceived notions about family. She had no real idea how to make a family anyway. But with Gervais…

"You're sure?" His forehead furrowed as he scrutinized her face. The look said everything. This was as far as he'd go without confirmation from her.

"Completely certain." She wanted to take a chance on him. On them. To give them an opportunity to be a couple.

And now that she'd made the decision after careful reasoning, she could finally allow her emotions to surface. She felt all her restraints melting away in the heat of the passion she'd been denying.

Even as she felt those walls disintegrate, she could sense a shift in Gervais. Like shedding a jacket and tie, he seemed to set aside his controlled exterior as a look of pure male desire flashed through his gaze. He closed the distance between them, his brown eyes dark and hungry while he raked his gaze over her.

He peeled the jersey up and over her head. She shook her hair free in waves that fanned behind her, leaving her rounded breasts bared to his devouring gaze. Heat pulsed through her veins—and relief. She had missed him since their incredible time together two and a half months ago, and she'd worked so hard to keep her desire for him in check for the sake of her babies so that she could make a smart decision where he was concerned. Now it felt so amazing to let go of those fears and simply fall into him.

She'd wondered what he would think of the subtle changes pregnancy had brought to her body. Her full breasts had fit in his palms before; now she knew they would overflow a hint more.

But Gervais's eyes were greedier for her than ever, and he stared at her with need he didn't bother to hide. Lowering her to rest on her back, he followed her down to the bed, his touch gentle but firm. His woodsy scent familiar and making her ache for him.

He hooked his thumbs in the sides of her pale blue panties, tugging gently until she raised her hips to accommodate. He slipped the scrap of satin down and off, flinging it aside to rest on top of the discarded Hurricanes jersey. His throat moved in a slow gulp. "That incredible image will be seared in my brain for all time."

He rocked back for a moment, his eyes roving over her.

Then his gaze fell to rest on the ever so slight curve of her stomach. The pregnancy was still early, but now she realized that the twins had been the reason her pants had grown a little snug faster than she would have expected.

A glint of protectiveness lit his eyes. "Are you sure this is safe? You passed out just last week. I don't want to do anything that could risk your health."

She thought she might die if he did not touch her, actually. But she kept that thought locked away.

"The doctor said I am healthy and cleared for all activities, including sex. Well, as long as we do not indulge in acrobatics." A wicked memory flashed through her brain. "Perhaps we should not re-create that interlude on the kitchen table in your London hotel room."

His heart slugged hard against his chest. Against hers. She wanted to arch into his warmth like a cat seeking the sun.

"No acrobatics. Understood." He trailed kisses beneath her ear and down her neck. "I look forward to treating you like spun glass."

A shiver tripped down her spine, her skin tingling with awareness. Tingles of heat gathered between her legs, making her long for more. For everything.

"I will not break," she promised, needing the pleasure only he could bring her.

He skimmed a fingertip down the length of her neck.

"Oh, careful, light touches can be every bit as arousing as our more aggressive weekend together."

She licked her lips. Swallowed over her suddenly dry throat.

"I look forward to your persuasion—once you take those clothes off." She ran her hands down his chest and back up his shoulders. "Because, Gervais..." She savored the feel of his name on her tongue. "You are seriously overdressed for the occasion. Undress for me."

His brown eyes went molten black with heat at her invitation, and his hands went to work on his tie, loosening the knot and tugging the length free, slowly, then draping the silver length over the chaise at the end of the bed. And oh my, how she enjoyed the way he took his time. One fastening at a time, he opened his white button-down until it flapped loose, revealing his broad, muscled chest in a T-shirt. In a deliberate motion he swept both aside and laid them carefully over his tie.

Her mouth went moist and she bit her bottom lip. She recalled exactly why she hadn't bothered with light, teasing touches the last time they were together. His body was so powerful, his every muscle honed. She hadn't been able to hold herself back the last time.

He winked at her with a playfulness that she didn't see in this intense man often.

She could not stop a wriggle of impatience, the Egyptian cotton sheets slick against her rapidly heating flesh.

Then all playfulness left his eyes as swiftly as he took off his shoes and pants, leaving his toned body naked and all for her.

The thick length of him strained upward against his

stomach. Unable to hold back, she sat up to run her hands up his chest, then down his sides, his hips, forward to clasp his steely strength in his hands. To stroke, again and again, teasing her thumb along the tip.

With a growl of approval and impatience, he stretched over her while keeping his full weight off her. He braced on his elbows, cupping her face and slanting his mouth along hers. His tongue filled her mouth and she knew soon, not soon enough, he would fill her body again.

His hands molded to her curves, exploring each of her erogenous zones with a perfection that told her he remembered every moment of their time together as much as she did. His hard thigh parted her legs, the firm pressure against her core sending her arching closer, wriggling against him, growing moist and needy. She clutched at his shoulders, breathy whispers sliding free as she urged him to take her. Now. No more waiting. He'd tormented her dreams long enough.

Then the blunt thickness of him pushed into her, inch by delicious inch. He was so gentle and strong at the same time. She knew she would have to be the one to demand more. Harder. Faster. And she did. With her words and body, rocking against him, her fingers digging into his taut ass to bring them both the completion they sought.

Her fingers crawled up his spine again and she pushed at his shoulders, nudging until he rolled to his back, taking her with him in flawless athleticism. His power, his strength, thrilled her. She straddled him, her sleek blond hair draped over her breasts, her nipples just peeking through and tightening. Gervais swept aside her hair and took one pink peak in his mouth. He circled with his tongue, sending bolts of pleasure radiating through her. Sighs of bliss slipped from between her lips. She rolled her hips faster, riding him to her completion. Wave after wave of her orgasm pulsed through her.

She heard his own hoarse shout of completion, the deep sounds sending a fresh wash of pleasure through her until she melted forward onto his chest. Sated. Every nerve tingling with awareness in the aftermath.

The swish of the ceiling fan sent goose bumps along her skin. The fine thread count of the sheets soothed her.

But most of all, the firm muscled length of him felt so good; the swirls of his body hair tempted her to writhe along him again.

If she could move.

And just like that, Erika realized how utterly complicated being with him was. Because like it or not, she had feelings for him. Feelings that were threatening to cloud her judgment.

And while this may have felt right for her, she needed to be sure it was right for him, too.

Gervais poured the flowery-scented shampoo into his hand. Her magnolia scent filled the steam and teased his senses as they stood under the shower spray in a vintage claw-foot tub. The sheer plastic curtain gave both privacy and a view of the room filled with fresh flowers he'd ordered sent up especially for her.

There was so very much he wanted to do for—and to—this incredible woman.

Drawing Erika close to him, he kissed her neck, nuzzled behind her ear, savored the wet satin of her skin against his bare flesh. Already he could feel the urge building inside him to lift her legs around his waist and surge inside her. To bring them both to completion again, but he was determined to take his time, to build the moment.

And yes, draw out the pleasure.

He lathered her hair, the bubbles and her hair slick between his fingers as he massaged her scalp. Her light moan of bliss encouraged him on, filling him with a sense of power over fulfilling all her needs. He continued to rub along her head, then gently along her neck, down to her shoulders in a slight massage. He wanted to pamper her, to show her he was serious about her and the babies.

She leaned into his touch but stayed silent. Feeling her let out a deep sigh, he decided he wanted to really get to know this beautiful, incredible woman. Sure, they'd spent some time together...but there was still so much he could learn about her. That he wanted to learn about *her*. Everything, not just about her beautiful body, but also about that magnificently brilliant mind of hers.

Such as why she had chosen a career in the military after growing up as royalty.

"So tell me about your time in the service. What did you really do?"

"Just what I told you that day we met."

"Truly? Nothing more? Not some secret spy role? Or dark ops career no one can ever know about?"

"How does the saying go in your country? I could tell you but then I would have to kill you."

He laughed softly against her mouth. "As long as we go while naked together, I'll die a happy man."

She swatted his butt playfully, then her smile faded. "Truthfully, there is nothing more to tell. I was a translator and handled some diplomacy meetings."

"I admire that about you." It had been a brave move. A noble, selfless act.

Shrugging, she tipped her shampooed head back into the water. Erika closed her eyes, clearly enjoying the feel of the steamy water. The suds caught on her curves, drawing his gaze. She was damn sexy.

"Why are you so dismissive of your service to your country?"

Eyes flashed open, defensive. He could tell it in the way she chewed on her lip before she answered, "I wanted to be a field medic and go into combat zones. But I was not allowed."

He nodded, trying to be sympathetic. To understand the complication of letting a princess, even from defunct royalty, into an active war zone.

"I can see how your presence could pose a security risk for those around you. You would be quite a high-value captive."

Her half smile carried a hint of cynicism. "While that is true, that was not the reason. My parents interfered. They did not want me to work or join at all. They wanted me to marry someone rich and influential, like I was some pawn in a royal chess game from a thousand years ago."

"Still, you made your own way. That's commendable. Why a field nurse and not in a military hospital?" He respected her drive. And her selfless career choices. She wanted to help people. Something told him she would have been a good field medic. Strong, knowledgeable, fearless.

"I did not want special treatment or protection because of my family's position. And still, I ended up as a translator not even allowed anywhere near a combat zone." Her voice took on a new determination. A tenacity he found incredibly attractive.

"So you made plans to continue your education after your service was finished." He knew she'd registered for coursework that would begin next month in the UK but had assumed she would ask for her spot to be held until after the children were born.

"I will not be deterred from my plans because of my family's interference." Eyes narrowed at him. Every bit a princess with that haughty stare. "I can support myself."

"Of course you can." He brought his negotiating skills to the conversation, hoping to make her see reason. "This is about more than money, though. You have a lot on your plate. Let me help you and the babies while you return to school."

"That makes it sound like I am incapable of taking care of myself the way my parents always said." Bitterness edged back into her voice. And something that sounded like dulled resignation.

"This isn't just about you. Or me. We have children to think of. You know I want you to marry me. I've made that clear. But if your answer is still no, at least move in with me. Make this easier for all—"

She pressed her mouth to his, silencing him until she leaned back, water dripping between them again.

"Gervais, please, this time is for us to get to know one another better. This kind of pressure from you about the future is counterproductive."

One thing was for sure—she had been opening up. Maybe asking her to marry him again was too much too soon. But he could feel the connection between them growing. So he would back off. But not forever. He just had to figure out a way to show her how good they were together. "Then how about we find food?"

Her smile was so gorgeous the water damn near steamed off his skin. "Food? Now that is music to this pregnant woman's ears."

The strands of Erika's hair fell damp against the cloth of the jersey. They sat in the suite's kitchen. She was on the countertop, cross-legged, peering over at Gervais's back.

He'd retrieved an assortment of ripe fruit—pitted cherries, chocolate-dipped strawberries, pineapple slices and peach slices. At the center of the platter was a bowl of indulgent-looking cream.

Stomach growling, she looked on in anticipation. He brought it next to her and pulled up a bar stool so that they were eye level.

Extending her hand to grab a cherry, he stopped her.

"Let me, Princess." With a playful smile, he lifted

a cherry to her lips. Inside, she felt that now-familiar heat pulse. He was tender, charming.

A threat to her plan of objectivity, too.

She popped a chocolate-dipped strawberry into his mouth. He licked the slightly melted chocolate off her fingertips, sending her mind back to the shower. Back to when she had thought this was uncomplicated.

Needing to take control of the situation, Erika cleared her throat. Her goal was the same as before. To get to know him. "What did you want to be as a little boy growing up?"

Finishing chewing, he tilted his head to the side. "Interesting question."

"How so?" It had seemed like a perfectly reasonable question. One she had been meaning to ask for a while now.

"Everyone assumes I wanted to be a pro football player."

To Erika, Gervais had seemed like the kind of man who wasn't nearly as cut-and-dried as that. He might live and breathe football, but it didn't seem as if it was the only dimension to him. Childhood dreams said a lot, after all. She'd wanted to be a shield maiden from long ago. To protect and shelter people. Her adult dream was still along those lines.

A nurse did such things. "And you did not want to be a football player like the rest of your family?"

"I enjoy the game. Clearly. I played all through elementary school into high school because I wanted to. I didn't have to accept the offer to play at the college level. I could afford any education I wanted."

"But your childhood dream?" She pressed on, before taking the cream-covered peach slice he'd offered her. She savored the taste of the sweetness of the peach against the salty flavor of his fingers.

Looking down at his feet, then back at her, he smiled sheepishly. "As a kid, I wanted to drive a garbage truck."

Her jaw dropped. Closed. Then opened again as she said, "Am I missing something in translation? You wished to drive a truck that picks up trash?"

"I did. When my parents argued, I would go outside to hide from the noise. Sometimes it got so loud I had to leave. So I rode my bike to follow the garbage truck. I would watch how that crusher took everyone's trash and crushed it down to almost nothing. As a kid that sounded very appealing."

Thinking of him pedaling full-tilt down the roads as a child put an ache in her heart she couldn't deny. "I am sorry your parents hurt you that way."

"I just want you to understand I take marriage and our children's happiness seriously."

His brown eyes met hers. They were heated with a ferocity she hadn't seen before.

This offer of a life together was real to him. His offer was genuine, determined. And from a very driven man. She needed to make up her mind, and soon, or she could fast lose all objectivity around Gervais.

Ten

It had only been three days since he'd gotten home from the loss in St. Louis. He needed time to think of his next strategy. And not just for the Hurricanes. With Erika, too.

Which was exactly why he'd pulled on his running shorts and shirt. Laced up his shoes and hit the pavement, footsteps keeping him steady.

Focused.

Sweat curled off his upper lip, the taste of salt heavy in his mouth. The humid Louisiana twilight hummed with the songs of the summer bugs and birds.

This always set his mind right. The sound of foot to pavement. Inhale. Exhale. The feel of sweat on his back.

He'd been quite the runner growing up. Always could

best his brothers in distance and speed. Especially Jean-Pierre, his youngest brother.

Jean-Pierre had to work harder than all his older brothers to keep up with them as they ran. Running had been something of a Reynaud rite of passage. Or so Gervais had made it out to be. He'd always pushed his brothers for a run. It was an escape from the yelling and fighting that went on at their home. Whether the family was at the ranch in Texas, on the expansive property on Lake Pontchartrain or on the other side of the globe, there was always room to run, and Gervais had made use of those secured lands to give them all some breathing space from the parental drama.

Slowing his pace, he stopped to tighten his shoelace. Looking at the sparkling water of the lake, he realized it had been too long since he talked to Jean-Pierre. Months.

Gervais knew he needed to call him…but things hadn't been the same since Jean-Pierre left Louisiana Tech to play for the Gladiators in New York. Sure, Jean-Pierre maintained a presence on the family compound, sharing upkeep of one of the homes where he stayed when he flew into town. But how often had that been over the past few years? Even in the off-season, Jean-Pierre tended to stick close to New York and his teammates on the Gladiators. When he did show up in New Orleans, it was to take his offensive line out on his boat or for a raucous party that was more for friends than family.

How Jean-Pierre managed to stay away from this quirky, lively city was beyond Gervais. When they were younger, the family had spent a lot of time in Texas. Which, make no mistake, Gervais loved, but there was a charm to New Orleans, a quality that left the place rarified.

He wanted to share those things with Erika. The cultural scene was unbeatable, and the food. Well, he'd yet to take her to his favorite dessert and dancing place. He pictured taking her out for another night on the Big Easy with him. She'd love it if she'd give him a chance to show her.

And though they'd fallen into a pattern over the past few days, he felt as distant as ever and all because she wouldn't commit even though they had children on the way. Sure, they made love nightly now. And he relished the way her body writhed beneath his touch. But it wasn't enough. He bit his tongue about the future and she didn't say anything about leaving.

Or staying.

And he wanted her to stay. Starting to run again, he picked up the intensity. Ran harder, faster.

He didn't want her to leave. He didn't want a repeat of London. Before he'd even woken up, she'd packed her things and let herself out of the hotel suite. Though it had been only one weekend, he had fallen for her. Now they'd spent days together.

Rather blissful days. Mind wandering, he thought to the last night in St. Louis when they'd explored the rooftop garden that was attached to their hotel suite. There'd been a slight chill in the air, but things between them had been on fire. In his memory, he traced the curves on her body.

Though she might be pumping the brakes on the future, he was getting to know her. To see past her no-nonsense facade to the woman who was a little sarcastic, kindhearted and generous.

The thought of her just leaving again like in London... it made his gut sink.

Rounding the last corner on his run, he didn't hold back. He sprinted all out, as if that would allow him to hold on to Erika.

This was damn awful timing, too. He knew he needed to focus on his career. To turn the Hurricanes into a financial dynasty to back the championship team Dempsey assured them they had in place. And this thing with Erika—whatever it might be—was not helping him. Sure, he'd nabbed that sponsor in Chicago. But every day he spent with her was a day that he wasn't securing another sponsor that would make the Hurricanes invincible as a business and not just a team. They'd been teetering on the brink of folding when he'd purchased them, and he'd reinvigorated every facet since then, but his work was far from done to keep them in the black.

But damn. He could not. No. He *would* not just let her leave as she had before. This wasn't just about the fact they were having a family, or that they were amazing together in bed.

Quickening his pace, he saw the Reynaud compound come into sight. The light was on in Erika's bedroom.

His grandfather had taught him a few things when he was a kid. Two of the most important: *build your dream* and *family is everything*. Two simple statements. And he wanted Erika to be a part of that. To create the kind of home that his own kids would never want to run from.

Sitting cross-legged on a cushioned chair in the massive dining room, Erika absently spread raspberry jam on her puffy biscuit. Try as she might, she couldn't force her mind to be present. To be in the moment.

Instead, her thoughts drifted back to Gervais and last night. He'd knocked on her door after his run. She'd opened the door, let him in. And he'd showered her in determined, passion-filled kisses. There was an urgency, a sincerity in their lovemaking last night. A new dimension to sex she had never thought possible.

Last night had made it even harder for her to be objective about their situation. She wanted Gervais. But she also wanted what was best for them both. Balancing that need seemed almost impossible.

A motion in the corner of her eye brought her back to the present. She found Gervais's grandfather filling his plate at the buffet with pork grillades and grits, a buttered biscuit on the side.

Gracious, she could barely wait for the morning to wane so the queasy feeling would subside and she could indulge in more of the amazing food of this region. Everything tasted so good, or perhaps that was her pregnancy hormones on overload. Regardless, she was hungry but didn't dare try more for a couple more hours yet.

She looked back at Gervais's grandfather, keeping her eyes off the plate of food. Leon hadn't gone with them to St. Louis, but Gervais had explained how travel anywhere other than from his homes in New Orleans and Texas left the old man disoriented.

He took his place at the head of the table, just to the left of her, and poured himself a cup of thick black coffee from the silver carafe. "So you're carrying my first great-grandchild—" He tapped his temple near his gray hair. "Grandchildren. You're having twins. I remember that. Some days my memory's not so good, but that's sticking in my brain and making me happy. A legacy. And if you won't find it disrespectful of me to say so, I believe it's going to be a brilliant, good-looking legacy." He toasted her with his china coffee cup.

"Thank you, sir. No disrespect taken at all. That's a delightful thing to say, especially the smart part." She gave him a wink as she picked at her biscuit. Praise of her intelligence was important. Erika had worked hard to be more than a pretty princess. Wanted her worth and merit to be attached to her mind's tenacity. To realize her dreams of setting up a nurse-practitioner practice of her own someday, one with an entire section devoted to homeopathic medicines and mood-leveling aromatherapy.

"That's important." He sipped more of his coffee before digging into his breakfast. "We have a large family empire to pass along, and I want it to go into good hands. I didn't do so well with my own children. But my grandkids, I'm damn proud of them."

"Gervais will make a good father." Of that she had no doubt. He was already so attentive.

"He works too much and takes on too much responsibility to prove he's not like his old man, but yes, he will take parenthood seriously. He may need some books, though. To study up, since he didn't have much of a role model. He sure knows what not to do, though." A laugh rasped from the man's cracked lips and he finished more of his coffee.

"I believe you played a strong part in bringing up your grandchildren." She reached for the carafe and offered to refill his cup, even though she wasn't drinking coffee. She stuck to juice and water these days.

He nodded at her, eyes turning inward as if he was reading something she couldn't see. "I tried to step in where I could. Didn't want to bring up spoiled, silver-spoon-entitled brats again." His focus returned to her. "I like that you went into the military. That speaks well of your parents."

Her mother and father had pitched an unholy fit over that decision, but she would not need to say as much. "It was an honor to serve my country."

"Good girl. What do you plan to do now that your studies are on hold?"

Technically, they weren't. She would be back in university in autumn.

"When I return to school, I will undertake the program to become a nurse-practitioner, even as a single mother." And she would. No matter how long it took.

"Really? I didn't expect you to, um—"

"Work for a living? Few do, even after my military service." Her voice went softer than she would have liked.

"You'll take good care of my grandson when I'm

gone?" His question pierced her tender heart on a morning when her emotions were already close to the surface.

"Sir, you appear quite spry to me."

"That's not what I mean and if you're wanting to be a nurse-practitioner, you probably know that." He tapped his temple again. "It's here that I worry about giving out too soon. The doctors aren't sure how fast. Sometimes I prefer the days I don't remember talking to those experts."

"I am so very sorry." She hadn't spent a lot of time with Leon Reynaud. But she could tell he was a good man who cared a lot about his family. And the stories Gervais told her only confirmed that.

"Thank you. Meanwhile, I want to get to know you and spend time with you so you can tell my great-grans all about me." He pointed with his biscuit for emphasis and she couldn't help but smile.

"That sounds delightful," she said to Gramps, but her eyes trailed over his head. To Gervais, who strode into the dining hall.

Sexy. That was the only word that pulsed in her mind as she looked at him. Dressed in a blue button-down shirt, he looked powerful.

"Don't mind me," he mumbled, smiling at her. "Just grabbing some breakfast before heading to the office. You can go back to telling embarrassing stories about me, Gramps."

Gramps chuckled. "I was just getting ready to tell my favorite."

Gervais gave him a faux-injured grin, swiping a muffin and apple from the table.

He stopped next to her. Gave her a hug and a kiss. Not a deep kiss or even lingering. Instead, he gave her one of those familiar kisses. A kiss that spoke of how they'd been together before. That they knew each other's bodies and taste well. She bit her bottom lip where the taste of him lingered, minty, like his toothpaste.

As he walked away, everything felt…right. Being with him seemed so natural, as if they had been doing this for years. It'd be so easy—too easy—to slide right into this life with him.

And that scared her clean through to her toes.

It had been a long day at the office, one of the longest since their return from St. Louis. Gervais had tried his best to secure a new technology sponsor for the Hurricanes, a west coast company with deep pockets that was currently expanding their presence in New Orleans. The fit was perfect, but the corporate red tape was nightmarish, and the CEO at the helm hadn't been as forward thinking as the CFO, whom Gervais had met on another deal the year before. Not everyone understood the tremendous advertising power of connecting with an NFL team, and the CEO of the tech company had been reluctant. Stubborn. It had been a hellish day, but at least the guy hadn't balked at the deal. Yet.

Gervais had left work midday to talk with some of Gramps's doctors. They were discussing treatment plans and some of the effects of his new medicines. All he wanted to do was give the best he could to his family.

Family. Gramps. Hurricanes. Jean-Pierre. Work and Reynaud business had swirled in his mind all day. The only thing he wanted to do this evening was see Erika. The thought of her, waiting at home for him, had kept him fighting all day. Besides, he had a gift for her and he couldn't wait to present it to her.

Walking into her room, he felt better just seeing her. She was sitting on the chaise longue, staring blankly at her suitcase.

Her unzipped suitcase.

That fleeting moment of good feeling vanished. Was she leaving? If he had come home later, would she have already been gone, just like London?

Taking a deep breath, he set aside his gift for her and surveyed the room. The two arrangements of hydrangeas and magnolias were on her dresser alongside an edible bouquet of fruit. He'd had them sent to her today while he was at work. For her to think about their time in St. Louis together.

As he continued to look around the room, he didn't see any clothes pulled out. So they were all either in the drawers or in her bag.

He hoped they were still in the drawers. Gervais didn't want her to go. Instead, he wanted her to stay here. With him. Be part of his family.

Tapping the suitcase, he stared at Erika "That's not full, is it?"

He tried to sound light. Casual. The opposite of his current mental state.

She looked up quickly, her eyes such a startling shade of blue. "No, of course not. Why would you think that?"

"You left once before without a word." He wanted to

take her in his arms and coax her into bed for the day, not think about her leaving.

"I promised you I would stay for two weeks and I meant it. After that, though, I have to make a decision."

He tensed.

"Why? Why the push?"

"I need to move forward with my life at some point." Chewing her lip, she gestured at the suitcase.

"I've asked you to marry me and move in with me, yet still you hold back. Let me help support you while you make a decision, with time if not money, wherever you are." He would do that for her and more.

She looked at him with a steady, level gaze. "Seriously? Haven't we had this discussion already? We have time to make these decisions."

"The sooner we plan, the sooner we can put things into place."

"Do not rush, damn it. That is not the way I am. My parents learned that when they tried to push me into their way of life, their plans for me." Her gaze was level, icy.

"So you plan to leave, just not now?"

"I do not know what I am planning." Her voice came out in a whisper, a slight crack, as well. "I am methodical. I need to think through all of the options and consequences."

"Is that what you did the morning you left me? Stayed up and thought about why we needed to turn our backs on the best sex ever?" Dropping onto the edge of the bed across from her, he caught her gaze. Looked at the intensity of her blue eyes. She was damn sexy.

Beautiful. And he wasn't going to let her walk away as if this was nothing.

"Best sex ever? I like the sound of that." She licked her lips seductively, leaned toward him, her breasts pressing against her glittery tank top.

So tempting. And definitely not the direction he needed to take with her.

He raised his brow at her. "You're trying to distract me with your beautiful body."

"And you are using flattery. We need more than that." Crossing her arms, she scrutinized his face.

"I've made it clear I understand that. That's what our time together has been about. But I am willing to use everything I have at my disposal. I am not giving up."

"Everything?" She gestured to the flowers, the candy and a small jewelry box.

He'd forgotten about the gift he'd brought for her.

Pushing off the bed, he approached her, leaned on the arms of the chaise longue. He kissed her forehead, one arm around her, the other still cradling the box. "Flattery, which is easy because you are so very lovely. Charming words are tougher for me because I am a businessman, but for you, I will work so very hard with the words. And, yes, with gifts, too. Will you at least open it?"

She took the box from his hands, eyes fixed on his. Her fingers found the small bow. Gently, she slowly pulled the white bow off. The Tiffany box was bare, undressed now.

Erika lifted the lid, let out a small gasp. Two heart earrings encrusted in diamonds glinted back at her.

Gervais's voice dropped half an octave. "It made me think of our children. Two beautiful hearts."

He tucked a knuckle under her chin and raised it to see her face. Tears welled in her eyes.

Pulse pounding, he put his arms around her, held her tight to his chest. "I didn't mean to make you cry."

She shook her head, her silky blond hair tickling his nose. "It is sweet, truly. Thoughtful. A wonderful gift."

Kneeling in front of her, he wiped the tears off her pale cheeks. He'd wanted to get her something meaningful. Drawing her hands in his, he kissed the back of each one, then the insides of her wrists in the way he knew sent her pulse leaping. He could feel it even now as he rubbed his thumbs against her silky skin. "I want this to work. Tell me what I can do to make that happen. It is yours."

Her eyes flooded with conflicting feelings. It was as if he could see into her thought process where she worked so hard to weigh the pros and cons of a future. Somehow he knew she was at the precipice of the answer she'd been looking for. One he was scared as hell to receive.

And, cursing himself for his weakness, he couldn't resist this one last chance to sway the outcome. To make her want to stay. So he kissed her deeply, ebbing away the pressure of speech to make room for the pleasure they both needed.

Eleven

Gervais had Erika in his arms and he wanted that to go on for... He couldn't think of a time he wouldn't want her. Every cell inside him ached to have her. So much so his senses homed in to her. Almost to the exclusion of all else. Almost to the point where he lost sight of the fact he'd left the door ajar.

And now someone was knocking lightly on that door.

With more than a little regret, he set her away from him and struggled to regulate his breathing before turning to the door to find...a security guard?

Hell. How could he have forgotten for even a second that his family's wealth and power carried risk? They needed to stay on watch at all times.

Security guard James Smithson stood on the other side of the half-open door, his chiseled face grave.

Gervais had always liked James—a young guy, athletic and focused. James had almost made the cut for the team. The poor kid was in an interesting position; he'd declined a college football scholarship when his high school girlfriend became pregnant. James attended an online school while helping raise their son, but he'd shown up at a couple of Hurricanes training camps with impressive drive, even though his stats weren't quite strong enough.

So before Dempsey could send him home, Gervais had taken him aside and found out he had skills off the field, too. He'd offered him help forming his own security company, making him a part of the Hurricanes family.

"Sorry to disturb you, sir, but we have some unexpected company."

"I don't accept unexpected guests. You know that." Gervais stared at the guard. Who, to be fair, was doing a damn good job at not looking at Erika in her tight-fitting sparkly tank top that revealed her killer curves. Even so, he found himself wanting to wrap her up in a sheet. Just to be safe.

"I understand that, sir," James assured him. "But..."

Erika looked back and forth between the guard and Gervais. "I'll leave the two of you to talk." She closed the jewelry box and clutched it to her chest. "If you'll excuse me."

James held up a hand. "Ma'am, I believe you'll want to stay."

Ericka's face twisted in confusion. "I'm not sure how I can be of help—"

James scrubbed his jaw awkwardly. "It's your family. Their limos are just now coming through the front gate."

Gervais blinked slowly. "Limos?" Plural?

"My family?" Erika stammered, color draining from her skin. "*All* of my family?"

James gave a swift nod, his gun just visible in a shoulder harness under his sports jacket. "It appears so, ma'am. Both of your parents, four sisters, three of them married and some children, I believe?"

Gervais scratched the back of his head right about where an ache began. Talk about a baptism of fire meeting all the in-laws at once. So many. "I think we're going to need to air out the guesthouse."

The pressure of a headache billowed between Erika's temples. As she stood in the grand living room, attention drawn outside, past the confines of this room, she felt everything hit her at once. First, her conflicting feelings for Gervais, and now this.

Her entire family, down to her nieces, was here. Now. Her eyes trailed past the bay windows to where Gervais, her father, Gervais's brothers and his grandfather stood on the patio. Having drinks as if this was the most casual affair ever. As if this was something they had done together for years. Gervais had a gift with that, taking charge of a situation and putting everyone at ease.

She'd spent so much time focusing on the reasons to hold back, she forgot to look for the reasons they should. There was a lot to admire about this man. His obvious love of his family. His honorability in his standing up to care for his children. And the way he handled his business affairs with a mix of savvy and compassion. Her heart was softening toward him daily, and her resolve was all but gone.

And of course there was the passionate, thorough way he made love to her. A delicious memory tingled through her. She tore her eyes from him before she lost the ability to think reasonably at all.

Her father, Bjorn Mitras, slapped his knee enthusiastically at something Gervais had said. So they were getting along.

The mood inside the living room was decidedly less jovial. She could feel her sisters and mother sizing her up. Determining what Erika ought to do. And if she had to bet, getting her Master's in Nursing wasn't even on the table anymore. They'd never supported her ambitions. And if she was carrying a male child...well, they'd certainly have a lot of opinions to throw at her.

For the first time since learning she was pregnant, Erika felt alone.

She had hoped for an ally in Fiona, but Fiona hadn't come to meet everyone. She wasn't feeling well. Erika was not feeling all that great herself right now. Her family overwhelmed her in force.

Turning reluctantly from the bay windows, she studied her mother. Arnora Mitras had always been a slight, slim woman. Unlike other royals, she recycled outfits. But Arnora was a friend of many fashion designers. She was always draped in finery, things quite literally off the runway.

Her four sisters—Liv, Astrid, Helga and Hilda—stood in the far corner, discussing things in hushed tones. The twins, Helga and Hilda, both had the same nervous tic, tracing the outline of their bracelets. It was something that they had both done since they were little girls. Erika squinted at them, trying to figure out what had them on edge.

But it was Astrid who caught her gaze. Blue eyes of equal intensity shone back at her. Astrid gave a curt nod, her honey-blond bob falling into her face.

It was a brief moment of recognition, but then Astrid turned back to the conversation. Back to whispering.

Three of her sisters had married into comfort, but not luxury. Not like what the Reynauds offered. And they lived across Europe, leading quieter lives. No male heirs, no extravagance. A part of Erika envied that anonymity, especially now.

Of course, Gervais had seen to every detail. And in record time. He called in all the staff and security. Arranged what looked like a small state dinner in record time. He even had nannies brought in for her nieces.

Beignets, fruit and pralines were decadently arranged into shapes and designed. It looked almost too beautiful to eat. Erika watched as her sisters loaded their plates with the pastries and fruit, but they eyed the pralines with distrust. They weren't an open-minded bunch. They preferred to stick to what they knew. Which was also probably why they skipped over the iced tea and went straight for the coffee. That was familiar.

"Mother—" the word tumbled out of Erika's mouth "—some advance notice of your visit would have been nice."

"And give you the opportunity to make excuses to put us off? I think not."

Sighing unabashedly, Erika trudged on. "I was not putting you off, Mother. I was simply…"

"Avoiding us all," Helga finished for her as she approached. The rest of the Mitras women a step behind her.

"Hardly. I wanted time to prepare for your visit and to ensure that every detail was properly attended to."

Helga gave a wave to the spread of food and raised her brow. She clearly didn't believe Erika's protest. "This place is amazing. You landed well, sister."

"I am only visiting and getting things in order for our babies' sake." Erika's words were clipped, her emotions much more of a tangle.

"Well, you most certainly have something in common. Relationships have been built on less. I say go for it. Chase that man down until he proposes." The last word felt like nails on a chalkboard in Erika's ears. She schooled her features neutral, just as she had done when she was a translator. No emotions walked across her face.

Erika stayed diplomatically quiet.

Her mother's delicately arched eyebrow lifted, and she set her bone china coffee cup down with a slow and careful air. "He has already proposed? You two are getting married?"

"No, I did not say we are getting married."

"But he *has* proposed," Hilda pressed gently.

"Stop. This is why I would have preferred you wait to meet him. Give Gervais and me a chance to work out the details of our lives without family interference, and then we will share our plan."

Liv waggled her fingers toward the French doors leading to the vast patio. "*His* family is here."

"And they are not pushy," Erika retorted with conviction. She wasn't backing down from this. Not a chance.

"We are not pushy, either. We just want what is best for you." Hilda's porcelain complexion turned ruddy, eyes widening with hurt and frustration like during their childhood whenever people laughed at her lisp. She always had been the most sensitive of the lot.

Smoothing her green dress, Liv—always the prettiest, and the most rebellious, the infamous sex tape being the least of her escapades—took a deep breath and touched her hair. "I think all of this travel has made me a bit weary. I shall rest and we will talk later."

And with that her mother, Liv, Helga and Hilda all left the grand living room, heels clacking against the ground.

But Astrid didn't leave. She hung back, eyes fixed on Erika.

Anger burned in Erika's belly. Astrid was her oldest sister. The one who always told her what to do. She had been the sister to lecture her as a child. Erika fully anticipated some version of that pseudo-parental "advice" to spill out of Astrid's lips.

"Keep standing up for yourself. You are doing the right thing."

Gaping, Erika steadied herself on the back of the tapestry sofa. "Seriously? I appreciate the support but

I have to say it would be nice to have with Mother present."

Astrid shrugged. "She is frightening and strong willed. We all know that. But you do understand, you are strong, too. That is why we pushed you off the balcony first."

"Wow, thanks," Erika grumbled, recalling the terrifying drop from balcony to homemade trampoline.

"You are welcome." Astrid closed her in a tight embrace. In a half whisper, she added, "I love you, sister."

"I love you, too." That much of life was simple.

If only the other relationships—her relationship with Gervais—could be as easily understood. Or maybe they could. Perhaps the time had come to stop fighting her emotions and to embrace them.

Starting with embracing Gervais.

With the arrival of Erika's family, work for the Hurricanes had taken a backseat. Not that he would have had it any other way. They were his children's aunts and grandparents. They were important to him. He had to win them over—particularly her father, the king, not that King Bjorn had shown any sign of disapproval.

But important or not, they were the reason he was just now getting to his charts and proposals in the wee small hours of the morning.

Gervais pressed Play on the remote. He was holed up in the mini theater. He had a few hours of preseason games from around the league to catch up on. This was where he'd been slacking the most. Hadn't spent much time previewing the talent on the other teams yet. Because while Dempsey would fine-tune a solid fifty-three-man roster from the talent currently working out with the team, Gervais needed to cultivate a backup plan for injuries and for talent that didn't pan out. That meant he needed to familiarize himself with what else was out there, which underrated players might need a new home with the Hurricanes before the October trade deadline.

A creak from the door behind him caused him to turn around in his seat. Erika was there, in the doorway. A bag of popcorn in one hand, with two sodas in the other.

She certainly was a sight for his tired eyes. He drank her in appreciatively, noting the way her bright pink sundress fit her curves, the gauzy fabric swishing when she walked. The halter neck was the sort of thing he could untie with a flick of fabric, and he was seized with the urge to do just that.

As soon as possible. Damn.

"I thought this could be like a date." She gave him a sly smile, bringing her magnolia scent with her as she neared him, a lock of blond hair grazing his arm.

He took the sodas from her and set them in the cup holders on either side of the leather chairs in the media room.

"Well, then, best date ever."

"That seems untrue." Worry and exhaustion lined her voice. "I am sorry about my family arriving unexpectedly. And for how much time they are taking out of your workday."

"It's no trouble at all. They are my children's grandparents. That's huge." Pausing the game, he gave her a genuine smile, conceding that he wouldn't be giving the footage his full attention now. But he had notes on the talent across the league, of course. As an owner, he didn't run the team alone.

And right now nothing was more important to him than Erika and his children.

Settling deeper into the chair beside him, Erika flipped her long hair in front of one shoulder and centered the bag of popcorn between them.

"I also appreciate how patient you have been. And my sisters loved the tours through New Orleans." Erika leaned on his shoulder, the scent of her shampoo flooding his mind with memories of London. St. Louis. And last night. Making love, their bodies and scents and need mingling, taking them both to a higher level of satisfaction than he'd ever experienced.

Damn. He loved that. Loved that this smell made her present in his mind.

"Of course." He breathed, kissed her head, inhaled the scent of her hair and thought of their shower together.

Her breath puffed a little faster from her mouth. She nibbled her bottom lip and gestured to the screen. "May I ask what you are doing?"

Gervais hit Play, a game springing to life. "Well, I have to get a feel for who is out there. I have a team to build. So I may have to replace my current rookies with some of these guys."

Erika nodded. "And why is this so important to you? Why do you spend so much time on football when, according to the press, they are worth only a fraction of your overall portfolio?"

"Someone's been doing her research," he noted. Impressed.

"I was not joking when I told you that I am trying to figure out where to go from here. I am thinking through all possible paths." Her blue gaze locked on him. "Including the one you have proposed."

His chest ached with the need to convince her that was the best. But he restrained himself. Focused on her question.

"Why the focus on football?" he repeated, reaching into the popcorn bag for a piece to feed her. "My family is a lot like yours. They come with expectations. But I have my own expectations, and I've always wanted to carve out something that was all mine within the vast Reynaud holdings. Some success that I made myself, that was not handed to me. Does that make any sense?"

He presented her with the popcorn and she opened her lips. His touch lingered a bit longer than necessary against her soft mouth.

She chewed before she answered. "You want to stand on your own two legs?"

Gervais smiled inwardly. Her idiom use was so close. "Something like that. If I can stand on my own two feet, make this team into something…" His mind searched for the correct words.

"Then no one can take that away from you. It is yours alone."

Gervais nodded, stroking her arm. "Exactly. I imagine that's why you want your Master's in Nursing so badly. So that is holistically yours."

"Mmm," she said, tracing light lines on his chest.

"Very wise of you. You have been listening to me, I see."

Her touch stirred him. Heat rushed through his veins as he set aside the remote.

"We are more alike than you think." He curled an arm around her shoulders and drew her closer, his fingers skimming through her silky hair to the impossibly soft skin of her upper arm.

"Because we are both stubborn and independent?" She slid her finger into the knot of his tie and loosened the material.

"It's more than that." He wrenched the tie off, consigning the expensive Italian silk to the floor.

"We are both struggling to meet the expectations of too much helpful family?" She arched a pale brow at him, all the while fingering open buttons on his shirt.

The hell with waiting.

He slid an arm under her knees and lifted her up and onto his lap, straddling him. Her long sundress spilled over her thighs, covering her while exposing just the smallest hint of satin panties where she sat on his thighs.

"And we both need to lose ourselves in each other right now." His fingers sifted through her hair, seeking the ribbon that secured the halter top of her sundress.

"You are correct," she assured him, edging down his thighs so that their hips met.

Her breasts flattened to his chest.

A hungry groan tore from his throat.

He kissed her hard, his control fractured after so many days of thinking through every move with her, of strategizing this relationship like the most important deal of his life. Because while it was all that and more, Erika was also the hottest, most incredible woman he'd ever met, and he wanted her so badly he ached.

She met each hungry swipe of his tongue with soft sighs and teasing moans that threatened to send him right over the edge. Already, her fingers worked the fastening of his belt, her thighs squeezing his hips.

"This day has been too much," she admitted, her whispered confession one of the few times she'd confided her feelings. "I need you. This."

And he wanted to give it to her. Now and forever.

But he knew better than to rattle her with talk of forever. Understood she was still coming to terms with a future together. So he forced himself to be everything she needed right now.

Flicking free the tie at her neck, he edged away from the kiss just enough to admire the fall of the gauzy top away from her beautiful breasts. Her skin was so pale she almost glowed in the darkened theater, his tanned hands a dark shadow against her as he cupped the full weight of one breast.

Molding her to his palm, he teased his thumb across the pebbled tip, liking the way her hips thrust harder against his as he did. She was more sensitive than ever, the least little touch making her breath come faster. Making her release quicker.

Just thinking about that forced him to move faster, one hand skimming down her calf to slip beneath the hem of her long dress. He stroked her bare knee. Smoothed up her slender thigh. Skimmed the satin of panties already damp for him.

She cried out his name as he worked her through the thin fabric, coaxing an orgasm from her with just a few strokes. Her back arched as the tension pulsed through her in waves, her knees hugging him until the spasms slowed.

He didn't waste time searching out a condom, since they no longer needed one. He let her go just long enough to shove aside the placket of his pants and free his erection.

She took over then, her fingers curling the hard length and stroking up to the tip until his heart damn near beat its way out of his chest. He kissed her deeply, distracting her from her erotic mission, leaving him free to enter her.

And oh, damn.

The slick heat of her squeezed him, the scent of her skin and taste of her lips like a drug for his senses. He gripped her hips, guiding her where he wanted. Where he needed. And looking up at her in the half-light reflected from the dim screen, he could see that she was as lost as him. Her plump lips were moist and open, her eyes closed as she rode him, finding her pleasure with as much focus and intensity as him.

He must have said her name, because her eyes opened then. Her blue gaze locked on his.

And that did it.

More than any touch. Any kiss. Any sexy maneuver in the dark. Just having Erika right there with him drove him over the edge. The pleasure flared over his skin and up his spine, rocking him. He held on tight to her, surprised to realize she had found her own peak again right along with him, their bodies in perfect sync.

After the waves of pleasure began to fade and the sweat on their bodies cooled, he stroked her spine through that long veil of her hair, savoring the feel of her in his arms, her warm weight so welcome in his lap. He wanted her every night. Wanted to be the one to take care of her and ease her. Pleasure her.

But even as his feelings surged, he could tell she was pulling back. Throwing up a seemingly impenetrable wall of ice as she edged back and tugged her dress into place. Her family's arrival had shaken her. Awakened an instinct to define herself in opposition to their expectations.

A part of him understood that. And was damn proud of her, too. But that same urge that motivated her to stand her ground, meet her parents and family dead-on, might also be the reason he felt frozen out.

The more he thought about it, the more real seemed the idea of losing not just his children, but her, too.

And as if she sensed his thoughts, she got to her feet. "Gervais, my family's here, so I would appreciate it if we didn't sleep together with them nearby."

"Seriously?" He propped himself up on his elbows.

"I know it may seem silly with the babies on the way, but...them being here? I need space."

He studied her face, her platinum-blond hair tumbling around her shoulders. "Damn it, Erika, all I've done is honor your need for space, taking cues off you."

"A few short days. Less than a month. And you call that space? Time?" Her throat moved. "Clearly we have very different ideas about taking our time. Maybe we don't understand each other nearly as well as you think."

Frustration fired inside him as he felt victory slip away word by word. He tugged on his pants, all the while searching for the right words and coming up short.

Not that it mattered, since before he could speak, she'd left the room. The click of that door made it clear.

She was running scared and he wasn't welcome to join her now.

If ever.

Twelve

The excitement of the fans at the home Hurricanes game was dwarfed in comparison to the buzz going on in the owners' box.

Erika sat against the leather chair, taking it all in, her heart in her throat after the way she'd left things with Gervais last night. But the way he made her feel scared her down to her toes. He made her want too much at a time when she had to be more careful than ever about protecting her heart and her future.

Gramps Leon called out to the Mitras clan. "Did Erika tell you how the Reynauds came into their fortune?"

"No, Leon, she hasn't shared much of anything with us. We'd love to know. American origin stories are so fascinating," Hilda said darkly, shooting her a daggered look across the spread of shrimp gumbo and decadent brownies. Erika rolled her eyes, moving closer to the glass to get a look at the field. Somehow, this game she had disliked so much was starting to make sense to her.

"Grampa Leon, we all know that story," Fiona said with a light laugh, her hands wringing together. She was nervous but Erika couldn't tell why.

"Yes, but the beautiful princesses and queen haven't. And they want to. Who am I to deny them that?" he said with a wink at Hilda, whose face was already turning into a toothy grin.

"It was a high-stakes poker game. My surly old Cajun ancestor was sweating as he stared at his hand of cards. The stakes were incredibly high, you see," Gramps Leon began, leaning on his knees.

"What were the stakes, Leon?" Queen Arnora asked, on her best behavior, since Erika had been emphatic with her mother that histrionics would not be tolerated. The babies were Erika and Gervais's, not potential little royal pawns.

Arnora had vowed she simply wanted to bond with their expanding family and was thrilled over impending grandparenthood.

"If my riverboat grandpa won, he would get a ship out of the deal. But if he lost, he would have to sign a non-compete. And stay working for the tyrant captain who kept him away from home for months on end. Needless to say, the cards laid out right for him and he won the first ship in the fleet. The Reynaud family empire was born. Just like that." He snapped his fingers, eyes alight with a new audience to entertain. "The rest is history. The family has been successful ever since. Especially my grandboys."

King Bjorn inclined his head. "You feel responsible for your grandchildren's success?"

"Yessir, King Bjorn. I'm proud of all of those boys. Feel like I practically raised them myself. Though I kind of did," Gramps Leon wheezed, eyes drifting to Theo, who shrank in the back corner, "My son almost made it big…eh. No matter. My grandboys did. That's what matters in the end."

Erika watched as Theo fidgeted with his drink, balling up a cocktail napkin in his right fist. She knew he hadn't been the best father, but a small part of her felt sympathy for him.

"And what did all your grandchildren do?" Arnora asked lightly, swirling the champagne in her glass.

Erika had often wondered how her mother had such ease with others but not as much with her children. Her mom took her role as a royal, a liaison to the world, seriously. Erika looked around at the Reynaud family and saw their bond, but not only that. She saw their relaxed air. The way they kept life…real. Connected. She wanted that for her children, as well.

And yet she'd pushed her babies' father away the night before out of fear of living like her parents.

Gramps Leon's dark eyes gleamed with pride and affection. "Well, you know Gervais bought his own team. I figure they'll make it big soon the way that boy works. And Dempsey is the youngest coach in the league's history. Henri is already a franchise quarterback looking for his first championship ring. Even Jean-Pierre is doing good things as a quarterback for that northern Yankee team. Where is he again?"

Theo cleared his throat. "New York. Jean-Pierre is the starting quarterback for the New York Gladiators." Pride pierced his words, and he lifted his eyes to meet Leon's. So he did care, Erika thought. It was just masked.

She wished it was that easy to tell what was going on with Gervais. Nothing he'd said so far betrayed any level of an emotional depth. Just sex. But that wasn't enough for her. And that was the reason she hadn't been able to help but pull away the night before.

Last night when she'd gone to him, she'd believed he might really care for her. Sure, the sex was great and he wanted to provide for their children. But she'd started to think that he also genuinely liked her, sex and children aside.

Before then, she'd been so sure of him. Of the decision she was close to making.

As she sat in the owners' box again, she realized she couldn't stop replaying seeing the bed empty when she woke up, knowing it was her fault for pushing him away but not knowing what she could have done differently. Erika would have continued to analyze the situation if it wasn't for the approach of Liv, her sister. The one that had been through the sex tape fiasco.

The scandal had almost cost Liv everything.

Liv narrowed her gunmetal eyes at Erika, pinning her. She sat next to Erika, hands firmly grasping the wineglass's stem. The smell of alcohol assaulted Erika's sense of smell, turning her stomach sour.

"Sister," she said lazily, "this family..."

Erika straightened, finishing the sentence for her. "Is filled with wonderful, loving people."

Liv nodded solemnly. "Yes. And how do you say—American royalty?"

Erika's eyes remained out toward the field, toward where Gervais stood with a reporter giving an interview, players and photographers around them. She would not be dignifying her sister's comment with a response.

"All I am trying to say, dear sister, is that you need to be here. You could be royalty for real if you did." Liv's words, spoken in a hushed tone, had a bit of a slur to them.

"That's not what matters to me. What matters is—" But the words caught in her throat as she watched Gervais get hit by two men locked in a tackle. Gervais was on the sidelines, knocked to his feet, his bare skull slamming back into the ground. Hard. Tackled on the sidelines with no equipment.

She barely registered what the Mitrases or the Reynauds were doing. In an instant, the panic that stayed her breath and speech was replaced by a need to move. A need for action. The damn need to get to his side.

Pushing her way to the door that led down to the stands, she ran smack into James, the security guard who had first alerted them that the whole Mitras clan was arriving. He stood at the door to the tunnels leading through the bowels of the stadium and out onto the field. His credentials were clipped to his jacket, a communication piece in his ear. "Princess, I am afraid I can't allow you onto the field. Please wait here. I promise to keep you updated about Mr. Reynaud."

James put a hand on her shoulder. Consoling? Or to restrain? Either way, it didn't matter to her because this man kept her from Gervais.

Years of practice drills during her time in the military pressed her muscles into action. Without sparing a second thought, she grabbed his hand and bent back his pinkie. A minor move but one that could quickly drive a man to his knees if she pushed farther. "James, I am a nurse, but I am also former military. I can flip you onto your back in a heartbeat and you cannot—will not—fight me because I am pregnant. Now, we can do this simply or we can make this difficult, but one way or another, I am going to Gervais."

James's eyes narrowed, then he exhaled through gritted teeth. "I could lose my job for this." He shook his head, rolling his eyes. "But come with me. You'll need my credentials to get through to the field."

She bit her lip hard in relief. "Thank you."

"Um, ma'am, could you let go of my pinkie?"

"Oh." She blinked fast, having forgotten she'd even still held him pinned. She released his hand and stepped back.

Wincing, he shook his hand. "Follow me."

She followed him through the corridors, urging him to go faster and barely allowing herself to breathe until she saw Gervais with her own eyes. He waved off his personal security team as soon as she came into sight, his face twisted in pain as the team doctor shone a small flashlight in front of his eyes, checking his pupils.

Her medical training came to the fore and took in his pale face. He sat on the ground, upright, and was not swaying. His respiration was even, steady. Reassuring signs. Her heart slowed from a gallop. He would need a more thorough exam, certainly, but at least he was conscious. Cognizant.

"Gervais? Are you okay?" Erika knelt beside him, then turned to the team's doctor, her voice calm and collected now. "Is he all right?"

On the field beside him, the game continued, the fans cheering over a play while Erika's focus remained on Gervais and all that mattered to her.

"I'm fine," Gervais growled, then winced, pressing his hand to the back of his head.

The doctor tucked away his flashlight into his bag. "He's injured, no question, given the size of that goose egg coming up. Probably a concussion. He should go to the emergency room to be checked over."

"Then let us go." She barked the command at the doctor. Meanwhile, the game had resumed playing, and she trailed behind him.

As she stepped out of the arena with Gervais, leaving her family behind, reality crashed into her. Her heart was in her throat for this man. He was the father of her children. But she barely knew him and already he'd turned her world upside down. She felt as if she, too, had taken a blow to the head and her judgment was scrambled. How could she care so much so soon?

What was she doing here? She had started to love him, but maybe she just loved the surface image. Maybe she'd done what her family had done—just looked at the surface. After all, he'd offered no feelings, no emotions to her. Just convenient arrangements for their children and sex. His marriage proposal had never included mention of love.

And she couldn't settle for less than everything from him, just as she wanted to give him her all.

What if in spite of all logic, she had fallen in love with him and he could never offer her his full heart?

There were only a few times in his life that Gervais had felt extreme elation and intense concern all at the same time. This was certainly being added to that tally.

Later that night as he stretched out in his own bed, Erika hovering, he was still replaying that moment Erika had rushed out to him. His head throbbed but his memories were crystal clear.

Watching Erika care enough about him to rush to his side filled him with a renewed purpose. He'd been blown away and more than a little unnerved watching her rush to his side, somehow having persuaded James to let her through security and out onto the field.

Make no mistake, he always wanted her there. By his side. But he didn't want any harm to come to her or their children, either. The thought of harm befalling her or their children by her own rash actions gnawed at him. The security was there for a reason. God, she was everything to him. Everything. And he wasn't sure how he could have missed out on realizing the depth of that.

They could be so good together, but it also seemed as if the risk of her pulling back was at an all-time high. All of her interactions with him since the CT scan came back had been rigid. Formalized. As if she was a nurse doing a job, not a woman tending to her lover.

That reaction clapped him upside the head harder than the wall of a football player that had crashed into him. Her reactions didn't add up. She had been so upset on the sidelines, so freaked out about what was happening to him. And now she was answering in snippets of sentences. He didn't want to upset her more, or keep her awake all night. But his family had been in and out of the room for hours. It was nearing morning before he finally had a moment alone with her.

His head throbbed far more from this situation than his minor concussion.

Propped up on the bed, he quietly said, "How did you get James to let you join me on the field?"

She flushed the most lovely shade of pink, her hand fidgeting with her blond hair draped over her shoulder. "I used some of my military skills to persuade him. Nothing extreme, given my condition, of course, just a small but painful maneuver."

"Seriously? Apparently, I need to have you train my security."

"And give away my secrets?" She gave him a princess-like annoyed scoff. "I think not. Besides, he should not have tried to keep me from you."

"While I find that sexy on one level, you have to be careful and think about the babies. What if you had been hurt?"

She shrugged, looking him square in the eye. "I was careful. You are the injured one. Now, relax. You may not be stressed but you have to stay awake. Do as the doctor instructed or I am taking you back to the hospital."

He felt the prickles of her emotions. Had to change the direction. Bring it back to breezy. Shooting her a sly smile, he said, "We could have sex. That would keep me awake."

"You're supposed to rest." Eyes narrowing with annoyance, Erika crossed her arms.

"Then take advantage of me. I'll just lie back and be very still." He closed his eyes, then half opened one of them to look at her. Hoping to elicit some sort of response out of her. Hoping to see that radiant smile spread across her face. Damn. He loved that smile.

"Oh, you think you are funny. But I am not laughing right now. You are injured and I am here to make sure you take care of yourself."

"You could tie me up so I don't get too…boisterous."

"Boisterous? Now, that's an interesting word choice and a challenge. But sadly, for your own health, I will have to hold strong against your boisterous charms. Let us play cards." There was no jest in her voice.

"Cards? Strip poker, maybe."

"No, thank you."

"Then I'll pass on the cards. I gotta confess, my vision is a little blurry." He held up his hand, trying to focus on his fingers. A dull ache pulled at him.

Turning, practically out the door to the room, Erika said, "I should get the doctor."

"The doctor has checked me. I've had an X-ray and MRI and CT scan. I'm fine. Concussed, but nothing the players don't face all the time. I'm not going to be a wimp in front of my team."

"They wear helmets."

"I have a thick head. Just ask anyone I work with. Or those I don't work with." He tried his best to crack that smile wide-open, but Erika's face was as solemn as ever. She was shutting him out and he didn't understand why.

"I'm not laughing."

"You want to be serious? Then let's be serious. Erika, I want you to move in with me. Hell, to be honest, I want you to marry me, but I will settle for you moving in here. Go to school here. Let's be together. Life is complicated enough. Let's enjoy more popcorn dates and sex in the screen room and every other room in this place. And in my cars. I have many, you know." The declaration was earnest. He wanted her. For now. Forever. And not just because they were having children together.

Erika slammed her hand on the desk, a quiet rage burning in her fine, regal features. "I am still not laughing, Gervais. We cannot build a relationship on sex. I need something meaningful. I have fought so hard to build a life for myself, to be seen as someone more than ornamental. A royal jewel in the crown meant to bear an heir to the line, defunct or not."

"Erika. It's not like that. I don't think of you as a crown jewel." Gervais searched her face, trying to understand her.

"All you have done since I told you I was pregnant is press for marriage. I have worked hard to gain my independence, my happiness, and I will fight for my children, as well. They deserve something more."

"Erika, I—" Gervais, the man who always had a plan, stammered, fighting for words.

Tears glistened in her eyes, but she stood tall, her shoulders braced as she backed away. "I will wake one of your brothers. It is morning anyway." Erika turned, was already to the threshold and then gone before he could even think of words to delay her.

He had botched this chance to win her over. And what a helluva time to realize just how much he loved her, this proud, strong woman. He loved her intelligence, her passion, even her stubbornness. He adored every hair on her head.

He loved her so deeply he knew any fear of repeating his father's mistakes would not happen. Gervais loved Erika. Real love. The kind that he knew damn well was rare in this world.

And in rushing her, he may have ruined his chance to have her.

As Erika let her feet dangle over the edge of the dock, she focused her attention out on the lake's waters. The late-afternoon sun cast golden shimmers on the surface of the water.

She felt as if the whole day had been a training exercise. Nothing had felt real to her. Since she stormed out of Gervais's room last night, Erika had felt disoriented.

The problem was simple. Despite logic and reason, she was madly in love with Gervais. These past few days had proved how easy it would be to fall into a routine together.

But they had also shown her how difficult it would be for them to become more than…well, whatever this was.

A breeze stirred her loose blond hair, pushing strands in front of her eyes. Though it was humid, and the bugs played a loud symphony, she was comforted by the noises, smells and sights of this foreign land. It was starting to feel a bit like home. Another confusing feeling to muddle through.

The wind gusted stronger, stirring the marsh grass into a beautiful shudder. Boats zipped a ways off from the dock, and she watched the wakes crest and crash into each other.

It was practically silent, except for the boats and bugs. Everyone had gone. She'd packed her family into their limos, watched from the dock until the landscape of New Orleans swallowed them up.

The Reynauds were gone on a day trip. Theo's idea, actually. He'd even taken Gramps with them. All the Reynaud men, save for Jean-Pierre, on one trip in one spot. Probably something that didn't happen too often.

Inching backward on the dock, she pulled her knees to her chest. Erika was at a complete loss of what to do.

If only it could be as simple as the word *love*. She loved her children. She loved their father. But she still didn't know if he loved her back. On the one hand they hadn't known each other long, yet she was certain of her feelings. She needed him to be just as sure.

Her head spun with it all.

And her heart twisted.

She knew what she wanted, but it didn't make sense. She wanted to say to hell with logic and stay here with Gervais. To move in. To love him. To build their family together and pray it would all work out.

Footsteps echoed along the dock, startling her an instant before she heard Gervais's deep voice.

"You did not leave with your family."

Whipping her head up, she took him in. Fully. And a lump formed in the back of her throat.

"Did you think that I would do that without saying goodbye to you?" She would never have done something so cruel. Not after what she felt for him and all they'd been through together.

His chin tipped, the moonlight beaming around him. "Is this your farewell, then?"

"I am not going home with them."

He pressed further, drawing near to her. "And to school in the UK?"

Decision upon decision. Layer upon layer. "Do you think I should?"

"I want you to stay here but I cannot make this decision for you. I don't want to rush you."

His answer surprised her. "I expected you to try to persuade me."

"I've made my wishes clear. I want you to stay. I want us to build a life. But I can see you're afraid. I'll wait as long as you need." He knelt to her level, touched her face with his steady hand.

She bristled. "I am not afraid. I am wary. There is a difference."

"Is there?"

She churned over his words. "If you want to mince words in translation, then all right. I am afraid of making the wrong choice and having our children suffer because of it."

"And you think we are the wrong choice?"

"I think that I love you." There. It was out there. This was how she'd make her decision. Let him know exactly where she stood.

"I know that I love you."

She swallowed hard and blinked back tears, barely daring to believe what she was hearing. "You do?"

"I absolutely do. No question in my mind." His voice wrapped around her heart like a blanket, soothing and private and intimate all at once. He was...everything.

"I believe you and I want so very much to believe that will be enough."

"Then be willing to challenge that warrior spirit of yours and fight for what we feel for each other."

Fight? Erika had been used to fighting for the things that mattered to her. Maybe this battleground wasn't so foreign, after all. "Fight."

"Yes, stay here. Get to know me. Let me get to know you. And every day for the rest of our lives we'll get to know more and more about each other. That's how it works."

"I will move in with you?" The idea was tantalizing this time and she wondered why she had dismissed it so readily before. Out of pride? The thought of losing herself in her family again reminded her how hard she had fought for her freedom to live her life. And truth be told, she wanted to live here, in this fascinating town with this even more fascinating man. She wanted to give her children a family life like the Reynauds.

She wanted Gervais.

Looking over his shoulder, her eyes took in the mansion.

"Yes. If that is what you wish."

"I can go to school here?" She hadn't even looked into programs around here, but she could. There were ways to make this work. Now that she knew, beyond a shadow of a doubt, that he loved her.

"Yes. If that is what you wish," he said again, those final words making it clear he understood her need for control over her life.

"We bring up our children here?"

"Yes, and in your country, too, whenever possible, if you wish. And most of all I hope that you'll do all of that as my wife." He squeezed her hand, brought her to a standing position.

Erika looked up at him, reading his eyes. "As simple as that?"

Pulling her into him, he shook his head. "Not simple at all. But very logical."

"Love as a logical emotion?" The idea tickled her.

"The love I feel for you defies any logic it's so incredible. It fills every corner of me. But I do know that my plan to work harder than I've ever worked at anything in my life to make you happy? Yes, that will be a plan I'm not leaving to chance. I will make that a conscious choice. But if you need time to decide—"

She cupped his face in her hands. "I do not need any more time at all. Yes."

"Yes?" Lines of excitement and relief tugged at his face.

She breathed in the scent of him, feeling balanced and renewed. Sure, for the first time in weeks, that this was where she was supposed to be.

"Yes, I love you and I will move in with you. I will go to school here. I will have our children here. And most of all, yes, I will marry you."

He gathered her closer, a sigh of relief racking his big, strong body. "Thank God."

"How did I ever get so lucky to meet and fall for such a wonderfully stubborn man?"

"We knew that day we met."

"In spite of logic."

"Instincts. With instincts like ours, we will make a winning team—" he rested his mouth on hers "—for life."

* * * * *

THE HEIR THE PRINCE SECURES

JENNIE LUCAS

To Katharine, who inspires me every day, and who daily shows how the impossible can be achieved with both kindness and grace.

CHAPTER ONE

Love meant everything to Tess Foster.

Not just love. *Romance.* Pink roses. Castles and hearts.

As a lonely teenager living in the attic of her aunt and uncle's Brooklyn bakery, Tess tried to keep her romantic dreams secret. In a modern world of easy hookups and one-night stands, it was embarrassing, even shameful, to be an idealistic virgin waiting for true love. As other girls giggled over their first fumbling sexual experiences in the back seats of cars, Tess kept quiet and hoped no one would notice that she spent her own Saturday nights with dusty books in the library, dreaming of handsome princes.

She'd known, even then, that when she finally gave herself to a man, it would only be to someone she truly loved. She'd wear white on her wedding day and lose her virginity on their honeymoon. She'd settle for nothing less than the fairy tale.

Then, at twenty-four, she met Stefano.

One moment, she'd been working as a waitress at a glamorous cocktail party hosted by a Spanish media mogul. Carrying a silver tray of champagne flutes through a crowd of movie stars and tycoons, Tess had been lost in thought, worrying whether she'd be able to afford another semester of design school.

Then a handsome stranger's dark, smoldering gaze had pierced her heart, making her lose her breath.

That had been it. That one look from him had almost brought her to her knees.

Because no one had ever looked at her like that. It was as if Tess, the hopeless, invisible wallflower, had suddenly become the most desirable, fascinating woman in all the world.

And the man who was looking at her...

Dark and sexy, he'd stood arrogantly apart, his perfectly cut tuxedo a mere veneer of civilization over his powerful, muscular body. His dark eyes had burned through her as he came toward her, moving with an almost feline grace.

"Buonasera," he'd said huskily.

Tess had turned the silver tray toward him so fast the flutes nearly knocked over. Her voice had squeaked. "Champagne?"

"No." With a sensual smile, he'd glanced at the martini already in his hand. "I don't want champagne."

"Something else, then?"

His voice was husky, with the barest trace of an accent. "I want your name."

And that had been the start of the most spectacular night of Tess's life. When she'd finished her shift at the party, he'd whisked her off in his chauffeured town car to an elegant, romantic dinner at the most exclusive restaurant in New York. Afterward, he'd suggested they go dancing. When she'd said she didn't have a dress, he'd stopped at a designer boutique and bought her one that sparkled and swayed against her skin.

She'd tried to resist, but she couldn't. Not when he'd looked at her like that.

Tess had danced in his arms for hours before he'd kissed her, leaving her intoxicated, breathless. He'd invited her to his suite at the luxurious Leighton Hotel. Looking into his dark, hungry eyes, she'd known only one answer.

"Yes," she'd whispered.

In just one night, he'd ruthlessly taken her virginity. And more than that: he'd dazzled her lonely, romantic heart into loving him.

But the next morning, waking up alone in the cold, gray dawn, she realized that she'd never even learned his full name.

A few weeks later, she'd found out she was pregnant. Her uncle had been furious, her aunt disappointed in her.

For the last fourteen months, even as Tess's two best friends, Hallie Hatfield and Lola Price, had rolled their eyes, she'd stubbornly insisted that Stefano would someday return to claim her and their baby. After all, even if she didn't know his last name, he knew hers. Stefano could find her anytime he wanted.

If he hadn't come yet, there had to be a good reason. Maybe he had amnesia, or his plane had crashed on a desert island. Those things happened, didn't they? Tess imagined every reason she could think of, except for the obvious one. Her friends thought she was nuts.

But Tess had to believe Stefano would return. Because, otherwise, she'd surrendered all her dreams for nothing. She'd given up her chance for a career, for marriage, for one love that would last her whole life—all for a one-night stand that had left her pregnant, abandoned and alone.

If Stefano didn't come back, it would mean the world was a cold and unforgiving place, and all the fairy tales her mother had read her as a child were wrong. Tess didn't want to live in a world like that. So she'd done her best to believe.

Suddenly, tonight, she couldn't.

Not for one more second.

Tess's shoulders drooped as she wearily pushed her five-month-old baby's stroller out of the Campania Hotel New York. It was ten o'clock on a warm, humid night in early September, but the night was just getting started. The streets were crowded with people leaving restaurants and streaming out of Broadway theaters, their faces animated and bright as they passed beneath the sparkling lights of the hotel's porte cochere.

Tess felt empty and sad. She'd just watched her friend Hallie sing at her husband's luxury hotel. After Hallie's amazing performance, Cristiano had publicly declared his love for his wife.

She was glad for Hallie, truly she was. Her friend deserved every happiness, especially after what she'd gone through. Normally, Tess would have told herself that seeing a couple so deeply in love proved that it might still happen for her, too.

But not tonight.

She'd been up since four that morning, working at her uncle's bakery while also caring for her baby. She felt sweaty and exhausted. Tendrils of her long red hair were plastered to her neck. Even Tess's jaunty handmade outfit, a vintage-style shirt and midi pencil skirt with mixing patterns, was wrinkled. She looked down at her adorable sleeping baby, her plump cheeks and dark hair, and a hard lump rose to her throat.

For over a year, she'd ignored her uncle's criticism, her aunt's disappointed sighs and her friends' teasing. She'd told herself Stefano would come back to her. But after seeing Hallie and Cristiano together, so happy together in their own little world, Tess had realized she was fooling herself.

Give it up. A memory came of Lola's tart voice. *He's never coming back, Tess.*

Tess stopped. As streams of people passed by her stroller on both sides of the sidewalk, she savagely wiped tears off her cheeks. She'd planned to take the subway back to Brooklyn with her baby rather than ask Hallie for a ride and risk crying in front of her. Her friends always teased her about being too cheerful and optimistic. She couldn't let them know how she really felt inside.

But that was wrong. Hallie was her friend, and Tess had left without so much as a farewell. Taking a deep breath, she tried to smooth her face into a smile. She'd go back inside now and congratulate Hallie. And if she asked why Tess was crying—

As Tess started to turn, she walked into a wall.

Not a wall. *A man.*

For a second, she saw stars from the blunt force of hitting her head against his chest. Dizzy, she shook her head, mortified.

"I'm so sorry," she blurted out. "It was my fault—"

Then she saw him.

For a second, Tess couldn't breathe. Her heart pounded in her throat as she tilted her head back to stare at the man's handsome face, his sharp cheekbones and jawline shadowed by the lights of the hotel's grand porte cochere.

Tall and dark-haired, the man wore a sleek black jacket that emphasized his broad shoulders, and trousers that fit snugly over powerful thighs. His tailored shirt was open a single button at the neck.

He wasn't strictly handsome, perhaps. His aquiline profile was a bit too arrogant, the set of his square jaw too thuggish. But he gave the impression of intense masculine beauty. His face was arresting, his body powerful, giving him the look of a dark angel.

The man's eyes widened, the irises so dark as to be almost black against his olive-colored skin.

Tess's lips parted.

"Stefano?" she whispered, gripping the handle of the stroller for balance. "Is it really you?"

She knew those dark eyes. That handsome face. Those cruel, sensual lips. She knew every bit of him. She'd dreamed of him, day and night, for over a year.

"Tess," he murmured.

His low, husky voice caressed the short syllable of her name. So he was real, then. *He was real.*

"You came back for me," she whispered. Joy rose inside her, brighter than all the lights of Broadway and Times Square put together. "You came back!"

His jaw tightened. He looked down at her from his lofty height, his broad shoulders towering over her. "What do you want?"

What did she want? She wanted to throw her arms around him, to cry out her happiness to all the world. After a difficult year, with everyone mocking her, this proved that happy endings still happened as long as your heart was true and you had faith. She'd been right!

But, as Tess moved to throw her arms around him, Stefano stepped back from her.

Something was wrong. She bit her lip, bewildered. "I am so happy to see you. Did you just get back?"

"Get back?"

"To New York." When he didn't answer, she continued with a blush, "Our night together, you said that you had to return to Europe but you'd be back soon—"

"Oh. Yes." His chiseled face was dark with shadow beneath his hard cheekbones as the lights of passing traffic moved past them on the avenue. "I've been in New York often this summer. And now for Fashion Week, of course."

"You've been here all this time?" A chill went through her as her joy withered inside her. She whispered, "And you didn't want to see me?"

Stefano frowned. His voice was a low baritone. "I liked you very much, Tess. It was an amazing night. But..."

"But?" she croaked.

Coming closer, he looked down at her, his dark eyes glittering. "But it was just a night."

To him it had just been a one-night stand, nothing more? One night, easily enjoyed and easily forgotten?

Tess's cheeks went hot as she remembered telling him in bed, in the hushed quiet before dawn with their naked bodies still intertwined, "I'm already falling in love with you."

In her innocence, Tess had meant every word. She'd been intoxicated by sensual pleasure she'd never imagined. In just twelve hours, he'd given her the most intense happiness of her life, more emotion and joy and beauty than she'd known for twelve *years* before. If that wasn't love, what was?

Now, looking at his coldly handsome face, Tess realized that her honesty had been a fatal mistake. Because when she woke the next morning, he'd been gone.

"Your Highness!" A young girl caught up behind him on the sidewalk. She was obviously a model—tall, slender, dark-haired and incredibly beautiful in a white dress that set off her dark skin. She held out a small notebook to Stefano. "You forgot this."

"Thanks, Kebe," he said gruffly.

She tossed her dark curls. "See you in Paris."

She left in a perfect catwalk stride.

"Who was that?" Tess whispered.

"A friend," he said. His dark eyes flicked briefly to the sleeping baby in the stroller behind her. "Well. It was nice to see you again." His expression was cool. Courteous. Distant. "Goodbye."

Pain and shock spread through Tess's body, making her knees shake.

He hadn't been looking for her.

At all.

He'd rejected her long ago. She just hadn't known it till now. Stinging tears filled her eyes.

All this time she'd dreamed of him as a romantic hero

who was desperate to return to her. The truth was that Stefano simply hadn't wanted to see her again.

Over the last year, as Tess had dropped out of college to work full-time at her uncle's bakery, struggling to provide and care for their baby, Stefano had been traveling the world, enjoying himself. In fact, it seemed he'd just been out on a date with a beautiful girl who looked barely eighteen. Whom he'd promised to see again in Paris.

Stricken, she looked at him with tears in her eyes.

Stefano's expression hardened. "Tess, it was for the best."

Wordlessly shaking her head, she backed away. For so long, she'd held out hope, imagining one perfect love brought by destiny, by fate. She'd remained faithful to Stefano's memory, dreaming of the day her handsome prince would return on a white horse to whisk her and the baby to his castle.

But Stefano was no prince.

Her friends and family had been right.

Tess gripped the stroller for support as anguish and exhaustion punched through her.

They'd been right.

"Come now. Don't act like your heart's broken," he said sharply. "How long did it take you to get over me? A few days?"

"How can you say that?" she whispered.

He looked pointedly at the baby in the stroller. "She's yours, isn't she?"

Yes. And yours. The words rose inside her, but got caught in her throat.

"And what about her father?" he demanded. "How would he feel if he knew you were here now, talking to me?"

"You tell me."

"How would I know?" Reaching out, he cupped her cheek. For a moment, in spite of everything, she closed her eyes, shivering at his touch as a flash of heat pulsed through her.

Stefano dropped his hand. "Let's not try to make more of our night than it was." He glanced at the baby. "Obviously, you quickly moved on. So did I. Our night was enjoyable enough. But it was meaningless."

Enjoyable enough?

Meaningless?

It was the final straw. She felt a flash of despair, the destructive kind that froze to the bone.

"Our night didn't mean anything to you?" Heart in her throat, she whispered, "You changed my life."

"Sorry," he said coldly.

She felt the word like a bullet.

"Fine." She closed her eyes briefly, shuddering. "We'll survive alone."

Knees shaking, she turned and walked away from him as fast as she could, away from her broken heart, from her shame that she'd so foolishly believed in the fairy tale. She fled the glittering lights of the Campania toward a shadowy side street, desperate to reach the far-off subway entrance, where she could sob in peace.

Prince Stefano Zacco di Gioreale stared after Tess, shocked by the jolt of her words, by the raw emotion he'd seen on her face and, most of all, by his body's reaction to seeing her again.

Tess Foster was even more beautiful than he remembered. He'd lied when he'd said he'd quickly moved on. The truth was that he'd spent the last year trying not to recall her hauntingly lovely heart-shaped face, her red hair, her bright emerald eyes, her sweet pink lips. He'd tried to forget her lush body and the way she'd felt naked in his arms.

Most of all, he'd tried to erase the memory of her intense, heartfelt whisper the next morning. *I'm already falling in love with you.*

For the last year, he'd done his best to forget. He'd told himself he had. Still, when he'd returned to New York in July to preside over the launch of Mercurio's flagship store, there was a reason he'd chosen to stay at the Campania Hotel rather than return to the Leighton, which had all those sweet, savage memories of their night together.

From the moment he'd first seen her carrying a tray of champagne at Rodrigo Cabrera's cocktail party, he'd known he wanted her. He'd felt drawn to Tess in a way he'd never experienced before. Or since.

He'd made it his mission to seduce her. As beautiful and vivacious as Tess was, it had never occurred to him she might be a virgin. Not until it was too late, not until he'd already pushed himself into her, both of them gasping with ecstasy. His body shivered at the memory.

He'd felt guilty afterward, though. There was a reason he didn't seduce virgins. They fell in love too easily and cloyingly imagined a future that bored Stefano to tears. He avoided them at all costs. Virgins didn't know how to play the game. Play it? They often didn't even know there *was* a game.

His worst fears had been proven true when, after the most spectacular sexual experience of his life, Tess had ruined everything with her outrageous declaration of love.

So he'd left. He took no pleasure in it. He would have preferred to see her again for many more sensual nights.

But she'd given him no choice. If she was already imagining herself in love with him after *twelve hours*, what would she do when he eventually ended their affair? Throw herself off the Empire State Building?

So Stefano had left. For her own good. He had nothing to offer a dreamy-eyed idealist with a heart full of love. Better to set her free immediately, before anyone got hurt.

The existence of the baby proved he'd made the right choice. Judging by the infant's size, Tess couldn't have waited long before she took another lover.

An image came to Stefano of another man taking Tess in his arms, doing exactly what he'd done, possessing her in furious, desperate need, in a hot tangle of limbs and sweat and pleasure. Scowling, he pushed the thought away.

At least Stefano had used protection. Obviously, the other man hadn't been so careful. The unknown man had gotten her pregnant with his dark-eyed baby.

He was surprised Tess wasn't wearing a wedding ring. He would have thought a romantic girl like her wouldn't be satisfied with anything less than happily-ever-after.

Stefano, a billionaire prince who'd been raised in a Sicilian castle, didn't believe in such fairy tales.

But he couldn't stop his eyes from watching Tess hungrily as her small figure disappeared down the dark street, her shoulders drooping and red hair flying as she pushed the stroller ahead of her.

Stefano's hand tingled. Raising his hand, he looked at his fingertips beneath the hotel's bright lights.

All he'd done was touch her cheek. That brief, simple touch had scorched his hand. All the emotion and desire he'd repressed for a year had suddenly roared into greedy life, burning him like a fire. Shocked, he'd dropped his hand.

As he watched Tess disappear down the block, he felt a new sense of loss. Why? Why did he still feel so drawn to her? He'd had beautiful women in his bed before. Why couldn't he forget this particular one?

Stefano forced himself to turn away. It was better this way, he repeated to himself. He started to walk toward the hotel's entrance. He stopped.

Something didn't make sense. He frowned.

If Tess was so happy in her new relationship, raising

another man's child, why had she been so overjoyed to see Stefano? She'd looked at him like unicorns were dancing on rainbows. Like all her dreams had suddenly come true.

Our night didn't mean anything to you?

He could still hear the tremble of her voice, still see the shadows cross her lovely, troubled face.

You changed my life.

And as she'd spoken she'd looked away.

Toward the stroller.

Toward her baby.

Her dark-haired, plump-cheeked baby.

"We'll survive alone," she'd said.

We. Not *I.*

A low growl came from the back of Stefano's throat. Turning, he pursued her grimly down the street.

Even with his longer stride, it took him time to catch up with her. He reached her at the end of the dark street, almost at the edge of Times Square. Grabbing Tess by the shoulder, he forced her to face him as the colorful lights of the electronic billboards lit up the sky brilliantly behind her.

"Wait," he ground out.

Tess had been crying, he saw. Her green eyes glittered like emeralds in her pale face. She lifted her chin fiercely. "Wait for what? For you?" She wiped her eyes. "What do you think I've been doing for the last year?"

Her voice was quietly accusing. Against his will, Stefano's gaze fell to her full, pink lips, and lower still.

Tess's hourglass figure should have been illegal in the modern world. Her flowy long-sleeved blouse was tucked into a midi pencil skirt, like a sexpot librarian. It showed her curves to perfection—her full breasts, tiny waist, and big hips a man could wrap his hands around. Her red hair tumbled over her shoulders, the color of roses, the color of fire.

She was different from any other woman he'd ever seen.

He wanted her. Even more than before. More than he'd ever wanted any woman.

With all his relationships over the years, his mistresses always knew love wasn't part of the equation. He only dated experienced, beautiful women he enjoyed having in his bed and on his arm. In return, they enjoyed his body, his prestige and the lifestyle he could provide.

If he was honest with himself, it had all grown rather tedious. Mechanical. He'd started to wonder which of them was using the other one more. Which was why he'd stopped having love affairs, even one-night stands, after his night with Tess. He hadn't wanted any other woman.

Why? Why did he want only her? Was it simply because he knew she was forbidden? Surely he couldn't be selfish enough to desire something only because he knew he couldn't have it?

Even now, he found his gaze lingering on her full hips, her plump, generous breasts. Her colorful outfit, with its ridiculously whimsical fabric, set off her amazing figure. His eyes lifted from her breasts to her bare collarbone, up her swanlike throat to her lovely heart-shaped face.

Her pink tongue nervously licked the corners of her mouth. His whole body felt electrified. All he wanted to do was kiss her.

Clenching his hands at his sides, he forced himself to turn toward the dark-haired baby in the stroller. She was still sleeping peacefully, her old-fashioned, collared dress half-covered with a blanket, clutching a stuffed giraffe toy in her plump arms.

No. She couldn't be. But even as Stefano told himself there was no resemblance, suspicion pulsed through his body, tightening his chest from his shoulders to his taut belly.

"Tell me about the baby," he said.

"What do you want to know?"

"Her name."

"Esme."

"Her surname?"

"Foster, like mine."

His jaw tightened. "And her father?"

Tess stared at him, then looked away, her lips pressed in a thin line. Groups of tourists walked by them on the sidewalk, laughing and chatting in bursts of different languages. She stubbornly refused to look at him, or answer.

"Tess," he demanded, coming close enough to touch her, his tall, broad-shouldered form casting a shadow over her smaller one.

Colorful lights swept over her red hair like a halo, as Tess finally looked at him. Her green eyes were half filled with hope, half with anger, as she said in a low whisper, "You, Stefano."

CHAPTER TWO

Tess had imagined so many times the moment she'd finally tell Stefano about their precious baby.

She'd pictured him crying out with joy and kissing her passionately, then taking Esme proudly in his arms. She'd dreamed of him falling to his knees to plead for her forgiveness for neglecting her so long—unavoidable as he was trapped on the desert island—and then begging her to be his bride.

She'd never imagined this.

"No." Stefano's black eyes were wide as he took a single step back on the sidewalk, his sleek jacket and trousers blending into the dark shadows. He looked down at the sleeping baby. "It can't be true."

Her heart twisted. She whispered, "It's true."

"How can you be sure?"

She hid the pang she felt at his careless insult. "You're the only man I've ever been with, Stefano. Ever, in my whole life."

"But we were careful. We used protection."

Stefano's hard, handsome face looked so shocked Tess almost felt bad for him. She almost wanted to comfort him, to tell him everything would be all right.

But even Tess's tender heart couldn't quite manage that. Not when the man she'd waited for all this time, the man in whom she'd placed her hope and faith, was making his rejection so clear—not just of Tess, but of Esme, too. She lifted her chin.

"I was surprised, too," she said evenly. "But it turns out condoms aren't always one hundred percent effective."

"Why didn't you tell me?" he demanded.

Her jaw dropped.

"How could I? I didn't know your last name or where you lived." She lifted her chin. "You always knew where to find me. You just didn't want to. I waited for over a year, believing you'd return." She hated the tears rising behind her eyes. "Everyone mocked me and teased me for it. I was in love with you, having your baby, and I didn't even know your last name!"

Tess was relieved for the distraction when her baby started to whimper. Blinking rapidly, she picked up the stuffed giraffe Esme had dropped on the sidewalk, then placed it tenderly in the baby's arms.

"It's Zacco," Stefano said abruptly. "My last name."

She looked up. "Zacco? Like the fashion brand?"

Even Tess had heard of the legendary luxury brand, famous for its haute couture and iconic handbags printed with flamboyant interlocking Zs.

"Yes," he said, then shook his head. "My great-great-grandfather started it. I will buy it back soon."

"You don't own it anymore? How could you lose rights to a company named after your own family?"

His jaw tightened, and he looked at their baby. "How could you get pregnant?"

The coldness in his voice pierced her heart. It was one thing for Stefano to treat Tess badly; another to be scornful of their baby.

Sweet five-month-old Esme, so plump and adorable and always happy, at least when she wasn't tired or hungry or teething, was already the person Tess loved most on this planet. Esme was her whole reason for living.

"I've just told you that you have a daughter." Tess felt a wave of dizziness that nearly brought her to her knees. She reached wildly for the stroller handle, gripping it tight so she didn't fall. "And that's all you have to say?"

His eyes narrowed. "How do I know she's mine?"

"Stop asking that! I told you!"

"I need more proof than just your word."

A white-haired couple holding theater playbills walked past, hand in hand. Seeing the way the couple smiled at each other, Tess's heart ached. That was what she'd wanted for herself. A lifetime love.

She'd wanted it so badly she'd been desperate to believe Stefano was the one, in spite of all evidence to the contrary. She'd be regretting it the rest of her life.

"Forget it." Her throat ached as she turned away. "We don't need you."

Stefano ground out, "I'm sorry if I hurt you—"

"Sorry?" Her voice trembled. "You're not sorry!"

"You're wrong," he said harshly. "I'm sorry I didn't realize you were a virgin until too late. Sorry you imagined yourself in love with me when you didn't even know me. Sorry you're now trying to claim your baby is mine!"

"Claim?" Tess's tears blurred his image as colorful flashing lights from the billboards of Times Square moved over his hard, handsome face. "You're right," she whispered. "I don't know you."

She couldn't believe she'd been so horribly wrong about everything. Even now, Stefano still looked like a handsome dream—tall and powerful in his sleek suit. Even his scent, like Italian oranges and hot summer nights, made her heart twist with longing and grief for what she could not have, what had never truly existed.

Reaching out, he gripped her shoulders. His dark eyes burned through her. "I never promised a future."

As she felt the weight of his hands on her shoulders, electricity pulsed through her, leaving her breathless.

Her gaze fell to his cruel, sensual lips as she whispered, "I know."

She heard his intake of breath. His grip on her shoulders tightened. "Stop it."

"What?"

"You know what."

His eyes were dark pools of hunger. As their eyes locked, sensual awareness coursed through her, sending sparks up and down her body, causing tension to coil low and deep inside her. Unthinkingly, she licked the corners of her lips. First one side, then the other.

With a low growl, he pulled her hard against his body and savagely lowered his mouth to hers.

She was lost in a rush of ecstasy as desire and anguished longing roared through her blood. She surrendered to the pleasure, to his power, his strength, relishing the feel of his arms wrapped around her.

Then, as if from a distance, she heard a choked moan rising from her own throat, wistful and broken, and she remembered how he'd just crushed her heart to a million pieces.

No. No!

Ripping away, she stared up at him in horror, her lips still tingling with pleasure, her heart bruised by that brief fiery joy.

"Don't you dare kiss me!"

His expression changed. "Tess—"

"Leave me alone." Her voice wobbled. She was afraid she might burst into sobs, and baby Esme's tired, hungry whine was threatening to become a wail.

Tess wiped her mouth with her sleeve, trying to forget the sweet taste of his lips, but she couldn't. A tsunami of grief and regret and exhaustion roared through her, leaving her trembling and dizzy.

She suddenly knew she wasn't going to make it to the subway. She was going to collapse right here on the street in front of the man who'd caused it all.

No. She had to somehow get back to her friends. She didn't care anymore if Hallie and Lola said *I told you so*. They were her only hope now that her whole world was falling down around her.

Swaying unsteadily, she turned, stumbling as she pushed the stroller back down the way she'd come. She could see the distant lights of the Campania at the end of the street.

"Tess." Catching up with her, Stefano grabbed the handle of the stroller. "Stop. Damn you."

His face was in shadow. The lights of a single passing car seemed long, smudging before her eyes. The world swam around her as the last of her strength fled. She closed her eyes.

For the last year, she'd tried to have faith while she waited for Stefano to come back and save her. But now that he'd returned, all he'd done was take away the dreams that had sustained her.

"Please," she whispered, blinking fast, feeling dizzy and sick. "Don't."

He frowned, looking down at her. "What's wrong?"

The dizziness increased, building to a pounding roar in her ears. She felt her knees start to collapse.

His strong arms shot out, keeping her from plummeting to the sidewalk. "Tess?"

The last thing she saw was the worried gleam of his dark eyes as the night folded in around her.

Tess was swaying, cradled in someone's arms.

Her eyelids fluttered open, then went wide with shock. Stefano was carrying her in his arms, against his hard chest.

They'd already reached the end of the block and were almost at the hotel.

"Esme," Tess gasped, twisting in his arms.

"She's safe, behind us." Stefano's voice was surprisingly gentle. Peeking over his broad shoulders, she saw a doorman she recognized from the Campania pushing the stroller. She'd met Dalton several times when she'd visited Hallie at the hotel. He gave her an encouraging smile.

"It's all right, Miss Foster." He glanced down at the baby. "She's right here."

"Thank you, Dalton," she whispered. Then she glared at the powerful man carrying her. "Put me down."

"No." Stefano kept walking. His handsome face was implacable. "You fainted on the street."

"I'm better now," she said, struggling in his arms. "Put me down."

His arms tightened around her. "When is the last time you ate?"

Tess struggled to remember. "This morning?"

"Aren't you sure?"

She shook her head weakly. "I started work at four. The bakery opens at six, and my uncle doesn't approve of eating in front of customers. On breaks I'm busy with Esme." She looked away. "I meant to eat something tonight, but I had to feed Esme. So I just had a glass of champagne." She put her hand on her forehead, still feeling dizzy. "She's been teething, so I didn't sleep much last night..."

Stefano shook his head as they approached the hotel's gilded revolving door. "I'm taking you upstairs until a doctor looks you over."

"It's not necessary," she said desperately. The last thing she wanted was to be vulnerable—in his arms or his hotel suite.

"A doctor," he repeated, his glare fierce. "He'll make sure you're all right. Then we'll get a paternity test."

She stiffened in his arms even as he carried her through the door. How could he ask for a test? Her word should be enough!

The grand lobby of the Campania was huge and luxurious, with midcentury decor and turn-of-the-century architecture. Molded plaster ceilings with crystal chandeliers soared high above the marble floor and paneled walls. Glamorous hotel guests and patrons crowded around the gleaming oak bar at the center.

Tess felt conspicuous as they walked past. They made a strange parade, with Stefano carrying her in his arms and the doorman pushing the stroller behind them. People turned to stare.

A group of gorgeous, very tall, very thin young women gaped at them openly from their table at the lobby bar. *Models*, Tess thought. They were their own tribe in this city, and you could always tell.

"Good evening, Your Highness," a man said as he passed, his eyes wide.

"Your Highness," a woman greeted him, looking as if she were dying to ask all kinds of questions.

Stefano responded only with a nod and kept walking.

"Your Highness?" Tess looked up at him. "That other girl called you that earlier. I thought it was a joke."

"I'm technically a prince," he said tersely.

"Technically?"

"Italy is a republic. Aristocratic titles are now merely honorary," he said flatly. "But my ancestors have been princes of Gioreale for hundreds of years."

"Gioreale is a place?"

"In Sicily. Once it was an important market village. Now it's a ghost of its former self. That is what I am." His lips curved. "Prince of ghosts."

Prince of ghosts. She thought she saw something haunted in his eyes. What was it? Emptiness? Pain? Despair?

"Miss Foster." Mr. Loggia, the hotel's general manager, came forward with an anxious frown. "What has happened? Are you injured?"

"She fainted, sir," the doorman said from behind them. "Prince Stefano alerted me from down the street, and I rushed to help."

"I see." The manager, who'd never been anything but kind to Tess, turned to Stefano with a scowl. "What did you do?"

Stefano replied coldly in Italian, and the manager responded in the same language, lifting his chin.

Mr. Loggia whirled to face her. "Is he taking you against your will?"

Stefano bit out something in Italian that sounded very rude.

"Miss Foster?" the manager demanded.

Tess felt Stefano's strong arms tighten around her, pressing her body against his powerful chest. As she looked at him, her lips tingled from his savage kiss by Times Square.

"No," she admitted, her heart in her throat. "He's right. I fainted."

Stefano turned icily to the manager. "I'm taking her to my suite, Loggia. Send up the doctor. And room service. What would you like?" he asked Tess.

Food. He was talking about food? She shook her head dimly. "I don't care."

"Are you sure you don't want me to call Mrs. Moretti?" the manager asked her with a frown.

For a moment, Tess was tempted to take the offered escape. Then she glanced back at her whining, hungry baby in the stroller. She knew what it was like to grow up without a father. If there was even a chance that Stefano wanted to be part of their baby's life, didn't she have to find out?

Even if that meant she had to take a paternity test to make him finally believe her.

"It's all right, Mr. Loggia," she said, quietly resigned. "I want to go with him."

She felt Stefano's arms relax slightly.

"If you're sure," the manager said, looking between them in disbelief. "I'll have room service send up your usual at once. And the hotel doctor, as well."

"Grazie," Stefano bit out sardonically, and turned away, carrying her to the elevator. The doorman pushed the stroller behind them.

"Mr. Loggia doesn't seem to like you much," Tess said.

"No," he agreed, not seeming perturbed about it. "In spite of the fact I'm their highest-paying guest. But his bastard boss despises me."

"Cristiano hates you?" Tess blinked in surprise. "Why would he?"

"You know Moretti?"

"His wife Hallie is one of my best friends."

"Ah." He shrugged. "He and I were drivers in a charity car race last year. We were fighting for the win. His car was in my way, so I—very gently—bumped him over."

"You hit his car?"

"He was blocking me. Cheating. He left me no choice. After I won, he tried to punch me in the face."

Tess couldn't imagine Cristiano losing his temper. He seemed so nice, especially tonight, when he'd declared his love for Hallie. "He *punched* you?"

"I said he tried to." Stefano hid a smug smile. "His friends held him back. I felt no need to return his attack. He simply couldn't accept that his attempts to sabotage me in the race had failed and I'd still managed to win."

"Winning isn't everything."

He looked at her in disbelief. "Of course it is."

The elevator door opened, and he carried her inside, with the doorman and the stroller behind them.

"If you dislike Cristiano Moretti so much, why do you stay at his hotel?"

"Because it amuses me to force him and his manager to serve me."

"They might spit in your food."

"They would not dare. Would they, Dalton?"

"Certainly not," the doorman replied indignantly. He added with a grin, "You tip far too well for that, Your Highness."

Stefano returned his grin, then looked at Tess. "Besides. I know Moretti, and he has too much pride in his hotel to ever serve any guest badly. Even me. He contents himself by merely marking up my bill to an exorbitant amount."

Tess glanced at Dalton, feeling awkward to be discussing Cristiano like this, in front of one of his employees. She asked Stefano helplessly, "Don't you mind all the conflict?"

"No."

"You like it!" she accused.

Stefano said with a careless smile, "A man can be measured by the quality of his enemies."

"My mother used to say that you can be measured by the strength of your love for family and friends."

He snorted. "That is the most sentimental thing I have ever heard in my life. What was your mother's profession?"

"Theater actress." A flash of grief went through her as she thought of her loving but impractical mother, dragging her as a child through summer stock plays and minor roles in small New England towns. She added softly, "Though she was never very successful at it."

"And your father?"

She felt a different kind of grief. "My mother raised me alone." She raised her chin. "You can set me down anytime. I'm perfectly able to stand."

"Not yet," he said shortly. "Not until we reach my suite."

With a sigh, Tess watched the elevator numbers go

higher. Her baby gave another soft whine from the stroller. Esme was tired and she needed to be fed. At this rate, they wouldn't be home till midnight. Tess hated the thought of coming home so late and facing her uncle's wrath.

The elevator door slid open, and Stefano carried her down the hall. As Dalton held open the door, he took her into the suite.

Tess looked around her in amazement.

The royal suite was lavish, spread out across the corner of one of the Campania's highest floors. Floor-to-ceiling windows provided views of Manhattan from every room. Carrying her into the elegant living room, which had a grand piano in the corner, Stefano finally set her down gently on a white sofa.

"Are you cold? Do you want a blanket?"

"You're being ridiculous. I'm not an invalid." She started to get up from the sofa, then felt dizzy and fell back against the pillows. "I just want my baby—"

Without a word, Stefano went back to the foyer. She saw him reach into his pocket.

"Thank you," he said, handing Dalton a folded fistful of bills.

"You're so welcome," the doorman replied fervently, and, with a respectful nod toward Tess, he left.

Kneeling in front of the stroller, Stefano unbuckled the unhappy baby, lifting her up into his arms.

Father and daughter looked at each other with the same dark eyes. Esme's whimpering stopped. The baby reached out a flailing arm and touched her father's face.

Stefano laughed, looking down at her. His expression changed. It became almost…tender. Watching them, Tess felt her heart twist in her chest.

Clearing his throat, he returned to the sofa and placed the baby in Tess's arms. Esme immediately nuzzled toward her.

"Do you want anything else?" he asked.

With a lump in her throat, Tess shook her head. She couldn't tell him the truth.

There was something she wanted, almost more than she could bear. Watching Stefano hold her baby, she'd wanted him to be the man she'd once believed him to be.

Two hours later, as Stefano shut the door behind the departing doctor, he looked back across the shadows of the royal suite. Tess and the baby had fallen asleep on the white sofa with the wide view of sparkling city lights. Beside her, there was an empty tray, with only crumbs left of her sandwich and soup. She'd gulped down three glasses of water, too.

Slowly he came closer, looking down at her. Even now, as Tess slept, he could see the dark smudges beneath her eyes. Her beautiful face looked exhausted. She'd fallen asleep in the few minutes he'd spoken privately with the doctor.

"She needs rest," the doctor had told him at the door. "She's been working too hard. She has nothing left in reserve. Take care of her."

Tess had such power over him. Stefano could still feel their kiss and remember how it had felt to hold her soft body in his arms, to plunder the sweet softness of her lips. He wanted her. And she was here. In his suite.

His gaze shifted to the bedroom door at the end of the hall.

Shaking his head hard, he pushed the thought away. Only one thing mattered now. It had nothing to do with sex and everything to do with honor.

Stefano's gaze slid to the baby still cuddled in Tess's arms. Esme had fallen asleep hours ago, as soon as she'd been changed and fed. That seemed appropriate given that it was past midnight. He didn't know much about children, but even in his own disastrous childhood, Stefano had always been tucked safely in his bed every night by a nanny. For all his parents' selfishness, they'd managed at least that much for their only child.

Which was more than Stefano himself could say if the paternity test proved Esme was his daughter. Had he unknowingly abandoned Tess, pregnant with his baby, without any money or any means to contact him?

His hands tightened.

He'd never wanted to hurt her. He'd tried his best to protect her, by leaving her. Before her love for him could get any worse.

Stefano still wasn't sure what love was, exactly. Was love real, and was he deficient in some way since he'd never felt it? Or was it an illusion, and were other people deluding themselves?

He preferred to think the latter.

But he'd never known a woman like Tess. The women he dated were usually exactly like him—selfish and ruthless, looking out only for themselves and determined to win at any cost.

Was Tess truly so innocent that she'd given him her heart and virginity, then raised his baby with faith he would return, loving him with such unimaginable loyalty?

He'd never known anyone that unselfish. Ever. Including—and especially—his own parents.

Stefano's father, Prince Umberto, had only cared about sordid extravagances, and thrilling affairs with women he swore he loved, then quickly discarded. He hadn't just cheated on his wife, he'd cheated on his mistresses. He'd ruined the family's famous company, the luxury Zacco brand, through his neglect, then sold it outright during the divorce.

After that, Stefano's mother, Antonella, had gone on to marry five more times, to progressively younger men, each living off her money during marriage and demanding a fat payout at the end of it. Stefano's parents had been too self-involved to bother personally with the care of their son, choosing to leave him at their castle in Sicily to be raised by paid servants. At twelve, they'd sent him off to an American boarding school, and left him there, even during the summers.

The Zacco legacy, the legendary hundred-year-old company—even the corporate rights to their very *name*—had been lost to his parents' selfishness. After his father's death when Stefano was finishing college at twenty-two, he'd inherited almost nothing: a falling-down castle in Sicily, some heavily mortgaged real estate, and the nearly bankrupt leather goods company that eventually became Mercurio.

In life, it was every man—and every woman—for themselves. Stefano had learned the lesson well. And life was a game he intended to win.

Over the last sixteen years, Stefano had laboriously rebuilt everything his parents had lost. His international conglomerate, Gioreale S.p.A., was now worth billions, containing luxury brands that sold everything from sports cars to champagne to jewels. And he was building the exclusive fashion line, Mercurio.

It was true, Mercurio's launch last year hadn't gone as well as he'd hoped, but he'd just hired a hot new designer, the eccentric, trendy Caspar von Schreck. His first clothing collection would be shown next month at Paris Fashion Week.

And soon, if everything went as planned, Stefano would finally acquire what he wanted most—he'd buy back the Zacco brand. Everything was coming together.

He should have been happy, or at least pleased.

But the truth was, at thirty-eight, Stefano was feeling strangely tired of all of it. It was why he'd left tonight's party early, even arranging for his driver to give teenage model Kebe Kedane a ride back to her anxiously waiting mother on the Upper West Side.

Once, Stefano had loved the thrill of New York Fashion Week, the parties, the clubs, the gorgeous women. Lately, everything he'd given his life to conquer...left him numb. He found himself wanting something else. Something more.

Taking back the Zacco brand would change everything, he told himself firmly. Next week he'd start negotiations with Fenella Montfort to buy back his family's legacy. Once it was his, he'd finally feel satisfied. He'd finally feel at peace.

He'd finally have won.

"Oh," Tess murmured, yawning as she stirred on the sofa. She blinked, cradling her baby gently as she sat up, rubbing her eyes. "I must have fallen asleep."

"You're tired." He looked down at her. "I'd like you to stay here tonight."

Her cheeks went pink. She looked down shyly, her dark eyelashes fluttering against her skin. "That's very kind of you, but—"

"It's not kind. I want this settled, one way or the other, before I leave for London tomorrow."

"London?"

"For Fashion Week."

She blinked in surprise. "Are you attending all of them?"

"Yes, back to back. New York, London, Milan, Paris." He gave her a humorless smile. "I do own a fashion brand."

"But it's not Zacco?" She said, looking bewildered.

"Mercurio." His smile dropped. "My father sold Zacco almost twenty years ago. I intend to buy it back. I'll start the negotiations in London."

"Good for you." The deal that meant so much to him obviously meant nothing to her. She stretched her shoulders back, drawing her shoulder blades together, which pushed her breasts forward, stretching the fabric of her modest vintage shirt. Unwillingly, his eyes traced over the shape of her breasts. Catching himself, he forced his attention back to her face.

But her eyes were even more dangerous than her body. They were deep emerald pools, like oceans for an unwary man to drown in.

"When will you be back from Europe?"

"I don't know."

Careful not to jostle the sleeping baby in her arms, she rose from the sofa. "Thank you for dinner, and for offering to let me stay, but Esme and I really should be getting home."

She started toward the foyer where the stroller waited, but he moved to block her. "You're not going anywhere."

His voice was harsher than he'd intended. Tess's lips parted, angry sparks rising in her green eyes.

"Please," he said, amending his tone. "I want you to stay. Dr. Miller promised the paternity results first thing in the morning."

"Why should I stay? It'll only prove what I already know. You're Esme's father. I have no reason to wait all night to get the news." She looked at the floor. "I've waited for you long enough."

An unsettled feeling filled Stefano. If she was telling the truth, then it meant he'd unthinkingly, cruelly abandoned her, pregnant with his baby. He couldn't let himself even reflect about what that might mean or the choice he'd have to make.

Stefano came closer. "Please stay. Until we know for sure."

Tess lifted her chin. "I have to get up early tomorrow."

"Again?"

"I work fifty hours a week."

"Why? Does it pay well?"

Tess gave a smile tinged with bitterness. "Minimum wage. Plus room and board for myself and Esme."

"Minimum wage?" He was outraged. "Why would you work so hard for so little?"

"There aren't many jobs I'm qualified for and where I can keep Esme with me."

"You should have stayed in design school."

"Wow," she said sarcastically. "Thank you for pointing that out to me." Her cheeks burned. "But I couldn't afford both tuition and day care, or manage sixteen-hour days of work and school away from her."

Stefano stared at Tess.

He could instantly picture what her life had been like since he'd left her last year, pregnant, penniless and alone. She'd worked a menial job for little pay, giving up her dreams of college, struggling to provide for her baby with no hope for the future.

All because he'd made sure she had no way to contact him ever again.

His stomach clenched. "If what you say is true and she's my child...it will change everything. Surely you know that."

Biting her lip, she glanced down at the sleeping baby in her arms, then said in a small voice, "It would?"

Placing his hands gently on her shoulders, Stefano said quietly, "Please stay, Tess. You're tired and so is Esme. Just stay. You can have the bedroom. I'll sleep on the sofa."

She gave him a startled glance, then looked at her sleeping baby cuddled against her chest. With visible reluctance, she sighed. "All right. Fine." Going to the stroller, she returned with a diaper bag slung over her shoulder. "Where is the bedroom?"

He felt an unexpected rush of triumph that he'd convinced her to stay. "This way."

Stefano led her down a short hallway to the hotel suite's bedroom with its huge four-poster bed, marble bathroom and view of the sparkling city lights. He pointed toward the bathroom. "There's a new toothbrush, toiletries, everything you might need." He paused uncertainly. "Do you want me to have the concierge send up pajamas? A crib for the baby?"

She shook her head, her eyes looking tired. "Just leave us."

With a nod, Stefano departed, softly closing the door behind him. As he returned to the main room, his shoulders were tense. He felt strangely restless. He played a few notes on the grand piano, then stopped, remembering Tess and the baby were trying to sleep. Turning to the wet bar, he poured himself a short Scotch and went to the windows, looking at the darkly glittering New York night.

Taking a drink, he stared out bleakly into the night, letting the potent forty-year-old Scotch burn down his throat.

Tess. The bright-eyed redhead was different than any woman he'd ever met, funny and sweet and sexy as hell. The morning he'd woken up in her arms, he'd already been planning to have her in his bed every night until he was satiated with her. Then she'd told him she was falling in love with him, and the whole world had stopped.

Stefano abruptly turned from the window. Work. Work was what he should be focusing on right now. As always.

Setting down his half-empty glass, he grabbed his laptop and sat down on the sofa. Blankly, he read through emails, including reviews of rival companies' shows during New York Fashion Week and details about Mercurio's upcoming event in Paris.

As Stefano read through the reports that had seemed so urgent only hours before, all the analysis and numbers seemed like meaningless symbols on the screen. From the bedroom, he thought he heard Tess's voice singing lullabies to the baby.

His baby.

He didn't know that yet for sure, Stefano reminded himself fiercely. Yet—he thought of baby Esme's dark eyes—he *knew*.

And if it was proved that five-month-old Esme Foster was his child? What would he do then?

Tess's singing faded and the hotel suite fell silent. Stefano stared at the cold glow of his laptop, wishing Tess would come out to talk to him.

He took a blanket and pillow from the closet and went back to the sofa. He stopped when he realized he'd forgotten to get pajamas. He didn't want to go to the bedroom and risk waking her, but he could hardly sleep naked, either, with her here.

He compromised by taking off only his shirt. He stretched out on the sofa beneath the blanket. He folded his hands on the pillow, behind his head, and stared at the ceiling, his jaw set.

His life didn't need to change, he told himself. He could simply tell his lawyers to arrange a generous financial settlement for Tess and the baby, and he could fly off to London as planned.

Tess was obviously a good mother. He could trust her to take care of Esme. Once they had unlimited money, they'd be fine. Tess would be free to do whatever she wanted. They didn't need Stefano.

Still, Stefano tossed and turned, remembering how alone he'd felt as a child, abandoned by his parents. Would Esme always think her father had deliberately chosen to abandon her? And if she did, wasn't it true?

Stefano woke from an unsettling dream to hear his phone ringing. He wrenched it to his ear. "Hello."

"It's Dr. Miller. I hope I didn't wake you. You said you wanted to know as soon as possible."

Looking out the windows, Stefano saw the light of early dawn. He gripped his phone. "Yes?"

"Esme Foster is your daughter. There can be no doubt."

Stefano closed his eyes. Part of him had already known—from the moment he'd really looked into the baby's dark eyes, exactly like his own.

You're Esme's father, Tess had said. *I have no reason to wait all night to get the news. I've waited for you long enough.*

"Your Highness?" the doctor said.

"Thank you," Stefano said flatly. "Send me your bill." He hung up.

Blinking, he sat up on the sofa, staring at the gray dawn over New York City, at the fine mist of September drizzle. Rising to his feet, he rolled his tense shoulders. He quietly went into the bedroom, careful not to wake Tess, who was sleeping half-upright, with their baby cuddled on her chest.

After taking clean clothes from the wardrobe, he went into the en suite bathroom. He closed and locked the door behind him, and took a shower so hot it scalded his skin. He shaved. He brushed his teeth. He wiped the steam off the mirror. He met his own eyes.

Nothing had to change, he repeated to himself. Nothing at all. He could still leave for London today. Let his lawyers handle this. He could continue to live his life as always.

A life of power and money.

Where he risked nothing.

Felt nothing.

Stefano's expression in the reflection was emotionless and cold. It was a trick he'd perfected long ago, imitating his father.

Once he was dressed in a crisp white shirt, dark trousers and a dark jacket, he went back into his bedroom. Reaching out, he gently shook Tess's shoulder.

Her eyes flew open, startled. When she saw him, standing over her in the shadows beside the bed, for a moment, she smiled in pure joy, as if all her dreams had come true.

Then she blinked, remembered and looked sad.

"What is it?" she said.

"The baby's mine."

She gave him a wistful smile. "I know." She waited, with painful hope in her eyes.

For what? What was Tess hoping? That he could settle down? Marry her? Help her raise the baby? Give them a home? A name?

Ridiculous.

Stefano had no idea how to be a good husband or father. He'd never even seen it done. Money was all he had to offer them. He'd give Tess a fortune and set her free.

But his body was fighting that decision. Even now, desire shuddered through him as he looked at her. She'd just woken up, but even in her rumpled clothes, tired and cuddling their sleeping baby in her arms, she was the most tantalizing woman he'd ever known.

What would it be like to wake up with her every morning? To have her in his bed every night? What would it be like to possess her completely?

Stefano pushed the thought aside savagely. Setting them free was the right thing to do. It would give Tess and their daughter the chance to be cherished and loved. By someone else.

And Stefano—

He'd focus on his upcoming negotiations. As Tess had said earlier, it was unacceptable that Stefano no longer even owned the corporate rights to his own name. He'd focus on that. Only on that.

And that was final.

"Come on, Tess," he said roughly, turning away. "I'll take you home."

CHAPTER THREE

TESS COULDN'T BELIEVE IT.

She glanced at Stefano out of the corner of her eye. They were sitting in the back seat of his expensive Rolls-Royce, with their baby in a car seat between them, as his uniformed driver maneuvered the morning rush-hour traffic already clogging the streets and avenues of New York in every direction.

She'd thought—really thought—that once he had proof he was Esme's father that he would offer to help her *somehow*. Hadn't he said that if he was the father, it would change everything?

Instead, he was taking her and Esme back to Brooklyn, to drop her off at her uncle's bakery on his way to the airport. Leaving Tess to face her uncle's wrath alone, while he flew off to London as planned.

Stefano had changed nothing.

Her disillusionment was complete.

"You're very quiet," Stefano said.

She couldn't even talk to him right now. Leaning forward, she spoke to the driver. "Thanks for the ride. I can't even imagine what it's like to drive in Manhattan."

"You don't know how to drive?" Stefano said.

She shook her head, still not looking at him. "I'm a New York girl. I take the subway."

But, as she spoke, her hand unconsciously stroked the

smooth leather of the seat. It was a strangely sensual experience. But she'd only been in a luxury car like this once before. The night he'd seduced her. The night she'd conceived Esme.

"Ba-ba-ba," the baby said wonderingly beside her, waving her fat arms. Tess looked down at Esme with a tender smile.

"Yes. Exactly."

After Stefano had woken her up that morning, she'd fed and changed Esme, and brushed her own hair and teeth. A chauffeured Rolls-Royce had been waiting at the curb as they'd come out the front door of the Campania Hotel, and she'd found a brand-new infant car seat had already been installed in the back seat.

This must be what it's like to be rich, Tess thought. Your path through life was always smooth, because paid employees ran ahead of you, clearing and tidying up every problem or delay. Even a child was no problem, apparently. You could just drop her off with a clear conscience and fly away on your jet.

"You're angry with me," Stefano said quietly.

As they traveled over the Brooklyn Bridge, Tess looked at him and immediately regretted it. "Why would I be angry?"

His eyes were dark and serious. "It's better this way."

"Better for who?"

"For you." He looked at the happy, gurgling baby. "For her."

Tess forced herself to smile. "You're probably right."

This would probably be the last time she'd ever see him, she realized. Stefano had made that clear since he'd woken her up and told her coldly that Esme was definitely his child, which, duh, she'd already known. What she'd hadn't known, what she'd waited with painful hope to hear, was how he would react to the news.

But all he'd said was that he was taking her home. After that, he'd avoided looking at her while the hotel staff had brought down his luggage from his suite.

Which was its own answer, really. Even now that Stefano had proof that Esme was his child, in spite of his earlier words, he didn't actually intend to do anything about it.

Tess was on her own.

It was a bitter pill to swallow. For over a year, she'd dreamed of Stefano returning to claim her, taking her in his arms, kissing her, begging her to be his bride. She'd dreamed of taking only one lover her whole life, and loving him for a lifetime. Being a family.

From the moment she'd met him on the street yesterday, she'd been forced to accept that, though Stefano Zacco might be a prince, he wasn't anything like the Prince Charming she'd imagined him to be. Still, part of her, deep inside, had hoped that once he knew without a doubt that Esme was his child, he'd change.

She was so stupid. Why did she always seek hope even at times she should have clearly accepted defeat?

"I want only the best for you both," Stefano said now. His black eyes pierced her heart.

His every action proved those words a lie. Taking a deep breath, she looked out at the passing buildings and said in a small voice, "So you're off to London now?"

"Yes. To negotiate for Zacco."

Her voice trembled a little as she said, "Good luck."

"Grazie," he said flatly.

They made their way through the most fashionable section of Brooklyn, toward the slightly less upscale neighborhood where her uncle's bakery had been started by his grandfather in 1940. Heads on the sidewalks turned as the gleaming car passed by.

She felt a hollow pang in her belly as she whispered, "My uncle is going to be furious because I was out all night..."

"Why do you care? You are only here to collect your things, and the baby's."

Frowning, Tess looked at him. "What are you talking about?"

Stefano snorted. "Surely you cannot wish to remain here, working yourself to exhaustion for little pay."

What choice do I have? She bit back the bitter words. She wouldn't let Stefano think she was asking for his money or anything else not freely given.

She was being foolish, she knew. Her practical, financially focused friend Lola would be screaming at her right now to demand a hefty dose of child support, as was her right, and as he could easily afford.

But she couldn't do it.

Tess had once wondered how her friend Hallie could have ever refused money from Cristiano Moretti under similar circumstances. Now, for the first time, she understood. It was because, after losing so much, sometimes a woman had only her pride left to cling to.

She set her jaw. "We'll be fine."

"Yes, I know. I've already called my lawyer."

Confused, she turned to him. "A lawyer? Why?"

"Now that I have proof of Esme's paternity, I cannot evade responsibility."

She sucked in her breath. "What do you mean?"

"Tess." Stefano's dark eyes glittered in the gray morning light. "Did you really think I'd leave you and Esme without a penny? My driver will return later this morning to collect you and Esme, and take you to my lawyer's office in Midtown. He'll arrange for your bank account and funds to buy a nice apartment in any neighborhood you desire. My driver will be at your disposal anytime, day or night. All your needs will be provided for, anything you need to make your life more comfortable. A housekeeper, a cook, charge accounts at every department store, private school for Esme."

Tess's mouth was open. "What?"

Stefano gave a hard, careless smile. "Why does this surprise you? It is now my duty to provide for you. You will never have to work again, Tess. Or do anything you do not wish to do."

Behind him, dimly Tess could see the Brooklyn Bridge and Manhattan skyline across the East River as the Rolls-Royce turned into her neighborhood.

When he'd said he wanted to take responsibility, for a moment she'd actually thought he intended to help raise their child, to be a real father; instead, he just meant money.

She should have been thrilled by his offer. Lola would have told her so in no uncertain terms. But she wasn't. Stefano made her feel as if she and Esme were merely another unpleasant obligation, like an electricity bill.

Sadness filled her heart. Her shoulders sagged as she turned away, staring out at the Brooklyn street. Her street.

"Tess?"

As they pulled up in front of the bakery, she said in a low voice, "I don't want your money."

"Don't be ridiculous. It's all arranged. Watson will be back in about two hours, won't you, Watson?"

"Maybe three, depending on the traffic, Your Highness."

Stefano reached over the baby's car seat to take Tess's hand in his own. "You're free," he said in a low voice. "You and the baby can enjoy your lives." He paused. "Someday you'll find a man who deserves you both."

"Thanks," she said over the lump in her throat, pulling her hand away. His patronizing words burned her to the core. She would have preferred it if he'd told her that he found her boring and that he'd rather eat glass than raise a child. At least then she could have respected his honesty. Instead, he was trying to make it sound like he was abandoning Tess for *her* sake, which shamed her. "I guess this is goodbye, then." She tried to toss her head, to smile. "And good riddance, right?"

"What does that mean?"

"A man like you would never want to commit to a family. Especially not a family like us." Avoiding his eyes, she unbuckled Esme and lifted her into her arms, along with the diaper bag. Getting out of the back seat of the Rolls-Royce, she looked back at Stefano, so thuggishly handsome in his well-cut suit. The man she'd loved with such fierce, unwavering loyalty for so long.

That man had never truly existed. He was a man she'd made up in her own heart, someone noble and strong who just happened to have Stefano's face and voice.

Looking one last time into his dark eyes, she whispered, "Goodbye, Stefano."

She closed the car door firmly, shutting the door on her heart's fairy-tale dreams.

"Here you go, miss." The chauffeur set down her beat-up old stroller from the trunk, opening it for her on the sidewalk. "I'll return to Brooklyn for you and Miss Esme shortly."

"Thank you," she said, proud of herself for keeping her voice steady. As she settled her baby in the stroller, two young men passed by on the sidewalk, smiling at her. She vaguely recognized them as customers from the neighborhood and tried to smile back at them, but she couldn't manage it. Her heart was too sad. Squaring her shoulders, she looked ahead.

Foster Bros. Bakery, the sign proclaimed in neon, over the faded paint of a sign original to 1940. The bakery had been expanded in the 1970s, and the window display now showed artificial wedding cakes with old, cracked white frosting over foam foundations. With a deep breath, Tess pushed open the door, causing the bell to chime.

Inside, the tables scattered across the rose-colored tile floor were far emptier than usual. There was only one customer, a white-haired poorly dressed regular named Peg, who came in each morning and paid for her coffee with nickels and dimes, then sat invisibly in the corner for hours, drinking coffee refills and reading newspapers other customers left behind.

Uncle Ray's head popped up over the bakery case.

"Where have you been?" he demanded as Tess came forward with the stroller. "Your aunt was so worried. We woke up this morning and had no idea where you were. Do you know how many messages we've left on your phone? She was about to call the police. The hospital. The morgue!"

Tess hung her head. "I'm sorry, Uncle Ray. I should have called."

He glared at her. "You shouldn't have stayed out all night! And with Esme, too." He looked down at the baby with a frown. "You should be ashamed, Tess. And since you weren't here to bake this morning, we have no pastries. Dozens of people walked out after they saw I had almost nothing to sell!"

The glass bakery case was indeed mostly empty, without Tess's pumpkin and maple scones, or pecan rolls or cherry Danish twists. The only pastry on offer was her aunt's morning glory super-bran honey-sweetened, carrot-and-zucchini muffin, which was a little too healthy for most.

"You could have asked Emily or Natalie. They're amazing bakers and—"

"They needed their sleep. They have class. I can't let them lose their only chance of college." *Not like you did*, his eyes seemed to say.

Tess's cheeks went hot. But she couldn't blame him for being upset. This bakery had been handed down from father to son for generations. Her uncle took it seriously.

After Tess's mother died when Tess was twelve, her aunt

and uncle had brought her here to live with them. Tess had often puzzled over her uncle's appearance. He didn't look like bakers should look. Bakers were supposed to be fat and jolly, spreading joy to the world with cake and bread. Instead, Raymond Foster had the ascetic look of a marathon runner, spare and muscular, with a gaunt face and the downturned mouth of someone disappointed with his life. And now, because of her, he was even more disappointed.

Tess's shoulders slumped. "I'll go back and start baking, Uncle Ray."

"It's too late for pastries," her uncle barked. "Make cookies. Maybe we can sell them at lunch and after school."

"All right." Biting her lip, she paused. "Last night...it's not what you think. There was a good reason I didn't come home. I... I saw Esme's father."

Her uncle's eyes widened. "You did?"

She nodded.

Uncle Ray looked around. "So where is he?"

She swallowed. "He had to leave for London."

"Ah." Her uncle's eyes narrowed. "Right."

"I did see him! I did!" she said, hating the pleading sound of her own voice.

Her uncle sighed. "Then he obviously wants no part of you or Esme," he said quietly. "It's time to move on."

"He did offer to—"

"Enough, Tess. These romantic fantasies have ruined your life for long enough. I won't let them ruin our family's business, too."

She flinched, even knowing he was right. Stefano hadn't wanted any part of her or Esme. He hadn't even asked about seeing his daughter again. All he'd wanted to do was pay them off. To make them disappear. While she...

She wanted a father for her daughter. She wanted a real home. She wanted a partner she could trust, someone she could share her life with. She'd wanted them to be a family.

Forget it, she told herself harshly. Her uncle was right. Romantic fantasies had ruined her life for long enough—

The bell chimed behind her. The bakery's door opened, and the cool September wind blew in. She heard a heavy step against the tile floor.

Maybe it was the faint scent of his cologne. The sound of his step.

But without even turning around, Tess sucked in her breath as prickles went up and down her body.

Her uncle's expression changed into a beaming smile as he looked past Tess to the new customer. "Yes, sir? How can I help you? We're out of pastries this morning, I'm afraid, but we have coffee and some very healthy muffins... How can I help you?"

"You can't." Stefano's voice was a growl. She closed her eyes, shivering. Coming directly behind her, he said in a low voice, "Tess. Look at me."

Slowly she turned.

Stefano looked like a dream to her, the handsome Sicilian prince staring down at her so hungrily, his muscular body powerful in a sleek designer suit.

"I thought you were leaving for London," she said, her voice trembling in spite of her best efforts.

"I am. But I forgot something."

"What?"

His sensual lips curved. "You."

"Me?" Tess whispered.

From the corner of her eye, she saw her uncle Ray's jaw drop.

Stefano put his hand on her cheek. "I can't leave you. I tried. I can't."

Electricity pulsed through her body at his touch. She breathed, "It seemed easy enough for you a minute ago."

He eyed the baby in the stroller, who looked back at him

with dark eyes exactly like his own. He said simply, "I need you and Esme with me."

"In London?"

Leaning forward, he whispered, "Everywhere."

She felt the warmth of his breath against her skin, and her heartbeat quickened. For so long, Tess would have done anything to hear Stefano speak those words.

But she'd suffered too much shock and grief today. He couldn't tempt her to forget so easily how badly he'd treated her. She pulled away.

"Why would I come with you?"

Stefano's eyes widened. She saw she'd surprised him. And he wasn't the only one. Her uncle and the white-haired customer were now staring at them, wide-eyed.

Giving her a crooked grin, he said, "I can think of a few reasons."

"If you want to spend time with Esme, I will be happy to arrange that. But if you think I'll give up my family and friends and home—" she lifted her chin "—and come with you to Europe as some kind of paid nanny—"

"No. Not my nanny." Stefano's thumb lightly traced her tender lower lip. "I have something else in mind."

Unwilling desire shot down her body, making her nipples taut as tension coiled low in her belly. Her pride was screaming for her to push him away but it was difficult to hear her pride over the rising pleas of her body.

"I—I won't be your mistress, either," she stammered, shivering, searching his gaze.

"No." With a smile that made his dark eyes gleam, Stefano shook his head. "Not my mistress."

Tess heard a gasp. Glancing back at the cash register, she saw that her aunt and cousins had come downstairs from the upstairs apartment. They were standing next to her uncle, wearing the same stunned expressions.

"Then…then what?" Tess stammered, feeling foolish

for even suggesting a handsome billionaire prince like Stefano would want a regular girl like her as his mistress. Her cheeks were hot. "You don't want me as your nanny, not as your mistress, so—what? You just want me to come to London as someone who watches your baby for free?" Her voice shook. "Some kind of...p-poor relation?"

"No." Taking her in his arms, Stefano said quietly, "Tess. Look at me."

Although she didn't want to obey, she could not resist. She opened her eyes, and the intensity of his glittering eyes scared her.

"I don't want you to be my mistress, Tess. I don't want you to be my nanny." His dark eyes burned through her. "I want you to be my wife."

Tess's beautiful face looked pale against her scarlet-red hair as she stood in the faded bakery. Her green eyes were shocked, even horrified.

Stefano was a little shocked himself. He marveled at how quickly everything had changed. Yesterday, before he'd known about the baby, marriage had been the last thing on his mind.

His own parents had hardly made him think well of the institution, and none of the ice-cold heiresses and greedy, pouting models Stefano had dated had ever tempted him to change his mind. Taking them to bed was more than enough.

Even an hour ago, knowing that Esme was his child, he'd grimly intended to let Tess go, leaving just his money to sustain them.

But when he'd watched Tess put their baby in a stroller and leave him, walking toward the bakery, he'd felt a jolt like a cold knife slicing through his solar plexus.

He hadn't wanted her to go.

Then he'd seen two men pass her on the sidewalk, slowing their walk to smile at her. Farther down the street, they'd turned back to look at her again. Their polite smiles changed to leers as they elbowed each other. Stefano could only imagine what the two men were saying about her. Or what they'd like to do to her.

The knife in Stefano's gut had twisted deeper. He didn't want to imagine Tess with another man. Ever. And yet he'd let her go so she could find a man who could love her. A better man.

But what if the next man wasn't better?

What if he was worse?

Admittedly love was a mysterious emotion to Stefano, as he'd never experienced it. From the outside, it seemed like a self-inflicted delusion, an addictive madness that people used as an excuse to behave badly. Love came like a hurricane and left like a tornado, leaving people trampled and homes destroyed.

It had been that way with his parents, and to an entire army of their discarded lovers and spouses, in their exhaustive quest for love. And all the while, they'd left their only child to languish in an isolated castle in the care of paid servants. To them, children were an unacceptable impediment to enjoying a love affair.

What if the man Tess chose was similarly selfish and cruel? What if he treated her badly? What if he cheated on her? Stole from her? Hit her?

What if, far from him being a better father than Stefano, he resented raising another man's child and mistreated Esme? What if he abused her?

A cold shudder had gone down Stefano's spine.

He'd thought giving up Tess and the baby was the right thing to do—for their sakes. In that moment, however, he'd suddenly realized he was leaving them to the mercy of wolves. And Tess, with her kind nature and optimistic heart, might not know the difference until it was too late.

After all, she'd thought Stefano was worth a year of

total loyalty. How badly astray could those rose-colored glasses lead her?

There was only one way to be permanently sure of their security. One way to keep them safe.

He had to marry her.

Perhaps Stefano couldn't love her. Even so, he could damn sure take care of her. And his child.

As he'd sat in the back seat of the Rolls-Royce, the desire—the need—to permanently claim Tess as his own had rushed through him with the force of a tidal wave. When she had disappeared into the bakery, his driver had started to pull away from the curb.

"Stop!" Stefano had shouted.

He'd couldn't let her go. He couldn't let them both disappear and trust that the next man would deserve Tess more than he did. He'd thought he could.

He was wrong.

Now Stefano looked down at her in the bakery's soft light. He was dimly aware of some old love song playing on the radio. From behind the counter, four people, a man and woman and two teenaged girls with backpacks, watched with their mouths wide. Ah, yes, Stefano thought. That must be the aunt and uncle and cousins who'd made Tess speak with such fear about being a *poor relation*. Stefano could hardly wait to take her away from the bakery and treat her as she deserved—like a princess.

"Well?" he said gently. "What is your answer?"

She shifted her feet uncertainly on the tile floor. "You—you want to marry me?"

"Yes."

"You can't mean it," she choked out, searching his gaze desperately. "A man like you could never be faithful to just one woman."

"You're wrong," he said flatly. "I've seen the damage of that in my parents' marriage. I would never betray you."

Tess bit her lip, looking up at him.

"Say yes, dearie!" cried the bakery's only customer, an elderly woman nursing a coffee at the furthest table. "He's a hunk!"

"I..." Tess looked down. Her dark eyelashes swept against the smattering of freckles on her pale cheeks. "I don't understand. The only good reason to marry," she said in a small voice, "is for love."

"You once said you loved me," he pointed out.

Her lips curved. "As you pointed out, that was before I even knew you."

The edges of his lips quirked. "So, get to know me."

Her eyes widened, then she shook her head, repeating stubbornly, "Love is the only reason for marriage."

Stefano thought about arguing with her, of pointing out that, in his opinion, romantic love was at best a biological reaction brought on by hormones and pheromones to coax a couple into settling into domestic life; at worst it was a delusion, an intoxicating dream that people used like a drug to escape real life. But with Tess's romantic heart, suddenly he knew all rational arguments would be wasted. Only an emotional appeal would work.

Deliberately, he lowered his head so his lips nearly brushed against her ear. He felt her shiver as he breathed in the scent of her red hair, like vanilla and flowers.

"You are the only woman I've ever wanted to be my wife. Only you."

He felt her shiver as she pulled away. Her emerald eyes were almost pleading. "But..."

He cupped her cheek. "I can make you and Esme happy," he said softly. "You'll always be protected and safe. We'll travel the world by private jet. You'll have homes in Paris and Rome and St. Barts. A castle in Sicily."

Her lips parted. "You have a *castle*?"

"It's a bit of a ruin." He gave her a wickedly seductive smile. "But yes."

"A castle," she whispered to herself.

Still, Tess didn't say yes. Other women might have been lured with dreams of wealth and status—not her.

Stefano took a different tack.

"You had to drop out of design school," he murmured, twisting a tendril of her red hair around his finger. "As my wife, you'll be far more influential in the fashion world than any mere designer. You'll be invited to every event. Runway shows. Fashion awards. Berlin. The Met Gala."

"I will?" she breathed.

He drew her closer into his arms, not caring who saw. Even baby Esme seemed almost solemn, watching from the stroller.

"Let me make you a princess." His hand gently stroked down her cheek to the edge of her throat, to her shoulder. His gaze fell to her pink lips as he whispered, "Let me give you the fairy tale."

Tess's eyes were huge. He could see she was tempted. But, still, she didn't say yes.

Why?

He thought of everything he'd ever done to persuade a woman into his bed. He'd never imagined, he thought with grim amusement, that he'd someday need even greater charm to persuade a woman to *wed*.

What else could he offer, aside from the heart he did not have? What could he propose that wasn't a lie?

Then he remembered what Tess cared about most.

"Let me give our daughter a name," he said huskily. "Let me give her a home. Let me be her father. I want you as my wife. My family."

Pulling the solid gold signet ring off his finger, Stefano slowly went down on one knee. All the women in the bakery gasped, but he had eyes only for her. He took her hand, looking up at her.

"Marry me, Tess."

She sucked in her breath. He saw tears in her eyes, and he knew he had her.

"Until I can get you a diamond ring, I offer this." He held up the signet ring. "It's been in my family for generations. I give it as my pledge of fidelity. My promise of forever." He looked up at her. "Will you, Tess? Will you be mine, not just now, but forever?"

For a moment, she seemed to hold her breath, as if caught between desire and fear.

"Say yes," squealed one of her young cousins.

"Yes!" cried the other one.

"Do it, Tess," her aunt said hoarsely. "Seize your dreams before it's too late."

The uncle was silent, watching them.

Tess shivered. Then her fingers tightened over his.

"Yes," she whispered.

Triumph rushed through Stefano, greater than he'd ever felt before, even when he'd made his first million, when he'd made his first *billion*. This was better. What he'd assumed was an entitlement to be merely demanded—Tess's hand in marriage—had become, with her hesitation, a prize to be fought for and won.

Still kneeling, he fervently kissed her hand, then slid on the gold signet ring engraved with the Zacco coat of arms. Her fingers were too delicate, so it would fit only on her thumb, and even then, she had to keep her hand closed.

"We'll get you another ring immediately," he promised, rising to his feet. But he didn't release her hand. He loved the feel of her smaller hand in his own, and soon he would have more of her.

All of her.

Tess gave him a shy smile. "I like your ring fine."

"Plain gold? No. You'll have a diamond. The best in the city." Only one woman in a million, he thought, would have said she didn't need a big diamond ring. Only one woman would have been reluctant to marry him unless it was for the right reasons. A woman who put her child above herself, and who was loyal and kind and true.

As he stood beside her in the weak September light from the bakery's windows, her family rushed forward to congratulate them. Stefano looked at Tess, now being hugged tearfully by her aunt and cousins.

He could hardly wait to marry her.

"You'd better take good care of her," the uncle said gruffly behind him. "After the year of hell you put her through."

Stefano turned with a single brusque nod. "I will."

"When will you marry?" the aunt asked, smiling.

He turned to Tess. "Tomorrow."

They all looked at one another, astonished. "Tomorrow?"

"Yes. I'll take you to London as my wife."

Her beautiful face appeared entranced as she nodded, ducking her head. "All right," she whispered. "Tomorrow."

"I cannot wait," he said huskily, feeling a swell of pride and the glory of conquest. Cupping her face in his hands, he lowered his mouth passionately to hers. Tomorrow couldn't come soon enough.

CHAPTER FOUR

"Are you sure about this, Tess?"

Tess looked up in surprise. She was wearing a wedding dress, sitting in a chair in an elegant private sitting room of the Campania Hotel, getting the final touches of her makeup done by a stylist. Doubt was the last thing she'd ever expected from *Lola*, of all people. Especially now, just minutes before the wedding ceremony was set to begin!

"Of course I'm sure," Tess said uneasily. "Why wouldn't I want to marry Stefano? He's Esme's father!"

Lola lifted a skeptical eyebrow. "I didn't hear you say anything about love."

"Of course Tess loves him," Hallie protested, sipping a mimosa nearby. "She's loved him for a year. Even when we teased her about it!"

"Yeah, I know. We thought you were crazy." Lola's eyes challenged Tess in the mirror. "So he's everything you imagined him to be?"

Tess's cheeks burned. "Pretty much."

"He told you he loves you?"

Tess bit her lip. "Um…"

"Has he or hasn't he?"

Looking between them, the stylist packed up her gear and excused herself, closing the door of the sitting room quietly behind her. With a deep breath, Tess looked at her two friends.

Lola and Hallie were wearing bridesmaid dresses in her favorite color, emerald green. Their three babies were already in the grand ballroom with Tess's cousins and Hallie's husband, Cristiano. The wedding was set to begin in minutes. Any moment now, the Campania's wedding planner would burst in with her headset and clipboard to tell them it was time for the whirlwind ceremony to begin.

Tess said slowly, "I've realized we don't really know each other that well. But we have a child now, so I...hope love will come in time."

Hallie and Lola glanced at each other uneasily.

"He hasn't told you he loves you?" Hallie said. "And now you're saying you don't love him?"

Turning in the chair, Tess glared at her friends.

"How long did it take for Cristiano to tell you he loved you, Hallie?" The brunette hung her head in answer. "And you." Tess narrowed her eyes at Lola. "Aren't you the one who's always going on about how mothers have an obligation to be financially stable for their children?"

"That *is* what you always say, Lola," Hallie said.

"But you're not like me, Tess," she said. "You don't care about money. You just want to be loved."

Tess felt a sharp pain in her throat.

"I want you to be careful, that's all. Don't do anything you'll regret." The blonde looked away. "Don't love him if you know he'll never love you back."

"Is that what happened to you, Lola?" Tess said timidly. "You've never said what happened with Jett's father..."

"We're talking about you, not me." She looked down. Her voice became sad. "I don't want to see you make a mistake, that's all."

Tess and Hallie looked at each other. This wasn't like their brash friend. Usually Lola couldn't wait to boss them around. *Speaking the brutal truth with love*, Lola called it, although her words were sometimes far more brutal than loving.

But then Lola hadn't seemed quite herself lately. No wonder, Tess thought. Lola had a newborn. That kind of exhaustion would put any woman off her game.

Tess hadn't slept very well last night, either. Knowing it was her last evening in her aunt and uncle's Brooklyn apartment, she'd stared up at the shadowy ceiling, tormented by anxiety. Without Stefano's overwhelming presence to reassure her, she'd felt a strange fear over this sudden marriage.

It's just cold feet, she'd tried to tell herself then. But now she wondered—what if it wasn't?

She'd never thought getting married would scare her. She'd always been sure that when she wed, she'd be so deeply in love she'd rush into the ceremony with a pure, joyful heart.

Today she was marrying a man she barely knew. Not for love, but because they had a child.

Maybe Stefano *could* love me, she told herself desperately. Someday. And if he did, who knew? Maybe she could someday be brave enough to forget how he'd hurt her. Maybe she could be brave enough to open up her heart again, too.

But was she willing to take the gamble? Because if Stefano couldn't love her, why would she be stupid enough to open herself up to more heartbreak? She wouldn't. Lola was right. She could never let herself love Stefano again, even if she wanted to. Not unless he loved her first.

But what if he didn't? Could she live her whole life without love?

Tess glanced at the empty champagne glasses on the table, next to the bouquets made by the hotel florist. Yesterday she'd relished her friends' shock and delight when she'd told them that her baby's long-lost father had returned, revealing himself to be a billionaire prince. And, not only that, he wished to marry Tess immediately!

Lola and Hallie's giddy squeals had been music to Tess's ears. She'd loved showing off the sparkling ten-carat diamond engagement ring Stefano had bought her on Fifth Avenue, after they'd left City Hall with their marriage license. She was wearing the diamond ring now, and though part of her already missed the simple integrity of Stefano's gold signet ring, obviously she couldn't go around wearing it on her thumb. She'd told herself she'd get used to the cold weight of the diamond in time.

Getting ready for the wedding with her two best friends had seemed like a good idea. And at first it had been wonderful. They'd giggled, drinking mimosas, and Tess had felt contented.

But now the gorgeous platinum-set ten-carat diamond ring hung heavily on Tess's left hand.

Shaking, she rose to her feet.

"Fine bridesmaids you two make," she said accusingly, "trying to talk me into jilting him at the last minute."

The other two hung their heads.

"Sorry, Tess," Hallie said. "He is your baby's father, after all."

"Sorry," Lola muttered.

Tess lifted her chin. "I never had a father or a real home. Don't you think I want that for Esme?"

"Of course you do," Hallie said soothingly.

"I'm sure you'll be very happy." But Lola didn't sound sure at all.

Tess swallowed. "Stefano has promised to be faithful. All he wants is to make me happy." Her voice trembled. "He's going to whisk me away to London and Milan and Paris for our honeymoon—"

"Some honeymoon." Lola snorted. "A fashion CEO

dragging you to all the Fashion Weeks. That's not a honeymoon—it's a business trip!"

"I studied fashion design," Tess said defensively. "I can't wait to be a part of it!"

"Sure, as his trophy wife. Not a designer."

Tears rose to Tess's eyes.

"You hush," Hallie told Lola harshly. "Don't listen to her," she said, patting Tess's hand.

"I'm just trying to save you from a lot of grief," Lola said flatly. "The fact that he's a billionaire only makes it worse. Because billionaires don't know how to love anyone." Her eyes were bleak. "I know."

"Excuse *me*," Hallie said.

"Except your husband, Hallie. He's one in a million." Lola's face gentled into a smile. Then she shook her head. "Doesn't Cristiano have anything to say about this wedding? He hates Stefano Zacco!"

Hallie shrugged. "Cristiano says since Tess has a child with Stefano, she must see something good in him, and on her own head be it." She grinned. "I think my husband must be remembering that I didn't always think so highly of *him*, either."

Slowly Lola picked up her bridesmaid's bouquet in a rustle of rose petals. "I think it's a mistake to leave your family and friends, and get married after a one-day engagement to a man you barely know." Wiping her eyes, she tried to smile. "But, of all people, you deserve the fairy tale, Tess. If you're sure Stefano's the one, then I wish you every happiness. I…" Her voice broke. "I'll see you in there."

The blonde hurried out of the room.

"She's just worried about you," Hallie said.

Tess looked at herself in the full-length mirror. Stefano had arranged for one of his smaller luxury fashion brands, Fontana, to make her a lavish wedding dress. The gown was exquisite, made of white satin, with full skirts and a corset bodice with a sweetheart neckline. The edges were embroidered with tiny diamonds, and so was the long white veil that trailed down her back, over her red hair that was pulled back into a chignon. Anchoring the veil was a 300-year-old diamond tiara, an heirloom of the Zacco family.

Her green eyes were lined with black kohl and mascara, her lips ruby red with lipstick. As Tess looked at herself in the mirror, she barely recognized herself. But in spite of the gown, the veil and the tiara, she suddenly thought she didn't look right for a bride. There wasn't any joy in her expression. Her eyes were scared.

"This is your life, and Esme's," Hallie said quietly, handing Tess her bridal bouquet of pink roses. "Trust your heart. It will tell you what's right."

Slowly taking her bouquet, Tess thought of how she'd felt when Stefano had pulled her into his arms in the bakery and demanded that she become his bride. Everyone had been so happy for her. In that moment, she'd felt like the luckiest girl on earth. Wasn't she?

And the decision was already made.

Wasn't it?

Taking a deep breath, Tess turned to Hallie. "Could you ask Stefano to come talk to me?"

"Right now?"

"Yes. Just for a moment, here in private?"

Hallie's eyes widened, then she said quietly, "Of course. I'll go get him. Then I'll wait in the hall for...for whatever you decide," she finished lamely. She left, closing the door softly behind her.

Tess looked out at the golden afternoon sunlight pouring through the window. Setting down her bouquet, she placed her hands against the corset boning of her gown's bodice, trying to make herself take long, slow breaths instead of panicked little gasps. Why was she suddenly so afraid?

Closing her eyes, Tess had the sudden memory of the day long ago when her mother had collapsed on their old shabby sofa, sobbing, unable to catch her breath.

"It's over," Serena Foster had choked out, whispering, "He's never coming back."

"Who?" Tess had asked anxiously. Just eight years old, she'd been alarmed to see her determinedly cheerful mother fall apart without warning.

Shaking her head, her mother had wiped her eyes and tried to smile. "It doesn't matter."

"Pinkie loves you, Mama," Tess had said desperately, pushing her ragged pink unicorn into her mother's arms. "And so do I."

"Thank you, darling." Hugging Tess fiercely, Serena had wiped her eyes. "I was stupid to love him. But he's a bigger fool by far..."

Tess opened her eyes when she heard a single knock at the door. It creaked half open.

"This is a bad idea," came Stefano's gravelly voice from the other side. "I don't generally care about wedding traditions, but even I know the groom isn't supposed to see the bride before the ceremony."

Her heart lifted at hearing his voice. She knew once they talked she'd feel better. "I don't care. Just come in. I need you."

Stefano peeked his head around the door, then came toward her in the hotel's luxurious private sitting room.

In his well-cut tuxedo, Stefano looked powerful, broad shouldered and devastatingly handsome. His dark eyes widened above his chiseled cheekbones when he saw Tess in her wedding gown. "You are so beautiful, *cara*." As he took her in his arms, the hard lines of his face glowed with fierce pride. "I can hardly wait to take you as my wife."

Taking a deep breath, she said timidly, "But you don't love me, do you?"

Stefano blinked, then pulled back, his forehead furrowed. "What?"

Nervously she licked her lips. "I'm just wondering if we're doing the right thing," she whispered, staring down at the elegant Turkish rug on the gleaming hardwood floor. "I mean, we don't love each other. I'm wondering...if someday you think we might... I'm just scared this whole thing might be a terrible mistake."

Her words seemed to echo against the walls. She waited desperately for him to kiss her, to reassure her. Instead, he said nothing. Finally she looked up.

Stefano's dark eyes were cold as ice. The expression on his handsome face chilled her to the bone.

"You wish to cancel the wedding?" he said softly. "To disgrace my name? To take my child away?"

What she'd wanted was reassurance. This was exactly the opposite. "All I want is for us to talk—"

"Is there another man?"

"No, of course not!"

"But you are having second thoughts." He gave her a bitter smile. "Or is this a ploy to renegotiate the prenuptial agreement you signed yesterday?"

"No!" Why would she want to alter the prenup? She'd barely read it. She took a deep breath. "I'm afraid."

"And I am afraid," he said with dangerous silkiness, "that you already gave me your word. We have a verbal contract. It's done."

Tess herself had thought something similar just moments before—that the decision had already been made, so there was no backing out. But hearing him speak the words like a threat made her back stiffen. "What are you saying?"

His eyes narrowed.

"You're wearing my ring." He looked down at the big diamond on her left hand. "You will take my name. You will be my wife, and we will raise our daughter. Our wedding will go forward as planned."

She tried to toss her head, not easy when it was weighed down with a heavy diamond tiara. "Maybe I won't!"

His lips twisted. Reaching out, he cupped her cheek, running his thumb along her shaking lower lip.

"And maybe," he said tenderly, "I'll hire a team of lawyers to utterly destroy you and your family. Maybe I'll take our daughter and make sure you never see her again."

Then Stefano drew back, his dark eyes smiling down at her as if he'd been flirting.

The room, with all its elegant furnishings, seemed to spin around her. Tess stared up at him, her eyes wide with horror.

"Are you ready, Miss Foster?"

Tess turned to see the hotel's wedding planner with her headset standing in the doorway. Behind her, Uncle Ray hovered.

"Yes. She's ready." Stefano's eyes were callous as he looked down at Tess. "Aren't you?"

Feeling sick inside, she gave an unsteady nod.

"What are you doing here, Your Highness?" the wedding planner chided. "You're supposed to be waiting in the ballroom."

"Of course." Deliberately, Stefano reached down and pulled the translucent white veil over Tess's tiara, over her face. He said lightly, "I can't wait to marry you, *cara mia.*"

And, after kissing her cheek through the veil, he left.

Tess stood in shock as her uncle came forward with tears in his eyes.

"You look beautiful, Tessie." He held out his arm awkwardly in the new designer tuxedo that Stefano had provided for him. "Are you ready for this?"

Numbly Tess took her uncle's arm. She picked up her bouquet.

"Thank you for walking me down the aisle, Uncle Ray," she said, barely knowing what she was saying. She felt frozen, like she was in a bad dream.

"My little sister would be so proud of you," her uncle said, blinking back tears. "Of the woman you've become."

"I wish Mama was still here," Tess whispered. After Tess's father had left, her mother had gone through many other short-lived romances—surely Serena would have known what to do now.

They followed the wedding planner down the elegant hallway, toward the entrance to the grand hotel ballroom, where her two bridesmaids waited outside the door. Lola refused to meet her eyes. Hallie took one look at Tess and demanded, "What's wrong?"

"Nothing," Tess said, looking away.

"Stefano just rushed by us. I guess that means you guys worked it out?" she said hopefully.

"You might say that," Tess said. *Maybe I'll take our daughter and make sure you never see her again.*

The double doors opened and a wave of music swelled as the orchestra started the first notes of the wedding march. Bouquets held high, Lola walked in, followed by Hallie.

"Here we go," her uncle whispered. Tess nodded, and clutching his arm like a life preserver, she walked forward.

Hundreds of guests rose to their feet in the gilded ballroom, beneath soaring ceilings and sparkling crystal chandeliers. Tess looked around desperately for a friendly face among the glamorous strangers staring at her incredulously, as if wondering why on earth a handsome billionaire prince would lower himself to marrying the likes of her.

They didn't know how much Tess desperately wished she wasn't marrying him now.

Lola had been right. Why, oh, why hadn't Tess gotten to know Stefano better before she'd agreed to be his wife? Why had she let herself get swept up in the romantic moment?

Why had she let her blindly, stupidly optimistic heart make the decision, instead of her brain?

Tess's knees shook. Looking through the crowd, she finally saw her own friends and family, who gave her encouraging smiles. Her aunt had tears in her eyes. She saw her cousin Natalie, holding Esme, whispering happily to the baby as she pointed at Tess. Nearby, friends from her neighborhood waved at her. Women she knew from the single moms support group she'd attended last year beamed at her as she walked by, including the woman who'd introduced her to Hallie and Lola. Lacey Tremaine Drakos stood with her ruggedly handsome Greek husband, holding their baby in her arms.

Then Tess looked forward, saw Stefano, and everything else faded to a blur.

He stood alone beside the minister, without a best man, in front of the guests, beneath a canopy of roses. His dark eyes gleamed down at her.

The bastard.

Tess's hands tightened on her bouquet. She would have dearly loved to smash his smug face with it.

As she reached the front, she barely heard the minister's words. "Who gives this woman to be married to this man?" Or her uncle's answer: "Her aunt and I do." She barely noticed the minister's long-winded advice on the duties of marriage. He might as well have been reading from a technical manual written in hieroglyphics.

As the minister spoke the words that would make them husband and wife, all of Tess's feelings and thoughts melted to one single overwhelming emotion for the man beside her.

Hate.

Stefano's expression was cool and impersonal. As their gaze locked and held, it changed. His eyes turned dark, hungry.

Tess was suddenly aware that they were flying like an out-of-control train toward the end of the ceremony, when Stefano would claim her as his wife and kiss her.

Then, tonight, on their wedding night, he would do far more than kiss her.

Tess's toes curled in her expensive white high heels. Out of pure hate, she told herself.

But the truth was more complicated. Even in her rage, as she watched the flick of his tongue against his cruel, sensual lips, her own lips tingled in response. Against her will, her whole body sizzled at his closeness, aching in its most secret places.

"And do you, Tesslyn Mae Foster, take this man to be your lawfully wedded husband?"

Gazing up at Stefano, Tess hesitated, heart pounding in her throat. She could refuse him now. In front of everyone. Tell him to go to hell. She *could*.

Stefano waited, his eyes narrowing. Three hundred guests held their breath.

I'll hire a team of lawyers to utterly destroy you and your family... I'll take our daughter and make sure you never see her again.

"I do," she ground out, furious and wretched.

"I now pronounce you husband and wife." The minister beamed at them. "You may kiss the bride."

Stefano lifted her long, translucent white veil off her face, back over the diamond tiara. Reaching down, he cupped her face with his hands.

Her knees went wobbly. Part of her wanted to turn away, to kick him in the shins. To scream in his face.

But not all of her. Part of her still wanted him. *Even now.* Heaven help her.

As Stefano pulled her into his arms, so close she could almost hear the beat of his heart, she felt the warmth of his breath, sweet and spicy as cloves. She shivered, holding her breath, frozen beneath her tight bodice.

With agonizing slowness, he lowered his head. Then his lips touched hers, and electricity pulsed through her body. He deepened the kiss, twisting his tongue against hers, publicly claiming her as his possession. She gasped beneath the brutal onslaught of pleasure, and to her shame, a soft moan came from the back of her throat.

When he finally pulled away, applause mounted like a storm swell as guests rose to their feet with a cheer.

Stefano lowered his head, nuzzling her ear. He whispered huskily, "That was quite a kiss."

Tess stared at him, trembling between fury and desire. Fury won.

Smiling for the crowd, she ground out through her teeth, "I hope you enjoyed it. Because that's the last time I'll ever let you kiss me."

His eyes narrowed.

"Allow me to present," the minister cried, "Their Highnesses Prince Stefano and Princess Tess Zacco di Gioreale!"

Holding her hand tightly, Stefano turned and waved at his friends, smiling like a happy bridegroom.

Tess knew a storm was coming. She could feel it building, like low-rolling thunder rattling toward them without mercy.

Her new husband intended to seduce her. To possess her. *She couldn't let him.*

It was all she could think about during the wedding reception immediately afterward in the grand ballroom. She felt the hum of her body's desire and grimly fought it, tooth and nail, until she nearly panted with exhaustion, even as she went through the motions of what was supposed to be the happiest day of her life.

Tess forced herself to smile until her cheeks ached as she accepted the congratulations of her family and friends. She held poses for endless wedding photographs. She mechanically ate an elegant dinner of salmon, baby potatoes and asparagus in a lemon-butter sauce, followed by wedding cake. She sipped champagne as toasts were offered by strangers.

She forced herself to make polite responses as Stefano introduced her to many fashion industry insiders, including the extremely thin, severely chic Fenella Montfort, whom he introduced as the majority shareholder of the Zacco brand. He'd added with a charming smile, "Though we'll talk more about that in London, won't we, Fenella?"

"If we must," the older woman said coolly.

As Tess's desire fought against her howling fury, her mind scrambled for a way to escape this marriage. Could she go to Hallie and Cristiano for help? Ask them to assist her in filing for a divorce?

But even if Cristiano Moretti gave her all his man-eating lawyers, she knew that divorce would be an endless, bloody war, with Esme its greatest victim.

Lost in her own churning emotions, Tess barely noticed when, after she tossed the wedding bouquet and Lola accidentally caught it, the blonde turned pale and immediately dropped it to the floor. Lola practically ran out of the reception, pausing only to grab her baby's stroller as other female guests fought for the bouquet in a flurry of rose petals. Normally Tess would have been alarmed for her friend.

But not today. Today nothing could reach her through her own haze of rage and fear.

Until this.

The tradition of the groom pulling the garter off the

bride's leg was supposed to be a harmless bit of fun, a sly nod to tradition to entertain wedding guests. Now, as Stefano knelt before Tess, who was seated in a chair, her heartbeat went to a thousand as he pushed up her full skirts. His dark eyes burned through hers as he slowly pulled the blue satin garter down her leg. His fingertips brushed against her bare skin.

Time slowed. She forgot her anger and fear. In this moment, all she could see was the hunger in his eyes, pulling her down into the flames.

Though they were surrounded by hundreds of strangers, it was just the two of them. Alone.

When he finally turned away, to toss the garter into the crowd of eager single men, Tess rose abruptly to her feet with a strangled gasp. She muttered, "I have to check on Esme," and fled for the head table.

"I'll come with you," he replied.

As he followed her back to the table, Tess was careful not to let Stefano touch her, not even her hand.

When they reached the elaborate, flower-decorated table for the wedding party and close family, Tess was dismayed to find Esme sitting happily in her cousin Natalie's arms. If the baby had been fussy, it would have been an excellent excuse for Tess to take her and go.

But go where? She could hardly return to her aunt and uncle's apartment tonight. All of Tess and Esme's meager belongings had been packed in two shabby suitcases and were already upstairs in Stefano's hotel suite, where she was supposed to sleep tonight. Natalie had volunteered to babysit Esme until they collected her on their way to the airport in the morning.

"I can't believe you guys did it," Hallie said, sitting comfortably beside Cristiano at the table. She shook her head. "How on earth did you pull such a big wedding together in one day?"

"Ask Moretti," Stefano replied smoothly. Reaching for his flute, he took a sip of champagne. "All I did was tell him to arrange it."

"It wasn't difficult, Zacco," Cristiano said. "Not when the words you used were *make it happen at any price*." The hotel tycoon sat with one arm draped over his wife's shoulders, the other holding their adorable baby, Jack. He quirked an eyebrow. "There's nothing we enjoy more at the Campania than unreasonable requests, as long as money's no object. Even for a conniving bastard like you, Zacco."

"Conniving?" Stefano bared his teeth into a smile. "You are the one who tried to cheat, by blocking my car in the race." He shrugged. "If you wanted to win, you should have gone faster."

"You could have caused an accident."

"I knew you were a decent enough driver that you wouldn't let that happen. Decent." Stefano saluted him with his champagne flute. "Just slow."

With a snort, Cristiano shook his head. "There are more important things in life than winning some cheap gold trophy in a charity race." He stroked his wife's shoulder. "It's a foolish man who's determined to win at any price."

"So losers always say."

The two powerful men glowered at each other, then suddenly they both laughed. Smiling, Hallie rose to her feet.

She looked at Tess. "It's time for your first dance as bride and groom, isn't it?"

The last thing Tess wanted to do right now was slow dance in her new husband's arms. Her cheeks went hot as she looked down at her clasped hands. "I think we've had enough traditions for one day…"

"Oh, please," Hallie begged. "I was planning to sing for your first dance. As a surprise."

Put that way, it seemed churlish to refuse.

"All right," Tess sighed. "Fine."

"Yay." Hallie looked down at her seated husband with a tender smile. "Wish me luck."

"You don't need it." Cristiano pulled her into his arms and lifted his lips to hers in a sensual kiss. "You'll knock 'em dead."

Watching the other couple, so deeply in love, Tess again felt a pang over what she now knew she would never have.

As Hallie hurried toward the microphone on the grand ballroom's stage, Stefano held out his hand.

"Shall we?" he said, smiling down at her as if he hadn't just blackmailed her into marriage and threatened to destroy her family and take her child away.

Glaring at him, Tess grudgingly put her hand in his and tried not to feel the electricity of his touch.

"And now," Hallie announced over the microphone, "for their very first dance, the Prince and Princess of Gioreale!"

A hush fell across the crowd as Stefano led her, in a swirl of her white satin skirts, onto the dance floor.

To the outside world, Tess knew it must look like a romantic moment, the handsome prince in his sleek, well-cut tuxedo, the bride in a lavish wedding gown sparkling with diamonds, dancing in his arms. The truth was anything but romantic.

The orchestra began playing the music of the song Tess had requested, one made famous by Etta James and that she'd loved since she was a child—"At Last." Hallie's beautiful voice started singing the haunting words, telling the rapturous tale of long-lost love finally requited.

Yesterday Tess had dreamily thought it was perfect. Now, in her husband's arms, all she felt was bitterness.

She looked up at his face.

"I hate you," she whispered. "You know that, don't you?"

Stefano looked down at her as they swayed, his handsome face arrogant. "You don't hate me. You're just angry. It will pass."

"Are you crazy? You forced me to marry you."

"I didn't force you. I offered you a choice."

"What—marry you or lose everything?"

His eyes gleamed in the spotlight as they danced to the music. "I knew you'd make the right decision."

Tess yearned to stomp hard on his foot with one of her stiletto heels. Instead, she bared her teeth into a smile for the benefit of the guests watching them as he whirled her around the dance floor.

"You are a monster," she said sweetly.

"Cheer up." He pulled her hard against his body. "I told you the truth. I intend to make you very happy in our marriage. Starting tonight."

He cupped her cheek, and desire crackled through her body, from her scalp to her toes and everywhere in between.

Breathing hard, she turned away.

"Go to hell," she spit out, trying to hide her conflicting feelings. How could her body still want him, when she despised him?

"I intend to satisfy you in every way possible." He stopped on the dance floor, looking down at her. "Tonight, you will be in my bed. Willingly and completely."

Trembling, she lifted her chin. In spite of her best efforts, her voice trembled as she taunted, "In your dreams."

"My dreams always come true." Stefano cupped her face in both his hands. "I always win, like Moretti said. I take what I want, at any price. And what I want—" he slowly lowered his mouth to hers "—is you."

Tess held her breath. She knew she should push him away, resist, but she couldn't. When his lips finally pressed against hers, the intoxication of his caress made her feel dizzy. She had to clutch his shoulders to keep from falling. The world spun around her as if she'd drunk far more than one glass of champagne.

Dimly she heard whistling and hooting from the crowd,

but they all seemed far away. In Stefano's arms, swaying to this beautiful song she'd loved all her life, her anger faded for a moment and her old dream resurfaced in her heart. She'd yearned for him for so long. Her perfect man. Her handsome prince. Their kiss brought it all back, sending her soaring into the sky.

As the song ended, he pulled away and Tess slowly opened her eyes.

Stefano stared down at her, his dark eyes wide as if he'd felt the same shock, the two of them in their own private world.

Applause thundered around them—for their first dance as husband and wife, and for Hallie's amazing performance.

Stricken, Tess touched her bruised lips. How could she keep kissing him like that? With everything in her heart? Her body ached for him, and her nipples felt tight beneath the smooth silk bodice.

For over a year, she'd been tormented by hot, sensual dreams of Stefano, of the night he'd taken her virginity and they'd conceived a child. She'd yearned for the man she'd imagined him to be. Now she knew the truth.

The dream still held sway over her.

She *wanted* to be in his bed. No matter how she tried to fight it. No matter how she pretended otherwise. Even now, looking up at him, she unconsciously licked her lips. She heard his soft groan and felt lost in his dark, hungry gaze.

Stefano took her hand. Without a word, he led her past the crowd, off the dance floor. He drew Tess past the tables and guests. Her full white satin skirts shimmered beneath the lights of the glittering crystal chandeliers as he pulled her away from the gilded ballroom and out a side door, into a shadowy back service hallway.

Once they were alone, his restraint fled.

He pushed her roughly against the wall, kissing her hard, gripping her wrists. She kissed him back with fury, surrendering to the angry force of her own desire.

"You're mine," he growled, kissing down her throat. "Say it, Tess."

Her head fell back as her veil tumbled and twisted around them.

"Yours," she breathed, and knew she was lost.

CHAPTER FIVE

As Stefano kissed down her throat, stroking the silky fabric of her dress, Tess closed her eyes, her body taut with need. She gasped as she felt the rough heat of his hands beneath the sweetheart neckline of her bodice, against her naked breasts.

Through the closed side door, she could hear the muffled sounds of music, laughter, dancing from the distant ballroom. The sounds of their wedding reception, still carrying on without them.

Here in this quiet, darkened hallway, they were alone. He swayed against her, and even through her thick white skirts, she could feel the force of his desire for her. They gripped each other, panting in the intensity of their need.

Abruptly he lifted her up against the wall. Her white skirts parted, her legs wrapped around his hips of their own accord. She felt his shaft pressing hard against her, through his trousers and the flimsy fabric of her panties.

Lowering his head, he kissed her passionately. Her fingertips dug into the shoulders of his tuxedo jacket. She wanted him closer, wanted *more*. With a low growl, he unzipped his fly.

Holding her backside, he pressed her hard against the wall. He shoved her delicate lace panties aside and pushed his enormous shaft inside her, filling her slowly, inch by delicious inch.

She gasped as she felt him hard and thick inside her, stretching her to the limit. Drawing back, he thrust again, even more deeply inside her wet, aching core. Desperate need pounded through her. She choked out a cry, gripping his shoulders.

His thrusts became harder, faster, as her white satin skirts shook and fluttered around them, the fabric opalescent and gleaming in the pale shadows of the hallway. Her breaths came in ragged gasps, her full breasts overflowing the low-cut neckline of the boned corset, a sliver of her pink nipples now visible.

Feeling him so deep inside her, all the way to her heart, pleasure blazed through her like a wildfire, consuming her. She'd wanted him for so long.

The wickedness of letting him do this to her when she hated him, when any moment someone might come into the hallway and see them, should have made her pull back and push him away. Instead, she only wanted him more.

Three more deep thrusts and she exploded in a shuddering cry, digging her nails into the expensive fabric of his tuxedo jacket. At that, he shoved himself inside her with a harsh shout, gripping her against the wall, his eyes closed with fierce ecstasy.

Tess slowly came back to earth, literally, as he released his grip on her thighs, letting her feet slide back to the floor.

His large hands smoothed her frothy white skirts neatly back down, as if nothing had happened. Turning away, he zipped up his tuxedo trousers. Watching him, Tess leaned back heavily against the wall, hardly able to believe what had just happened.

"I was never going to let you touch me again," she whispered.

Stefano glanced at her out of the corner of his eye. His cruel, sensual lips lifted into a cold smile. "If this is you hating me, I like it so far."

With a humiliated gasp, Tess turned away. He grabbed her wrist.

"Wait." His voice was low, and his earlier expression was gone, replaced with some emotion she couldn't identify. "Don't go. I didn't mean it."

"You did that just to show your control over me," she choked out, wiping her eyes, knowing she was probably streaking mascara across her face.

"Is that what you think?"

"What else could it be?"

He snorted, shaking his head. "I didn't even show control over *myself*. I meant to take you upstairs to the suite." He gave a rueful laugh. "I didn't quite make it."

Tess's cheeks were hot as she looked down at the patterns of the carpet. "You blackmailed me into marriage," she said in a low voice. "You threatened to destroy my family, to take Esme away."

"It was an empty threat." He looked at her with glittering eyes. "I would never take Esme away from you, Tess. Not for any reason."

Shocked at this admission, Tess demanded, "Then why did you say it?"

"You were threatening to call off our wedding."

"We barely know each other. All I did was share some doubts. And you proved my fears right!"

"I don't want you to be afraid of me," he said quietly. "But I couldn't let you leave. Or Esme. I can't just abandon you to the whims of fate and hope you'll be safe. Marrying you is the only way I know to keep you safe." He gave her a regretful smile. "I'm sorry if my method was a bit unorthodox—"

"Unorthodox?"

"I'll make it up to you," he said in a low voice. "We have a lifetime. I know I can make you happy."

A lump rose in her throat at the certainty in his voice. "How can you be so sure?"

"You said you spent the last year thinking of me." Lifting his hand gently to her cheek, he said softly, "What you don't know is that I spent the last year trying not to think of you. And failing."

"What are you saying?"

"I never forgot you, Tess." He paused. "There's been no one else."

Was he saying...?

"Impossible," she breathed. "The model I saw you with yesterday—"

"Kebe?" He snorted. "She's just a kid. I was giving her a ride home from a party. Although," he murmured, grinning, "I like that you were jealous."

"I wasn't," she lied.

"Didn't my marriage proposal prove you're the only woman I'm interested in?"

"You proposed because of Esme."

"She's not the only reason." His hand stroked from the edge of her jawline to her sensitive lower lip. "You asked yesterday if I could be faithful to you. The truth is..." His dark gaze lifted to hers. "I have been. For over a year."

There was a noisy burst of conversation from the other end of the service hall as a group of uniformed waiters appeared, carrying trays. But Tess couldn't look away from his gaze. She was in shock.

Stefano took her hand with his own. "Come with me."

"We should go back to the reception," she said, trying to ignore the thrum of her heart. "People will be wondering where we are—"

"So?"

"Aren't they your friends?" she said, bewildered.

"Acquaintances. I don't give a damn about them. You're the only one I want to please."

"And Esme—"

"She's fine with your cousin, isn't she?"

"But..." She bit her lip. "What will my family think? Leaving my own wedding reception without a farewell?"

"It's your day, Tess. Your choice." His dark eyes seared her. "Do you want to go back and make small talk? Forget about what you think you're *supposed* to want. What do you *actually* want?"

Tess's lips parted. For so long, she'd worried about pleasing others. Always being cheerful, pleasant and helpful, no matter what. Maybe part of her had always been afraid that if she put one toe out of line her uncle and aunt might abandon her, as her father had, and send her away.

Raw emotion filled her. What did she want?

No one had ever really asked that before.

"I want to leave with you," she whispered. His dark eyes gleamed.

"Then come." His large hand enfolded her smaller one. As he pulled her down the shadowy hall, past the chattering waitstaff, it occurred to Tess that if their passionate interlude had taken any longer they would have put on a shockingly good show for a bunch of strangers. She should have felt ashamed.

But she wasn't. After a lifetime of feeling invisible and desperate to please, something had made her reckless and bold.

Not *something*.

Someone.

Stefano wasn't afraid of her expressing her true feelings, either good or bad. He was strong enough to take it. He didn't judge her. He wasn't going to punish her. He wasn't going to leave her.

You asked yesterday if I could be faithful to you. The truth is I have been. For over a year.

His husky words echoed through her as Stefano led her into the Campania's lobby. She shivered, hardly able to believe it was true. Stefano had been faithful to her for over a year?

Her hand tensed in his as he led her toward the elevator. Wealthy guests and elegant patrons at the lobby bar turned to gape openly at them, the famous billionaire prince and his redheaded bride in a diamond tiara and wedding gown. People started to whisper, to lift their phones to take pictures.

"Hurry," Stefano said in a low voice, picking up the pace. She raced with him, clinging to his hand, her white veil and white wedding skirts flying behind her.

As the elevator door closed behind them, he pulled her hungrily into his arms. He kissed her forehead, her temples, her eyelids. He cradled her in his arms as if she were a treasure and he never wanted to let her go. And then he kissed her lips.

As the elevator traveled upward, Tess felt her body surrender in his powerful arms. When he kissed her, she was lost.

How she wished she could still believe in her romantic fantasy of him, that he was a handsome prince on a white horse, a strong, romantic hero she could trust. How she wished she could just let herself go, let herself love that man...

But she couldn't. As he drew away from the kiss, Tess looked up at him. She couldn't even *think* about loving him. Not unless she wanted her heart to be broken again.

Because however she might feel in his arms, Stefano was no knight in shining armor. Just hours before, he'd blackmailed her into speaking their vows at their wedding ceremony. What should have been the happiest moment of Tess's life had instead been misery, an agony of hate and despair.

She couldn't let herself truly trust him. She couldn't let herself believe in the romance or give him her heart.

But as Stefano smiled down at her, his dark eyes gleaming wickedly, she felt breathless. Her heart pounded with emotion and desire.

She hated that he'd blackmailed her into marriage. But at least he'd done it for the right reason, she told herself. He wanted to protect her and Esme, and claimed that he would spend the rest of his life making them happy. Could Tess truly fault him for that?

Especially when he made her feel like this...

As the elevator reached their floor, the door opened with a ding. Still holding her hand, Stefano led her toward his suite. After unlocking the door, he pushed it open. When Tess started to walk inside, he stopped her with a chiding smile. "That's not how it's done."

He picked her up in his arms as if she weighed nothing. Her long white veil and white skirts trailed behind them as he carried her over the threshold.

Inside, the suite, already so luxurious, had been utterly transformed. She gasped when she saw the lavish vases of long-stemmed red roses and soft glow of white candles.

"What have you done?" she breathed, looking up at him.

His eyes were dark, caressing her face. "For you," he said in a low voice. "All for you."

As the door closed behind them, he carried her past the main room, with its glittering view of the New York skyline at twilight, toward the bedroom.

Breathing in the scent of roses, Tess looked up at him as he carried her to bed. The flickering candles moved shadows across the chiseled planes of Stefano's high cheekbones and jawline. Like a medieval knight, she thought dreamily.

The bedroom, too, was filled with candles and roses. He set her gently on her feet, and she stepped out of her expensive white high heels. Looking down at her hungrily, he gently pulled out the pins that attached the diamond tiara and veil to her hair. He set them on the nightstand. The diamonds gleamed in the candlelight, the translucent veil lingering like a ghost against the marble floor.

Never looking away from her, he slowly took off his tuxedo jacket. He removed his platinum cuff links, one by one, setting them beside the tiara. He kicked off his expensive shoes, dropping his black tie to the floor.

All the while, she stood shivering in front of him in her wedding dress, knowing what was about to happen. Wanting it to happen.

Coming forward, he reached his arms around her and slowly unzipped the back of her wedding dress, letting it fall softly to the floor. Her shivering intensified as she stepped out of the gown and stood before him in her wedding lingerie.

She wasn't cold. His gaze was a blast of heat against her skin.

He'd picked out her lingerie. She'd blushed when she'd first tried it on. The structured bodice of her wedding gown had hidden a strapless bra that barely covered half of her breasts. And, more shocking still, there were slits in the white silk so her pink nipples peeked through the fabric.

Her panties were nearly as bad, just a little sliver of silk, loosely attached to white garters that held her shimmering stockings to her thighs.

Feeling his gaze in the flickering candlelight, she started to take off her bra.

"No," he said hoarsely. "Leave it."

Reaching up, Stefano loosened her chignon so that her red hair tumbled down around her shoulders in a cloud of scarlet.

"So beautiful," he breathed. Lifting her gently in his arms, he set her down on the enormous bed.

"So are you," she said shyly.

"You're mine now. To do with as I please."

She lifted her chin, and repeated, "So are you."

With a jagged intake of breath, he ripped off his crisp white shirt so swiftly she heard buttons hit the floor. Climbing beside her on the bed, he pushed her back against the mattress, lowering his mouth hungrily to hers.

She braced herself, expecting his embrace to be savage, for him to demand, to ruthlessly *take*, as he had in the hallway outside the ballroom.

But this time was different.

He gave, rather than took; he tempted, rather than plundered. His hands were gentle, caressing every inch of her naked body, even and especially the secret places barely covered by the sliding whispers of silk.

He seduced her slowly. Unsnapping her garter belt, he pulled down her thigh-high stockings, one by one, teasing her until she was panting with need.

He didn't demand what was his by right. Instead, he begged her with his touch.

And all along, she could feel his desire for her, fiercely contained. How was it possible that he already wanted her again? But he did. He did not bother to hide it. He caressed her with agonizing slowness, taking his time, as if he intended to make their pleasures last forever.

They could, she realized. They were married. They had all the time in the world.

Reaching up, she kissed him, caressing his sharp jawline, rough with five-o'clock shadow. She ran her hands down his back, over his warm skin, feeling the hard power of the muscles of his shoulders and biceps.

With a low growl, he rolled her over so she was above him on the bed. A moment before, trapped beneath his weight, she'd felt bold, unrestrained. Now, as she sat astride him, she stroked her fingertips tentatively down his bare chest, then stopped, biting her lip.

"What do you want me to do?" she whispered.

His dark eyes glinted up at her in the flickering candlelight. "Take what you want."

Reaching up to cup her full breasts through the bra, he lifted his head and gave one pebbled nipple a lick where it peeked through the slit in the silk, then moved to the other. She closed her eyes at the hot sizzle of pleasure spiraling in waves down her body.

Hesitantly she ran her hand down his powerful chest, lightly dusted with dark hair, to his flat, muscular belly. With her legs straddled over his hips, she could feel the hard thickness of his desire, feel the involuntary movement of him between her thighs.

Lowering her head with a tumble of her red hair against the pillow, she kissed his mouth, daringly teasing him with her tongue. He responded hungrily, kissing her long and hard. Reaching around her, he roughly unhooked the peek-a-boo bra and tossed the flimsy fabric to the floor. She relished the feel of her full naked breasts crushed against him, her tight, aching nipples brushing his hard chest. Instinctively, her hips swayed.

A choked gasp came from the back of his throat. Innocent as she still was, she suddenly realized her power over him. And she gloried in it.

She reached down to unzip his fly. With deliberate slowness, turnabout being fair game, she slid his tuxedo trousers and silk boxers down his legs, inch by inch.

Tossing them to the floor, she looked down at him in the candlelit shadows of the bedroom. He was a completely naked, magnificent male, his shaft jutting huge and hard from his body. She moved forward, intending to taste him even there, to tease him with her lips and hands. But, here, his patience ended.

With a low growl, he ripped off her white silk panties in a violent gesture, leaving the expensive garment nothing but tatters and ripped threads. Reaching around her hips, he lifted her up from his body, then pushed her back down against him, entering her.

Slowly.

Deliciously.

She gasped with pleasure, closing her eyes with ecstasy as he filled her so deeply—deeper still—stretching her all the way to the hilt.

As tension coiled tightly inside her, he gripped her hips, guiding her to ride him. She panted with the agonizing sweetness of the sensation. He felt huge beneath her, inside her. Leaning forward, she kissed him, trying desperately to hold herself back, to control the rhythm. But the pleasure was too great. Her body tightened, going higher and higher with rapidly exploding desire, and spiraled out of her control.

"Tess," he breathed beneath her in the dark. Thrusting deeply, he groaned her name. *"Tess."*

Something broke in her heart, rising from her soul like the sun after a storm. Joy burst through her, and all the broken little pieces of her soul came together in a bright blinding light. They were married. The two of them together made one—

A cry came from the back of her throat, rising to a scream that she did not recognize as her own as she exploded. In the same instant, he roared in harmony to her cry.

With a harsh intake of breath, she collapsed over him, exhausted, spent. Her limbs felt boneless.

Slowly his powerful arms reached up to wrap around her tenderly. For a long time, he held her, both of them naked in the candlelit bedroom. She heard only his rough breath, felt only the power of his body, lifting her with the rise and fall of his chest.

The next evening, as the chauffeur drove them through the streets of London, Stefano saw the awe in Tess's eyes and felt a strange thrill of wonder. It was almost like he, too, was seeing the glittering sights of London for the first time. Big Ben, Tower Bridge, the Tower of London, Trafalgar Square, Buckingham Palace.

"I've never seen anything like it," she breathed.

"You're a New York girl," he teased. "Surely you're not so easily impressed."

"This city is thousands of years old," she informed him archly.

"What were you reading on the plane? The history of London?"

"I was reading a novel. Louisa told me." Louisa was the flight attendant on their private jet. "London was founded by the ancient Romans!"

"So really," he said lazily, "we should get credit."

"You?"

"Italians." He reached past the baby to put his hand tenderly on his wife's knee. "Just wait until London Fashion Week. Are you excited?"

"Yes." Looking at his hand, she blushed, biting her lip. "Very."

And well she should blush, Stefano thought smugly, after the night they'd had. It had been the most amazing twenty-four hours of his life, even better than their first time. He'd made love to her four times last night in the hotel, then twice in the private bedroom in the back of the jet as they crossed the Atlantic. *His wife.* He couldn't get enough of her.

He shivered, remembering.

"I can't wait to see everything," she said softly, looking out at the city. "London, Milan, Paris. I can't believe I'll be attending three different Fashion Weeks, back to back."

"You never attended the one in New York?"

She snorted. "Fashion Week is for famous people, not poor design students. I've seen pictures on social media, though. I always wondered what it would be like."

"To see a runway show?"

"To hold one of my own." She gave him a wistful smile. "To be a designer for a major house."

Was she hinting that she wanted a job at Mercurio or Fontana? No, surely not. Why would Tess want to work, to hold down a grueling job with long hours that often paid little, when she could live with him in luxury? Stefano smiled at her. "You'll meet Mercurio's new designer in Paris," he said huskily. "And see all the shows up close."

Tess returned his smile. "Do you usually sit in the front row?"

He shrugged. "I could. But I generally leave that to celebrities. I prefer to be in the second row. I don't need to be photographed. I'm there for business."

"And to check out your rivals?" she said, handing their cooing baby a giraffe toy.

He gave Tess a startled look. She grinned, then said cheerfully, "I used to buy pastries from the bakery down the block for that exact same reason."

How funny she was, Stefano thought, his gaze tracing her sweet, pretty face, her pink lips, swollen from a night of kisses. His body stirred again.

It amazed him that he could still want her, after the night they'd had. He'd married Tess out of sense of duty, and because he desired her. What he hadn't expected was that he'd enjoy her company so much, even in the daytime. Talking with her. Being with her.

Somehow, Tess made everything in Stefano's life, everything he'd previously been bored with, seem different and new.

Climbing aboard their private jet in New York that morning, Tess had exclaimed over its large, luxurious cabin, newly outfitted with a travel crib and baby toys. Her eyes had been wide as saucers.

"First time on a private jet?" he'd asked her, smiling.

"First time on a plane!"

It was no wonder she'd been excited. When the flight attendant had offered to make them drinks and dinner, Tess had followed Louisa into the galley, to "help." Stefano was mystified. He always kept a distance from his own employees, even if they'd worked for him for years. His executive assistant, Agathe Durand, had been with him for fifteen years, but until her grandson became seriously ill last year, Stefano had known almost nothing about her family. He respected his employees' right to privacy and expected them to respect his. Tess obviously felt differently. By the end of the flight, Tess and the flight attendant were apparently best friends.

The flight attendant glowed under Tess's friendly attention, and so did the two pilots, at her over-the-top praise. Tess's sweet, hopeful nature was like sunshine, he realized, making everyone happier around her. Opening people's hearts.

Not his, of course. He didn't have a heart, so he was immune. But he enjoyed the effect she had on others. He was amused by her company and enjoyed the novelty of looking at the world through her less cynical eyes. Her warmth and idealistic heart were good qualities for a wife and mother.

Plus, she blew his mind in bed.

Stefano glanced at her now, sitting on the other side of the baby's car seat in the back of the Bentley. She was exclaiming over everything—even ordinary things such as red post boxes and black taxi cabs. Feeling his gaze, she gave him a happy smile, but he saw faint shadows beneath her eyes. As much time as they'd spent in bed, they hadn't slept a great deal. He was used to taking business calls and discussing the latest numbers at all hours, but he'd been surprised to discover Tess was awake just as much with the baby. He was accustomed to pushing himself to the limit, but he wanted Tess to be comfortable. He'd already sent a message to his assistant to find a nanny as soon as possible.

"What's that?" As the car slowed, Tess craned her neck to look out their window.

He smiled. "Our hotel."

"Wow," she breathed, looking up at the grand Victorian hotel, its stone turrets towering over them.

After the Bentley stopped, the hotel's uniformed doorman opened the door. After unbuckling the baby seat, Tess let him help her out, with Esme in her arms.

"Welcome to the Leighton Hotel London, madam," the doorman said, then bowed to Stefano. "Welcome back, Your Highness."

"Hello, Walter. This is my wife."

The doorman's eyes widened and he corrected himself, bowing to her, too. "Your Highness, welcome."

"Nice to meet you, Walter," she said warmly, then took Stefano's arm as he led her into the Leighton's grand, gilded lobby. The service was impeccable, as always. They were whisked upstairs without even having to pause at the registration desk, with their luggage and new stroller brought behind them.

Stefano always stayed in the same penthouse suite in London. As they entered the door, he smiled at her, his eyes twinkling. "Will this do for a honeymoon?"

Holding their babbling baby against her hip, Tess walked through the suite's five elegant rooms and terrace overlooking Hyde Park. "Wow," she breathed again. Then she saw the flower arrangements and fruit baskets on the suite's gleaming wooden table. "What are these?"

"Congratulations on our marriage, I imagine. From friends who couldn't attend the ceremony. And business acquaintances." Coming forward, he kissed her. "Welcome to London, *cara mia*." He kissed Esme's fat cheek tenderly. "And you, *mia figlia*."

"Bah," said the baby, waving her chunky arms at his nose.

There was a peremptory knock at the door of the suite, and a chic white-haired woman entered, followed by a plump middle-aged blonde.

"Tess," he said, and took his wife's hand, "I'd like you to meet my executive assistant, Agathe Durand."

"Congratulations again, Your Highness," said the white-haired woman.

"Thank you, Agathe." He looked next at the plump blonde. "This is the nanny?"

"Yes, sir."

"Nanny?" said Tess.

"I am most pleased to meet you, Your Highness," the executive assistant said to Tess with a nod, then motioned to the middle-aged woman behind her. "This is Ann Carter, from the most respected nanny service in London. She'll be traveling with your family for the next month."

"Lovely to meet you, Your Highness." The nanny's smile was kind. She looked at the baby. "And this is the little one?"

"Er...hello." Still holding Esme tight, Tess turned to Stefano with a bewildered frown. "Why do we need a nanny? Unless—" She brightened. "Are you offering me a job as a designer? Oh, Stefano!" Joy lit up her face. "You don't know what this means to me. I don't need any special treatment. I'll be happy to be assistant to an assistant—"

Stefano cut her off with a scowl. "You don't need to work, Tess. I can more than provide for you."

Her face fell. "Then why a nanny?"

He could hardly explain that he wanted to give her more time for sex and sleep, not with his employees listening to every word. So he stuck to half the truth. "As my wife, you'll often have PR events to attend. Runway shows. Parties. Charity balls." He grinned. "Art Basel. Weekends on the French Riviera or yachting on the Costa Smeralda."

"Me?" Tess looked flabbergasted. "I'll be doing those things?"

"You're joining my life, and that's how I live. Starting with a party tonight. You remember the woman who attended our wedding, Fenella Montfort?"

Tess's face was blank. "Um. Maybe?"

"It's fine. You were distracted." He smiled. "She's the primary shareholder of Zacco. Our lawyers have already started negotiations, but the company is hosting a party at her town house tonight, and I hoped…"

"You hoped to use your charm to jump-start the negotiations?"

"Exactly."

Tess looked at him and sighed. "Then of course we must go."

Taking her hand in his own, he kissed it. "Thank you, *cara*. I knew you would understand."

"Don't worry, Your Highness," Ann Carter said, holding out her arms for Esme.

With some visible reluctance, Tess handed her the baby as the nanny continued talking.

"I've been caring for babies my whole life." She smiled down at Esme. "We'll get along very well, won't we? Shall we go read stories in the nursery?"

The baby gurgled with delight, waving her pudgy arms.

Tess watched them, biting her lip. Stefano could see she was nervous at the thought of leaving their daughter with anyone besides family or friends.

"It'll be all right," Stefano said, touching her shoulder. "The party isn't far. We don't have to be out late."

She took a deep breath. "All right." She gave him a wan smile. "This party is important, right?"

"It is." Drawing her close, he kissed her on the forehead. "Thank you."

Thirty minutes later, he and Tess left the hotel in a luxury limousine. The burly bodyguard he kept on staff in Europe, Leon Rossi, sat in front beside the driver.

Leaning close to Stefano in the back seat, Tess whispered, "Why a bodyguard?"

"Don't worry." Stefano looked down at her. "He'll wait in the car. There's no threat. It's simply best practice."

"You mean, all the other billionaires had a bodyguard, so you wanted one, too."

"Well…yes." A smile lifted the corners of his lips. "And I wanted the best. I stole Leon away from his previous employer. Who was that again, Leon?"

"Cristiano Moretti, boss."

Folding her arms, Tess shook her head, her eyes gleaming with amusement. "You're incorrigible."

"See? You do know me."

Stefano couldn't stop looking at her. Tess was wearing a new dress, chosen from a selection sent up by the hotel's luxury boutique. He'd offered to arrange a stylist, but Tess had refused. She'd done her own hair and makeup in twenty minutes. And she was the most impossibly beautiful woman he'd ever seen.

Her bright red hair tumbled down her shoulders, and her ruby lips were full and ripe. Her bright green eyes stood out like emeralds, lined with black against her fair skin. Her hourglass figure was lush and enticing in the strapless sapphire-blue dress. A faux fur stole was draped around her bare shoulders to keep out the cool, slightly drizzly air of an autumn night in London.

Stefano felt intoxicated with pride. Lowering his head, he kissed her, relishing the sweet taste of her soft lips.

He drew back with a sigh. "I almost wish we didn't have to go tonight."

"This Montfort woman, what's she like?"

He smiled down at her, running his hands through her silky hair. "Even more ruthless than her father. He was the one who bought Zacco. She took over after he retired."

"Is she married?"

"Why?" His smile broadened. "Are you jealous?"

"Just wondering," she said evasively. The lights of the city passed over her lovely face as the limo drove through the London night.

"As far as I can tell, she's a workaholic. It's a pity." He sighed. "Zacco has done exceptionally well with her as CEO."

"Why is that a pity?"

"Business is booming, which is reflected in Zacco's stock price, and will make it harder to convince her to sell. But I assure you," he whispered, cradling her cheek, "you have nothing to worry about, *cara*. All I want from her is Zacco. Believe me."

She bit her plump, pink lower lip. "And what do you want from me?"

"From you?" he said huskily. "Everything."

He kissed her again, deeply. It was far easier to take her in his arms with no baby seat between them in the back seat. When the limo stopped, it took him a moment to notice. The back door opened, but he didn't feel the cold air.

The driver politely cleared his throat. "We're here, Your Highness."

Reluctantly Stefano pulled away from the embrace and tenderly rubbed away a smear of lipstick from Tess's cheek. At the same moment she reached up and wiped it off his lips. Looking at each other, they gave an awkward laugh. Then, after getting out of the car, he held out his arm. "Come," he said in a low voice. "I can hardly wait to introduce you."

CHAPTER SIX

STEFANO THOUGHT HE knew luxury, but this was truly over the top.

The Zacco party was in full swing at Fenella Montfort's luxurious, five-story town house near Kensington Palace. Everything was lavish, from the flowers to the champagne to the army of uniformed servants. He himself certainly had his share of household employees, but Fenella's party was staffed at levels that made *Downton Abbey* look chintzy.

Everywhere he looked, he saw the Zacco brand. Everything from pillows to brocade curtains was festooned with the famous curlicue Zs.

Stefano's stomach clenched. He thought of how his lawyers' negotiations had already stalled. Fenella's lawyers were stonewalling, claiming she had no desire to sell. Zacco, always glamorous, had become wildly fashionable since Fenella had become CEO.

The offbeat, colorful, ridiculously expensive clothes were now splashed all over magazine covers, trendy with Hollywood, old-money and social-media celebrities alike. The stock price had increased 20 percent in the last year.

In that same time, Stefano's own new fashion brand, Mercurio, had tanked. Their previous creative director's lackluster designs had done poorly in every market. It took a special sort of skill, he thought grimly, to bomb simultaneously on every continent at once.

He consoled himself with the thought that Mercurio's new collection, to be debuted in two weeks in Paris by the hot young designer he'd recently hired, would soon get the company back on track.

But the truth was Mercurio meant nothing to him compared to the brand that bore his family name. He had to get Zacco back at any price. If he couldn't, what had he been working for all these years? What was the point of success if he couldn't get what he wanted most?

"Your Highness!" a well-known German artist greeted him, shaking hands.

"Stefano—good to see you!" A famous model kissed him on each cheek, then, before Tess could decide to be jealous, the model kissed her exactly the same way and moved on to the next person.

A glamorous older woman with hip-length black hair walked by, trailing an entourage of wildly dressed young people. The woman paused when she saw Stefano.

"Your Highness," she said, nodding her head briefly.

"Mrs. Sakurai," he said, with the same respectful nod.

The woman glanced at Tess without recognition, then continued through the party with her entourage and a crowd of adoring fans in her wake.

Stefano turned to Tess. "That woman is—"

"Aiko Sakurai," she breathed, staring after her. Stefano's eyes widened.

"You know her?"

"I studied her in design school. She's amazing. Her designs—" Tess shook her head. "I could only wish to be half so talented as her."

"She's older than you," he pointed out. "She's had more experience."

"What she's done as Zacco's creative director isn't just experience. It's genius."

"Yes, unfortunately. Thanks to her, Zacco's valuation

has gone up billions and become completely unaffordable," he said grumpily. Catching himself, he looked down at Tess with a smile. "Come. There are others I want you to meet."

For the next hour, they drank cocktails as he introduced her to CEOs and friends and journalists, all members of the international fashion jet set. They congratulated them on their marriage and were eager to meet Tess. No wonder, he thought. With his wife's warmth and beauty and charm, not to mention the inherent star power of being the unknown working-class Brooklyn girl who'd managed to tame a playboy like Stefano, Tess was quickly the most popular person in the room.

Stefano watched Tess affectionately as she spoke earnestly to a famous South African designer. She wasn't intimidated by anyone. She treated everyone the same, from billionaires to waitstaff. Stefano liked that about her. Her honesty, her kindness. Even at a party filled with some of the most gorgeous, glamorous people in the world, he thought, no one could hold a candle to his wife.

But where was their hostess? He scoured the crowd for Fenella Montfort's tall, spare frame. He finally saw the woman talking to a prime minister and Rodrigo Cabrera, the Spanish media mogul.

Setting his jaw, Stefano went to join them.

"Good evening." He nodded at each. "Your Excellency... Cabrera." His eyes focused on his quarry. "Ms. Montfort."

"I hear you're married, Prince Stefano," Rodrigo Cabrera said, his eyes glinting. "Congratulations."

"Thank you." He lifted his eyebrows. "Actually, you should doubly be thanked, Cabrera, since I met my wife at your party."

The Spaniard looked intrigued. "My party?"

"Last summer, in New York. You were celebrating some movie of yours that had just reached a billion dollars box office worldwide. Tess was a waitress there."

"How extraordinary."

"Yes." But as Stefano spoke, he was wondering how he could speak with Fenella Montfort alone, though Zacco's London Fashion Week party did seem an inappropriate venue to convince her to sell her shares.

She gave him a cold smile, as if she knew exactly what he was thinking.

"Excuse us," she said abruptly to the other two men. "Prince Stefano and I have something important to discuss."

"Of course," said the prime minister with a bow.

"Congratulations again," Rodrigo Cabrera said coolly. "Actually making it to the altar is quite an accomplishment."

It seemed a strange comment, but Stefano forgot about it as he faced the woman who owned his family's company.

"Prince Stefano," she said coolly. "I'm so glad you brought your new wife. Such a fascinating creature." She glanced toward Tess. "A true original."

"Thank you."

"It wasn't a compliment." She jutted her sharp chin toward a young, dark-haired man flirting with models by the marble fireplace. "That's my date. Bruno."

"Ah," he replied, unsure of her point. Why would he care about her date?

Fenella gave a laugh. "He's a musician. But a good lover." She paused. "I can't imagine being stupid enough to marry him."

Stefano's shoulders tightened as he understood. She was insulting not just Tess, but also him, for marrying her.

What he didn't understand was why. He barely knew Fenella Montfort. They were business acquaintances only. What could be the point of an attack that was so personal and so pointless?

He tried to keep his voice conciliatory. "As fascinating as it is to discuss our love lives, we need to talk about your shares."

"Yes, we do." She tilted her head. "Please tell your lawyers to stop bothering us. It's tiresome."

"We can raise the offer."

"I don't intend to sell. At any price."

"You haven't heard the new offer," he said.

She shrugged. "I don't need to."

He narrowed his eyes. "Then why did you invite me tonight?"

"I wanted to tell you in person."

"No. There's something else."

Fenella's eyes gleamed. "You're right, of course." She tilted her head. "I'm throwing the fashion journalists a bone. Having you at the party gives them drama to write about. The handsome billionaire prince attending a party for the company his family lost. Your presence makes the Zacco brand seem even more valuable. That's what really matters, isn't it?" Watching him, she smiled. "The success of my brand."

Her brand.

She'd lured him here as an insult, he realized. A taunt.

A rush of anger went through Stefano's heart. He controlled it, giving her a ruthless smile. "In that case, I wish you good evening, Ms. Montfort."

She sipped her champagne. "And you, Your Highness."

Turning away stiffly, he set down his own half-empty glass and strode through the crowd of people until he found his wife. He took Tess by the elbow. "Let's go."

"Go?" She'd been having a good time talking to all the people around her. She looked disappointed. "Right now?"

"Right now," he said grimly.

As the limo returned them to Mayfair, Stefano stared out at the sparkling London night.

The handsome billionaire prince attending a party for

the company his family lost. Your presence makes the Zacco brand seem even more valuable. That's what really matters, isn't it? The success of my brand.

The memory of Fenella's taunting voice echoed through him as they drove through the city. Tess, after a few attempts to talk to him, finally gave up. The evening, which had begun in such hopeful pleasure, ended in silence.

Once they arrived back at their hotel suite, Tess rushed to check on their sleeping baby. Ann Carter rose to her feet from the chair where she'd been knitting some baby-sized slippers. Esme had obviously been well cared for.

Stefano spoke to her quietly, then the woman left for her own hotel suite on another floor. It would cost an exorbitant amount to have her on retainer for the next month, but, to Stefano, no price was too high for his child's or his wife's comfort. He'd always believed the cliché: *You get what you pay for.*

But he'd never imagined Fenella Montfort would refuse to sell at any price. How could she?

Pulling off his black tie, he walked heavily to the bedroom. He tossed down his jacket. His jaw was hard as he looked at himself in the shadowy mirror.

He had to find a way. He *would*. By right, Zacco belonged to him. It was his family's company, their legacy.

He had expected Tess to join him in the bedroom. When she did not, he went looking for her. The nursery was dark, the only sound Esme's gentle snores. The main room was empty.

He finally found Tess on the moonlit terrace overlooking Hyde Park. She was hugging the faux fur stole around her shoulders, looking out into the night.

"What are you doing out here?"

Squaring her shoulders, she faced him quietly. "What happened tonight?"

"What do you mean?"

"Why did we leave so suddenly?"

Stefano was tempted to deny, to bluster, to evade. To stonewall.

Instead, he heard himself say, "Fenella Montfort won't sell Zacco."

Tess's eyes widened. He waited for her to say something flippant. Instead, coming forward, wordlessly she wrapped her arms around him.

For a moment, he closed his eyes, accepting the offered comfort. Then he drew back, tightening his jaw. "I'll find a way to convince her."

"And if you don't?"

"I will."

"You already have so much," Tess said slowly. "Mercurio, Fontana. Real estate, companies that sell sports cars, jewelry. Do you really need Zacco back that badly?" Searching his gaze, she said, "Couldn't you just let it go?"

"No," he said.

"Why?"

He looked out briefly toward the darkness of Hyde Park.

"My father ignored everything except his pleasures—mistresses, love affairs. He left me to be raised by servants and sold off the family business to finance his sybaritic lifestyle." His hands clenched. "I want it back."

"I get it," Tess said suddenly. "You want to make it right. To get back what you lost."

Stefano looked at her sharply. She gave him a sympathetic smile.

"I never knew my father," she said. "My mother raised me alone. When I was twelve, she died." She looked down, her arms crossed over her chest, gripping the ends of the stole around her shoulders. "After her funeral, I thought my father would finally come for me. But he...he didn't. I found out later he was already married, with another family."

Stefano hated the pain in her eyes. "He was wrong. Both to you, and to his wife. He acted without honor."

"He was still my father." She gave a wistful, bitter smile. "After my mother's funeral, I tried to barricade myself in our apartment with books, so that my uncle wouldn't take me to Brooklyn. Because I was so sure my father would come. But he didn't want me to exist, so he pretended I didn't."

Moonlight illuminated her beautiful face, showing a single tear streaking down her cheek as they stood together on the dark, quiet terrace.

"He was a fool," he said quietly.

Tess took a deep breath. "The point is, sometimes you can't get back the things you've lost. No matter how hard you try. All you can do is try to move on, move forward." She looked out toward the moonlit park. "If my aunt and uncle hadn't taken me in, I don't know what would have happened to me. Although…"

"Although?"

She gave him a wistful smile. "Sometimes it was hard to always feel so indebted to them. To be afraid that if I made one false step they might send me away."

A silent curse went through him. No wonder she'd fallen in love so easily the night he'd seduced her. She'd been hungry for a place—a person—to call her own. Someone with her by choice, not duty. Taking her into his arms, he said quietly, "I'm sorry."

"Don't be." She lifted her gaze to his. "It's all worked out, hasn't it? We're married now. Raising Esme together." She interlaced his hands with her own. "We'll give her a better childhood than we had. She'll always know she's loved—by both of us."

"Yes," Stefano said. The word *love* made him uncomfortable. He cared for Esme, yes, and he felt his responsibility acutely to provide for her and protect her as a father. Was that the same as love?

"We're each other's family now," Tess said, her eyes shining, and his heart tightened even more. "All the pain is in the past. The future is filled with love—"

"Look, Tess," he interrupted. "You know I'm not good with..." He couldn't say the word *love*. "With feelings, right? Emotions?"

She looked at him, uncomprehending.

"I just don't want you to get the wrong idea," he said. "Like you did our first night, when you suddenly claimed you loved me. I wanted to see you again. But after that, I couldn't."

All the color drained from Tess's face.

"That's why you never called me again?" she whispered. "Because I said I was falling in love with you?"

He shrugged. "Look, I know that's all in the past. We're married now. We have a life together, a child. So I want to make sure we understand each other. I like you a lot, Tess." He gave her a wicked grin. "Especially in bed. But that's all I'm capable of. Passion. Partnership. Parenthood."

Her pale cheeks flushed red. She gave a strange laugh, pulling away. "I know that. Do you seriously think I don't know that? I'd never be tempted to love you again. Not now I know you!"

"Good," he agreed, relieved. "I just wanted to be sure. I'd never want to make you unhappy or break your heart."

"You, break my heart? Not likely!" Turning away, Tess changed the subject. "So what will you do about Zacco?"

"Convince her to sell," Stefano said.

"How?"

"The same way I do everything." He spoke lightly, but his smile was grim. "At any price."

Tess had gambled, marrying him. She'd gambled and lost.

Her husband would never love her. He couldn't love her.

When she'd naively blurted out that she was falling in love with him, after their first night together, he'd ruthlessly cut her out of his life.

Just that had made him disappear.

I like you a lot, Tess. Especially in bed. But that's all I'm capable of. Passion. Partnership. Parenthood.

For Tess's whole life, she'd dreamed of loving someone and being loved in return. But, now, she would never know what either felt like.

Because if her husband couldn't love her, then she couldn't love him.

They would be friends. Partners. Spouses. Lovers. That was all.

But it was hard.

During their week in London, Tess spent every moment at Stefano's side, both by day, as he took her to runway shows, and by night, as they attended parties, then afterward, in bed, when he set her world on fire.

She saw his kindness when he thought no one was looking. To the outside world, Stefano tried to always look ruthless and tough. And he was, she knew. But there was also another side to him. He secretly helped people, without any benefit to himself.

His executive assistant, Agathe, had told Tess privately that when her young grandson had fallen desperately ill the previous year, Stefano had flown the boy to Switzerland and paid for him to get experimental treatment. Tears rose to the Frenchwoman's eyes. "My grandson might not be alive now if not for Prince Stefano's kindness. But he won't let me thank him, or even mention it."

It was a story Tess would hear again and again. The very next day, the head of a children's charity had come up to Tess at a party. "Prince Stefano has given our charity millions, but he insists on complete anonymity. He won't let us thank him, so I'm thanking you. He's made such a difference." Wiping his eyes, the elderly man had smiled. "But you're his wife. You know how he is."

She hadn't, though she was quickly learning.

Returning to the Leighton from a party, Stefano and Tess had overheard the night manager talking anxiously on the phone. He had a relative trapped in another country, and war had broken out. Stefano had interrupted. "Call this number," he'd said, handing the distraught manager a card. "Your relative will be evacuated within the day."

When the older man tried to tearfully thank him, Stefano brushed him off. "It's nothing. Anyone would do the same."

Tess doubted that. After all, the manager wasn't Stefano's friend or even his employee. He was simply someone who happened to work at Stefano's favorite London hotel. But Stefano chose to get involved.

At his own company, Gioreale S.p.A., she learned Stefano was revered for the way he promoted his employees, based not on who they knew or where they'd gone to school, but purely on their hard work and talent. The company's social marketing manager, a former addict who'd gone to prison for two years before getting clean, had made a point of finding Tess at a runway show to tell her, "No one else wanted to hire me, but Prince Stefano gave me a chance. He changed my life."

Over and over, she heard these whispered stories of secret kindness, of changed lives. But whenever she tried to ask Stefano about it, he was brusque.

"Don't be ridiculous. I hired Thomas Martin because he's the best damn social media director in Europe." He gave a swift smile. "You know me. I just want the best."

For some reason, he seemed embarrassed by his kindness, as if it was a weakness. But his employees worked hard to please him, and he returned their loyalty in full, paying them double what other firms paid. It was almost shocking, Tess thought, in this modern age, to see a boss who cared more about his employees than about maximizing every penny of profit.

Who wouldn't love a man like that?

Not her, Tess told herself stonily. She felt nothing for him at all, except—except friendship. And pride, perhaps, but who could blame her?

Their last morning in London, Tess woke up before dawn in their hotel suite, thinking she'd heard a noise from Esme's room. She yawned, glancing at the clock. It was just past four.

Stefano's side of the bed was empty. He'd made love to Tess before midnight, then she'd fallen asleep in his arms. He must have gotten up to make an overseas phone call, she thought, perhaps to the Tokyo office. His appetite for work was superhuman. It was what had made him so successful, but sometimes she wondered how anyone could work so hard, and sleep so little.

Blearily she stuck her feet into slippers and pulled on a robe, then headed to Esme's room to feed and change her. She stopped when she heard a noise inside.

Peeking through the open door, she saw to her surprise that Stefano was sitting in the rocking chair, tenderly crooning an Italian lullaby to Esme. The baby, cradled against his powerful chest, was holding a bottle and staring up at her father with big, adoring eyes.

At the tender image, Tess's knees went weak. She closed her eyes, leaning against the hallway wall for support. Seeing the way he was caring for their child in the middle of the night, deliberately leaving Tess to sleep, made her eyes fill with tears.

Perhaps he didn't know how to love Tess. But he cared for her, and he loved their child.

Holding her breath, she watched as he rocked the baby to sleep, then took the empty bottle from her lips and lifted her carefully into the crib. For a moment, he watched their baby sleep, and Tess's heart swelled in her chest. Then, with a sigh, he started to turn.

Hurriedly Tess ducked back down the hall. Rushing back to their bedroom, she leaped into bed, pretending to be asleep in the dark. A moment later, she felt him climb into bed beside her.

"Stefano?" she whispered.

He paused. "I was just checking on the baby. She's fine." He kissed her forehead. "Go back to sleep."

Who wouldn't love a man like that?

Not her, Tess repeated to herself desperately. She'd been burned. She'd been warned outright. She wasn't stupid enough to go back for second helpings of pain!

She liked him, that was all. They shared a child. Shared a life. She liked how he listened when she talked, as if every word she said was fascinating. She liked how he looked at her, as if she was the most beautiful creature in the world. She liked how he cared for their baby so carefully, learning how to be a father when he'd barely had one himself.

She wouldn't love him. Of course she would not.

Fiercely determined, she held back her heart. She felt like she was clinging to the edge of an abyss, with white knuckles. It almost seemed like he was taunting her, the way he'd suddenly become the man she'd always dreamed of. Desperately she looked for his flaws.

After London, they spent an idyllic week in Milan, attending the most important runway shows and parties, staying in the best suite in the best hotel in the city. See? Flaw!

"You always want the best of everything," Tess grumbled, rolling her eyes.

"Yes, I do," he said huskily, pulling her into his arms. "Why do you think I married you?"

He kissed her, his lips hot and smooth as silk. Another flaw, she thought. His kisses. They tempted her to believe lies and to want things she could not have. Specifically: his heart.

It was like he wanted to destroy her.

She hid her growing misery over the next week in Milan as she wore new couture dresses every night, made by famous Italian designers that she'd previously only seen in magazines. Stylists did her makeup and hair. With their wonderful nanny watching their contented baby, Tess and Stefano went out every night. She met fascinating people, made lots of new friends, ate delicious food and, best of all, wore designer clothes to every event. Clothes that felt like art.

Clothes that, in her growing panic, suddenly felt like her only escape.

Growing up, Tess had often played dress-up, trying on her mother's old costumes from an ancient trunk that had always come with them wherever they traveled.

After her mother died, her uncle had refused to allow Tess to bring the trunk into the already crowded apartment above the bakery. But Tess had never forgotten the difference clothes could make.

On the nights her mother performed on stage, Tess had seen the transformation. Clothes could change who you were and who people took you to be. Clothes could make you appear—even make you *feel*—old or young, hopeful or sad, rich or poor. Clothes could make you stand out or they could make you disappear. During her lonely years in high school in Brooklyn, when she couldn't afford to buy new clothes, Tess had learned to sew.

Getting into fashion design school had been the happiest day of her life. She'd won a scholarship with her good grades, but she'd still had to scrimp and save for two years, which made her older than most of the other students. It had broken her heart when she'd had to give it up.

Now, as Tess attended runway shows and actually met

the people who designed the clothes, all her old dreams came flooding back. Even the most famous designers hadn't always been famous, she realized. Once they had been just like her, with nothing but a dream.

Each night, after they returned to their hotel suite, she'd peek into her old suitcase, at the handmade designs she couldn't leave behind. Her eyes always fell on a beautiful, shimmery green gown she'd made right after she'd dropped out of design school. Facing single motherhood without a career, she'd been discouraged and afraid. So she'd made the fairy-tale dress to give herself hope for the future.

She'd never gotten a chance to wear it. Since marrying Stefano, she'd only worn designer clothes from luxury brands. But each night she lightly touched the green dress. Maybe, someday, she'd wear it. Maybe, someday, she'd even design again. Maybe, someday, she'd be brave.

But not today. She was too busy spending every moment with the husband she wasn't allowed to love and with her baby, who had never seemed happier.

She could survive, Tess told herself. She could live without love. Her baby's happiness was worth any sacrifice.

She still got lots of attention. Whenever she and Stefano went out, people spoke to her warmly.

"Welcome, Your Highness."

"It's so good to see you again, Your Highness."

"You do us honor, Your Highness."

After so many years of living in her uncle's attic, feeling invisible and unwanted, it felt like warm sunshine after a long, cold winter.

Between fashion events, Stefano took Tess and Esme to see the sights of Milan. He seemed to relish her gasps at every tourist attraction. As she went into raptures over the Duomo or the Teatro alla Scala, he always kissed her, which made her blush. Which made him kiss her more.

Family was what mattered. Her baby's happiness mattered. Tess's romantic dreams? Those were in the past, to be put away like childhood toys.

But, sometimes, she had to hide how much it hurt.

Stefano wasn't always happy, either. She knew he was brooding about the upcoming Mercurio show and the stalled negotiations for Zacco. Sometimes, she caught him glaring at nothing, his hands clenched. Once she overheard him yelling at his lawyers. Apparently, they'd hit a brick wall. The Montfort woman was still flatly refusing to sell.

The afternoon before they left Milan, Stefano announced they needed a getaway and took them to a villa on Lake Como owned by one of his friends. There, their family had a picnic on the terrace, beneath a rose-covered trellis.

As their baby played, Tess looked out at the autumn sunlight shining off the lake, matching the soft glow in Stefano's dark eyes. Sitting beside her at the stone table, he took her in his arms as the first cold wind blew down from the mountains across Lake Como.

How can you be so cruel? Tess thought wildly, looking up into the gleam of his dark eyes. How can he look at me like that unless he loves me?

I just don't want you to get the wrong idea... I'd never want to make you unhappy or break your heart.

Remembering his words, she felt a chill. Whatever she imagined in his eyes, she couldn't let herself believe it. He'd told her outright not to love him. So she wouldn't. Her heart ached. What else could she believe in?

She had to find a new dream. But what?

Then she suddenly knew.

CHAPTER SEVEN

HANDS IN POCKETS, Stefano paced back and forth across his sprawling Paris apartment. He stopped, turning to glare at Tess, who was sitting in a chair, getting her hair and makeup done.

"Where is it?" he demanded for the tenth time. She gave him a tranquil smile.

"It will be here. Any minute."

"What's taking so long?" he growled, clawing back his hair. "We're supposed to leave in ten minutes."

"We have time."

He exhaled, grateful for Tess's calm smile. He didn't know what he'd do without her. It was funny, he thought. He'd owned this Paris apartment for years, the entire top floor of an exclusive building in the 7th arrondissement, with balconies overlooking the Eiffel Tower and autumn-hued trees of the Champ de Mars. It had never felt like home to him. Now, having a family here, it did. Esme didn't just have her own bedroom, she had her own nursery suite. Ann Carter was already there, playing with the baby.

"I'm dying to see Mercurio's new spring collection," said Genevieve Vincent, the stylist doing Tess's hair, a friend of his. She smiled, tilting her head. "I'm sure you've already seen it, Stefano. What's your honest opinion? I promise not to mention it in my blog—much."

"Sorry, Genevieve. I can't discuss it," Stefano said. "But it's going to be amazing."

"Really? So you *have* seen it." Genevieve looked hopeful. "*Amazing*, eh? Can I take that as a quote?"

He hesitated. The truth was, Caspar von Schreck, his new designer, had refused to let Stefano see any of the designs in advance, saying it would interfere with his creative process. But the man had promised to send samples of the best dresses for Tess to wear to the big runway show tonight.

The last thing Stefano needed was for rumors like "CEO tepid about new collection" to sink Mercurio's new season before it even started. Praise seemed safe enough.

"It's wonderful," he said firmly. "The whole world will be impressed. And, yes, quote me."

There was a hard knock at the door. The three of them looked at one another.

"See, Stefano?" Tess said cheerfully. "You worried over nothing!"

He heard his bodyguard in the foyer, answering the door. A moment later, Leon rolled in a large garment rack. The clothing was hidden by a thick canvas printed with the Mercurio logo of big block Ms.

"Finally," Stefano said under his breath. Hurrying forward, he yanked off the cover.

His eyes went wide. Only three hangers, looking forlorn, hung from the enormous rack. He grabbed the first dress, hoping to be reassured that the new collection would be the success that Mercurio—and he—so desperately needed.

But he couldn't make sense of it. He looked at the first dress, then the next, then the last. All three dresses were an unattractive shade of beige, with ragged, asymmetrical hems and strangely placed cutouts on the hips and breasts that seemed to defy the bounds of decency.

Genevieve stood beside him, her eyes wide. "Those are from Mercurio?"

Stefano bared his teeth in a smile. "Very…innovative, aren't they?"

"Innovative?" Tess stood on the other side of him now, her lovely face incredulous. "Are you crazy?" She looked at the three dresses with increasing desperation. "They're hideous!"

She was speaking his greatest fear aloud.

"Just choose one." His voice was harsh. "And get dressed. I'll check on the baby. Then we must go."

Stefano went down the hall, trying to keep calm. Outside the nursery door, he paused, taking several deep breaths, his hands clenched at his sides. His designer knew what he was doing. The man was widely in demand. Everyone had said Caspar von Schreck was the best.

Obviously, Stefano must not understand the latest trends. And Tess and Genevieve didn't, either.

At least he prayed it was so. Or he was about to be humiliated. And when his conglomerate's share price plummeted, he'd literally pay the price.

Pushing the thought away, he smiled and went into the nursery. His baby daughter's face lit up when she saw him.

"Bah-bah!" she said, reaching for him.

"Good evening, Your Highness," the nanny said. "We were just reading a book."

"I see that." Lifting Esme up in his arms, he hugged her, breathing in the sweet smell of the baby's dark hair. His heart swelled with some emotion he didn't recognize—pride? Yes. It had to be pride. "*Buonanotte*," he whispered to her, then returned the baby to Ann Carter's arms.

As the nanny went back to reading a book about a duck and a truck, Stefano hesitated in the hallway. To his surprise, he almost wished he could stay. He wished he and

Tess could be the ones to cuddle with Esme, and read her the story about the duck. Let Ann Carter go to the Mercurio show.

But that was ridiculous. What was he thinking? Straightening the cuffs of his sleek black jacket, he checked his platinum cuff links and wondered which dress Tess had chosen to wear. Luckily his wife was so beautiful that she'd make even a washed-out, raggedy gown look good.

When he came out of the hallway into the main room, he saw Genevieve packing up. Tess was ready, wrapped in a long black cape. He frowned.

"So, which dress did you choose?"

A determined look came over her beautiful face. "It's a surprise."

"But you did find one."

"Yes, I did." Her gaze was evasive. "I need to say goodnight to Esme."

A moment later, they left his luxury apartment. Their bodyguard held an umbrella overhead to keep out the cold October drizzle, soft as mist. As their limousine drove them across Paris, Tess held her long cape carefully over her gown. She wouldn't let Stefano see even an inch of it.

She obviously desired to reveal her dress dramatically on the red carpet, he thought. It might have amused him if the stakes hadn't been so high. After all, how much surprise was possible, really? One beige dress was very like another.

Stefano looked out at the sparkling City of Light, thinking how important tonight's event was, not just to Mercurio, but to him personally.

If Caspar von Schreck's new spring collection was a success, then Mercurio would flourish. Which meant the stock of Stefano's parent company, Gioreale S.p.A, would rise. He'd be able to use it as collateral to make a new, higher offer to acquire Zacco from Fenella Montfort.

But if tonight wasn't a success...

His hands tightened.

It just had to be.

Caspar von Schreck was the best, he repeated to himself. He was the hottest designer in the world. Everyone said so. How could it possibly fail?

The limo finally pulled up in front of the glamorous *palais* where the Mercurio show was being held. With all the secrecy and buzz, it had become the most-anticipated event of Paris Fashion Week.

The bodyguard opened his door. Buttoning his jacket, Stefano smoothed a confident smile over his features and stepped out.

The rain had stopped. Crowds cheered, recognizing him. So far, so good. Giving the crowd a short wave, he turned back to Tess. As he helped his wife out of the limo and onto the red carpet, cameras flashed and reporters shouted questions.

Ignoring them, Stefano looked down at his beautiful wife. He felt a flash of comfort. At least, no matter what, she was completely on his side.

Looking nervous but determined, Tess lifted her chin, then dropped the long black cape onto the red carpet.

Stefano's jaw dropped as he saw her dress.

Not beige.

Not ragged.

Not Mercurio.

Tess wore a shimmering, diaphanous emerald dress that flattered both her figure and her coloring. Her green eyes sparkled in the light. Her red hair tumbled down her shoulders, and her full, sensual lips were the color of raspberries against her pale skin. She looked like a star on the red carpet.

There was a gasp, a sudden whirl of paparazzi frantically taking pictures.

"What a beautiful dress, Princess! Is that from Mercurio's new spring collection?"

"Incredible!" another reporter shouted. "What a triumph!"

Slowly Tess turned to look at him, her eyes pleading. From the corner of his eye he saw their bodyguard collect her cape from the red carpet. Cameras flashed.

Stefano was frozen in shock.

His wife wasn't wearing a dress from Mercurio's new line. She wasn't wearing Mercurio at all—or Fortuna or any of the Gioreale brands. She wasn't even wearing Zacco.

He'd seen this exact dress in her suitcase. Seen her sighing over it once or twice, when she thought he wasn't looking. He knew exactly what it was.

This amazing dress was Tess's own design.

It was unheard-of to go rogue at an event like this. If you were an important guest of a fashion house's runway show, you always wore their clothes even if they were borrowed from the company. You wore them as a mark of respect, to play the PR game.

So what did it say that the CEO's new wife had snubbed the Mercurio brand to wear her own hand-stitched designs?

"Beautiful dress, Your Highness!" one of the reporters called to Tess. "So that's a preview of tonight's show?"

Tess blushed, looking more beautiful than ever. "No," she said shyly, "actually, it's—"

"It's her design," Stefano said, putting his arm around her shoulders. "My wife is an amazing new talent."

Tess looked shocked, but not as shocked as the reporters. Stefano knew, in supporting Tess, he'd seem to be insulting his own company and his new designer. Not only was Tess wearing her own clothes, but Stefano was outright promoting them on the red carpet instead of Mercurio's!

But what choice did he have? He set his jaw. How could

Tess have put him in this position? How could she stab him in the back, injuring Mercurio's reputation when everything was on the line?

Reporters surged breathlessly forward. "Prince Stefano, are you saying—"

"Is Caspar von Schreck's job in jeopardy, Your Highness?"

"Is the spring collection a disappointment?"

Baring his teeth in a smile, Stefano said, "We're very proud of Mercurio's spring line. And tonight, you'll see it for yourself. That's all. Thank you."

Gripping Tess's arm, he walked her down the red carpet, not letting her stop for any other shouted questions.

"Thank you, oh, thank you, Stefano," Tess whispered. She took a shuddering breath. "I was so scared what you'd say, but I couldn't wear those dresses, I just couldn't—"

"How could you, Tess?" he said under his breath. "The press think I am snubbing von Schreck and trying to launch you as a designer!"

She sucked in her breath. "So why did you support me?"

"The alternative was to let them think we were already having problems in our marriage. I had to act proud of you!"

"Act?" She turned pale. "You mean you're not?"

Stefano ground his teeth. "You're talented, Tess. No one can dispute that. Your dress—" his eyes traced over her curves "—is spectacular."

Her eyes lit up. "Then—"

"But you can't seriously want to launch your own company. Do you want to work eighty-hour weeks in a studio, leaving Esme with a nanny? Do you know what it's like for a child to be raised that way? Because I do."

Her jaw tightened. "Have you forgotten I've spent most of Esme's life working flat out at my uncle's bakery?"

"No. I haven't," he said grimly. "Nor have I forgotten

the reason. Because I abandoned you without financial support." Just thinking of how he'd left Tess and Esme destitute still made his stomach clench. "As long as you are my wife, you will have a comfortable life."

"What if I don't want to take it easy?" she retorted. "What if I want to follow my dreams?"

"What dreams? Being 'an assistant to an assistant,' as you charmingly put it, working endless days fetching coffee, doing very little design, for almost no pay?" he said scorchingly. "That's your big dream, instead of caring for our daughter?"

Tess's expression fell as they walked through the crowded foyer of the *palais*. "If I could find a way to do both..."

"Tonight the story was supposed to be Mercurio," he ground out. "Instead, now it will be you."

She looked abashed. With quiet defiance, she lifted her chin. "I couldn't wear those dresses, Stefano. They were horrible. No woman alive would want to wear them."

Her simple, obvious statement made his heart stop.

Tess was right.

Stefano couldn't imagine Caspar von Schreck's beige, peculiar dresses on any woman of his acquaintance. What did that mean?

It meant that the new collection would fail.

It meant the stock price would fall.

It meant Zacco was lost for good.

As they entered the enormous ballroom in the palace, where Mercurio's runway show would be held, Stefano forced himself to greet people, to act confident, as if he didn't already know the battle was lost. As he spoke to acquaintances, he gripped his wife's hand. He was relieved when the lights started to flicker, an indication that the show was about to begin.

They found their seats. For this one show, he'd wanted

to sit in the front row. He looked around them at the cavernous space. Were those smoke machines?

Foreboding went through him.

A moment after they sat down, all the lights abruptly went off, turning the ballroom completely black.

For a moment, the hundreds of guests inside the *palais* were silent. He smelled smoke. Then dramatic electronic music began to thunder around them. A strobe light, high overhead, began to flash outrageous patterns against the smoke.

Pain rose to Stefano's temples, throbbing in time to the loud music and pulsing lights.

The first model started down the catwalk, wearing a dress just like the ones von Schreck had sent them earlier. It did not look any better on the model than it had on the hanger. The dress's cutouts highlighted strange parts of the model's body—her lower belly, beneath her armpit and half her breast—making her look awkward and peculiar. The sickening beige color made the girl's face look so washed-out she almost looked dead.

It's a disaster, Stefano thought wildly. But at least he'd been prepared. At least things couldn't get worse.

Then they got worse.

Avant-garde was how the most charitable magazines described the Mercurio show later. More typical words to describe it were *epic fail* and *instant internet meme*.

The electronic music and flashing lights that added such drama to the darkness abruptly faded with a loud scratching squeal. The Hokey Pokey played on the loudspeakers, the old children's song sounding somehow threatening rather than playful. The first model disappeared, and new models started rapidly coming down the catwalk one by one, wearing large, cartoonish animal masks that completely covered their heads, as if to distract the audience from all the lumpy beige and greige dresses.

A hush fell across the crowd, then tittering laughter. Camera phones came up.

And that was even before a model wearing a lion mask, who probably couldn't see well through the huge fuzzy mane, tripped on her high heels and fell off the catwalk, landing on the lap of a senior editor of *Vogue Italia*. The other models kept walking as if nothing had happened.

Stefano felt his wife's gentle hand on his arm. She was watching him with worried eyes. He realized his hands had tightened into fists.

The show seemed to last forever. When it was finally over, Caspar von Schreck, the young, trendy designer whom everyone on the Gioreale board of directors had pleaded for Stefano to hire, came out wearing a full lumberjack beard, baggy tweed trousers and an open shirt. Holding his little dog against his chest, he waved at the crowd and bowed as if he had done something amazing.

He had, Stefano realized. With one stroke, he'd just caused Stefano to lose his chance at buying back the company that had been in his family for generations.

No. That wasn't fair. It wasn't von Schreck's fault. It was Stefano's. He should have insisted on seeing the designs in advance. He should have known that just because the designer was talented, it didn't also mean that he wasn't crazy drunk on his own vanity.

"Oh, my God," a socialite breathed behind them, turning to speak into her camera for social media. "Did you all see that? My Halloween costume is sorted!"

Stefano rose abruptly to his feet, his jaw tight, and headed backstage.

He already knew that the stock price would plummet tomorrow. Even though Stefano was Gioreale's CEO and primary shareholder, he'd still have to explain this disgrace to other shareholders and the media, and explain how, under his leadership, Mercurio had gone from stock loser to international laughingstock.

"Stefano—"

Behind him, Tess's voice was pleading, but he didn't stop for her. He couldn't.

There was only one person he wanted to talk to right now. And it would be all he could do not to talk with his fists.

Tess felt sick to her stomach as she followed Stefano backstage. This was the Mercurio fashion show?

Where was the fashion?

All she'd seen was a bunch of starved-looking girls, many of them younger than her cousins, walking in clothes that looked like ripped-up grocery bags, stumbling down the catwalk in ridiculous animal helmets. It might be called performance art; to Tess it was just silly.

This was the show her husband had so badly wanted to be perfect. She glanced at Stefano's tight shoulders in his tailored black jacket as he strode ahead of her through the crowd. Although she felt badly for him, something told her that her sympathy would be unwelcome.

Backstage was a madhouse of stylists and models with racks of clothes and people everywhere.

An American reporter, the cohost of an influential morning talk show, stepped into his path, hovering with a live camera crew.

"Your Highness! Prince Stefano! May I get a comment? What did you think of Mercurio's spring collection?"

"We are, of course, very proud," Stefano ground out, "to have such a daring, avant-garde artist as our creative director. His vision is world changing."

Tess could see from her husband's taut jaw how he really felt about it, no matter the PR spin he was trying to put on it. Then she heard wild yelling and barking.

Turning, she saw Caspar von Schreck loudly berating a young woman. His little dog was barking, adding to the noise. The shamed girl stood in tears, holding the lion mask in her arms.

Tess recognized Kebe, the beautiful model Stefano had once given a ride home in New York. She was the model who'd tripped on stage, Tess realized. She barely looked older than her nineteen-year-old cousin Natalie.

"You *idiot*," Caspar von Schreck was screaming into her face, flecks of spittle flying. "You clumsy *clod*!"

"Please, Mr. von Schreck," the girl whispered. Her shoulders slumped. "It was an accident…"

"You ruined my show with your incompetence!" the bearded designer shrieked. "I'm going to make sure you never work in this business again!"

Tess moved without even realizing it. She stood between the tearful young girl and the world-famous designer.

The man's bloodshot eyes narrowed as he sneered at Tess. "And what do you want?"

Tess stuck out her chin. "You're the one who should never work in this business again, you horrible man!"

A gasp went through backstage, followed by a low, gleeful hiss. The designer's eyes widened as silence fell and everyone turned to watch.

Von Schreck glared at Tess.

"And who are *you*?" He looked dismissively over her shimmering green gown. "You didn't even wear Mercurio to the show. You are *nobody*!"

Tess felt suddenly calm.

"You're right," she said evenly. "I'm nobody. But I know good clothes when I see them, and the three dresses you sent us today were the ugliest clothes in *history*!"

"The three…" The designer's eyes widened. "Wait. Are you—?"

"And you must know it, because why else would you

force these poor girls to wear animal helmets? You should be ashamed of yourself!"

A low current of malicious laughter went through the backstage area. The designer was obviously not well liked even among his own people.

The designer's eyes narrowed dangerously as he took a step toward her. "Shut up."

"How dare you bully everyone!" He'd probably been cruel to his underlings, she thought, just like the poor tearful girl behind her. Imagining someone being so mean to her cousins or her daughter, Tess glared at him. "You might be famous," she said, her back snapping straight, "but the truth is, you're nothing but a no-talent hack!"

Von Schreck gave an enraged growl, drawing his hand back, as if to hit Tess across the face.

But his arm was caught.

"Don't even think about it," Stefano said coldly. He threw the man's arm aside. "You're fired, von Schreck."

The designer's face went pale. "Fired?"

"I agree with everything my wife just said." Stefano looked at him. "Now get the hell out."

Caspar von Schreck sucked in his breath, his cheeks red as he looked around them, at the live camera crew and the models recording the moment on their camera phones. He stiffened.

"You can't fire me. I quit!" The designer tossed his head, causing his beard to flutter like a flag. "Mercurio doesn't deserve my amazing talent." Looking around, he proclaimed loudly, "Last week, Fenella Montfort offered me a job at Zacco, and I'm going to take it! That's a real fashion house!" As his dog barked noisily in his arms, he added maliciously, "Didn't Zacco used to be *your* company, Your Highness?"

Stefano took a step toward him, his dark eyes glittering. "Get out."

"Good luck finding a designer half as genius as me!" With a final toss of his beard, Caspar von Schreck turned on his heel and left, his dog yipping back at them angrily.

Exhaling in relief, Tess smiled up at Stefano, feeling so proud of him her heart could burst. Turning to the tearstained young model behind her, she said, "Are you all right?"

Kebe nodded, her eyes big. "Thank you." She wiped her eyes. "You had no reason to take my side."

"I had every reason. You're my husband's friend." Tess shook her head. "And no one has the right to treat people that way!"

Feeling a jacket suddenly covering her own bare shoulders, Tess looked up at Stefano. A strange emotion glowed in his dark eyes. He said quietly, "I'm glad you were here."

Her heart warmed beneath his glance.

Stefano glanced at Kebe. "Your mother will be heartbroken when she hears how you were treated. I'm sorry."

"Don't worry. I'll tell her how you both rushed to my defense." Kebe grimaced. "But first I'm going to change out of this hideous dress."

"Prince Stefano!" The American reporter was panting in her rush to stick a microphone into his face. "There's a rumor going around that you deliberately fired von Schreck so you could replace him with your new wife, though she has no fashion experience whatsoever… Any comment?"

Tess's eyes went wide with shock. "No, it's not true."

"He was fired for gross incompetence," Stefano said evenly. "And for abusing the staff. Mercurio will start fresh next season. Though my wife is amazingly talented, she's focused on raising our daughter. Thank you."

"Your Highness!" Other reporters and bloggers were already fighting their way through the crowds backstage.

Stefano grabbed Tess's hand. "Excuse us."

Holding her hand tightly, he pulled her away. The front of the *palais* was just as much of a madhouse. People were yelling things out to them and blocking their path, and everywhere Tess looked she saw camera phones recording them.

For the first time, she understood the need for bodyguards as Leon suddenly appeared to help clear a path through the crowds. She didn't exhale until they were safely in the back seat of the limo.

The chauffeur drove them away, with Leon sitting in the front seat beside him.

Stefano turned to her. "I'm glad you were here tonight, Tess." Reaching out, he cupped her cheek. "Thank you for what you did."

"What did I do?"

"The right thing," he said quietly. "No matter the cost."

The sparkling city lights glittered beneath the autumn drizzle as the limo flew through the Paris night. Taking her into his strong arms, Stefano kissed her.

A week later, Stefano rose wearily from his desk in his private office of Gioreale's Paris headquarters. It was almost midnight, and the building was quiet. Even Agathe Durand had gone home, at his orders.

Rolling his shoulders, he went to the wet bar and poured himself a drink. No ice, not water. Just Scotch. Taking it back to the window, he stood looking out at the cold October night.

The large window overlooked the modern, bright steel-and-glass buildings of La Défense, Paris's business district to the west of the city. The moon seemed frosted with ice crystals in the darkness.

Stefano felt like a fool. He still had no designer for Mercurio. The luxury brand was in free fall. Before, it had been merely unfashionable; now it was a joke.

As threatened, Caspar von Schreck had gone to work for Zacco. Stefano took a gulp of Scotch. He thought of how often in the past he'd casually stolen key employees from rivals. In this case, he suspected Fenella Montfort might get more than she'd bargained for.

Her first mistake, he thought. Much good may it do her.

Stefano felt restless. He paced two steps in front of the window, then took another drink. He didn't feel like himself, because Prince Stefano Zacco di Gioreale always won, and this wasn't winning.

He'd spent the last week doing damage limitation, reassuring the press and Gioreale's shareholders that the Mercurio disaster was trivial and the future was bright.

Stefano took one more drink, staring out at the frosty Paris night. Enough, he thought. He set down the unfinished glass.

He was going home.

Locking up his office, he bade *bonsoir* to the overnight security guards. When he left the building, he felt the shock of cold air against his skin. Autumn was almost over, he realized. Winter was nearly here.

He looked back at the Gioreale building. He suddenly longed to be done with it. All of it. Fashion. Shareholders. Crazy designers. He closed his eyes, imagining a soft, warm land of orange groves, with vineyards ripening in the sunshine.

Gioreale. He'd named his company after his title. It was also the name of his family's ancient castle in Sicily, as well as the nearby village, neither of which he'd seen since he was a boy.

It was strange that he suddenly missed it now. For most of his life, he'd thought of Gioreale as the lonely prison of his childhood, before his parents had sent him to an American boarding school at twelve. Why did he now yearn for that warmth, for the scent of lemons and the exotic spice of the Mediterranean Sea?

Getting in his Ferrari, he drove back to the 7th arrondissement lost in thought. He reached his elegant residential building and parked in the garage, then took the private elevator to the penthouse floor. He felt he'd barely seen Tess or Esme all week.

He arrived to find his luxurious, sprawling apartment was dark. Of course. They'd gone to bed. He set down his briefcase and hung up his coat. Through the windows, he saw the illuminated Eiffel Tower shining brightly in the night. Then, late as it was, that too went dark.

He noticed a single light gleaming down the hall. His wife was awake. Tess had waited for him every night, no matter how late, no matter how often he told her she should get her rest.

"You're back earlier than usual," Tess said, smiling. Hiding a yawn, she sat up in bed, setting aside her novel. "I'm so happy you're home."

Her green eyes shone up at him adoringly. As if she—

As if she—

No. Stefano turned away, not wanting to see the love in her eyes. He told himself it wasn't there. Tess would be too smart to love him, knowing it could only bring her pain. He said shortly, "You didn't need to stay awake."

"I don't mind." She gave him a wistful smile. "It's the only way I can see you."

Looking at her, he caught his breath. She was wearing his favorite silk negligee, her brilliant red hair tumbling down her shoulders. His eyes drank her in hungrily, down her swanlike neck to the open neckline of her negligee, with the top of her breasts peeking out. Leaning down, he kissed her, and the tension in his shoulders eased.

When he finally pulled away, she gave a satisfied sigh.

Her eyes twinkled. "Now that was definitely worth staying up for."

He was tempted to press her back against the bed and make love to her, without another word. Instead, he sat down abruptly beside her. He pulled off one expensive Italian shoe, then the other, tossing them to the floor.

"What would you think," he said slowly, "about taking a vacation?"

"Like a honeymoon?"

Stefano blinked. "Honeymoon?"

"Don't get me wrong," she said quickly. "I loved Milan and London. And Paris is lovely. It's just…" She focused on the closed book in her lap. "So much of your time has been spent promoting Mercurio and negotiating for Zacco and working in your Paris office. It would be nice to have a little time just…with us."

Stefano stared at her.

She was right, he realized. They hadn't had a honeymoon, not a real one. He'd spent the last three weeks dragging her all over Europe, consumed by things that didn't matter, things that had all come to nothing.

He looked away. "Sure."

"Oh, do you mean it?" She clasped her hands eagerly. "Where?"

He knew he could suggest all kinds of places. His beach house in St. Barts. A villa in the south of France. A yachting trip around the coast of Sardinia. Exploring the autumn foliage of New England. The Greek Isles.

Instead, he heard himself say, "Would you like to see my castle in Sicily?"

Tess's eyes lit up. "You know I would."

"It's not glamorous. But I was raised there." He lazily twirled a tendril of her red hair. "You can see the sea. There's vineyards. A half-ruined village."

"Sounds dreamy."

He gave a low laugh. "I can't guarantee that. I haven't been back to Gioreale since I was twelve."

"Gioreale." Her eyes looked enraptured. "Like your title?"

"It's your title now, too," he reminded her. "Yes, the name is from the castle. And the village is also called Gioreale. But like I said...it's a ruin."

"I remember." She nodded solemnly. "Prince of ghosts."

He barely remembered saying that. But it was true. The last time he'd seen the village, through the back window of the car as his parents' chauffeur drove him to the airport where he would travel alone to America, Gioreale had looked desolate, the shops abandoned, the young people all gone.

Tess looked thrilled at the prospect of a visit. "When can we go?"

"Tomorrow." He hoped he wasn't making a mistake taking his family there. His childhood hadn't been a happy one. Still, Tess seemed overjoyed, and he wanted to get away from the world. What could be more remote than a half-ruined castle in the Sicilian countryside?

"Thank you," she whispered, putting her hand on his cheek, rough with five-o'clock shadow. "You're so good to me."

"Am I?" His gaze traced from her full lips to her bare throat. The strap of her lilac-colored negligee had slid down her shoulder. He kissed her bare skin, golden in the lamp's soft glow.

Tess's expression changed. Reaching up, she loosened his tie, tossing it to the floor. Then, with a sensual smile, she switched off the lamp so the only light in the bedroom was the silvery moonlight cascading through the translucent window curtains.

Desire rushed through him, and amazement. Tess had never initiated lovemaking before. He kissed her hungrily, pushing her back against the enormous bed.

His hands ran roughly over her silk nightgown, and the even softer silk of her skin. He kissed her with all the passion in his soul, determined to make her body sing. And as he did, he tried to ignore the way his own heart threatened to come alive.

CHAPTER EIGHT

TESS SIGHED WITH PLEASURE, closing her eyes as she turned her face to the warm Sicilian sun.

The wind blew through her hair as Stefano drove the vintage red convertible. Her hair was pulled back with a scarf, and she was wearing a sundress and sandals. From the front seat of the car, she glanced back, smiling as their baby cooed happily from her car seat.

As soon as they'd arrived in Sicily on Stefano's smallest private jet, Tess had felt free, like they'd left all their troubles behind, along with their bodyguards, assistants and even the trusted nanny. Stefano's suits had disappeared, and he wore a casual black T-shirt and jeans that seemed to caress his powerful muscles. It was a different world.

Leaving the airport behind, they'd driven through the small city of Ragusa, where she'd goggled at an old mansion with stone faces carved into the balconies.

"The Palazzo Zacco," he'd told her.

Her eyebrows rose almost to her hairline. *"Zacco?"*

He snorted. "Don't get excited. It's not ours. It was built by a totally different family. No—" he'd looked up, switching the car's gears with a grin "—our little place is up in the hills."

They'd traveled the slender coastal road on the edge of the cobalt blue sea. Now they were going deeper into the island, past orange and olive groves. As the road climbed up the hills, they passed vineyards heavy with the last grapes waiting for harvest. In the distance, she saw a village tucked into a small valley.

"The village of Gioreale," he said quietly. "Half destroyed by an earthquake in 1961. My father ruined the rest by neglect." As they drew closer, his hands tightened on the steering wheel, as if he were bracing himself.

But as they entered the village, Tess looked incredulously at the well-kept charming pink stucco buildings and freshly painted green shutters. There was a profusion of flowers, and the cars parked on the streets were gleaming and new.

At the center of the village, near a small, well-maintained church, outdoor cafés lined a square filled with tourists taking pictures of the lavishly sculpted stone fountain.

"I thought you said it was a ruin," Tess breathed as the convertible slowed. "A ghost town."

Stefano was staring around with amazement that exceeded her own. "It was." Blinking hard as if he didn't believe his own eyes, he looked back at it through the rear-view mirror. "The fountain—did you see that? It had water! It never did before."

Tess tilted her head. "So it's changed since you left?"

"Yes..." Stefano's eyes widened. "But I never thought..." Not finishing the thought, he pressed on the gas. The red convertible flew up the next hill, as, in the back seat, Esme giggled and clapped her hands, clearly relishing the wind on her face.

Tess smiled back at her baby, then looked out at the rolling hills and took a deep breath of the fresh, fragrant air.

"It's more beautiful than I ever imagined." She held her hand out, in the direction of the sheep placidly grazing in a nearby field, and felt almost like she was flying. She looked at him. "I can't believe I'm princess of this magical place."

"Magical is right." Shaking his head, he gave an amazed laugh. *"Tourists.* In Gioreale."

Leaning back against the soft leather seat, Tess closed her eyes. She tried to remember the last time she'd felt so happy. The drama of Paris already felt like a world away.

Stefano had told her that his company's stock price was down nine percent. Costing him hundreds of millions of euros.

Costing him Zacco.

Which wasn't to say Mercurio hadn't gotten lots of press. It had mostly just been negative. The story was everywhere, first of the runway show itself, with the models in animal masks, capped by poor Kebe tripping and falling into the audience; then of the aftermath. The video of Tess chewing out Caspar von Schreck had already been viewed a million times. Many people were calling her defense of the young model admirable, but a good few had been insulting and rude, asking how a mere *trophy wife* had the right to attack a *true artist* like von Schreck. The one thing everyone agreed on: Mercurio might not survive this disaster.

It was all so horrifying that Tess had quit social media entirely. On the flight to Sicily, she'd called Hallie and Lola. Her friends had both been indignant on her behalf.

"Some bully was yelling at a girl? Of course you had to say something," Hallie said.

"You can't let bullies win," Lola had said, her voice oddly restrained.

Tess had been happy to hear her friends' voices. Stefano had spent much of the flight pacing, speaking tersely to shareholders and board members from Buenos Aires to Berlin. Grimly he'd laid down the law: no new clothing would be manufactured or shipped out until they'd found a new designer. It would be a crushing blow for their business, especially the flagship boutique in New York.

But they'd left that all behind. In the convertible, Tess

glanced at Stefano out of the corner of her eye. He was so handsome, and never more so than now.

Golden sunlight frosted the edges of his strong features, his black eyes and olive-toned skin. His square jawline was already dark with five-o'clock shadow, though it was only noon. His short dark hair waved in the wind as his hands gripped the steering wheel.

How would Stefano feel if he lost Mercurio, on top of Zacco?

She couldn't bear to think of it. Not when he meant the world to her. Not when she...

"Look." He nodded forward. "The *castello di Gioreale*."

Following his gaze, she gasped.

At the top of the hill was an old fortified castle, surrounded by vineyards and lit up by sunshine.

"Wow," she breathed. Not only had he made her a princess, but he'd brought her to his castle, just like a fairy-tale prince. All her childhood dreams were coming true.

Especially this. Especially him. Looking at Stefano, her handsome prince, a lump rose in her throat. He was an incredible lover. An amazing husband. A wonderful father.

He could have been angry at her—for causing the scene with von Schreck, and for wearing her own design on the red carpet. Instead, he'd supported her. He'd announced proudly that the dress was Tess's own design. He'd protected her from von Schreck when the man had tried to hit her. And then he'd brought her here. Tess looked at him, her heart in her throat.

Dust kicked up around them as Stefano drove the vintage red convertible behind the castle. Stopping the car, he got out and rolled up a garage door, then drove into a stable that had been converted into a six-car garage.

"No wonder it's not locked." Turning off the gas, he looked around. The converted stable was mostly empty inside, with only a few old estate cars. "My father used to fill this with his Ferraris." He gave her a smile that didn't meet his eyes. "Let's see what else has changed."

Lifting their baby out of the car seat, Tess waited as he took three small suitcases from the tiny trunk of the convertible. Then she followed him out of the garage.

Outside, the stone castle was sprawling and magnificent. Manicured gardens stretched to the edge of endless vineyards, broken up by pretty clusters of trees. Far below, at the bottom of the hills, she could see the smoky blue haze of the sea.

Tilting back her head, she looked up at the castle in awe. Red bougainvillea climbed the walls like scarlet flames. Tears filled her eyes.

"What do you think?" Stefano said quietly.

Turning to face him, she tried to smile, holding their baby on her hip.

"I love it," she whispered. She lifted her tremulous gaze to his. "I just can't believe it's real."

He grinned. "Oh, it's real, all right. As you'll discover once you actually live in it. The castle was built in the late Middle Ages, but the foundations are much older. It was a palace in the days of the emirate."

"Emirate?"

"Sicily was the crossroads of the Mediterranean. Everyone's had a piece of it at one time or another. Ancient Greeks, Romans, Vikings, Arabs, Normans, Spaniards. And now Italians." He shrugged. "Conquerors come and go. My own ancestors came to Sicily six hundred years ago, in service to the king of Aragon."

It all sounded very romantic to Tess. She imagined the clash of swords between knights, a damsel languishing in a rose-covered bower. "It sounds lovely."

He gave her a strange look. "Lovely?"

"Romantic."

He snorted. "That's one way of looking at it, I suppose."

Gazing up at the castle, he said, "I haven't been home in a long time."

"Everyone will be so excited to see you!"

"They all hated my father." He lifted their suitcases higher against his shoulders. "I doubt they'll be glad to see me."

The back door of the castle was unlocked. Inside, it was dark and quiet. Tess craned her head. The closest she'd ever been to the inside of a castle was the time she'd visited the Cloisters, the medieval museum in northern Manhattan.

She looked down at her feet. Even the floor appeared ancient, with a worn, colorful mosaic that looked almost Byzantine. Everything was old. The walls were rough stone, and the furniture was obviously hundreds of years old. There was actually a suit of armor in the hallway.

Above them, the ceilings were shadowy and dark, with few windows and thick stone walls. The temperature seemed to drop.

"This is what a real castle feels like," Stefano said, observing her with a grin.

"Amazing," she said, shivering.

"Don't worry. There's a modern wing that's a little more livable. This way."

It was funny, she thought. For all her life, since her mother had read her fairy tales as a child, Tess had dreamed of castles. As a student, she'd pasted pictures of famous castles on the cover of her writing notebooks. From a distance, the castle of Gioreale had indeed looked majestic and awe-inspiring.

As she walked through the windowless hallways, she was forced to face the hard truth that old castles were indeed dark, cold and uncomfortable inside. Sometimes, it seemed, reality was not nearly as good as the fantasy.

But sometimes... Tess looked at Stefano's broad shoulders as he walked ahead of her, carrying their luggage. Sometimes it was even better.

"In here," Stefano said, pushing a thick oak door open. Following him, she gasped.

They were in a traditional great hall, with a fireplace as tall as Stefano. The high ceiling had exposed beams and was painted with old family crests and insignias. There were windows, and the furniture looked comfortable and new. Well, comparatively new. Golden light flooded in from lead-paned windows overlooking the cloistered courtyard.

"The modern wing," he said.

"Modern?" she said faintly.

"Sí." He grinned. "It's only three hundred years old."

"Only!"

Setting down their luggage, Stefano looked at the crackling fire in the fireplace. "It's strange we haven't seen any of the staff. Maybe they're in the kitchen."

With Esme in her arms, Tess followed him down a different hallway, then another. Finally he pushed open a door. Inside was a gleaming kitchen—far more modern than three hundred years old—filled with people. They were all bustling about, preparing food.

A woman gave a shocked cry as a dish shattered against the tile floor.

A short white-haired woman pushed through the crowded kitchen. Her wrinkled face lit up as she stared up at Stefano in shock. With a cry, she threw her arms around him. Tenderly he hugged her back, speaking in rapid Italian.

Stefano finally pulled away, looking a little sheepish, but happy for all that. "Tess, I'd like you to meet Gerlanda, my old nanny. She's now housekeeper here." He looked down at the white-haired woman, now wiping her tears with an apron. "Gerlanda, I'd like you to meet my bride from America, Tess, and our daughter, Esme."

The elderly woman's eyes went wide, and then she gave a joyful cry. Turning back to the others, she said a few quick words in a strange dialect of Italian—Sicilian?—and all the others began to exclaim joyfully as well. Tess found herself surrounded by smiling people, all patting her shoulder and stroking the baby's head, welcoming her in English, in Italian or just by the warmth on their faces.

"Thank you, thank you." Gerlanda shook her hand joyfully at Tess. "For bringing him here." Tears were streaking her kind face. "Welcome, my princess."

Awed by all the raucous, noisy delight now filling the gleaming kitchen, Tess turned to look at her husband.

They all hated my father, he'd said. *I doubt they'll be glad to see me.*

From the happy shouts and tears, she saw he'd been completely wrong.

"What are you all doing here?" Stefano said, looking at the platters of food being assembled on the marble counter. "Is there a party?"

The others burst into laughter and a cacophony of Italian and Sicilian.

"The festival of harvest," one of them explained, glancing in Tess's direction. She realized they were speaking in English so she'd understand and was touched at their kindness.

"It will be our biggest one ever, since we also celebrate the success of the winery."

"It's doing well?" Stefano sounded mystified. The people around him laughed, their faces in broad smiles.

"Our Moscato—it just got the top rating from a famous wine critic."

"The bottle price, it will go very high."

"Extremely high."

"More tourists will come to Gioreale. More hotels to

open, more restaurants, more everything," another said happily.

"The harvest festival is this afternoon," a young woman said. "Please, you must come!"

In the corner of her eye, she saw Stefano hesitate. He glanced questioningly at Tess.

"Please, Princess, make him come!" a girl pleaded. "And your sweet baby."

"Of course we'll come," Tess said, smiling at them.

Everyone cheered. Speaking in rapid Italian, Gerlanda pulled off her apron.

"But you have traveled far. You must be hungry. Your bags are inside? Salvatore," she snapped her fingers, speaking to a nearby man. The man immediately left the kitchen, smiling as he passed them.

Gerlanda turned back, cooing at the baby. "I will make you some lunch. Just to tide you over."

"We're not terribly hungry," Tess began. She was still full from the lovely breakfast that Louisa had prepared them on the private jet.

"Of course you are," the Sicilian housekeeper said briskly. "You are too skinny. You must keep up your strength! For Stefano! For Gioreale! And this sweet little one." She stroked Esme's dark curls. "The festival is hours away. You will starve. I will bring you food."

Tess tossed her husband a pleading glance.

"Thank you, Gerlanda," he interceded. "But I'd like to show my new bride around the estate. And perhaps," he said thoughtfully, "visit the winery."

"Yes!" The older woman's face lit up. "See what you have done for us."

"What has Stefano done?" Tess said.

"After his father died, Stefano always made sure to send money for the village. Even when his company was small and he had nothing. He always sent it to us. Always." Her eyes gleamed with tears as she looked up at him. "Now you are here, so you can see your sacrifice was not in vain. Or your belief in us." Abruptly she turned away. "You are not hungry, fine, so I will make you a picnic."

Stefano stared after her with a smile tracing his lips. "Same old Gerlanda."

"She calls you by your first name," Tess said wonderingly. "No one else does. Not even your assistant."

"Gerlanda was my nanny for two years, from the time I was eight until ten." His smile lifted to a grin. "I think in her mind, I am still ten years old."

"If she loved you, why did she leave?"

The smile dropped. "She didn't. My mother fired her. She always got rid of any servant I started to care about. She didn't want me to get too attached to them."

Tess stared up at him in disbelief. "What?" she breathed. "Your parents abandoned you—then wouldn't let you love any of your caregivers?"

"Not just caregivers." His voice was casual, but she saw the tightness around his eyes. "Anyone I loved would disappear. After Gerlanda was forced to leave, I made friends with kids in the village. But at the end of the summer, they were told not to play with me or their parents would lose their jobs. So I roamed over the countryside with the gardener's dog." He paused. "My parents thought it was vulgar. So they told the gardener to get rid of his dog. When he refused, he was fired."

"Oh, Stefano," Tess choked out, her heart breaking. How could anyone be so cruel, to systematically and deliberately remove all love from their own child's life?

"It's all in the past." Stefano's expression was cool. "I haven't thought about it for years." He took her hand. "Come."

But was it really in the past? As he showed her around the sprawling castle, Tess felt sick.

Because now she knew and could no longer deny it.

She loved him. She was totally and completely in love with her husband.

And he'd warned her against it from the start.

You know I'm not good with...with feelings, right? Emotions? I like you a lot, Tess. Especially in bed. But that's all I'm capable of. I just... I'd never want to make you unhappy or break your heart.

Loving Stefano, was Tess making the same mistake her mother had made—giving herself to a man who was totally unobtainable?

Had she just made the biggest mistake of her life?

"What do you think? Can you handle it?"

Tess jumped guiltily. "What? What do you mean?"

Smiling, Stefano took the baby from her, cradling Esme in his strong arms. "The castle. It's not too rustic for you?"

"Oh." She looked around the master bedroom. One of the staff—Salvatore?—had already brought up their three suitcases. She studied the twisted wood columns of the massive four-poster bed, and caught the view of the valley past the balcony. She tried to smile. "I think I can handle it."

But could she?

When they went back downstairs, they found Gerlanda waiting with a picnic basket. "And one of the village mothers thought you might find this useful for your walk."

Stefano looked doubtfully at a fabric contraption in the housekeeper's hand. "What is it?"

"A baby carrier!" Tess exclaimed. She'd wanted one for ages, but hadn't had the money. When she started to put it on, Gerlanda stopped her.

"It's man-size. For the father."

Tess turned to Stefano with a huge grin. "Even better!"

For the next few hours, they explored fields and vineyards, beneath the wide blue sky and golden light. Stefano held Tess's hand and carried their baby on his back. As Stefano pointed out interesting features of the estate and Esme jabbered behind them softly, Tess looked down at her hand wrapped in his larger one and felt tears in her eyes.

Stefano stopped abruptly. "What is it? What's wrong?"

She tried to smile. "Nothing. I'm just happy."

"So happy you're crying?" he said suspiciously.

"We're a family," she whispered, looking up at him.

Their eyes locked, and for a moment he looked stricken.

Then all trace of emotion was shuttered from his handsome face. "Of course we are." His voice was cool. He dropped her hand. "Ah. There's the winery."

Inside the squat, prosperous gray stone building, they found the winery staff busy serving the tourists in the tasting room, selling them bottles by the case. Seeing Stefano, one of the employees immediately took them back to the production area, where they found the vintner, a middle-aged man, looking harried amid all the vats.

The employee went ahead and quietly spoke in the man's ear. The vintner whirled and saw Stefano, and his face lit up. With a joyful clap, he strode forward and eagerly shook Stefano's hand, bowing again and again. Turning to Tess, he welcomed her with an embrace, a kiss on each cheek and a rush of words in Sicilian.

They spoke for an hour with the vintner and his staff, learning how the winery's production and fame had flourished and grown. Then Tess started to notice some of the tourists peeking into the production area and surreptitiously snapping photos—not just of Stefano, but also of Tess. For a moment she was bewildered, then she remembered that, back in the real world, she was all over social media right now, and probably TV, as well. Being even temporarily famous made her uncomfortable. She was relieved when they finally left the winery and returned to the castle's private land.

"The winery's doing well." Stefano sounded shocked. "I didn't realize. They're shipping all over the world. They can barely keep up production."

"You didn't know?" she said, surprised. "Don't you own it?"

"No, and that's probably why they're doing so well," he said dryly. "The village owns it, as a cooperative." He shook his head, a smile lifting up the corners of his lips. "All of Gioreale is thriving."

"Because you believed in them. Invested in them."

He frowned. "Of course I did. I grew up here. Who wouldn't?"

Your father, Tess thought, but she didn't say it. It wasn't her place. Family could be complicated, she knew. She didn't like to hear criticism of her own father, though he'd died three years ago without ever trying to contact her. Even after his death, she'd tried to respect his wishes—by not going to his funeral or ever telling his other family of her existence.

Was it right? Wrong? Tess didn't know. All she did know was that love could be complicated, and sometimes it could be hard to tell it apart from hate.

Which must be, she thought with a lump in her throat, why Stefano didn't want any part of it.

"I hope you're hungry," Stefano said suddenly, giving her a wicked grin. "If we don't eat this picnic, we'll never hear the end of it."

He led her to a grassy spot on the top of the highest hill, not too far from the castle. They spread a blanket so the baby could play. Six-month-old Esme's idea of play was to try to clap her hands and catch her own feet, which always left her in a paroxysm of giggles.

Beneath the October sunshine, they spread out the housekeeper's picnic of fruit, sausages, cheese and freshly baked bread, and shared a bottle of the famous red Moscato the vintner had pressed on them. Beneath them, in the castle courtyard, they could see servants preparing tables for the harvest festival—hanging fairy lights, flowers and colorful decorations. As the afternoon waned, more villagers started arriving by foot and horse and car, all of them loaded down with food and wine.

"You're sure you want to go tonight?" Stefano said, tilting his head. "This is supposed to be our honeymoon."

"I want to go. It looks fun. The villagers love you," Tess whispered, her heart in her throat. She took a deep breath. "And so do—" She lost her nerve. Stuffing her mouth with grapes and cheese, she swallowed. "Yum."

"It's all grown on this estate."

"Delicious."

His dark eyes lit up. He murmured, "You're delicious."

Leaning over on the blanket, he kissed her, and she felt her body rise. They kissed for a long time in the warmth of the October sun, until twilight approached and Esme needed to get ready for bed.

Tess trembled, thinking how she'd nearly told him she loved him. What would have happened? The best case, she thought, was that he'd have said, *Thanks, but no thanks*.

Worst case: he'd be packing now to leave her.

That night, as they attended the harvest festival, surrounded by people who couldn't wait to thank Stefano for all he'd done for them, she tried to convince herself that she could keep the secret for the rest of her life.

She didn't need Stefano to love her.

It was enough that she loved him.

Wasn't it?

Sitting beneath the fairy lights at the center table, Tess watched one person after another tell Stefano how he'd changed and bettered their lives. She tried not to love him. But it was hard, which was to say, impossible. And it hurt.

Because she knew he'd never love her back.

After all he'd gone through, who could blame his heart for turning numb? To Stefano, love must feel like pain. She could hardly bear to think of him as a lonely little boy, neglected and abandoned. Even his dog had been taken away.

If only my love could heal you.

Tess's eyes widened as she straightened in her chair.

If only she could show him that love wasn't something to be feared, but embraced.

If she could show him that true love could last a lifetime…

When the harvest festival was finally over and everyone started cleaning up, Tess rose to her feet and found Gerlanda, to ask how she could help. In response, the housekeeper gave a hearty belly laugh.

"You, do the cleaning? No. I forbid it. You do enough. You make our prince happy."

"*Sí,*" another woman said. "We want Prince Stefano's happiness, after everything he's done." Turning away, she smiled. "And by the way he looks at you now, Princess, you make him very happy indeed."

Following the woman's gaze, Tess turned. Stefano stood on the other side of the castle courtyard. His black eyes looked at her hungrily across the crowd. Their eyes locked in the velvety Sicilian night.

He came forward, and took her hand.

"It's late," he said huskily. She shivered at the heat of his touch. "Time for bed."

He led her into the castle and up the stairs. Their footsteps echoed against the worn stone. He never let go of her hand, only pausing to check on Esme, sleeping in the nursery next door. Then he led her to the bedroom.

Silvery moonlight flooded the large window. Glancing out, she saw the full moon frosting the dark valley, reflecting against the black sea. Coming behind her, he gently rubbed her shoulders, pulling her back against his body. "Are you happy, *cara*?"

She turned in her arms. "Very happy."

How long could she hide her love for him? She was suddenly scared as she glanced toward the enormous four-poster bed. Once she was naked in his arms, feeling him deep inside her, she feared the truth would explode from her lips, and it might cost her everything.

He must never know. He could never know.

Unless…unless she could somehow heal him. Change him. Or was that just her foolish heart believing what she wanted to believe, instead of cold reality?

Lowering his head to hers, Stefano kissed her passionately. She sighed, lost in his embrace. But, as he started to lead her toward the bed, she nervously pulled away, pretending to be interested in the shelves of leather-bound books stretching up the opposite wall.

"So many books," Tess said awkwardly, touching their spines. "They all look so old."

"They are, I suppose. I'll show you the library downstairs sometime," he replied in a low voice, pulling her back into his arms. "Thousands of books, some of them a thousand years old."

Her jaw dropped. "A *thousand*?"

His sensual lips lifted into a smile. "I love how innocent you are. The smallest things impress you."

"A small thing—a great room full of books a thousand years old!"

Stefano shrugged. "Small."

"Then what on earth would you call *amazing*?"

Lifting his hand to her ponytail, he pulled out the tie, and her red hair came tumbling down the back of her cotton sundress.

"Having you in my bed," he whispered.

Lifting her reverently in his arms, he carried her to the

enormous four-poster bed. As he lowered his head to kiss her, she felt a sea breeze come in through the open window, scented with jasmine and exotic spices from distant shores. She felt the roughness of his jaw against her skin as he whispered words like an Italian invocation and kissed down the length of her body. Slowly he removed her clothes, and then his own. He made her feel she was on fire, lit from within.

And through it all, with every beat of her heart, came the rhythm of the words she longed to say.

I love you. I love you.

But the last time she'd said those words, Stefano had left, intending never to return. Just because she'd said, *I'm already falling in love with you.*

Strange. At the time, she'd honestly believed her words. She'd thought she knew what love was.

Looking back, Tess realized she hadn't known at all. She'd just been in love with the idea of love, and dazzled by a romantic, sensual night with the most handsome, powerful man she'd ever known.

Real love was different.

It wasn't flowers or jewelry or poetic words. It wasn't the fairy tale of a grand wedding or becoming a princess in a castle. It wasn't even spectacular, mind-blowing sex.

Real love was quieter.

It grew when you weren't looking. From moments of laughter, of sharing. From small kindnesses. Like all the little things Stefano did that he thought she wouldn't notice, not just for her, but for others. For his employees. For his hometown. For their child.

Despite his attempts to hide it, she'd discovered his deepest secret. Stefano's title might be *Prince*, but in his heart, he was something even better.

He was a good man.

She knew him now, perhaps better than he knew himself. She knew him, and she loved him.

Did she dare tell him? Would that be foolhardy—or brave? Would her honesty ruin their fragile happiness? Or would it be the start of a life more joyful than either of them could imagine?

As Stefano held her in his arms that night, as she felt the weight of his body over hers and the soft Sicilian winds blowing in from the balcony against their hot skin, she felt tormented, even as she shuddered with pleasure beneath the slow stroke of her husband's hands.

Until, when he pushed himself inside her, making her cry out with ecstasy, she could take it no more. As he shuddered into her with a low roar, she gripped his shoulders and looked straight into his eyes.

"I love you," she whispered. "I love you, Stefano."

The next morning, Stefano woke with a strange feeling in his chest, finding he'd cradled Tess naked in his arms the whole night as they'd slept. A flash of vertigo went through him, leaving him woozy and sick.

I love you, Stefano.

He could still hear the tremble of Tess's voice last night, see the piercing emotion in her emerald eyes. He'd been deep inside her, his whole body shuddering with pleasure, but when she'd spoken the words, something had gone through him, something greater than joy. Overwhelmed, he'd kissed her, again and again as she'd softly wept.

"I was so scared to tell you," she whispered, pressing her cheek against his naked chest.

"Don't be scared," he'd said, his heart in his throat. And he'd found himself whispering love poetry in Italian he'd thought he'd forgotten. Since they'd arrived in Sicily, the prison of his childhood had become paradise.

He'd kissed her again, then held her until they'd both slept with their naked bodies intertwined. And for that brief moment, everything had felt right to him.

Waking in the morning was different.

I love you, Stefano.

A chill went down his spine. A pounding anxiety formed at the base of his brain. He looked at Tess, cuddled against him beneath the blanket, her beautiful face tender, smiling in her sleep.

Stefano couldn't breathe.

He had to get out of here.

Jumping up, he went to the closet. Pulling on boxers and dark trousers, he grabbed a suitcase that Salvatore had unpacked for them the night before. He came back toward the wardrobe.

"What are you doing?"

He saw Tess watching him in the shadowy pink light. Sleepy as a kitten, she looked soft and adorable and it made the feeling in his chest tighten a little more.

"Getting dressed."

She yawned, stretching her arms. "Is the baby awake?"

"No, not yet."

He thought of how he'd quoted love poetry last night, and he felt sick. It didn't mean anything, he told himself. A man could not be held to account for what he might say in the arms of a beautiful woman.

But he knew what was really happening. Why he'd slept in her arms last night better than he ever had before. And that he must not—could not—let it happen. Because the moment he relaxed, the moment he surrendered to emotional weakness, everything would crumble beneath his feet.

Stay in control, he ordered himself, clenching his hands at his sides. *You feel nothing.*

"Stefano?"

"I have to go," he said flatly.

"What?" She sat up in bed, looking shocked. "Go where?"

"I must return to Paris to start the search for Mercurio's new designer. And then London, to see if I can convince Fenella Montfort to sell her shares."

But even as he spoke, he knew there was no way to buy Zacco now. Not unless he sold everything he owned outright, and maybe not even then. The woman had made it clear she had no desire to sell.

But Stefano had to give Tess some reason for his departure, and he couldn't explain the real reason. Not when he barely understood it himself.

"Oh." Tess looked down at her body, still covered by the luxurious cotton sheets. She gave him a forced, cheerful smile. "I guess it was silly of me to think we could stay in Sicily forever. Of course not. You run a billion-dollar conglomerate. So when do we leave?"

"I'm leaving now." He paused. "You and Esme will remain."

"What?" She clutched the sheet higher, over her naked body that just hours before had been hot and tangled beneath his own. "No!"

"You will do as I tell you." He couldn't bear to look at her beautiful, anguished face. Turning away, he stuffed a few more things in his suitcase.

"This is because I told you I love you, isn't it?" Tess's voice trembled. "I knew this would happen! I knew it!"

Stefano looked away. Outside, he could see the hills leading to a pink horizon over the distant Mediterranean and, beyond that, Africa. Without a word, he pulled on a crisp white shirt and tucked it into his trousers. Sitting in a nearby chair, he laced up his black leather shoes.

"Please, Stefano," she whispered. "Just talk to me."

His stomach tightened, but he forced himself to face her.

Tess's hands were clasped, her thick black eyelashes fluttering against her pale cheeks.

Dawn broke, and sunlight flooded the bedroom from

the east-facing windows, frosting Tess's beautiful face with warm golden light. As their eyes locked, he felt strangely vulnerable. And no wonder. He'd never revealed so much of his heart to any other living soul.

Just that thought made the world start to spin again and that sick feeling rise in his chest.

"I just have to go." He looked away. "I will return in a few days. When I do…" He set his jaw. "We'll talk."

"Stefano, don't go," she whispered. "Please."

Stefano felt a hard, rough twist in his chest at the pain in her voice. He crushed his feelings just as he'd been trained to do. Snapping the small suitcase shut, he kissed her forehead, then left without another word and without looking back.

CHAPTER NINE

It was the longest four days of Tess's life.

Four days of being alone in a remote Sicilian castle, being asked by the villagers and servants where Stefano had gone. Four days of eating alone in the great hall with only her baby for company. Four days of looking anxiously online for news of Stefano and discovering none.

And four nights of sleeping alone in their big bed, dreaming of him. Four mornings of waking up with a knot in her throat, her heart hovering between hope and dread.

Did Tess have any reason to hope?

I will return in a few days. When I do, we'll talk.

He could love her, her heart stubbornly argued. She'd seen the way he looked at her when she'd told him she loved him. She'd felt the way he kissed her, whispering words in Italian that sounded like music. She loved him. And she thought he could love her if he let himself.

But, for him, all love had ever meant was loss and pain.

She could settle for him not loving her, she told herself on the first day. She could live her whole life without ever being loved, she told herself on the second. He couldn't help it, she insisted on the third.

But on the fourth...

Everything in Tess rose up in rebellion.

She thought of her mother, waiting eight years for a married man to leave his wife. She thought of herself, waiting over a year for Stefano to return to her, convincing herself that he was trapped on a desert island with amnesia.

This was her life. Her baby's life.

No more settling.

No more excuses.

Esme deserved better.

And, Tess realized with clarity, so did she.

If Stefano didn't love her and she stayed anyway, no matter how she tried to endure his coldness, eventually her love would turn to hate. What would their marriage be like then? A prison. For both of them.

What would that teach Esme?

Stefano had been nearly destroyed by his parents' selfish cruelty. Even Tess, unthinkingly, had followed her own mother's path when she'd let herself fall in love with an emotionally unavailable man like Stefano, who in spite of his warmth and goodness, seemed now as cold and unreachable as a distant star.

Tess had learned to give too much. Stefano had learned to be selfish. He put himself first. Tess and the baby were mere baggage. Whether he took her with him on his travels or left her behind on a whim, he expected her to be his accessory. He expected to be the boss.

Though my wife is amazingly talented, she's focused on raising our daughter.

She'd been a little hurt, but told herself it didn't matter. Because there was something she wanted even more than to be a designer. She wanted to be loved.

Now she knew she'd be neither.

Tess closed her eyes, suddenly wishing she was back in New York with her family and friends. Wishing she still had a job, even a poorly paid one, where she could earn money and self-respect, rather than being dependent on Stefano, when he didn't love her.

She'd told him she loved him, and after one precious

night, when he'd held her so tenderly, he'd left her in the morning. He'd abandoned her.

Again.

This was unbearable, she thought. She couldn't let it go on.

Now, standing on the balcony in the cool October night, Tess stared at Stefano's terse message for the tenth time since she'd gotten it an hour before.

On my way home. I think I know how to make you happy. Talk more tonight.

What did it mean? Tess shivered. Was he going to tell her he loved her after all?

Hearing her baby babble, she glanced back through the open door toward the master bedroom, where Esme, fresh from her bath and in footsie pajamas, was playing with soft blocks on the bedroom rug.

Tess looked hungrily toward the pale sliver of road between the violet-purple hills leading to the castle. She expected Stefano any moment. She wrapped her arms around her body, hugging herself for comfort. She'd hoped he would arrive before the baby's bedtime, but it was almost too late…

Then she saw the headlights. A car was racing toward the castle at a breakneck speed.

She jumped, as if afraid of being caught waiting for him again. She hurried back into the bedroom, her hands shaking as she slid the balcony door closed behind her. Inside, her eyes caught her reflection in the full-length mirror.

Tess's pride hadn't been able to talk her out of trying to look nice tonight. Her wild red curls tumbled over her shoulders, and she wore a simple dress of her own design, with pink roses patterned on black silk. Spots of feverish pink color stood out on her cheeks.

"Bah!" Esme said proudly, holding up her chubby arms. The baby had recently figured out how to sit, but Tess always made sure to surround her with pillows for those moments when Esme would topple over with a crash.

"You have a block! Good job!" Tess picked the baby up, cuddling her close, relishing her sweet smell. She thought of why she'd married Stefano. So they could be a family. So they could be happy.

So they could love each other.

Please, let him love me, Tess thought, closing her eyes. *Please, let my faith be rewarded.*

She heard noises downstairs, as Stefano's deep voice called out to staff in Italian and they answered. With his return, the castle seemed to come alive.

Or maybe it was just Tess. She waited, practically vibrating, until she heard his heavy step in the hallway. Trembling, she turned to face the bedroom door.

Stefano's tall, broad-shouldered silhouette filled the space. He was wearing a well-cut suit and tie that perfectly fit his powerful, muscular body. His handsome face was serious. His dark eyes cut through her heart.

"Hello, Tess," he said quietly.

"Hello," she said, her heart pounding.

Coming forward, he kissed her softly on the cheek. She inhaled his scent of soap and spice and power. She felt the warmth and heat of him so close to her.

Please, she thought. *Please, please, please.*

"And Esme." His eyes crinkled as he smiled at her. Gently he took the baby in his arms, giving her a kiss before turning back to Tess. "How was she?"

"She missed you," Tess said. "So did I."

Stefano's handsome face suddenly became a mask. "It's past her bedtime."

"I let her stay up, hoping you'd get here."

"Thank you." His voice was courteous, impersonal. Tess

bit her lip, feeling strangely awkward, as if she were speaking to a stranger, not her own husband.

Oh, this was ridiculous.

Biting her lip, she blurted out, "Stefano, you know we—"

"I'll put her to bed." Holding the yawning baby, he turned away, pausing at the door. "Gerlanda has arranged dinner in the great hall. I'll join you in a moment."

And he was gone.

Tess felt numb. For four days, she'd yearned for her husband's return. Now she felt afraid. What if her fears were right and her hopes were wrong?

I think I know how to make you happy, his message had said.

What could that mean, except that he was going to tell her he loved her? It had to be, she reassured herself. Straightening her shoulders, she went downstairs.

The great hall was newly decorated with vases of roses, reminding her with a pang of the roses on their wedding night. A fire crackled in the large fireplace, and shadows shifted across the exposed beams and painted ceiling above.

A small, intimate table for two had been set up beside the fireplace. Dinner had already been served and was waiting on china plates, beside linen napkins and sterling silver utensils. Nearby was a bottle of champagne on ice.

Seeing that, Tess exhaled with relief, her heart filling with joy. She knew instantly that everything was going to be all right.

Stefano loved her. That was what he'd come to tell her. Why else would they celebrate with expensive champagne?

All the pain she'd felt for the last four days—all the uncertainty and fear—disappeared in a puff of smoke. It had all been worth it, because now she knew he loved her, and—

"You look beautiful."

Hearing Stefano's voice behind her, Tess turned with a smile. "You're not so bad, either."

Shadows and firelight moved across the hard angles of his handsome face as he came forward. He pulled a black velvet box from the pocket of his black jacket. "I got you something."

"You didn't have to do that." *Just loving me is more than enough.*

"You deserve it." He opened the black box to reveal an exquisite diamond necklace, probably worth millions. He smiled when he saw her shocked expression. "Let's see how it looks on you."

Nervously Tess lifted her hair so he could wrap the expensive necklace around her throat. She shivered at the touch of his fingertips. Attaching the clasp, he stepped back to look at her.

"Beautiful," he whispered.

Numbly Tess reached up to touch the stones. She preferred the warmth of his hands. The diamonds felt cold and hard and heavy against her skin.

"Shall we have dinner?" he asked, gently putting his hand against her lower back to guide her.

He held out her chair, then sat down on the other chair across the small table. For a few moments, they ate the pasta without words. Tess felt the silence like a knife. Why wouldn't he just say it?

"I missed you," she blurted out.

"And I missed you." He paused. "I was wrong to leave you like that," he said quietly. "I'm sorry."

She exhaled. "It's all right. You're here now."

"Yes. And now," he said, his dark eyes smiling as he reached for the champagne bottle, "we celebrate."

"Celebrate what?" she said, her heart pounding.

After popping the bottle open, he poured two glasses

and handed one to her. "I was a fool. I should have seen this long ago."

"What?" she almost shouted.

He was going to tell her he loved her. He was going to say it right now. And then everything would be all right. They'd be happy for the rest of their lives.

Stefano looked at her. He was so handsome, his eyes so dark and devastating, that just looking at him made her heart squeeze roughly in her chest.

"I want you to know," he said, and leaned forward, "that I've just managed to hire Aiko Sakurai away from Zacco as Mercurio's new creative director."

It was so unexpected it took her several seconds to even make sense of his words. She said weakly, "You did?"

"Yes," he said proudly. Reaching over the table, he took her hand in his own. "But there's more."

Thank heaven. Tess nearly cried with relief. For a moment there she'd actually thought—

"I'd like to hire you," he said. "As associate designer at Mercurio."

Her jaw dropped. Her heart fell to the cold gray flagstones.

"What?"

"You'd answer directly to Mrs. Sakurai, whom you admire so much. No fetching coffee. Just doing the design work you love." He beamed at her, then held up his hand sharply as if to ward off her protests. "I know you don't have any experience, and it's a big leap. But just think of what you can learn. Perhaps, in a few years, you could take over one of the smaller houses. Perhaps you can eventually take over Mercurio entirely. I have faith in you."

"But," she said through numb lips, "you said it would be ridiculous for me to work at a major fashion house. You said I'd have to work such long hours, and be away from Esme…"

"All my companies have on-site day care."

"I'd still be away from her for—how long did you say? Sixty hours a week?" Her voice trembled. "And away from you."

He shifted in his chair. "That won't be a problem, at least for a few months. I've decided to sell controlling interest in my conglomerate."

"What!" she gasped. "Sell Gioreale? All your luxury brands? Even Mercurio?"

He gave a single nod. "I'll need to sell my shares at top price. Then I can make Fenella Montfort such an offer for Zacco that only a fool would refuse."

"So," she said slowly, "I wouldn't be an associate at Mercurio for long, would I?"

His jaw set. "I'm sure the new CEO will wish for Aiko Sakurai to remain as creative director. She had global success at Zacco. She only left because she didn't want to work with von Schreck." He considered. "If she likes your work, she'll want to keep you on her team."

Tess shook her head. "You'd really sell the company you built with your own two hands? Just for your family's old company, with von Schreck as creative director? How can that be worth it?"

He stared at her, then turned away, his jaw tight. "I'll be traveling to get my company in order and ready for prospective buyers. In the meantime, you and Esme can go live at our apartment in Paris—"

"Without you. So I can have a possibly temporary job that no one will think I'm qualified for."

Stefano was still holding up his champagne flute, obviously expecting her to clink her glass against his in a toast to their future. At that, he set it down.

"I'm giving you what you want most," he said slowly. "Am I not? Arranging a job with a mentor you admire.

Putting you on the path to becoming designer of a major fashion house. I thought you'd be thrilled."

Tess stared at him.

She couldn't believe she'd done this to herself *again*—twisting the bounds of reason to talk herself into believing what she wanted to believe.

He didn't love her.

He hadn't even tried.

Ice cut through her heart. She'd thought she knew him. In her mind, Prince Stefano Zacco was an honorable, dashing, scarred hero, Heathcliff and Mr. Darcy rolled into one. But the truth was that, throughout their marriage, as she'd made one compromise after another, sacrificing little fragments of herself for his sake, he hadn't done the same.

"I told you I loved you," she whispered, trying not to cry.

His jaw set. "And I told you, that's not something I can give you. I wish it were."

"You didn't even try," she said miserably.

Leaning forward, he grasped her hand over the table.

"I can't," he said quietly. "So just take what I can give you, Tess. Take it, and be happy."

For a moment, she looked at him, at this magnificent great hall in the Sicilian castle, surrounded by diamonds and flowers and silver and expensive champagne, a fire roaring in the fireplace.

All this elegance and grace, she thought dully. All something out of a fairy tale. A fashion magazine.

Once, she'd yearned to be part of this world. If she stayed, if she agreed to his terms, she could be. All her childhood dreams could come true.

Except the one that really mattered.

Could she choose this beautiful, glamorous life, one that others would envy, when it meant she'd never be really, truly loved? Never ever, not until the day she died?

The answer thundered in her heart.

No.

Love was what she wanted. Real love.

And if Stefano couldn't love her, she had to be true to her own heart.

Pulling her hand away, she looked at him with tears in her eyes. She couldn't believe she was doing this. She choked out, "I can't."

Stefano appeared astonished. Then his black eyes glittered in the firelight. "Can't, or won't?"

Her voice shook. "What's the difference?"

His dark brows lowered like a thundercloud. He growled, "Then what the hell do you want?"

Tess looked at him and, with a deep breath, she made one final attempt.

"What I want," she whispered, "is for you to be brave enough to admit you love me, too."

It was suddenly quiet in the great hall. Stefano heard the crackle of the fire as logs snapped and burned. He heard the roar of blood pounding in his ears.

What I want is for you to be brave enough to admit you love me.

Stefano had spent the last four days running from her. He'd fled first to Paris, then London and Madrid. He'd done it to check on the efficiency of Gioreale's regional offices.

No. That was a lie. He'd been desperate to escape Tess's words. He couldn't let her love him. He couldn't love her back.

And, yet, he couldn't leave her.

Today at dawn, he'd had the solution. Giving Tess, who'd never even graduated from design school, an important job at Mercurio was a huge risk. But it was a risk Stefano was willing to take. He wanted Tess to be happy. To be fulfilled.

Just as he would be, after he got back control of Zacco. His family's company was his destiny. His future legacy.

What his father had lost, Stefano would win.

But he wanted Tess at his side—smiling, adoring Tess, so caring and kind. To keep her as his wife, he was willing to do almost anything.

But it hadn't been enough. His name, his home, his jet, his fortune, and even his fashion house—all not enough for her. She continued to demand the one thing he could not, would not give her.

What I want is for you to be brave enough to admit you love me, too.

Cold fury built inside him.

"You think I'm not *brave* enough?" he said, narrowing his eyes. "You're calling me a coward?"

A lesser woman would have quailed, retreated.

Tess lifted her chin. "Yes."

He sucked in his breath, staring at her.

Tess was no longer the naive girl he'd married, he realized, the one with rose-colored glasses and pink-hued dreams. Her lips, formerly always so ready to smile, were now pressed together in a thin trembling line. Her green eyes, which had once danced with optimism and hope, were flat, as if all the dreams had been pulled out of them.

Because of him?

He wanted the old Tess back. He wanted them to be who they'd been. He wanted to mess up her hair, to see her smile, to see her face light up with joy as he lowered his head to kiss her. His jaw tightened.

"I can't give you what you want," he said in a low voice. "Why can't you understand that?"

"Why can't you change?"

Funny, he thought dimly. She'd been hoping all this time he'd change. He'd been hoping she wouldn't.

He said evenly, "Acquiring Zacco has to be my focus right now. Fenella Montfort is refusing to negotiate or even receive offers from my lawyers. It's going to take all my time and energy to convince her to even see me. I am trying to make you happy in my absence. Trying to—"

"I know what you're trying to do." Her eyes pierced his soul. "Buy me off. But I won't be part of it."

His dark eyebrows lowered fiercely. He growled, "Tess, damn you—"

"No."

Looking at her wan face, Stefano felt his heart twist. He suddenly wanted—

No. He fought the feeling, focusing on his anger.

"So what do you want me to do, Tess? Just stay here with you? Let Fenella Montfort keep Zacco? Surrender my family's name forever? Our legacy?"

"No," she said quietly. "What I want is for you to start a new legacy." She looked down at her hands. She was twisting her enormous diamond ring around her finger. "That company is not the only thing that bears your name."

She was talking about Esme, he realized. She and Tess also bore the Zacco name now.

Anger built higher. She was attacking him, and he had to defend himself. "I married you, isn't that enough? I've been a good father. I've given you both everything I can. Even you—I'm offering you a position that any other young designer would kill for!"

"I know," she said softly. "And I'm grateful."

That was more like it. He leaned forward. "Then—"

"But I don't want to be your employee. Only your wife." She blinked back tears. "I wanted so badly for you to love me, Stefano. I would have given everything—my heart, my soul—to make it come true." Reaching up, Tess unclasped the million-euro diamond necklace. "But I don't want this."

Gripping the jewelry in her hand, she held it out to him across the table.

"That necklace is a gift," he said, hurt. "I bought it for you."

"Take it back. Wait." He watched in shock as she pulled the diamond ring off her left hand and added it to the ball of precious jewels she extended toward him. "Take it all. I don't want it anymore."

Disoriented, he held out his hand, letting her drop the hard, cold diamonds into his palm.

"Not even the ring?" he said, his heart numb.

Her green eyes looked gray. "You don't love me."

"I never promised to love you. Just to honor and cherish. To romance you."

"I didn't know the difference then." She took a deep breath. "Now I do."

A roar of pain rushed through him, which swiftly turned to anger. Dropping the diamonds to the table with a clatter, he said, "If you're threatening to divorce me because I can't give you every single thing you want—"

"Every single thing?" she repeated incredulously.

"You're being unreasonable," he ground out. "What does love matter? It's just a word."

"Not to me." Anguished tears filled her eyes. "Please, Stefano. If you cannot love me, then please," she whispered, "let me go."

Let her go? *Let her go?* Every part of him rejected that ridiculous notion. She belonged to him! Tess was his wife. Esme was his child. They belonged with him. At his disposal. At his command.

He set his jaw. "No."

"You must." Her sad voice echoed in the great hall, beside the crackling fire. "If you don't let me go, it will destroy us both."

He stared at her. "You would throw our marriage away for nothing? Because I won't say those three words? Because I won't *lie*?"

"Because you're afraid."

"Afraid," he sneered.

She nodded. "I understand why, after everything you went through, but Stefano, don't you understand?" Shaking her head, she choked out, "*Loss happens anyway.* Whether you're brave enough to love or not. The answer isn't to feel nothing until we die. The answer is to seize our joy and *live*. To love as hard and long as we can." Tears streaked openly down her face. "As I wanted to love you."

Stefano's jaw clenched as he stared at her. Did she think he was a fool? Of course he wanted to love her! He just did not know how! If he could have spoken three words as a magic incantation to make her happy forever, he would have!

But he couldn't feel them, and he couldn't lie and pretend he did. He wished he could. Stefano took a deep breath, trying to force the words from his lips. *I love you.* No one else found it hard. Why did he?

The words choked in his throat.

Savagery filled his heart as he turned away. Fine. He would simply lay down the law. He would tell her how it would be. She was his wife, damn it. She would remain so. She would obey—

Then he heard the quiet heartbreak in her earlier words. *If you don't let me go, it will destroy us both.*

He thought of the optimistic, romantic, dreamy-eyed girl she'd been. He looked at the heartbroken woman in front of him now.

When he'd married Tess, he'd honestly thought it was for her own good. He'd believed he could take better care of her than any other man.

He was no longer sure of that.

He said in a low voice, "I have given you everything I have to give."

"I know," she whispered.

Stefano rose unsteadily to his feet. He felt dizzy and

powerless and cold all over, in a way he hadn't felt since he was a boy. He stared down at her.

"Go, then," he said hoarsely. "Take Esme and go."

Closing her eyes, she took a deep, shuddering breath. When she opened them, they were luminous with grief.

"Thank you." Rising from the table, she walked slowly up the stairs. Stefano stood by the enormous fireplace in the great hall, frozen in shock.

Surely Tess would come to her senses. Surely she'd realize that they were meant to be together.

But when she came back downstairs five minutes later, she was wearing a coat, with a diaper bag over her shoulder and Esme sleeping in her arms. "I saw Salvatore in the hall. He'll give me a ride to the airport."

Stefano looked at his wife and child, and his chest twisted painfully. He couldn't breathe. He didn't want them to go.

"Goodbye," Tess choked out. She turned to go.

"Wait."

She stopped, not turning around. Stefano still couldn't believe this was happening. He came up behind her.

"If you really love me," he said in a low voice, "how can you leave?"

Tess turned, and the look she gave him cut him to the core. Stefano realized her rose-colored glasses were finally gone. She now saw him exactly for the man he really was.

"I loved an illusion," she whispered, and left.

CHAPTER TEN

"You have some nerve. Stealing my designer."

Fenella Montfort softened her words with a feline smile. She was sitting behind her black lacquer desk in her office at London's Zacco headquarters.

"I didn't steal Aiko Sakurai," Stefano replied coldly. "She quit after you hired von Schreck to replace her."

"I intended for them to be co-designers. Creators of a brand-new synergistic vision."

He gave a grim smile. "Apparently Mrs. Sakurai didn't see it that way. Your loss. My gain."

"I still have von Schreck."

"Which is why you should sell all your shares now. Because once he shows his first collection, your numbers will drop."

Fenella narrowed her eyes. He returned her gaze coolly.

Stefano should have felt a thrill of triumph. For the last month, since Tess had left him, he'd focused on this goal, day and night. He'd done everything he could to get this meeting today.

His own company, Gioreale S.p.A., had already gotten offers from around the world for Stefano's controlling interest in the stock. He'd hired away Zacco's star designer, Aiko Sakurai, by tripling her salary and giving her a large amount of stock, so even if the company sold, she'd be wealthy enough to start her own brand, should she choose.

And Fenella Montfort must by now have some inkling how awful Caspar von Schreck would be for Zacco.

For once, Stefano held all the cards.

And he would have traded every one of them, he thought, to have his family back.

Just thinking of Tess caused a deep ache through his body, from his throat to his jaw to his chest to his hips. All of him.

Turning away, Stefano looked out the large window, toward the gray steel and glass of London's business district, and behind that, the gray November sky. All so gray, Stefano thought. Flat and gray.

"So cheeky," Fenella said.

Taking a deep breath, he tried to focus on her. "So that's why you finally agreed to a meeting? Because I stole your designer?" Stefano knew she was as competitive as he was.

"Not just that," Fenella said. Clicking on her computer, she turned the monitor to face him on the other side of the desk.

A shock rippled through his body.

Tess's picture was on the monitor. He hadn't expected to see her. He'd spent the last month trying not to think about her, or think at all. Since she'd abandoned him so brutally, their only connection had been through his New York lawyers, working out a custody agreement for Esme. He'd tried to arrange for Tess to receive a generous monthly stipend, not required by their prenuptial agreement. To Stefano's shock, Tess had refused it.

Even his money, it seemed, was no longer good enough.

Tightening his jaw, he glared at Fenella on the other side of her desk. "Why are you showing me a picture of my wife?"

"Didn't you read it?"

Stefano looked closer at the screen. It was an online article from a New York newspaper.

It seemed he hadn't been the only one who'd been busy this past month. Since she'd returned to New York, Tess had already begun her own small fashion studio. Tonight, according to the article, she'd be hosting a charity runway show for her first capsule collection at the Campania Hotel.

Stefano looked back at the picture of Tess. His heart lifted to his throat. She was sitting at a bright green desk in a colorful bohemian office, with their sweet baby daughter playing nearby on a fluffy white rug covered with baby toys. Tess's beautiful face beamed up at him, her red hair tumbling down her shoulders, her emerald eyes warm. So much light and color. She'd done it even without his help. She'd followed her dreams, on her own terms. He was proud of her, so proud.

Tess had never really needed him, he realized. She'd always had the strength to pursue her dream of being a fashion designer. Why had she ever been willing to accept less?

Because of him.

I don't want to be your employee. Only your wife. I wanted so badly for you to love me, Stefano. I would have given everything—my heart, my soul—to make it come true.

But he couldn't love her. So she'd left him. She'd started her own small business. A company with integrity. With heart.

Just like Tess.

She was better off without him.

Stefano was filled with grief he hadn't felt for a long, long time.

Without looking up, he said in a low voice, "Why did you show me this?"

"This is really why I invited you," Fenella said. "Not because of Aiko Sakurai—at least, not *only* because of her." Her cool eyes met his. "But because your wife has left you."

Stefano looked up sharply. "So?"

"That makes you interesting."

"How?" His lips twisted bitterly. "You sense weakness?"

"I sense strength." Tilting her head, Fenella said, "The possibility of a partnership."

Partnership. At the word, Stefano felt overwhelmed with memories of the partnership he'd had with his wife. The two of them laughing, talking, making love. Supporting each other. Caring for their baby. Pain went through his heart.

"What are you talking about?"

Leaning forward, she said coolly, "We have an opportunity."

"You're finally willing to negotiate for Zacco?" he said, leaning back in his chair so he didn't gag on the overwhelming floral smell of her perfume.

"Now that your unfortunate wife is gone—"

"Don't call her that—"

"You should replace her. With someone more appropriate."

Fenella's cold blue eyes met his, and he knew exactly whom she was suggesting.

A chill went through him. He rose to his feet, pacing to the window. He looked down at the gleaming steel and glass buildings beneath the lowering November sky. He finally said, "Are you trying to imply you care for me? Because we both know that's a lie."

"I care about success. And so do you." She rose to her feet. "We come from the same world, Stefano. Our families go back generations. We both know how to win—at any price."

A ray of sunlight burst through the gray clouds, illuminating the faint web of lines around her hard blue eyes.

"Forget love." She shook her head. "Love is for losers. You and I—we were born to rule. If we join our companies together, we'll be more successful than you can imagine. We have no limits. We can work twenty hours a day, every day, until we achieve it. We'll be so powerful, no one will ever be able to touch us." She took a step forward. "The world is ours to take."

Stefano stared at her.

Fenella Montfort was offering everything he'd once thought he wanted. Thought he needed. The pure control of single-minded focus that led to absolute power.

Wasn't that what he wanted—to never feel vulnerable again?

Tess had been right, he suddenly realized. He had been afraid. Of being powerless. Of feeling the pain of loss. So he'd pushed her away. Refused to love her.

Then why was it, that from the moment Tess had left, all he'd felt was the abyss of howling, terrifying loss?

His eyes went wide.

Loss happens anyway. He heard the echo of Tess's voice. *Whether you're brave enough to love or not. The answer isn't to feel nothing until we die. The answer is to seize our joy and live. To love as hard and long as we can.*

"Well?" Fenella purred as she came closer. "What do you say? Do we have a deal?"

With an intake of breath, Stefano looked up at the woman's cold, calculating gaze. If not for Tess, he might have accepted her offer. He might have given away his only chance of real happiness for the sake of power and fortune.

But power was an illusion. Fortune was empty. He knew that now. Because for the last month, without his wife and child, he'd felt nothing. Everything he'd once cared about was worthless. A booming stock price. Unimaginable wealth. Why did he need more of those things when they didn't make him happy?

Love was the only real legacy.

He closed his eyes, remembering Tess's quiet voice. *Start a new legacy*, she'd said.

He hadn't understood it then. Now he remembered days

of warmth and joy, of red wine and sunshine and blue skies. Nothing to do with money or power. A different kind of legacy.

He opened his eyes slowly.

Love.

Suddenly he had to see Tess. Now. Immediately. He felt dizzy with need. He needed her like sunlight. Like rain. Not because she loved him, but because he loved her.

He loved her.

Stefano looked at Fenella. "Not interested."

Her eyes narrowed. "Don't be a fool."

A beam of sunlight fell against his cheek, warming Stefano like the touch of Tess's hand, and he suddenly knew he was throwing away everything he'd once wanted for everything that truly mattered. He understood now.

Tess.

A smile rose straight from his heart. "Keep Zacco. I don't need it. I already have everything any man could dream of."

Stefano felt free. Joy thrummed through him like a song. Like a whirl of color. Red like Tess's hair, green like her eyes, their baby's laughter calling to him across the sea. "Goodbye, Ms. Montfort."

Grabbing his coat and briefcase, he strode out of his office, glancing back one last time at the Zacco headquarters. He knew he'd never see it again.

For all his adult life he'd thought winning the company was the only way to save the family legacy. To save himself.

Tess had shown him otherwise.

Life wasn't a game to be won or an asset to acquire. It wasn't a business based on profit or loss.

Life meant giving your heart. Taking the risk. Because though loss was guaranteed, joy was a choice. And joy came only from loving others.

Love was a gift, freely given. A leap of faith in this

cold modern world. It wasn't weakness. It wasn't illusion. It wasn't even an ocean to drown in.

Love was the life raft.

"I never should have agreed to this," Tess breathed, raking her hand through her untidy red waves. "Why did I think I could do this?"

Her two friends looked at each other.

"Because you can," said Lola firmly.

"Easy," said Hallie.

Tess's first runway show was due to start in five minutes, in the intimate venue of the hotel's elegant Edwardian tearoom. They were in a backstage area with the models and mirrors and racks of clothes. Their three babies were being watched by Cristiano and Tess's cousins.

Looking at her now, Hallie gave a low laugh, then covered her mouth with her hand. "Sorry. But you look so nervous." At Tess's glare, she added with a grin, "I'm just remembering how it felt. But you guys still made me go onstage and sing!"

"Because you're amazing," Tess said.

Hallie looked at her pointedly. "And so are you. Which is why I invested in your brand."

Tess's *brand*? She had a brand? All she'd done was design clothes she liked. But Hallie was right. She had a brand now. The thought made her want to run back to cower in the Morettis' old hotel suite upstairs, where Tess had been staying with Esme since Hallie's family had moved into their remodeled mansion in the West Village. "I never should have let you invest in my company, Hallie. I'm not ready!"

"Of course you are." Lola looked at the models around them, each of them carefully dressed in an outfit that Tess had designed and sewn herself. "Your clothes are so pretty." She looked down at her own outfit, also a Serena original. "And shockingly comfortable!"

"We're going to make a bundle," Hallie said gleefully, rubbing her hands together. "I can't let Cristiano be the only entrepreneur in the family."

Nervousness roiled in Tess's belly as she thought of how much money her friend had already invested in her. Grabbing a pin from her belt, she tightened the neckline of a model's brightly colored shirt. "What if my collection is a flop?"

"A *flop*?" Hallie said indignantly. "At the Campania? Impossible! And we're raising money for charity. How can it go wrong? Serena is going to be a huge hit!"

Serena. Tess shivered. She'd named her company after her mother, and this show would raise money to fight the disease that had killed her. Another layer of pressure if she failed.

The last month had been a whirlwind. Since she'd returned to New York, Tess had spent hours in her new baby-friendly office working on her designs. In the evenings, Hallie and Lola had joined her with their babies, drinking wine and listening to Tess talk tearfully about her marriage. Naturally, her friends had taken her side.

"That so-called prince is the biggest jerk in the world," Hallie had said.

"Second biggest," Lola had mumbled, but wouldn't explain. After all this time, she still refused to reveal the identity of her baby's father, forcing the other two to wonder. Hallie thought the man might be a famous celebrity. Tess guessed he might be a married jerk, like her own father who'd abandoned her. But Lola refused to say, making Tess wonder if baby Jett's father was even worse than they imagined...

But how would Tess know? She'd been wrong about so much, first and foremost Prince Stefano Zacco di Gioreale. Grief still twisted her heart. How could she face the world without him?

"I'm scared," she said to her friends, whispering so the models and hairstylists and makeup artists wouldn't hear.

Hallie squeezed her shoulder, then turned to speak quietly to an assistant, who hurried out of the room.

"Stop whining," Lola said. "Your clothes are good. You know they are. So just shut up and do it."

Slowly Tess walked past every model yet again, looking carefully at each outfit. Her clothes weren't expensive or intimidating. Instead, she'd created warm, colorful, comfortable outfits designed to make women happy, both with how they looked and how they felt.

Twelve outfits, each of them brightly colored, a mixture of old and new. She stopped at the very last model, who was wearing an ivory-colored wedding dress, embroidered with a small blue bird on the edge of the skirt. The bride held a bouquet of bright blue tulips.

Staring at the bouquet, Tess stopped, remembering her own wedding bouquet of pink roses. How happy she'd been, how sure that the two of them would live a fairy tale...

What was she saying? She'd wanted to kill Stefano with her shoe. She should have known a marriage begun in blackmail could only end badly.

And yet... A lump rose in her throat, and she had to blink back tears.

"Don't worry, Your Highness," said the girl in the wedding dress. "I won't let you down."

It was Kebe, the young model Tess had defended in Paris. When the girl had heard Tess was showing her debut collection in New York, she'd volunteered to walk the runway for free. She'd also promoted the event to her half-a-million followers on social media, causing the event to promptly sell out.

Tears rose to Tess's eyes at the girl's kindness even as she chided gently, "I told you, call me Tess. I'm not a princess anymore."

"You are to me," the girl said firmly.

"Tess?"

Turning around, Tess saw her uncle standing uncertainly in the doorway, holding baby Esme.

"Uncle Ray." Coming forward, she hugged him, then took her baby in her arms.

"Your friend—Mrs. Moretti—thought you might want to see Esme before the show," her uncle said awkwardly. He shook his head in amazement. "Look at you, Tessie. You're a designer. Just like you said you'd be."

Tess cuddled her baby in her arms. "I feel lucky."

"It's more than luck." Her uncle hung his head. "I should have believed in you more. Encouraged you."

She looked up at him in surprise. "You took me in, Uncle Ray. You gave me a home."

"I gave Serena a hard time, too. Because I never thought crazy dreams could actually come true." His eyes looked suspiciously wet. "But now, seeing you...it makes me wonder if maybe I should follow a crazy dream of my own." His voice became a whisper as he patted her shoulder. "Your mama would be so proud."

For a moment, Tess was too overwhelmed to speak.

Taking the baby back in his arms, Uncle Ray said gruffly, "We'll be cheering for you out there. Every step of the way." Smiling, he said to Esme, "Wait till you see all the amazing things your mama has done."

As Tess watched them leave, those words echoed in her ears. *Wait till you see all the amazing things your mama has done.*

At that, her shoulders straightened. Her fear melted away.

She wished—how she wished—that Stefano could have loved her. She still loved him in spite of her best efforts. No matter how many times she told herself that she'd loved an illusion. She loved the man he could have been, and suspected she always would.

But she'd be grateful for what remained. Her family. Her friends. Her daughter. She'd do everything she could to make them proud today. And even if she failed, she'd never stop trying.

"All right," she said firmly to the models. "Let's go!"

Tess hovered in the back of the large, elegant tearoom as the first model sashayed past the potted palm trees and gilded mirrors. The tea tables had been cleared out, replaced with a long catwalk surrounded by chairs.

The models entered one at a time, some of them dancing, all of them smiling. Music played, lighthearted and free. It was fun, playful, casual.

Tess blinked back tears as she watched the models wearing her designs. To her surprise and delight, with each new outfit, the audience's applause grew louder. Finally Kebe came out on the catwalk, gliding serenely in the wedding gown. The music built, and holding the blue tulips triumphantly over her head, she turned back to where Tess shyly hesitated.

"Come on, Princess!" she called. "Come up here!"

With a deep breath, Tess went out to face her public.

There was thunderous applause. She gave an awkward wave, then stopped as the tears in her eyes spilled over, as full as her grateful heart.

Perhaps she couldn't have what she'd wanted most. But at least there was this—this one moment—

She saw a flash of red as someone handed her a huge bouquet of red roses. Hallie must have arranged flowers. She looked past the long-stemmed red roses to smile at the person hidden behind them.

Then her breath left her.

It was Stefano.

Suddenly everything else fell away. The applause,

the lights, the music, the audience. There was only now. This. *Him.*

"Stefano?" she whispered uncertainly, trembling.

Coming closer, he looked at her, and she saw that his dark eyes were luminous with tears. He said in a low voice, "You're a star. As you always deserved to be."

"What are you doing here?"

Dropping the roses, he took her hands in his own. His touch burned through her, and so did his dark eyes. "I'm here for you."

She looked up at him in shock.

Reaching out, he cupped her cheek. "You were right, Tess. I was afraid. I couldn't let myself love you because I couldn't bear the pain of losing you. Then I lost you anyway." Pulling her into his arms, he said softly, "Now I realize that there's only one thing in life that's worth any price."

The audience in the tearoom had fallen utterly silent. Even the models were staring at them. Tess held her breath.

"I'm in love with you, Tess," he whispered.

Now she knew she really was dreaming.

"You," she said, faltering and licking her lips. "You love me?"

"I've never felt this way about anyone. And I never will again. Just you. I love you." Stefano blinked fast. "You're all I care about."

Her heart was pounding in her throat. "What about Zacco?"

"I don't need it. Don't want it."

"What?" she croaked, nearly staggering back in shock.

"I just need you. You were right," he said huskily. "My legacy isn't a company. It's not wealth or power." He glanced at their baby, sitting with her aunt and uncle in the front row. He turned back to Tess, and this time there could be no doubt that there were tears in his eyes. "My legacy is you. You and Esme. And I'm yours."

"Stefano—"

"Give me the chance to show you," he whispered, and lowered his head to hers. His lips seared hers, hot and persuasive, gentle as silk. He kissed her tenderly, and when he finally pulled away, Tess blinked, lost in a dream.

"Can you ever love me again?" he said wistfully, running his hand down her cheek. "Can you?"

"I never stopped loving you," she choked out.

Joy lit up his eyes. Lifting her in his arms, Stefano whirled her around, making her colorful skirt fly out. She heard the audience's applause and sighs of delight. But, for Tess, it was just the two of them, laughing together with pure joy.

When Stefano finally set her down, his handsome face was bright. He kissed her again, and a moment later, Kebe and the other models came to congratulate them, and Hallie, too. Joyful music played as confetti rained down from the high ceiling amid the audience's thunderous applause.

"See?" Hallie whispered smugly in Tess's ear. "I told you the show would be a success."

Tess felt like her heart could burst. She waved at her family to join them onstage with Esme, then looked around for Lola, wanting her to join them, too. But she saw the blonde leaving with her baby, departing through the door on the other side of the room. She wondered what could be so important that would make Lola leave.

Then she forgot all about it as her husband pulled her in his arms, tilting her back with a fierce kiss.

"Is this really real?" Tess said in a daze, looking up at his handsome face as colorful confetti fell around them like flower petals. "Or is it a dream?"

"It's both," he said.

She smiled through her tears. "What will I dream about now that all my dreams have come true?"

Stefano took their baby from her uncle. Turning to Tess,

he wrapped them both in the security of his powerful arms. His dark eyes were luminous with love and hope. "We'll find new dreams together."

With an unsteady laugh, Tess reached up and ran her hand over his rough, unshaven cheek. "I think that's the sexiest thing you've ever said to me."

"I love you, wife," he said huskily, instantly proving her statement wrong. Then he kissed her with all the sweetness and power of a dream that would last forever.

"Look, Esme!" Tess beamed as she pointed out the window toward the parade on Central Park West. "Santa!"

"She's just seven months old. I think she might be a little young to care about Christmas," Stefano said, smiling at them tenderly. Tess grinned back.

"It's never too soon to start family traditions."

They'd just bought their new co-op, and most of their furniture still hadn't arrived, but Tess had desperately wanted them to move in before the New York Thanksgiving Day parade in late November.

"So we can start our first holiday season right," she'd said. "Just think of all the memories we'll make!"

Of course, Stefano had agreed. He couldn't wait to make memories with Tess. In their bedroom. Tonight.

Coming forward now, he wrapped his wife and baby in his arms as they looked out the huge window at the view of the parade and Central Park beyond. The festive season had just begun.

Later today, friends and family would arrive for the traditional American feast of turkey and mashed potatoes and pumpkin pie. As their dishes and pots hadn't arrived yet—they were lucky to even have a big table and chairs—the meal would be catered from one of the city's finest restaurants.

Except for the desserts and rolls, of course. Those would be provided by Tess's family.

No longer Foster Bros. Bakery, it was changing to the Foster Sisters, as her two young cousins were eager to take over. They'd been bored by college, and had instead taken a loan from Tess and Stefano—at exceedingly generous terms—to buy the bakery from their father and mother, who'd just left to sail the world. The older couple, who'd always secretly yearned for adventure, were finally seizing the day.

It was never too late to change your life. Or to change yourself. Hadn't Stefano learned that better than anyone?

After his obsessive attention the previous month, his company, Gioreale, was running better than ever and had just hit its highest stock valuation in its history. Mercurio had received amazing press after hiring the respected, beloved designer, Aiko Sakurai. Mercurio's stock price had gone up. Zacco's had gone down.

But the Zacco brand now mattered as little to him as the Palazzo Zacco in Ragusa. Neither had anything to do with him, in spite of the name.

The name wasn't important, Stefano had realized. Only the *people*.

Every time he remembered his years—decades—of unspeakable loneliness, of hollow wealth and cheap pleasures as he tried to pursue a useless goal, he shuddered a little, and thanked fate for sending his wife to save his soul.

Otherwise, who knew? He might be married now to Fenella Montfort. Ice went down at his spine at the thought.

The woman had quickly recovered from Stefano's rejection and immediately started dating her company's new designer, Caspar von Schreck. It had only been a few weeks, but already there'd been public clashes, fights and rumors of infidelity on both sides. Another shudder went through Stefano.

He was so happy to be out of that world. And so thankful to be in this one.

He looked down at his wife, so soft and loving. The gold signet ring glinted on her left hand. It had been resized to fit her slender ring finger. "I don't want a diamond," she'd told him. "I just want this. Because it's part of you." Remembering, Stefano's arms tightened around Tess as their baby suddenly giggled, waving her stuffed giraffe.

"Mama," Esme blurted out happily, causing Tess to squeal with delight, as she always did. Esme beamed proudly. It was a new trick she'd just learned a few days ago. Her first word.

"Dada," Stefano said coaxingly now. "*Dada.*"

Perplexed, Esme stared at him, her fingers in her mouth. Then she pulled her hand away.

"Mama," she repeated proudly.

"Good job, sweet girl," Tess praised, covering her baby's fat cheeks with kisses. Still giggling, his wife looked back at him. "I see you haven't lost your competitive streak."

"Never have. Never will. And since you don't want me to invest in your company—"

"Hallie and I are doing very well, thank you."

"Then I need some other goal. Something spectacular. Something that will impress you."

"Impress me?" she said teasingly, "Most men would think it was enough to run a multibillion-dollar company."

"It's practically running itself, thankfully, so I can spend more time with you and Esme. But a man needs more than money," he informed her loftily. "He needs a challenge."

Tess considered. "You could decorate the apartment. Hire the household staff you keep claiming that we need. Start that venture capital fund you keep talking about."

Stefano tilted his head, considering. Then he smiled. "Maybe later. For tonight, I've got something else in mind."

He leaned forward. "This is what I have planned for you after the baby's asleep and everyone's gone home tonight…"

He whispered some very provocative things in her ear.

"Why, Your Highness," Tess said, pulling back with a blush. "I can't believe you'd say such things."

Stefano gave her a wicked grin. "Not just once," he informed her. "Twice."

Her eyes became round as saucers. "Are you serious?"

"Maybe three times, if I'm really on my game," he whispered, and lowered his head to kiss her.

Then the doorbell rang, and he reluctantly let her go. They went to answer the door, to welcome their friends and family for their first dinner in their new home—even Cristiano Moretti, who'd somehow become a friend.

"After all," Moretti had told him last week, shaking his head, "with wives like these, we men have to stick together, or we'll be totally bowled over." Stefano had nodded solemnly in agreement.

For the first time in his life, Stefano knew who he was meant to be. Tess had been right. A man wasn't measured by wealth or power or the quality of his enemies. A man was defined by his love for family and friends. By the strength of his heart.

Tess was right about all kinds of things, Stefano thought, his lips tracing a smile. He looked down at her tenderly. He must be very competitive. Because, as they opened the door to the welcoming cheer of friends, Stefano suddenly knew his spectacular goal: For the rest of his life, he'd love his family more than any family had ever been loved before.

* * * * *